ETERNAL LIGHT OF THE CRYPTS
(*Lux Aeterna de Cryptae*)

A Historical Fiction in the
Ruins of Charlemagne's Empire

By Alan Van't Land

Full Quiver Publishing
Pakenham ON

Eternal Light of the Crypts
Copyright 2021 Alan Van't Land

Published by
Full Quiver Publishing
PO Box 244
Pakenham, Ontario K0A 2X0
www.fullquiverpublishing.com

ISBN: 978-1-987970-28-9
Printed and bound in the USA
Cover design by: James Hrkach and Alan Van't Land
Photo of church: copyright seanliew, Adobe Stock
Drawings copyright Alan Van't Land

All quotations of the Bible are from the NIV, as follows:

THE HOLY BIBLE, NEW INTERNATIONAL VERSION®, NIV®
Copyright © 1973, 1978, 1984, 2011 by Biblica, Inc.® Used by permission.
All rights reserved worldwide.

NATIONAL LIBRARY OF CANADA
CATALOGUING IN PUBLICATION

Published by FQ Publishing
A Division of Innate Productions

To everyone who encouraged my writing, but especially to Michelle, who bore my musings of Charlemagne, relics, and thieves with patience and my wrestling for redemption with love.

OFFICE OF THE HOURS (approximate)

Matins: midnight
Lauds: 3 am, or around dawn
Prime: 6 am
Terce: 9 am
Sext: noon
None: 3 pm
Vespers: 6 pm, or around dusk
Compline: 9 pm

acta: the acts, or works, of a person; often the title of a work, such as the Biblical book *The Acts of the Apostles,* but its medieval usage often included a saint's miraculous works after death.

aether: the upper stratum of the sky / the material that comprises this region.

agricola: farmer.

antiphon: a song sung in two parts, each by half a choir.

apse: the east end of the church, containing the altar, and usually a semi-circular wall opening back to the main portion of the church (the nave); where most medieval churches are laid out like a cross, the apse is the head of the cross.

caritas: charity.

cellulae: the cells of the monastery; not a prison cell, but a small, simple room, for sleeping and isolated meditation and prayer.

colonus: a peasant, possibly around this time period having a status between a slave and a freeman.

colonae: plural of *colonus.*

comes: the Latin title meaning "companion," a person of high rank, which evolved into the modern title Count.

contra mundum: against the world.

corpus: body.

deniers: Carolingian silver coins, struck in various mints and not always controlled by the state.

diptych: a two-paneled, hinged tablet, that opened like a book and had icons carved or painted on the interior of the leaves. A triptych was similar, but had one main panel with two front pieces that hinged open to the left and right respectively.

dux: originally the Latin word for leader, or war leader. By the early middle ages it denoted a Duke, above a *comes*/count, but beholden (sometimes) to a *rex*/king.

episcopus: the bishop, from the similar word in Greek, meaning overseer.

fideles: the faithful; the trusted companions of a lord. See Note 21.

furta: theft.

herburgium: listed in the Laws of the Salian Franks as a sorcerer, a practitioner of condemned forms of healing.

incantatio: incantation / spell.

incubate: the practice of sleeping in a shrine in hopes of healing or a vision.

in pricipio: In the beginning, the start of Genesis 1:1 and John 1:1.

Kyrie Eleison: a liturgical prayer, meaning "Lord, have mercy," with Kyrie meaning Lord. Part of the Roman Rite of the Church used to this modern day, and first found in the 4th c. work *Apostolic Constitutions*. The Kyrie is repeated three times at Mass, usually with the second line being changed to *Christe eleison*, meaning "Christ, have mercy."

lacuna(e): a lacuna (plural lacunae) is a missing gap in the writing of old manuscripts, where the words are partially erased, destroyed, missing or illegible.

ligamina: a ligature, or cord, placed for spiritual / magical purposes.

locus: literally the location, or place; the precise burial site of the saint, but more importantly, the point of the strongest *praesentia* (presence) of the saint. See Note 10.

lux aeterna: eternal light.

malefici: malevolent, wicked, or evil people, particularly those accused of demonic powers.

maphorium: a veil worn by Byzantine women around the head.

medica: medical.

miracula: miracles.

nave: the main, long hall of the church, often supported by columns on either side; the long arm of the cross floorplan.

pace requiem: rest in peace.

scriptorium: the book copying center of a monastery.

Sheol: the Old Testament description for the abode of the dead.

sortes: the practice of seeking God's direction through the random selection of a passage from a work, usually of the Bible.

strix: a witch. See Note 46.

transept: the cross arms of the church, extending perpendicular (usually north and south) from the joining of the nave and apse.

translatio: literally the physical translation/movement of saints relics from one location to another; see Note 1.

tympanum: the semi-circular area over a doorway but below the arch; in medieval churches, these were often decorated with Biblical scenes.

villa: a village, usually collected in the manor-style of a collective farm.

vitae: the life of a person; literally the title of a biographical-hagiographical work.

MAPS

TO BRITTANY
TO PARIS
TOURS
NANTES
R. LEGER
NOIRMOUTIER
ST PHILIBERT
THOUARS
TO BURGUNDY
NORTHMEN
PICTAVENSIS
R. VINIANA
AQUITANIA
OCEANUS
LEMOVICENSIS
TO BORDEAUX
TO SEPTIMANIA AND
SPANISH MARCHES
20 MILES

ST-MARTIAL
TO TOWER
TO BRIDGE
9
8
16
3
1
2
10
6
15
7
4
5
13
12
14
11
11
1 CHURCH
2 APSE
3 BELL TOWER
4 SACRISTY
5 DORMITORY
6 CLOISTER
7 REFECTORY
8 ABBOT'S HOUSE
9 GUEST HOUSE
10 GRAVEYARD
11 GARDENS
12 SCRIPTORIUM
13 COOKHOUSE
14 STORAGE
15 STABLES
16 LIVESTOCK PENS

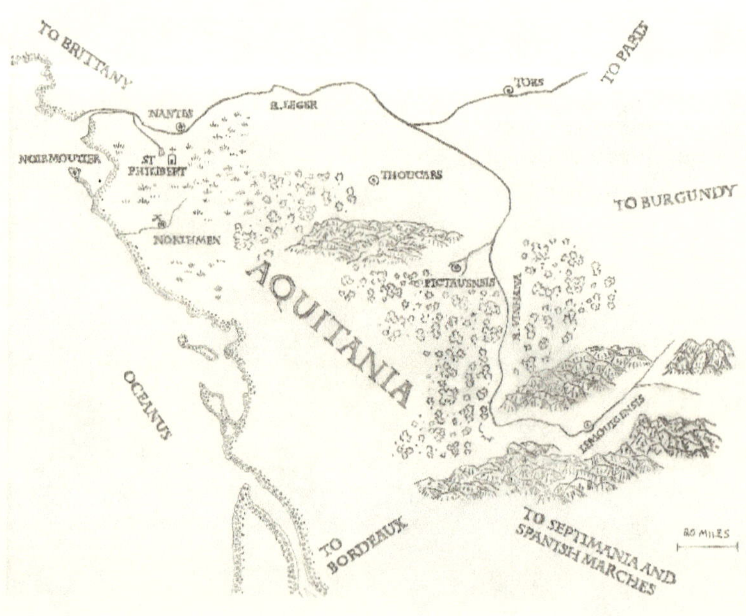

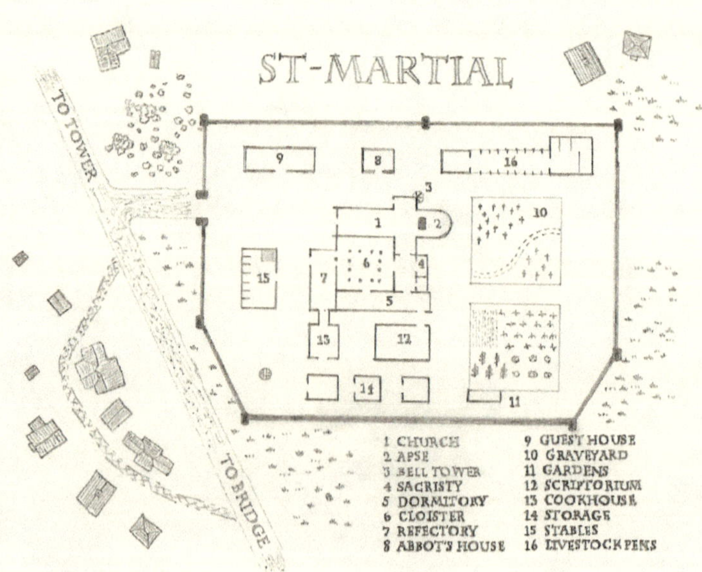

Faith during the early medieval period in Europe was murky, distorted, and at times ridiculous, but it was also unwavering and bold. Most importantly, it was full of wonder. It was sometimes very recognizably Christian, and other times far removed from anything that seemingly could have developed into Western civilization and the modern Church. But the key to medieval Christianity is the Incarnation. Ever since God joined His divine being to physical material, casting down the Gnostic assertion that spirit was good and matter was evil, the Church recognized that the spiritual enmeshes with the physical, both sacred reflections of the other in the natural world, in relationships, and in all activities of life.

Accordingly, saints were venerated at least annually at the anniversary of their deaths, in the reading of their *Acta* (works) or *Vitae* (lives), in ceremonies at gravesites or shrines, in the carrying of their bones and ashes and clothes, and in church song and liturgy. In a wild and unpredictable world, they were shafts of God's light piercing grim storms. Christians everywhere believed saints, particularly through their tombs and relics, to be more tangible access points for contact with the grace of God. Faith could be wept over before a marble sarcophagus, carried in a reliquary or on a phylactery pouch around one's neck, and smelled in incense and other foreign, heavenly spices. This faith was real: historical records show it produced real conversions, missionary fervor, true forgiveness, and personal redemption. It was through this faith, and no other, that Christianity, the Bible, and our knowledge of Christ came down to us today. Scour early medieval history (and for that matter, late antiquity), and you'll rarely find Christianity separate from the saints and their relics. Through God's delegated power, saints protected communities from marauders, healed the sick, brought thievery to light, held people to vows, gave guidance for the future, and influenced weather and disasters: in sum, they aided against the greatest uncertainties that plagued human life.

Without relic veneration in all its forms, the Church would have lost a vitality necessary for its survival *and expansion*. If it later became an oversized branch of the tree of Christian faith expression, gnarled, a bit rotting, and in need of trimming or truncating (depending on your view of the Reformation and Counter-Reformation), it was nevertheless, for far over a millennium, not just a major expression, but a *generator* of faith in Christ. Such a lengthy history of relic veneration, starting before the New Testament was codified, before even the Church penned the Nicene doctrine of the Trinity in the fourth century, seems less an aberration to be locked in the attic of embarrassing family secrets and more its own relic of our faith to be celebrated for the conduits of grace throughout the Church's European expansion.

As for Saint Valerie, after the destruction of St-Martial's abbey in consequence of the French Revolution, she and Saint Martial were rediscovered in their shrine in 1960 in Limoges (known at the time of this story as Lemouicensis). Saint Martial's history in that town was long attested to by the late ninth century when the death of the last Carolingian emperor, who we modernly name Charles the Bald, caused as many as five "kinglets" to spring up in the power vacuum. Saint Martial's centuries-old shrine had been converted to a full monastery about forty years before the fictitious visit of Egilolf and Aristeus. Saint Valerie's story, however, has no historical record until the ninth century, and its official details (brief and varied as they are) make it seem an invention of that time period. When my research showed Saint Philibert's relics had been moved from Noirmoutier (Herius) to Saint-Philibert-de-Grand-Lieu (Dee), and then on to Tournus, all in the relatively crammed history of a few decades, it seemed an intriguing pretext within which to explore a story for the sudden creation of Saint Valerie. Patrick Geary's modern historical work, *Furta Sacra*, accurately eliminates the possibility that some random farmer or cleric simply strode into Limoges one day, having dug up some bones he claimed were a long-lost saint. Whatever Saint Valerie's story was at the time of her discovery, it has been lost to the vagaries of oral storytelling or abandoned for the prescribed forms of hagiography. I hope readers find my fiction a suitable substitute that also reveals the esoteric but brilliant radiance of medieval faith.

My belief is true, nor is my faith in vain, that we live body and soul. For I recall how bodily, after harrowing Hell, with easy ascent God returned to Heaven. My remains hope the same, though obliged now to rest in holy-scented sarcophagus: my leader Christ, by similar renewal, will call me from dust to the radiant stars.

—Prudentius, *Liber Cathemerinon*, III. Late 4th c. AD

PROLOGUE: TO INSCRIBE WITH IRON ON LEAD

My pen threatened to drip if I didn't start writing. But where does Truth begin?

In pricipio: Egilolf and I stole some bones and quite innocently started two battles. Well, perhaps not innocently.

In the beginning was a word. Our word. Egilolf and I promised saint relics to an abbot, a priest, and a nobleman, but we only found bones for one of them. All were desperate. One deadly desperate. Actually, we found two sets of bones, but that is far too confusing of a start.

In the beginning was a sin. Egilolf had a terrible penance—recover the relics of a saint—for a sin he refused to disclose. And I? I suppose I stole bones for worse reasons. Daily bread. Ambivalence. Anger at God for the decimation of my monastery.

The fit of the stool, the yew desk worn smooth by the pass of scribes' hands, and the flickering light over two pages before me were more familiar than my father's house. Why then could I not write? Was it the absolute silence when I expected the background hum of others scratching at parchments, sanding them, rolling scrolls or cutting codices? Or was it that both pages were blank, that despite retreating to this *scriptorium*—almost a mirror of the one from when I was fifteen—I was not this time copying but creating?

I breathed the cloying scents of gall ink and vellum.

Translatio Sancta Valerie. I wrote the title across both pages. Beneath, I added myself as author. *Aristeus of…*of nowhere. Long gone was my monastery, longer still my father's farm. Even after hauling Saint Valerie's bones across the breadth of the land, I had no home.

At least I had a future now, one as wide as Francia.

Aristeus of Francia.

I still hesitated. The expected version would be shorter; after all, creations pare the sum of facts. Which version was more important? The official version, read annually to the clerics, the *comes* and perhaps *dux*, their noble families, and even to the rustics? Or the truth, likely forgotten—or worse, intentionally ignored—left to molder, never copied at this desk or another?

No one wants truth. Not *all* of it.

Tarrying, I stepped to the window and looked across the cemetery and gardens of the abbey of Saint Martial. The bright moon muted the stars. The ethereal, silver light diffused through cloud-cast on the cloister, the outer wall, and the forested hills cascading as waves to the horizon—I felt for a moment I could almost, almost, *desperately almost* grasp the secret knowledge of everything, as though I had nearly gained the far-sight of the angels. My knuckles whitened on the windowsill, clutching for the mind of God. But all too soon, a retracting, a retreat, the infinite world collapsed on me, a table, and a feather pen. I must decide without divine guidance.

Almost.

I returned to the desk and, in one straight sitting, wrote two pages on the official story of the recovery and procession of Saint Valerie's relics from her obscure crypt near the war-torn territory beyond Pictauensis to her new home at Lemouicensis, in the abbey of Saint Martial. I recorded the miracles I saw and heard, the usual cripples healed, feuds ended, and exorcisms performed. The usual. *Saint Irenaeus, intercede for me; help my unbelief,* I prayed. As though any intercession of God's great power in this sorry, sin-reft earth was *usual.* Yet compared to the greater truth, the one I planned to spend the rest of the night writing, perhaps for no greater audience than the angels hoarding their divine vision, those *were* the usual *miracula.* The greater miracles were unperceived: the wars avoided, the conversion of the damnable Northmen, the reconciliation of one lost sheep.

Or perhaps two.

I sanded and set aside the shorter version, leaving ornamentation to future scribes. Again I hesitated. I could think of no convention, no classic Latin forms, for what I needed to write. If this was a history, like Bishop Gregory of Tors wrote of the Franks nearly three hundred years ago, I would start with the Creation, continue through the stories of the Israelites, transition through Jesus and the Romans to the Frankish king successions up to the Great Emperor Charles, and thus bring my work to the present day with his not-quite-so-great offspring. If the protagonist was Saint Philibert, or even Saint Valerie, I should start with their *vitae* and continue with their *acta* after death, through their continued presence in their glorious remains: bones, grave dust, and clothing. If writing the annals of the reign of a modern king, one of those numerous and fractious progeny of Charles the Great, or the upstart dukes that raised themselves to full royalty (how Pelagian!) as the last of Charles' line fell, I would start with his coronation by the pope and recall his battles, betrayals, monuments, wives, and subsequent fractious offspring. As if there weren't enough Northmen to kill, that we had to pit Frank against Frank!

But these are mere scenery in this story of the grave robber Egilolf, a thief sanctified *because of,* not despite, his thieving. So perhaps I should start before the Valerie debacle when Egilolf first tried his hand at filching a saint from the grave.

CHAPTER 1:
HE DESCENDED TO THE DEAD

When Egilolf initially described his first relic theft attempt, undertaken in Rome some months before I met him in the spring of 890, I envisioned scenes from the ancient Christian poet Prudentius. His pilgrims pouring into the catacomb of the horse-torn martyr Hippolytus, turning the corners of ever-darkening flights of narrow stairs, diverse beams of weak sunlight allowing a vague impression of the cavern, the mosaic walls, the tear-washed marble tomb.

Egilolf's truth, of course, was harsher.

"Sometimes a saint wants to be remembered," Egilolf murmured, first once, and then, after a half step forward, again. Like the repeating *Kyrie*, he continued his mantra and, more hesitantly, placed step after half step. The chaplain priest who set him this penance of recovering a saint's relics had armed him with this sentiment, a feeble weapon amidst the cold, hallowed stones of the dead.

Some years past marrying age, though not so old that others would assume him wise, Egilolf groped forward in the wan light of a torch. Stooping despite the sufficient ceiling, his height was hard to determine. His sharp nose and fair hair declared him foreign, at least to the Eternal City above ground. The dust and dank air declared every visitor foreign to this crypt. From the bricked-up entrance to the solid stone sarcophagi, the place boldly whispered a forbidding peace. There had been no visitors here, not for an age.

Egilolf slid a foot forward, his boot hissing across the stone floor. He grated to a halt. "But I must. The priest said…" The stillness dragged his words into silence.

Like the witch of Endor, these sarcophagi called up Egilolf's own ghosts. Dead men by the scores, Franks and Moors and Northmen, their corpses like tidal driftwood on wave-thrashed beaches or sterile seeds strewn across scrub grass hills.

More personally, Egilolf's mother, buried in their village chapel, succumbed to an evil vapor. His fellow soldier, not killed in battle, but buried at the same chapel. The soldier's grieving widow, piercing Egilolf with her sorrow.

And hate.

He shook his head to clear it.

He inched past two chambers off the main hall, past three crowned men carved in stone kneeling before a woman and her infant, offering their royal gifts. His goal lay at the far end of the chamber, directly across from the stairs he had descended, where the grandest sarcophagus dominated the gloom. An elaborate vineyard motif carved across it entwined a bas-relief in three parts: a man thrown from a ship, a whale spewing forth the man from its mouth, and the man resting on land under a shading vine. *Jonah*, Egilolf thought. *The dead returned to life.* He looked up at the close, arched roof over his head and back toward the sole exit, masked in deep shadow. *I am in the whale, sealed in with the dead.*

He looked to the right end of the sarcophagus, where a stone man in a box-shaped boat received a bird with an olive branch. He tested the lid at this end, but it would not budge. When he tested the opposite end, he saw a carving of three youths, standing in a fire, arms raised. *Salvation from death.* His head drooped. Four intersecting arches, something like a cloverleaf, indented the lid near this end. The indentation sloped toward its own center, where a small hole descended into the sarcophagus over the entombed decedent's skull. A libation hole for the hungry dead.

Egilolf traced the script along the edge but could not decipher it, not because it was worn, nor because it was Latin, but because he could not read. Not Latin nor Greek nor any language, civilized or barbaric. Finding a bracket in a pillar for his torch, he emptied his small scrip of metal wedges, a mallet, and a patch of sheep hide, thick with wool. Covering the mallet head with the wool, he set the first wedge between lid and box. His tentative strike made a tick that in daylight and the company of living men would have gone unnoticed but in the utter stillness of the crypt seemed deafening. Slowly the hammering increased in volume and tempo, perhaps from confidence or else desperation. With relief, triumph, and trembling, he convinced the lid to shift. Using other wedges, he inched it along. Once it was a meager quarter open, he set down the mallet, took up the torch, and wielding it much like a sword, re-approached the opening step by half step. The last two feet he covered in a rush, thrusting the torch so nearly inside the dark sarcophagus that had it contained anything but bones and dust, it must have caught fire.

Egilolf found a mostly intact skull and crumbling ribs. Recalling the glory of bejeweled reliquaries he saw in every church, he sank back. He almost dropped the light but instead set it back into the sconce. He picked up his bag, took up the sheepskin, and paused. It was one thing to open a long-sealed crypt below a church, even worse to pry open a man's tomb. But to pick up the dead, to touch ancient bones.... He shuddered.

"Sometimes, a saint wants…"

The words stuck. Penance or not, it risked Heaven's wrath to disturb a grave. After a motionless minute with his hand suspended over the tomb, he snatched up the skull and a few long bones with the sheepskin, placed it all on the flagstone floor and began wrapping. His breathing quickened, running off the silence. Trembling, he dashed the sheepskin into his pack, spilling the bundle. He tied it up again with fumbling hands.

He returned to the sarcophagus, pulled a leather pouch from around his neck and scooped pinches of grave dust into it. When half full, he tied it shut with a thong and hung it back around his neck.

Grabbing the torch and pack, he turned to go. As quickly, he spun back to the sarcophagus and made the Sign of the Cross. Once, and then again. "*Gloria Patri, et Filio, et Spiritui Sancto...*" Hoping his prayer was sufficient, he shuffled toward the exit.

"A thief may flee to the sanctuary of a church," a voice rang out in Latin. Egilolf halted, waving the torch about the gloom, but it did not illuminate the far end of the crypt from where the shadows spoke. Where the stairs led back to the church. His sole exit. "But where," continued the voice, "can a thief find sanctuary if he steals from *within* the church?"

"Who's there?" Egilolf demanded, his Latin poorer than his native tongue but sufficient to understand menace. Two forms appeared in the dim light. Egilolf assessed their size and thought he could best them if it came to it. Then a third appeared from the stairwell, carrying his own torch. "I'm no thief. I'm tasked—"

"As though it mattered!" cut the voice, now discernible from the middle of the three. "Your boorish Latin and your looks brand you a Saxon or Frank. Undoubtedly some abbot or lord has paid you to come steal more of Rome's precious saints and cart them off to your un-patronized land. You think you're the first to try? That's not how it's done around here."

"Who are you?" asked Egilolf, weighing odds and buying time. Once a military scout, he had dodged a few ambushes in his life, but the crypt now felt small. Far too small.

"You've heard of the deacon Deusdona?"

Egilolf shook his head.

"No? And you think yourself a relic hunter? For a hundred years, since my great-great-grandfather started the business, this has been my family trade."

The man on the right, dressed not in tunic but in a Greek chlamys, gasped sharply at the first speaker. "What are you saying?"

The first man sneered, "Clerics!" and returned his attention to Egilolf. "In this city, you pay me to collect relics. Or you'll pay later. You think I don't have my informers, and that as soon as you asked in the market—subtly, you felt—I wasn't on to you? No one encroaches on my territory. Now hand over Saint Vincentius."

Egilolf noted the third man, the torchbearer, was spider-stepping his right hand across his waist toward his left hip. Toward an old gladius sword.

The cleric, facing the relic trader, protested, "You knew? You knew! We could have guarded the church instead of waiting until after the thief breached the crypt!"

Cocking his head toward the cleric, the trader replied, "Even an encroacher has his uses. Do you think my people haven't also searched for the crypt entrance before? The Frank found it for me. He's more resourceful than I'd credit his race. And now, since he's done me some service and since we are in a church, after all, I will spare him." To Egilolf, he repeated, "Hand over Saint Vincentius. Before I change my mind."

They were all well-armed, though only the silent torchbearer seemed to be eager for a fight. Egilolf set down his pack, removed the sheepskin, and offered the bundle.

The trader seized it and stepped back. He unwrapped the bundle, examined the contents, then wrapped it again. He then broke into a chuckle, which grew to a deep laugh. "You really—know nothing—do you?" he said between fits of laughter, wiping his eyes. With effort, he calmed himself. "You think you could convince anyone that this was a saint, with bones wrapped in—in sheep's skin?"

His laughing grew riotous. He knelt, set the bundle in the dust, and slung his own pack off his back. From it, he produced a cloth that shimmered in the torchlight, unlike anything Egilolf had seen before, except perhaps on King Charles' queen, whom he had glimpsed once briefly on campaign in northern Francia. "These could be your grandfather's bones for all anyone knows," he mocked. The leader laid the bones in the mystical cloth and unstopped a small jar, filling the tomb with the heady smells of incense.

"What are you doing?" asked the cleric. "Saint Vincentius must be returned!"

Ignoring him, the relic trader sprinkled the incense among the bones.

"Clearly, Saint Vincentius wanted to be found again, found and moved where others will remember and value him more than your church has." The trader sealed the incense jar, wrapped up the gold cloth, and stowed it all in his pack.

Egilolf watched mutely. The torchbearer clenched and unclenched his hand as if daring Egilolf to fight.

"Don't fear, I'll find a suitable new *locus* for him." The trader kicked the sheepskin aside as he stood.

"But the people," sputtered the cleric, "they—they'll—"

"Sure, they'll be upset. Fortunately, you already caught the thief." The trader jerked a thumb at Egilolf over his shoulder as he retreated.

The cleric caught the edge of his cloak at the base of the stairs. "You came to me about a thief planning to steal Saint Vincentius. You said you would stop him!"

"Didn't I do just that?"

Egilolf glanced between the two arguing men and the still-silent guard, now gripping the old sword. He did not think he could best the guard, even without worrying about the cleric and trader.

The trader bartered over his shoulder as he climbed the stairs. "There's a merchant group leaving next week for the Avars, who last season were paying twice the going rate of the Magyars for relics. You'll get your cut as soon as I've had a translation story written up and completed the sale. Besides, you think Saint Vincentius wants to remain with people who don't care enough to protect him from a Frankish thief?"

The cleric's protests grew fainter as he followed the trader up.

The guard backed to the base of the stairs, always facing Egilolf, and silently withdrew.

Egilolf followed up the narrow staircase, uncertain if a sword awaited him. His caution vied with an urge to escape the crypt's black horrors. Escape and, just maybe, recover the relics. *Miracles could happen. Jonah betrayed God, drowned in the sea and still the whale spat him onto dry land.* He needed those relics. His penance—his salvation—depended on it. He ducked through his recently made opening, stepped over the toppled bricks, and emerged into a small alcove.

He was beyond the altar in one of the apse recesses, the east end of the church. The cleric caught up to the relic trader at the main doorway at the west end of the nave, and the guard trailed behind. The church was small, as confining as the once-sealed crypt beneath it.

"Two-tenths," growled the trader, "Or nothing." When the cleric nodded, the trader ordered the guard, "I've changed my mind. This whole night's been more hassle than profit. Kill him here. Drag him out the doorway. I wouldn't want it said we killed him in the church. But wait after I've taken Saint Vincentius well away. He doesn't need to see this." Not waiting for acknowledgment, he stomped out the doors.

Egilolf eyed the transepts north and south for other exits but saw none. He scanned the altar area for any weapon better than his belt knife. The guard drew his sword and swaggered down the center aisle, his eyes fixed on the thief. Egilolf kept the width of the altar between them, dodging left and right in hopes to unbalance his would-be killer and dash past him. But the guard was good and countered every feint. Probably served in the military himself once. Egilolf wondered how long this ring-around-the-table could forestall his death. Suddenly the cleric, forgotten by thief and would-be killer, threw himself in front of the guard. "You can't kill him *in* the church!" he shouted. "Have you no sense?"

The guard didn't reply, nor did he take his eyes off Egilolf. Victims had been dragged from churches and killed on the steps, and some not brought that far. Soldiers knew God didn't always punish sacrilege. As the guard stepped around the nuisance, the cleric threw himself on the guard's sword arm. Reflexively, the guard fended the cleric off with his other hand—the hand holding his torch.

The cleric's thin chlamys lit instantly. He began to scream out, "O God! O God!" as he fell to the floor, the flames spreading as fast as his cries. The screams, echoing off the perfect semi-circle of the apse, reverberated with the harmonics of an unholy chant.

The guard dropped both sword and torch and, perhaps not prepared to test God so much as to kill a cleric in a church, beat at the flames.

Egilolf leapt onto the altar and vaulted over the maelstrom of limbs and fire. He sprinted to the door, tossing his own torch behind him to discourage pursuit. Once out the door, he dashed down the steps, double-checked the knots of the pouch at his neck, and slipped into the alleys.

Heads popped out of windows, questioning the screams rising from the church.

The burnt cleric hobbled out the doorway, collapsing as he cried out, "They stole Saint Vincentius!"

One of the times he told this story, at a home where he shared perhaps too much wine, Egilolf described slipping out of Rome via a broken aqueduct, disused since the Goth invasions nearly five hundred years ago. But at the first telling, he stared into our campfire in the Septimanian Forest, and he spoke hollowly of running and running. Not until many more months of our own escapes together and staring into more shared fires did he speak of what drove him to steal bones. But before the reason for his penance trickled out, Egilolf shared that his first attempt to steal relics preceded his sojourn into the Spanish

Marches, then beyond, into Moorish Spain. There he learned that Spanish relics were not any easier to obtain. Not that Frankish ones proved easy either, but Spain is where I met him. After that, our story really began.

CHAPTER 2:
WONDERS IN THE HEAVENS ABOVE,
SIGNS ON THE EARTH BELOW

Ah, Cordoba, city of learning, and tolerance, and absolutism! Not thirty years had passed since the last wave of Moorish persecution and Christian martyrdom in that Spanish stronghold. When I wore thin my shoe leather, adrift after the loss of my abbey and brother monks, I found in that great city the books I sought—books of reason, ruled in precise lettering. I found order.

Alongside these, I found stern lessons from the local Christians on how not to anger the accursed Moors. Sermons abounded on the topic, replete with simple instructions such as not calling them "accursed," and commands not to insult their prophet. I could sooner question their god than his prophet. I avoided such affairs, since such conflicts precipitated the martyrdoms of mid-century. While I was surviving, barely, by selling my scribing services, Egilolf approached me in the late spring of 890 with an offer: half of the reward if I aided him in crafting a translatio *story of a Cordoban martyr saint which he planned to take to Aquitania.*

Reluctant to leave the libraries of Cordoba but motivated, I confess, by the prospect of a greater income, and also perhaps pining for Francia again, I agreed. It was much later before I found out that was only Egilolf's second theft attempt. Even later, before I learned the perilous results of the first misadventure in Rome. But the theft of Saint Perfectus succeeded, though my new companion bemoaned the outcome. We escaped Cordoba unmolested with the relics, but through too much talk at dinner in an abbey, we were waylaid in the Marches and brought to Comes Guifre. *There, despite Egilolf's objections that Saint Perfectus wanted to proceed to Aquitania, the* Comes *declared the Spanish Perfectus, martyred for his resistance of Moorish tyranny, the ideal patron for the new abbey he was building for his son. Or perhaps it was a nunnery for his daughter. He spoke on for a while, laying out his restoration plans for some Visigothic monastic ruins to the point that I ceased listening. Either way, Saint Perfectus found his new* locus, *and we received a reward sufficient to fund another two or three months on the road. We proceeded, first into Gascony, then farther north.*

Egilolf soon sought another saint to reclaim, and though I misunderstood his purpose for it—he had not mentioned his penance yet—I was glad to have returned to Aquitania and the fringes of Francia and Burgundia with a new aim to life. And so, though we perceived it not, God's divine direction brought us in the early summer of 890, Anno Gratia, the fifth day after the Feast of the Nativity of Saint John the Baptizer, to the abbey of Saint Martial, in Lemouicensis.

"Having exhorted and blessed you all by recounting some of Saint Foy's great miracles," a road-worn pilgrim standing at a lectern at the far end of the refectory announced, "I would now share with you a song we have prepared on her great blessedness."

As the speaker paused for a sip of his watered wine, Egilolf spun on the bench toward me. "Aristeus, he matches you for long-windedness!" A tinker and his wife sharing table with us chuckled. I didn't bother replying, but at the table next to ours other pilgrims, wearing crosses similar to the speaker, glared at my companion. Behind us, a group of brothers from the abbey looked up, some struggling to keep the Rule of composure and serenity. Egilolf opened his mouth again but shut it when the abbot scowled our way. Full, the dining hall could have held eighty or so. Partially empty this evening, half the room was taken by members of the abbey, ordained and lay. Another table seated a dozen pilgrims. A few other travelers, including an old man who wore a gray priest's robe but sat apart from the brothers, filled the tables closest to us. Egilolf resumed his dinner as the speaker continued. I considered my own shabby barley loaf, which called to my mind how long I had been away from simple, coarse monastic meals. The cheap bread, however, was offset nicely with a beetroot and leek soup in which floated two bites of pork.

"Far back before the age of Constantine, when pagan emperors slew Christians at every whim, a small child, more powerful in spirit than her age and weak sex would have you believe, defied the persecutor Dacian…"

As the speaker harped on, ruining a beautiful story by emphasizing every word equally—clearly, he had no rhetorical training and attempted to atone for his lack with volume—the tinker pulled Egilolf into a quieter conversation. "Are you pilgrims, then, headed to Spain?"

"No," Egilolf chuckled a bit to himself. "Not pilgrims. Just came from Spain."

"Oh, from where? Which pass did you come over?"

"By the Augustan road. The *Comes'* soldiers patrol it better this summer. We've come from Cordoba. Where I met Aristeus." He tipped his chin toward me.

"Cordoba? That's deeper into the Moors' land. What took you there?"

Egilolf had just taken a bite and didn't seem in a hurry to finish it, so I spoke up for him. "I was a scribe there. I am sure you know it for a city of letters and ideas."

The wife, modestly silent to this point, freed her curiosity: "It is a good city for scribes. Why did you leave?"

"He wasn't making as much as he'd like you to believe," Egilolf gave a small laugh.

"So, what took you back to the road?" The tinker spun an easy conversation, likely a life's habit of seeking a sale from simple exchanges.

Egilolf stiffened a bit, but I had come to find him overly suspicious of everyone we met, a lingering habit from his military scouting past. He hung his head back into his soup and left me to answer.

"Saint Perfectus, really." The tinker and wife both shared a quizzical look, so I continued. "He was martyred in Cordoba thirty-eight years ago for the crime of speaking the truth. Not about the Moor's god, you understand, but about their prophet. They're quite sensitive about him. But we brought him north out of that city—"

Egilolf gave me a sharp and sharper kick beneath the table, and I bit back a yelp.

The wife's face twisted with loathing and fear. The tinker kept his face still but leaned away from us. "Oh, uh, we were not stealing him. It was rather more like a rescue, bringing him out of the oppression to the Marches." Under the table edge, Egilolf crushed my forearm. The wife glanced nervously at her husband, and an awkward silence hung at our table despite the pilgrim-preacher blathering from his stand.

The tinker nodded politely and returned to his meal, at a loss for words perhaps. I learned, the hard way, discretion when discussing relic recovery.

In the silence at our table, I gazed about the room, rubbing the bruising spot on my arm. My eyes caught the old priest, the one in gray robes at the table next to us, staring at Egilolf. I had not noticed when his interest sparked. He appeared bald but kept his head deep under his hood even while dining. His beard, more white than gray, grew more than a hand's-breadth below his chin, extending over his robe in a counterpoint to the shadows on his face. His eyes flickered sharply between his food and my companion.

In the pause, the lecturer shouted the praises of Saint Foy's beheading without pause: "But due to the great persecutions, and the pagans not even allowing proper burial of the martyrs' remains, her relics remained hidden until the persecutions had passed! Then the bishop-saint Dulcidius built a new basilica for her in Agen!"

A rather large pilgrim suddenly loomed over me, interrupting my conjectures on the old priest. "Can I join you a minute?" asked the pilgrim, his bulk forcing Egilolf to move down the bench before his question was fully out. "Have you heard of the great translation of Saint Foy from Agen to Conques?"

Hoping for news of Lyons, I ignored his question: "Who has not? Having come from Conques, have you heard anything about *Dux* Rudolf? I heard rumors he elevated himself to *Rex* of Burgundy."

The pilgrim, too eager a missionary, or perhaps ignorant of the broader world, refused to change topic. "We return from the small but great abbey at Conques. Like their Saint Foy, small but mighty. In my grandfather's day, the monks tell, she was brought from Agen."

I suppose I didn't look impressed. Egilolf made his disinterest obvious, spinning his knife on the table. "I have read most of her works myself, even copied a chapter or two," I replied to awe this rustic peasant into silence on his newly-beloved saint. "Do you have any news of Burgundy?"

In the background, the lecturer was trying to dramatize the dilemma of Bishop Dulcidius, debating if he could move Saint Foy's body without losing its parts. I say *trying* to dramatize because he was unable to exceed his previous tempo and volume.

"No," the heavy pilgrim answered me shortly and then addressed the rest of the table. "We were there for the first procession of her new statue!"

After having sighed and sought anything more interesting around the room, I inadvertently swung back to him at this announcement.

He mistook my motion for wonder.

"Truly, her reliquary is unique and inspiring. Her relics have been incorporated into a statue, completely made of gold!"

"A statue?" I asked. I expected Egilolf to perk up at the mention of gold, but he made no response. Despite his explained motives in Cordoba, I did not believe he undertook these risks solely for the recovered saints' benefactions. I assumed it was just his way of making his day's wage.

"She sits about three feet high on a throne. The brother monks then carry her through the village outside the abbey for all to see. She has protected her region from drought, famine, and robber barons, among her numerous other miracles."

I paused to consider how best to confront this. The lecturer's proclamation was wrapping up, but I only half heard him describing Saint Foy as both present with her Bridegroom in heaven and also with her relics on earth.

"How can you think it acceptable to venerate a saint through a statue?" I asked. Apostasy is best denounced directly. "It reeks of the paganism of Aaron's golden calf that caused Moses to cast down the tablets. It goes well beyond even the Greek form of *ikon* worship, which, as everyone knows, was proscribed—" I cut myself off as the pilgrim began choking in shock.

Egilolf muttered, "Sure, bash the hornet's nest."

The pilgrim gasped air and scrambled to his feet. "The abbot of Conques himself approved the design! Who are you to challenge it?" he shouted.

"Pope Saint Gregory the Great," I instructed, maintaining a lecturer's calm, "spoke of evangelizing new peoples at their level of ignorance, paralleling their practices into true Christian beliefs, which method is likely the only practical one to convert the rustics. And yet—"

"Rustics?" the pilgrim shouted.

"You know, those uneducated commoners who believe—"

"Rustics!" With surprising speed for his mass, he reached over Egilolf and hauled me to my feet by a fistful of my robe.

"In the name of God!" boomed the abbot. The hall went silent. I hung awkwardly by the front of my tightly gripped robe, only now realizing the pilgrim's other fist was arrested solely by the abbot's authority. Our confrontation had happened too quickly for Egilolf to intervene.

The man who ruled hall and abbey seemed far too old and frail to shout so loudly. His face appeared less road-worn than the old priest, and yet the yellow, saggy skin whispered of the encroachment of mortality. I hung in space as he addressed us.

"Might I remind you, although I allow the teaching of edifying works over meals, and I am more patient than most in tolerating travelers' conversations—a policy I might have to reconsider—this is still holy ground for contemplation, not a tavern for drunken shouting and cockfights!"

The large pilgrim released me and slunk back into his seat. "Thank you, pilgrims,"—here I found the abbot's smile to the pilgrim lecturer exaggerated—"for sharing with us the great miracles of Saint Foy. May she bless us all. We shall all depart, in *silence*, to contemplate Christ's grace, which oft comes through Saint Foy and many other saints." The *silence* was obviously stressed but had I not been listening intently, I would have missed the abbot's slight twitch at the word *other*. There being nothing else to do, we all stood and filed out, the large pilgrim without a backward glance, though Egilolf and I did exchange a mute farewell with the tinker.

Contrary to my previously long-kept schedule of holy hours, with its routine of early rising, I find the waning eve most conducive to complex thought. Egilolf had also proved himself capable of keeping watch at all hours, so without speaking, we did not follow the hushed pilgrims back to the guesthouse but instead wended our way among the abbey grounds. The summer solstice, having passed eight days before, the evening took its own eternity transitioning to starlight.

"Had to have the better story, didn't he?" asked Egilolf.

"Who, the pilgrim?"

"Who else? Ah, I suppose I'd be eager too. Retell the pilgrimage memory on the long trek home." We circled the outer grounds, from south to east, and Egilolf paused to watch the sky darken beyond the eastern hills. "Why'd you rile up the man?"

"I was not riling him up. I was instructing the ignorant. It's something of a delicate balance, I suppose, deciding what can be spared from pagan customs. The Church has spent centuries, and still, the art is imperfect. Saint Gregory the Great, of course, recommended sanctifying pagan temples into churches, so the local rustics would feel welcome in buildings they knew. He prescribed the same for their holy days, so as not to deny them a celebration but to replace it with something pointing to Christ. Easier than getting a man to cast aside both beliefs and practices. And yet, something about a statue for Saint Foy crawls across the nape of my neck."

I too faced the gold-red sunset. "Does it not you?"

"Don't know the things you talk about. Ancient things, like your great man Gregory."

"He is not ancient. He lived but a few hundred years ago. Ancient is the early church, over eight hundred years ago when the Apostles made the first bishops. We must reach back to them, the first generations who wrote and collected the New Testament, to learn the difference between veneration and worship. Did you know when the early believers were martyred, the pagans often prevented the collection of bodies, knowing the relics were precious to Christians? As a child, I read of the first martyrs of Lyons, and I would consider worthwhile all my years of copying if the only work I ever scribed was their *acta*."

I watched Egilolf, who still faced the graveyard. Was he listening? "Lyons threw the martyrs' ashes in the river, fearing that the Church members would worship them otherwise. They confused worship, obviously, with veneration, but still, when we incorporate relics into statues, I wonder if we stray too far."

"Lost me as usual, Aristeus. Calming, though. To listen to you ponder things that don't matter."

"Don't matter? Is anything more important than orthodoxy, than discerning heresy from truth? Saint Augustine himself said that anything not eternal was too brief! Eternal truth is of the greatest importance and when relic veneration degenerates into worship–" I sputtered in my anger.

Egilolf, perhaps startled by the edge to my tone, shook himself, then offered me a half-smile. "Yes, it's the eternal that matters."

Despite the agreement, I could tell his thoughts were elsewhere. Reflective, but elsewhere. "Sorry. Thinking of the wars, again?"

Reticent on the road from Spain, Egilolf had dropped only scraps of his past, and these disparate, but they were enough to illuminate years of scouting in multiple Frankish armies across the span of the old empire and at times beyond.

"Yes. That, and…" He strode forward, and I had to lengthen my stride to match him around the north side of the church. Once, he looked at me, opened his mouth, shut it and kept walking. He pointed to a crumbling section in the north abbey wall and then to a lower ruined window in the church's bell tower, an archer slit damaged and cracked wide. "Been long since war came here." I must have looked confused, for he added, "Otherwise, the abbot would have repaired his defenses."

With this abrupt change of topic, I pried no further—that night.

As we circled the north transept entrance, we approached the abbot's house, its roofline a shadow below the last deep blue of day's end.

A monk approached us from the direction of the guesthouse. "Are you the travelers Egilolf and Aristeus?" he asked.

When we confirmed, he asked us to follow him to see the abbot.

If the monastic father truly wanted to see us, he was in no rush about it. The monk motioned us to a bench outside the doorway to the abbot's open office, then disappeared into the night. Despite being lax in the refectory, the abbot kept the Benedictine rule of sparse quarters: a writing desk next to a shelf holding an impressive ten codices, a corner shelf with a solitary unlit candle and a crucifix, and a door beyond which I could only see the edge of a bed. Abbot

Gonsindus hunched over the desk, lit by three candles, his face a hand's-breadth from the page he scribed. Next to him stood a brother monk who, by conversation, must have been the prior or the cellarer, but who by his stiff neck and haughty speech could only be the prior.

Our seating arrangement made us audience to a debate taking place, a discourse on bread. "…we *will* discuss the bread first before I make any rulings on the beer and wine, or the cheese and beans." The abbot spoke like a mother to her petulant child. He never looked up from his writing as he lectured. "You will not order Brother Borfurt to halve the ration to the poor without—"

"But our pilgrim numbers dwindle!" the prior interrupted. "If we cut the alms bread for the poor, we could feed the pilgrims better than, say, Conques. Word would spread, and we could regain our losses."

The abbot set aside his quill. "Don't interrupt, Ageric. Impatience nestles into your soul. I will not diminish the bread to the poor." His tone switched to that of a cantor, reciting: "Adalhard's ratios to Corbie are well-reasoned. Forty-five loaves of wheat and rye, each to weigh three and one-half pounds. Additionally, five loaves of wheat or spelt. The total to be divided as follows: twelve to the poor that spend the night, and half again for the next day's journey, six for—"

"Gonsindus, the coffers rise or fall by the pilgrims that pass through, and their numbers have done nothing but fall since the theft of Saint F—"

The abbot cut the prior off with a sharp gesture. "You forget yourself, brother. Perhaps you should examine your soul." He softened. "Forget your worry of pilgrims and coins. I have an inspiration waiting right now outside the door."

The prior held the scowl from his face until he left the room and stalked past us.

The abbot beckoned us in and resumed his reading. Without glancing up, Abbot Gonsindus asked, "Did you really obtain Saint Perfectus' relics from Cordoba, or are you tale-makers?"

"Count Guifre believed them real."

The abbot finished copying his line and set down his pen before turning to Egilolf.

"Yes. Count Guifre, by all accounts, is a fair warrior who has shed enough Moorish blood to allow Odo, Charles, Lothar, Rudolf and everyone else to fight each other for a now-non-existent throne. As he ages, he undoubtedly seeks eternal prayers for his soul. Hence his nunnery. That much I know by my sources to be true. But what I asked was—" here he peered at Egilolf, and I glimpsed the stern wisdom of Solomon questioning the women over the dead child— "did you really obtain Saint Perfectus from Cordoba?"

"I don't lie. Not about God or saints," retorted Egilolf. "Not learned, but I'm honorable. Prudent."

"Yes." The abbot allowed himself a thin smile. "Some of the saints are rather prone to scourging the wicked. Even while they heal the penitent with holy pity."

Egilolf prickled at this.

"How did you come to seek for Saint Perfectus?" the abbot probed. "Or any saint, for that matter?"

Knowing how sharply Egilolf avoided that question whenever I asked it on the road, I interjected. "For your purposes tonight, Father, is that particular question necessary?"

The abbot appraised me, then Egilolf again. "I am Abbot Gonsindus. Amidst the thorough extolling of Saint Foy's virtues tonight, I overheard you speak of Saint Perfectus. I know not how you came to be a relic—*seeker*, shall we say?—but perhaps you are granted this gift by the grace of the Holy Spirit and the intercession of the saints." He clasped and unclasped his hands, looked at his papers, and then back at us.

"My problem is this: Lemouicensis has always been a waypoint on the pilgrimage route to the tomb of Saint James in Spain. But ever since the theft of Saint Foy—and I will say theft, for she was guarded by her keepers, and only by cunning and false-friendship over years was her guardian's trust overcome—because of the theft, I say, of Saint Foy and her translation to Conques, more pilgrims detour to the south, especially now that she has a new statue. As though novelty equaled holiness!"

"I, too, was greatly concerned when I heard about the statue—" I began, but his glance shut my mouth.

"Not that I would malign the good Saint Foy. I have heard she tends to punish anyone who speaks against her or at least play tricks on those obstinate in their unbelief. Our patron Martial sees to the needs of his abbey, but for over three hundred years, this place was little more than a shrine and quarters for a handful of monks. It has been less than fifty years since the second Charles funded a full monastery here. Perhaps we require another saint's assistance. One not only a bishop and teacher, though that guidance is also necessary for an abbey, but someone closer to the needs of the people. Pilgrims flock to Saint Foy because of her uniqueness as a female child, but what do people really want?"

"Peace," Egilolf spoke softly.

"Yes. At least, most do. English saint-kings, men both holy and warriors, generously helped their people in life and defended them from ravagers foreign and close. We have need of such a saint now in these unstable times. Someone to aid us against the Northmen, and the Moors, and also during these squabbles for the Frankish throne." He collected himself with a shake of his head. "I will need you to write the *translatio* story, certainly. Something suitable and holy."

"In Spain, I heard *Dux* Ranulf declared himself King of Aquitania. Is that truth or rumor?" I asked.

Abbot Gonsindus waved his hand as though batting aside a gnat.

"You want us to bring a saint here?" Egilolf asked guardedly.

I didn't see a trap anywhere in this; in fact, he and I had been hoping for employment. Still, if Egilolf scanned for a trap, perhaps I should too.

"Preferably a Frankish one. From the Merovingian days. From before all this in-fighting, and cousin slaying uncle, and brother against brother. Before Moors and Northmen brought so much death. Bring me relics and the story of their recovery."

I almost pointed out that Gregory, bishop and historian of Tors, had written entire books of similar intrigue, plotting, and death three centuries ago. But I caught myself before belittling a learned man with his lack of knowledge—especially since we were now in his employ.

After a brief reassurance that a worker was worth his wages, and a fatherly reminder that *compline* would soon be upon us, the abbot showed us to the door. The waning half-moon had not yet risen, and the torch at the abbot's door lit only the first few paces of the pathway.

To allow time for my eyes to adjust, I posited, "It would almost have been better to find a saint first and then the receiver, but I suppose half the problem solved is better than none."

Egilolf's response was to grab my arm. He raised his other hand to my lips to silence me. He tilted his head, listening. I did the same but heard nothing. Still motioning me to silence, he released me and took a step toward the east side of the house. Something scuttled in the shadows.

"Who's there?" Egilolf commanded. He took the torch from its sconce and advanced. A louder shuffle of feet answered, and Egilolf thrust the torch forward. A curly brown head and peasant's wool tunic crouched below the abbot's window then fled.

"Come, Aristeus!" Egilolf yelled and sprinted after the eavesdropper, heading toward the livestock barns and fences.

Without considering the consequences of trailing an aimless light in darkness, I stumbled after him across the field. Egilolf's light disappeared around the first barn, then reappeared as I rounded the same corner. Inexplicably, the light ahead rose into the air about a man's height, then dropped suddenly. I sprinted after it, but five steps later, simultaneous sharp blows to my chest and hip knocked me to the ground. My breath struck from me; I gasped for air and struggled to my feet, raising my arms to block any more strikes.

No blows came, and though Egilolf's light was far ahead, and I could see little, I heard no one around me. With groping arms splayed, I identified wood rails before me. I had struck the livestock fence at full sprint. The rise and fall of light had been Egilolf climbing over.

With darkness and bruising wounds arguing against pursuit, I watched the image from Egilolf's torch moving to and fro as he chased the eavesdropping man. The light disappeared briefly behind the second building, hopped back and forth over fence lines a few more times, and swiped back and forth in arcs when my companion searched nooks and corners.

After a minute, the torchlight steadied and then made its casual way back to me. Egilolf called my name and I directed him to me.

"Where'd you go?" he asked.

I bit off a lecture about the futility of pursuing a receding light in dark and unfamiliar territory and instead asked the more pressing question. "Were you able to determine anything regarding our interloper? Anything to identify him by?"

"Gave me the slip among the hogs," he replied, directing me back toward the abbot's house. "Didn't see a weapon drawn. A spy, not a killer."

This was not reassuring news, and I informed Egilolf as much. "How would anyone have known why the abbot called us this evening?"

"Maybe he didn't. Maybe he often listens at the abbot's window. Most wouldn't notice him there."

"And how were you alerted to his presence?"

"Didn't scout armies much by day."

We returned the torch to the abbot's doorway and stepped back into the shadows. It took a minute or more to once again see the ridgeline of the church against the night stars.

"The guest quarters are off to our right. Shall we stumble that direction?" I suggested.

"Not just yet. Need to think. About a coincidence, or God's guidance."

Egilolf, as I believe I've mentioned, was frequently cryptic at this point in our relationship, but he seemed tolerably rational despite his lack of education, so I was curious to see what he might reveal next. He led us back east, and I thought he was laying a trap for our eavesdropper. When I asked as much, Egilolf barked a short laugh. "That spy will be long gone. You see his panic?"

The path had a slight difference in its shade of black, enough to follow with cautious steps. As we approached the graveyard, I heard a low murmuring. I strained my ears and caught phrases of Saturn, the *aether*, and evil spirits. Someone was teaching cosmographic lessons under the night sky.

The thought of the spy lurking nearby made me nervous, yet what could be unsafe about an academic gathering? "Are you all right if I leave you to your contemplation while I attend this lesson?" I asked. I took his silence for assent and, testing my footing, proceeded into the graveyard.

"But if the stars decree the fates of men…" I heard one of the group begin, but a small wind in the grass took the rest. An old voice answered, in which I detected authority resisting the frailty of age, but I missed the reply. As I continued closer, I glanced back and barely made out Egilolf's dark outline, still pacing by the church.

"…by themselves don't determine the fate of all men and their actions," spoke the old voice, "yet, made of heavenly fire themselves and fixed in the outer *aether*, their immutability testifies to the eternity of God. All great events of this world God wrote there at the Creation, at the foundation when He spoke into being Light itself. It is in the seven planets, moving between us and the backdrop of the *aether*, that we see more clearly the frequent interactions, the portent-laden signs, the channeling of men's wills. Who recalls the influence of the lowest planet?"

Another voice spoke out as if by rote, almost too loudly for the still night, "The moon is the lowest planet, so low that it pulls at the sea. Due to its proximity to the spirits of the air, haven to most *daemonic* powers, the moon is to some extent corrupted, as is evidenced by its luminous intensity at night. Some argue this explains the propensity for man to be influenced to evil at night, and even more so when the moon is full."

"Almost verbatim," sneered a third voice. "But Brother Helias, if man's propensity to evil is due to the heavenly planets or to *daemons*, is sin really the fault of man?"

I stopped in the shadows behind the group and studied the planets while listening. Mars I found readily, baleful and inflamed.

The old voice responded, "Sin has always been the fault of man. The choice is always there, but we dwell on a battlefield, amidst an eternal war. Before the serpent tempted the woman, God had already presented the option of disobedience to Adam: do not eat. The serpent prodded the woman and she, in turn, tempted the man. But temptation forced neither. So it is with the heavens: God foreordained some of existence when He created the stars and all the heavens. The planets influence by their alignments, their ascension or waning through the quadrants of the sky. The heavenly servants also tug, not just the *daemons* of the air but also the nine orders of heavenly powers. Who can name them?"

The first eager voice piped up, "Cherubim, seraphim, thrones, powers, princes, the heavenly army, the lowest angels, and…"

"You missed a few," came the old voice. "Can anyone help Clovis?"

After a few seconds of silence, I could not resist, "The dominions and virtues." I sensed the group of students jump, but the old man either heard my approach or else did not recognize a newcomer.

"Yes, well done. The highest levels, naturally, attend to praising God in heaven, beyond the stars. They have no need to consider our lowly earth and human doings. But the angels, along with the heavenly army and the Archangel, God gave us against evil powers. We must always be mindful of the cosmographic battle raging around us, aware of those who aid man and those who joined the Accuser.

"What of diviners, the magi, and those who can commune with the dead? What do we make of them, knowing now the order of the heavens? Anyone?"

I confess that the rare opportunity for an intellectual exchange drove out any thought of Egilolf, his unspoken concern, and our great new commission. "Most are mere charlatans, using some flutter of hand and ancient words to fool the rustics," I said, stepping up to the circle of students. "Though some, having exchanged any hope of eternity, opened themselves to the direct power of *daemons*, greater than those of man, yet still more limited than that of the angels. The return of dead spirits, I have read, is often in truth a shade of those renegade angels taking on bodily form."

"Yes, generally—" the old man began replying before another student interrupted.

"Brother Helias, is all foreseeing evil then? The diviners and magi, I mean. The priest in my village used a *lunaria* to help calculate auspicious days for marrying, curing, harvesting, and such. Cannot the angels also foresee?"

"Certainly, Clovis," began the old monk, though I noted the asker was not Clovis, "the angels can foresee, else they would lose to the *daemons* who also have limited powers in these areas. But our great aids in life are the saints, for their benevolences cover all aspects of life. Who has not known a thief unmasked by a saint? Or of a saint who helped heal a grievous injury? Or gave a vision about a momentous decision to one who slept at a *basilica*? I cannot discount completely the *lunaria* because I have visited some monasteries that prescribe their use and copy them extensively, but it seems a residue of pagan days. Even then, the saints, relaying God's mercy, may be the medium for providing true guidance, so that ignorant pagans more easily accept Christ, seeing His aid through ways yet familiar."

"Grace even unto the blind and ignorant," I agreed. Many seasons more gray than gold had passed since I last joined such a discussion. I recalled dialogues with Brother Angius, lofty logic and ancient theories whispered under the cloister sky long ago. I smiled at the memory—and spat out my grief. No stars or signs heralded his death, and no saint had guarded him or the other brethren.

I sealed up those memories so they would not ruin this rare discourse. "What is your opinion, then, of the *Sortes Sanctorum?* Divining not by the moon in the heavens, but by the Word of God Himself?"

The old man shifted in his seat. "Some denounce this practice, though I suspect they actually revile the form. Saint Augustine himself allowed it if done via the Gospels and not some lesser book. Though his description is concessionary."

"What texts have you encountered regarding dream interpret—" I began.

"Aristeus!" Egilolf's cry cut the vast night and intimate discussion.

"I regret I must depart to aid my friend. Thank you for your insight."

"Freely received, freely given, Clovis. Go with God's blessings, and thank Him for His great grace, ministered to us through his saints and angels. Consider it whenever you look to the stars."

I crossed myself and stumbled back toward the church, calling out softly for Egilolf. Once I found him, I tried to share my new thoughts on fate and divine foresight while we headed to the guesthouse. *Compline* had long since come and gone.

He remained silent until he paused at the door. "What if someone set you to a great task, then seasons later, someone else set you to the same task? Would you think God reminded, or *daemons* tempted?"

"I suppose that would depend on the nature of the task." Venturing a guess, I asked, "Is this about Abbot Gonsindus' request for relics?" Egilolf paused, his hand on the latch. I waited for him to reply, but after only silence, he continued inside. I remained outdoors for half an hour more, pondering the stars until the moon rose over the cemetery. The night had cooled enough that, having stood still under the night sky, I shivered as I curled up in my pallet.

That night I dreamt of the stars dodging a baleful moon as they descended to dine with saints in a shrine of *aether*, huddling over the tombs and eating Northmen skulls, while spiced wine poured out of the sarcophagi and the saints crumbled to dust, the blood-wine washing over a multitude, healing the deformed and converting the leprous into fine wheat stalks, and setting fire to white-washed women crushing serpents under their heels. The fire was my *scriptoria* burning, the whole monastery burning, Northmen's battle cries amidst screaming prayers of brothers as they were hacked into holocaust offerings, the cries and sparks rising mingled, fading into the night sky, bereft now of its stars, as I darted from shadow to shadow away from the hellish end of my lost haven.

I woke sharply from the tendrils of this dream to sounds of rapid, gasping breaths. I thought it my own until I heard it from Egilolf's direction. Faintly the monks' chant of *lauds* echoed out our window. Dawn was stayed by yet a few hours, but Egilolf rose and left. Wondering but befuddled by my dream, I drifted back to sleep.

When I woke in the morning, I sought my companion, and I found him in the refectory at table, his face haggard. He had not returned to sleep since his rising at *lauds*. We sat by ourselves, sopping our bread in silence.

My thoughts kept tumbling over until they spilled out. "Where should we seek this saint-king for the abbot?"

Egilolf dunked another piece into his gruel and put it to his mouth, methodical as only a man can be when he runs from his thoughts.

I grabbed his wrist and repeated my question.

He blinked twice, as if awakening anew. "By the abbot's words, easiest would be some Briton or Saxon shrine. But Northmen harry both coasts, especially this year. We shouldn't risk it." Egilolf focused slightly as he talked. He tore at his bread, but his eyes relaxed. "We could start toward Brittany. See what comes our way. It's the right direction, at least." He chewed his bread and thoughts, and after a slow minute, he added, "I'm tempted to find some old bones. Wrap them up properly. If you wrote a good story, like Saint Perfectus, it would work for the abbot."

"You would dare forge some relics? Present some farmer's bones as holy! I did not think you to be—"

"I said I was tempted!" he retorted, drawing looks from the next table. He quieted before continuing, "But though it'd gain us some *deniers*, there'd be no miracles. No exorcisms. Wouldn't prove much to the abbot. Wouldn't do much for our souls." Egilolf quickly spoke past my puzzlement. "Easy refuses to ever be right. Yet if it's the only way…"

"Broad the path and wide the gate—"

"I know, I know." He tore his next bite harshly. "It's too early for you to preach. You're a scribe, not my confessor."

"Last night in the graveyard, actually, we were discussing the best ways to receive divine foresight and how to sift the divine from the demonic. I would appeal to Saint Irenaeus and the martyrs of Lyons, except I have not heard before of asking one patron's aid in finding another."

Egilolf snorted. "Remember the last time you asked for Saint Irenaeus' aid? As we escaped Cordoba? Look where that got us."

"We got paid, and Saint Perfectus was brought safely to where he needed to go."

"Your opinion. I wanted him in Francia." He crammed his last bite into his mouth and talked between bites. "Let's not open that pit again. Spent *lauds* praying for God's guidance. Still no answer."

"Oh? I presumed you attended *lauds* because you could not sleep after nightmares."

Egilolf glared at me blackly, and I nearly crossed myself to ward off evil. I was flailing for a suitable apology when a hand clamped my shoulder.

Are bones just bones if they lack a story? If one looked quickly, seeing only veneer, I could understand such a conclusion. Anyone can find dead bones, and they remain just that. But living bones—the saints found again, undisturbed or forgotten for centuries—are still as powerful as when they were buried, perhaps more so for being full-rested. That lesson was impressed upon me when I first read Einhard's translatio *of Saints Marcellinus and Peter, from Rome all the way to Seligenstatd, in those glorious days of Charles the Great. I often strived to recreate its intensity. From death, life; from wretched sin, glorious salvation; from perishable, the imperishable. Aid for a heavenly future, and the earthbound present. The translation of a saint was a powerful thing, almost a resurgence of the power of the saint himself.*

If I could but find a saint in need of moving.

CHAPTER 3:
REAPING WHERE YOU DID NOT SOW

Peter strides beside Jesus, leading the other disciples and a large crowd along a wide and easy road. The gentle sun, the slight breeze, the cloudless sky are all perfect. Yesterday Jesus told off the rich Pharisees, not exchanging his first followers for those educated or rich. Peter is reassured. He, once a poor fisherman at the lowliest banquet seat, has moved up to the better place. Even a gentle rain fell last night, forestalling the dust that usually choked so great a following. Peter catches a smile from John that agrees: this is why they left their boats and nets. They stroll the veritable road to heaven.

Jesus ascends a small hillock to address the crowd. "Unless you hate your own life, you cannot follow me." Peter catches John's look of puzzlement but awaits the explanation. Peter was used to Jesus' parables starting obscurely.

But like that time He insisted that everyone gnaw his flesh, Jesus doesn't soften. "If you're a king bent on war, but count the enemy as twice greater than you, won't you seek a peace? Those who don't give up everything cannot follow me." Peter, feeling smug, recalls the day he left his family and fishing boats. He's already counted his cost.

He doesn't quite hear Jesus' last words. Something about carrying a Roman cross.

A hooded priest used my shoulder as a crutch to lower himself on the bench at my right. I recognized him as the elderly priest who watched us at dinner.

"God sent his sheep out among wolves, and yet they returned rejoicing," he began in a voice much stronger than I expected. His trembling hands, however, made a mess as he ate between phrases. "Having spent a lifetime listening and watching, I am confident in my deductions. You spoke of relic-finding last night, and the good Abbot Gonsindus showed great interest as you spoke, amidst his annoyance, which he tried to hide as the pilgrims extolled Saint Foy. You later met with him, and now you debate sharply amongst yourselves. You've been tasked to seek more relics, which of itself cannot be the problem. So, you debate where and how and whom to seek."

I was admiring the man's deductions, visualizing his logical organization, and therefore missed what he next said.

Egilolf interjected, "How'd you know we met the abbot?"

I could have forgotten about the eavesdropper but for my bruised hip.

"I spoke with him this morning. He tolerates me for my age. But as I said, I am your solution. I know of relics that need recovery. If you're as capable as you say you are."

Egilolf pulled out his pouch of Saint Vincentius' ashes from around his neck and shook it. "I got these ashes from a forgotten crypt in Rome. I acquired the bones of—"

The old man ambivalently waved him to silence. "I believe you, or I would not have approached."

My companion glanced at the monks and pilgrims also breaking their fast at nearby tables. "Wasn't you at the abbot's window last night, for sure. But someone was."

"Listening ears, yes? Perhaps a stroll around the gardens."

We rose and followed him out, Egilolf offering the priest his arm, which was refused. The old man seemed sound in his gait, but surely not enough to have outraced a military scout through livestock pens.

We followed the priest from the refectory out to the garden. Along the way, we introduced ourselves.

The priest replied, "I am Leovigildus. Though you can see why some just call me Leo, yes?" Two monks hoed the west rows of bulbous root plants. We passed them and slowed among the early summer beans, their height giving a semblance of privacy.

"What of these relics, Father?"

The old priest ignored us and knelt to pray silently. When he stood, he faced us. "I hope I am not misplacing my trust. I do know of relics, but they are not to be recovered for Abbot Gonsindus, nor for this monastery. I have spent most of the night praying to Saint Philibert for his guidance and to Saint Michael the Archangel, that he smite you if you prove false. You've heard of Herius, yes?"

"Northmen raider base. Island off the coast?" asked Egilolf.

"More a peninsula that lies off the coast of Bordeaux," I corrected.

"Somewhat. It lies farther north, more west of Pictauensis but still south of Brittany. It was not always a raiders' harbor. In the time of Louis the Pious, before the empire split, the island was home to a monastery wholly dedicated to God and to Saint Philibert."

"The one now at Tournus?" I asked.

"The same. In the twenty-third year of the reign of Louis the Pious, Herius was finally abandoned after raids by the Northmen."

"Your saint is stuck on some rock in the sea, a Northmen base? Briton would've been more possible!" Egilolf snarled.

"Let me finish without interruption from both of you. We were able to take Saint Philibert with us when we left Herius—and, yes, I can see your question; I was sixteen years old then and am now seventy. We settled near the mouth of the *Leger* but far enough away from the river so as to not invite Northmen. We created a new monastery at Dee. I thought it a blessing at the time. With Saint Philibert closer to the people and the Northmen continuing to raid the coast and even up some rivers, pilgrims flocked there often for his protection. We were able to upgrade the church several times and needed to, really, for the growing number of pilgrims. In the face of growing raids, though, I assisted the abbot late one night transferring Saint Philibert's relics from his tomb into an even older crypt under the church, a hole under the old shrine over which we had built the new church. The abbot's fear was that the Northmen would come without warning, and Saint Philibert would be lost to them. The empty reliquary was left in the usual crypt, for the pilgrims still coming.

"The monastery did have to be abandoned, though not in the emergency of a raid. It happened while I was on a delegation to Rome and beyond, for what was supposed to be a few years but turned into a few decades. Imagine my surprise when I returned to track down the monastery at Tournus and find that, not only had my abbot died without telling anyone about hiding Saint Philibert, but those sons of heretics wouldn't believe me when I told them! Few of that group remember Dee or our first home of Herius. As if Saint Paul had not written to Timothy that the young should praise their elders like fathers and not rebuke them harshly. I left there angry enough to die. They had relics, you see, that they claimed were in the reliquary when they took it and left. I know they weren't true, because no one knew of the lower crypt. All they had were some peasant bones that another brother put in there, no doubt. You can see no one remembers the truth, yes?"

Father Leo rubbed his shaking hands together. For a moment, I thought him finished.

"I came to see, though, while contemplating Jonah, that the ignorance of fools should be pitied, and that though I wished, I confess, for fire, plague, Northmen or some other judgment of God to wipe out that pit of vipers, they were but sheep astray. And no wonder, for blessed Philibert is not restored to them. His relics lie buried still, I have no doubt, in the hidden crypt at Dee. You see now, don't you, how Saint Philibert has guided me and you together, yes? This can be no coincidence."

"What would be our reward for this service?" I asked.

"I should be angry for you even mentioning such a thing, but I have already considered your ignorance to be like those hell-bound monks at Tournus. No doubt Abbot Gonsindus offered you something. I have no great wealth, and the spiritual blessings of Saint Philibert should not be overlooked. This is a fallen age, though, focused on earthly tangibles, and to abuse Saint Paul's word, he who works deserves to eat. On that delegation to Rome, I was caught up as part of a council to the eastern patriarch in Constantinople. I suppose they wanted to display the variety and vastness of western Christianity. While cutting down a side street one day in that great city, I saw two men fighting over a white tablet. I was about to pass by when one threw the other hard to the ground, where he lay senseless. The victor called to me, and though my Greek is limited, he conveyed the other man was his brother, and they were split, like most Greeks, over the veneration of saint images. They call them *ikons*. What I thought a simple white tablet he then gave to me and asked me to bear it far away, to save it from destruction."

The priest brought out from his robe a thin box the color of cream, about one-and-a-half-hands high, and a hands-breadth wide. He passed it to Egilolf, who laid it on the table. The exterior was unadorned, but I noted that small hinges were set cunningly into the side so that it opened like a book. Though it was clearly not a book; inside were carvings, one on each side. Though it lay upside down on the table, I recognized the Holy Mother holding the Child in the right panel.

"Who is on the left?" I asked.

"Saint Michael and, in the small insert below, Saint Mercurius. The Greeks have much need of fighting saints, and Mercurius was an ancient Roman legionnaire, executed in the days of pagan Rome. Or so I was told in Constantinople. The inscriptions over them bear their names in Greek. But the greater treasure lies in the *Hodegetria*."

"Who's that?" asked Egilolf, stabbing a finger at the Virgin.

"The Blessed Mother, yes? Are you blind?" Father Leo had little patience for ignorance.

"Yes, I see. But who was she modeled after? Are you sure this is from the far east?" Though he had done nothing but stare at the carved woman since he opened the book, Egilolf leaned across the table into the priest's face. "This was carved somewhere near here, wasn't it?"

"Wrong! I don't know what you're getting at, but this is not some cheap trash," said the priest, reaching a protective hand over the carving. "You'd have to exhume the treasuries of many nobles before you'd find this much ivory, particularly in a backwater place like Lemouicensis. Not to mention finding someone with the skill, knowledge of the Greek carving style, and the Greek language. But dismiss it if you want to. This *diptych* is extremely valuable for its material alone. I thought you'd treasure it as I have these many years, but if it's nothing to you, sell it if you will. *After* you bring me Saint Philibert relics, yes?" He snatched back the carving, lovingly closed it, then tucked it back into his robes.

"I—I'm sorry. The carving resembles someone I know."

"You know the Virgin Mother, do you?" I laughed, trying to lighten the tone and not scare off this new employer.

"I'm no artist, but everyone follows a model. The carver copied some beautiful woman. Sorry…"

"You're rather struck by the likeness, yes?" asked the priest. "Who was she to you, this woman that looks like the Blessed Virgin?"

But Egilolf gnawed at his lip and would say no more.

To fill the silence, I said, "You mentioned some Greek word I am not familiar with."

"The *Hodegetria*, that pose of Mary with the Christ Child, is a classic form in Constantinople, the way Mary holds him in her left arm while pointing to him with her right. We would not think of it here in the West, but the Eastern church looks upon Mary as a great protectress, a powerful general. I was there, you know, for the great Russian siege of 860, when that city's fate fell blacker than ever before. Which says a lot for a city attacked repeatedly through the centuries. Then came Photius the Patriarch, leading the defense more than the soldiers. He carried the *maphorium*—the Blessed Mother's veil—in a procession along the heights of the city wall. That iconoclasm business was supposedly ended by then, but there were still plenty who thought it idol worship. Thus the fight between the brothers that brought this treasure to me."

Egilolf's eyes flicked towards me. The *diptych* was valuable and would command a good price to the right buyer. I nodded, and my companion answered for us. "I'll need maps to your Philibert."

The remainder of the morning, Father Leo drew diagrams in the dirt of the church at Dee and maps of its region beyond Pictauensis, south of Nantes. Pictauensis was as far westward as either of us knew the land, and my knowledge came only from annals.

Egilolf spent half an hour committing the maps to memory and questioning the old priest. "This lowland here. Marshy this time of year?"

Father Leo shook his head.

"And this river by the church. How long to follow its bank down to the *Leger* river?"

"I never hiked the river, but travel to the ruins of Nantes would take most of a day. The road once was wide and—"

Egilolf cupped a hand over the priest's mouth, cutting him off. As quickly, he pointed down the row. Unnoticed before, a monk picked beans at the end of our row. The beans were not fully ripe, and this monk had his hood up despite the late morning sun. Egilolf stalked toward the hunched figure, who kept his back to us. "Heyya, Brother. A question."

He got no closer. The figure jumped up and ran. Egilolf pursued, and his quarry dodged between bean stakes. His hood caught wind, pushing it down to his shoulders, and I saw the same brown hair from the night before, its curls distinct. The spy fled toward the south entrance to the dormitory. If he reached it, his exits would be numerous, but the most likely would be the refectory, as fleeing through the church risked sacrilege.

"Wait here, Father," I called and sprinted off, circling outside the *scriptorium* and ducking into the kitchen. Preparation for the evening meal had not begun, so the kitchen was empty. I slammed through the door to the refectory, leaving it swinging wild behind me. The orderly array of dining tables cut long aisles toward the northern doors. I reached the cloister doorway in time to hear the slapping of feet on stone, approaching my door through the colonnade outside. I set myself just inside the doorway, waiting to block the fugitive's path. The steps slapped loud as I stepped into the gap, holding up an imperious hand while announcing, "Halt, you impertinent—"

A jarring impact laid me out on the hard floor, knocking me half senseless. "You, you—" I sputtered, my head ringing.

"Where'd he go?" Egilolf, my accidental assailant, stood over me. "He must've run in here. I'm sure of it." He searched under and around tables frantically, ignoring my hand pleading for his aid.

Receiving none, I heaved myself off the floor. "I can assure you he did not come through this exit. At which point did you see him last?" My head spun, and I steadied myself against a dining table.

"Dormitory. Caught a look of his face as he made the corner. Next time…" Egilolf glowered and spat in disgust. If I had known how the next time would turn out, I'd have done more than spit.

That afternoon, Egilolf and I again found ourselves circling the grounds around the church while discussing our choices. We should seek Saint Philibert, that was obvious, though Egilolf kept reiterating that he was not the warrior-king that Abbott Gonsindus desired. Still, a few hours ago, we sought a saint and were now directed to one. The only part not miraculous was the dilemma of distribution.

"For my part," I replied as we made our third pass before the church nave doors, "I think we must return Saint Philibert to Father Leo. Otherwise, we should anger the saint, and that is not something I would risk. That does not really further our means for living, but we could always sell the *diptych*, perhaps if we were to journey somewhat into Lombardy. There must be some Byzantines there willing to purchase it."

"That's the problem. Don't care about the coin. If I got the *diptych*, I would keep it. But I have other reasons to deliver the relics to Abbot Gonsindus." He tried to smile. "He'd probably accept an old, fairly well-known Frankish saint, even if he wasn't a warrior."

"You have reasons besides coin? Like what?"

Egilolf's face went flat. His eyes narrowed, wary as a beaten cur's.

"No, do not give me that look," I softened. "If you persist in being reticent, I will not ask further. Are we at an impasse then? I need you to actually obtain the relics; you need me to write the *translatio*, so everyone knows they're not just some bones."

Egilolf glared at me and I at him. Though he was my only companion since the loss of my monastery, we had known each other for less than a season. "Perhaps we at least start for Saint Philibert and decide later what to do with him. We can seek divine guidance as we proceed."

He grunted, which I took for agreement.

Hope alone, I once read, builds no bridges.

CHAPTER 4:
NO ONE CAN SERVE THREE MASTERS

First principles build the foundation for all conclusions. I wondered later if we initially reasoned well but started with a wrong premise. Why would God grant us what we needed, only to give us even greater dilemmas?

The ancients and pagans looked for signs in flights of birds, entrails of livestock, the movements of horses, even how and when people sneezed. In our age, monks and priests, hermits and nuns, seek God's will through silence, prayer, Scriptures, and the exhortations of the Early Church Fathers. But not all can withdraw from the world. Those less educated or without access to the church's written deposit of faith seek visions of the saints or the intervention of angels. The stars, the planets. Written words: carved, impressed, painted, and scrawled. Spoken words: chanted, repeated, sung, preached.

And some, wretches lost to all hope, delve shapeless powers, sorcery, and atrocious potions. Even viler, the necromanticum *with their blood-*magia *tamper with death. What drives fallen mankind to this? Knowledge is but the intermediate goal, in itself neither virtuous nor sinful. It goads not alone. Ultimately we grope for control. Because we do not want to submit. Not to the elements. Not to foreigners or lords. And not to God.*

I awoke the next day praising God for sparing me from nightmares and found it was a cool day, a grace in the growing season. After singing *prime*, we broke our fast in the refectory. Suppressing feelings of duplicity, Egilolf and I agreed to both Father Leo and Abbot Gonsindus. The latter provided supplies from the abbey's storage, both victuals and a red silk cloth in which to recover the relics. He blessed us in the recesses of the storage hall, glancing over his shoulder at the doorway. Given the importance of our mission, I thought he should supply us with horses or at least a pack animal, but perhaps he did not think we would seek, much less find, and would gamble no more from his storehouses. When I shared this sentiment with Egilolf, he just replied, "O, he of little faith!"

We set foot to road well before *terce*. Outside the abbey gate, I surveyed the valley east, toward the town and cathedral, and beyond to the river. The sun rose cheerfully, lying about the day's events. Some of that talk of planets' influence was horse-dung.

The town of Lemouicensis was built in the valley of the *Vinhana* river, predominantly on the western bank. The road from the east spanned the river by an old Roman bridge and traveled along the south edge of the abbey before rising into the low foothills, where the region's tower fort kept watch. If we had been allowed to follow the road farther, it would have led us northwest, breaking from the westerly path of the *Vinhana*, only to meet and cross the same river after a few days' travel.

I say if we had been allowed to follow it because when we were less than a mile out of town, past the fort and into the wooded foothills overlooking civilization, a half-dozen riders came galloping along the road behind us. We stepped off the road to let them pass.

As they came within a few hundred paces, one began yelling, "That's them! The thieves!"

Four riders wore leather and gripped spears. A fifth wore a mail shirt over leather with a Frankish longsword at his waist. The one yelling was the only one unarmored. His monk's robe, hood and all, flowed behind him as he galloped, revealing brown, curling hair. My stomach dropped, and my limbs locked.

Egilolf grabbed my arm and dragged me toward the woods.

"Running only confirms guilt!" I protested. My eyes remained fixed on the riders' approach, even as my feet blindly followed him into the trees. Egilolf wove the erratic pattern of a pursued hare between oaks and bushes. I was winded within the first minute. Nevertheless, the trees slowed the riders and may have gained us enough time to escape if I had not tripped over a leaf-hidden root. My already-bruised hip landed on a rock, and by the time I was able to rise, three pursuers surrounded me. Egilolf was gone.

The mail-shirted one stood before me; his armor and graying hair marked him as the leader and possibly the most intelligent of the group. I was mistakenly comforted that his sword was still sheathed. His pale face reminded me of an abbey brother I once worked with, who cut his leg horribly and grew ashen and wan as he bled out.

"My lord, I am a monk, Aristeus by name, and I can assure you I am innocent of whatever injury, in property or body, you think—"

His fist to my stomach doubled me over. His hand to my throat hauled me back erect. Holding me by the neck at arm's length, he addressed the woods. "You that ran and hid!" He punched me again in the stomach. "Come out!" Another punch. His strikes ignored the thin shield of my arms over my middle. "I can do this all day!" He paused. Punch. The remainder of the guards fanned out into the underbrush. The robed spy kept silent astride his horse. My stomach screamed and heaved, and I think only the hand pressing my throat kept me from vomiting. The leader raised his fist again.

"Hold," came a low command at my back.

My captor shoved me to the dirt while he spun and drew his sword frantically. The other guards ran back, caught unaware as much as their leader.

Egilolf stood warily at the edge of a dense bramble patch.

That he had managed to circle behind the guards undetected clearly infuriated my armored assailant. He addressed us with the point of his blade. "You two came from Saint Martial's. Named Egilolf and Aristeus."

"What's it to you?" asked Egilolf, bolder than I'd have felt even if not beaten.

"I am Sichar, first *fideles* of *Comes* Fulgaud of Lemouicensis. Captain of his guard. My lord wants a word."

"About?"

"That's his business. My task is to get you there."

Egilolf and I exchanged glances as if we had any choice. Egilolf shrugged, held his arms away from his belt knife, and let two soldiers approach and disarm him. A third directed me back to my feet and the road with the butt of his spear.

"What of my money?" cried the brown-haired man.

"Ask the *comes*. He'll see you're paid," Sichar replied.

Furious but biting his lip, the spy rode back to town.

Egilolf and I were loosely bound, my left arm to his right. Surrounded by Sichar and his fellow guards, who remounted, we returned down the road we had but started.

"Who was that?" Egilolf asked the *fidelis*.

"Someone my lord said knew you by sight."

"His name?"

"Like I care."

I considered asking if we were accused of a crime but didn't want to plant ideas not sown. As we returned to the fort, the gate guard didn't seem particularly interested in us, which I took as a good sign. Once within the wooden palisade, Sichar and one of the other guards prodded us to a half-stone, half-wood hall next to the base of the stone tower. Compared to a cathedral or abbey, the construction was rough and unadorned, built completely for defense.

Inside, the hall adjoined the first floor of the tower. Poorly lit by a few slit windows, the corners seemed to hold spare shields and spears. The room was otherwise empty but for one long table. Its sole occupant rose from the study of a map as Sichar halted us. *Comes* Fulgaud suffered from being a very small man, likely with just enough power to dream of more. Despite the dim light, his eyes darted between many considerations and plans. "You are the relic thieves, correct?" His tone was more genial than his words implied.

Egilolf shook his head.

I answered, "Egilolf was once a soldier and now travels seeking his fortune, while I, a scribe, was dispossessed of my monastery and *scriptorium* by marauding Northmen. A common plight, I am sure, so I do not know why your lordship would waste his time noticing such a lowly pair."

The lord's tone both sharpened and quickened, as if matching his eyes. "Spare me your self-debasing lies. I haven't brought you here on account of the law. This is my land, and I keep my rule by knowing things of my enemies even before they do. And things of my allies." He paused. Did he offer something? I wondered why he called us thieves if we weren't here over the law.

"Most interesting," I babbled over a rising panic. "Just the other day, I was discussing with fellow religious brothers the various methods of foreknowledge, whether scrying the heavens or—"

"I amend my order—spare me *all* your prattle. To make the matter simple, I am building a chapel here within the fort. I cannot possibly protect the cathedral outside my walls, nor man walls long enough to encompass it, but I would not readily abandon God's aid. Our Bishop Anselm, hoping in a war that I would nevertheless attempt to protect his defenseless church, has pointed out the decision of some council of Carthage, five hundred years old, requiring relics in every altar. I suspect this ruling is not everywhere enforced and has probably been at one time or another countermanded, but he will not bless any new church of mine unless I find a saint. Though I have the *deniers* for building, the church can withhold all relics to their ends."

This lord seemed better educated than most and more reliant than his captain on words over fists. "Which is why I brought you to me. My ears informed me that you boasted at Saint Martial's about the recovery of a Spanish saint. Abbot Gonsindus heard it too. For a year now, he's cried about the loss of pilgrims to his house. Don't look surprised. I protect this land not with the greatest army nor the strongest tower, but, as I said before, by staying ahead of my enemies.

"Now, you set out. But not back to Spain, nor east into the Burgundian mess. What takes you west?"

I perked my ears. "Burgundy, my lord? I seek word of my homeland, if you would share it."

"Are you the only Frank that hasn't heard *Dux* Rudolf declared himself king too? Against the claims of *Rex* Odo at Paris and Ranulf in Aquitania. Ha! It matches our sorry generation that shortly after Charles succeeded in restoring the empire of his great-grandfather, he tolerates that traitor Arnulf and then quite inconveniently dies without child. If anyone has to be emperor, I'd prefer Odo, who at least has the backbone to fight the Northmen off." He picked up a letter. "And then, to seal us completely in the tomb, Ranulf manages to claim he's fostering the third Charles, to raise him as emperor when he comes of age. Last I heard, he hasn't solved yet the problem of that bastard son of his, who has more ambition and health than he has legitimate blood."

He leaned in, earnest and urgent. "Now, perhaps, you see the predicament of my region. Rudolf to the east. Ranulf to the west. Odo should lead us from the north, but God alone knows where he fights. I'm caught on the edge of two dukes, neither content to let someone else be king. You," he pointed suddenly to Egilolf, "speak like a native of this area. Do you care at all for your homeland? Did your father raise you to honor it? Or is your allegiance solely to the church? Or yourself?"

Egilolf cleared his throat, but the *comes* continued without waiting for an answer. "We have need of a great patron here. The abbey has Saint Martial, but this area needs most of all a divine protector."

"I will not deny, lord," I replied, "that Abbot Gonsindus has tasked us with seeking the relics of a saint for the benefit of the abbey. Perhaps we could bring you a part of what we—"

"Part," he sneered. "If you brought part of an apostle, that would be sufficient." Sichar shifted behind us—it sounded like he put a hand to his sword-hilt. "But for any other saint, it will do me little good to share it with the abbey. Or the bishop. Anselm would hold that over me the rest of his days." His voice hardened. "I could, if you force me, hold to the *Lex Salica Karolina*. I'm sure you've heard the penalty for disturbing a grave, and even more so, for despoiling the dead in a *basilica*."

Perspiring slightly, I stammered, "I am not sure, lord, of the applicability of those laws – however binding they are on all Francia – when dealing with a saint who *wants* to be re-located—"

"Exactly." He strode back to his table. "You shall find, when you return with your relics to Lemouicensis, that this saint will *want* a new chapel for himself, not overshadowed by the long-reverenced Saint Martial at his abbey, nor crowded out by the multitude of relic bits at the cathedral. My ears are everywhere, and Sichar is relentless. Your saint comes here."

He returned to his map. Sichar jerked a pointing finger to the door, and in a matter of minutes, with no opportunity to say much to the contrary, our simple plans had boiled into a maelstrom. Egilolf and I exited in silence, back to the sunlight and the small courtyard within the wall.

My companion faced Sichar. "We'd travel faster by horse."

"Get, thief." He turned his back on us and marched away.

Egilolf sagged, like he was the one who had been struck in the gut. I grabbed his shoulder and led him out the gate.

"Is that how people see us? Thieves?" Egilolf asked, his eyes on the dirt road at his feet. "I wonder..." he continued, raising his head. He halted both his speech and gait.

"You wonder what?"

He quickly put his head down and dashed off. When I caught up to him, he muttered, "Have we seen that guard before? The blond youth by the gate?"

"That is what you wonder?" He glared even as I continued, "No, no, I jest. I have little desire to draw the *comes*'s attention to us further by gawking at his guard, but I did not recognize anyone there. Where do you think you have seen him?"

"I don't know." He kept up his pace but glanced back twice more. The turmoil on Egilolf's face said it was the wrong time to share more details of the *Lex Salica* that *Comes* Fulgaud's threats had recalled.

An hour back down our original roads — passed fortunately without soldiers and spies — Egilolf spoke again without preamble. "Now what? Half a week ago, we wondered where to get relics. Now we've got a source, but three demands."

Whether he wanted a reply or not, I had none, so we continued in silence, past small farmholds tucked between an ever-encroaching forest. The oak here grew thick but spared room for elm and linden. It made for a shaded march, which, as the afternoon wore on, could have been considered a small blessing if I had been in the mindset to consider it. Shortly after passing the ruins of a small chapel, partially burned but mostly dismantled for the home of a *colonus* across the vale, Egilolf spoke again. "You ever read anything about when a lord can overrule the church? Or the church a lord?"

"Hmm. That has been a quagmire at various times. Christ directed us to render to Caesar what was Caesar's, and to God, what was God's. The apostle Paul told us to obey authorities. When the Roman Emperor Theodosius ordered the massacre of Thessalonica, Bishop Ambrose cut him off from the Mass, until he, the emperor, repented on his knees in submission to the bishop. As the historian wrote, some authorities are given to bishops and some to emperors. Ideally, as with Charles the Great, a lord is selected by God, and thus follows divine direction, revealed through the pope. The same should parallel for dukes and counts, to follow the direction of bishops and abbots."

Egilolf grunted his disgust. "Assuming everyone follows God's direction. What if a bishop imposes one action and a lord the opposite?"

"Well, the Roman martyrs, defying the proconsuls by their refusals to sacrifice incense to their gods or Caesar, would seem to offer one example."

"A corpse at a gallows offers another," he scowled.

I suppose I should have been able to put together more pieces of Egilolf's past by this point, if I had tallied the worries he crossed sword and raised shield against. But I figured everyone has a roughened past—Saint Paul murdered Saint Stephen, after all—so I did not ponder overmuch. Until it required me to kill someone for him.

CHAPTER 5:
A FIVE STONE FAITH

The sickle hung in the air, like a hawk poised to swoop. The wielder looked down on golden heads of wheat and smiled. He grimaced at the sickly green tangle of brambles lurking below the ripe heads. Perhaps the Master had been right, that the whole field would have been churned and lost in attempts to extricate the weeds during summer. He had done his best to prune the thorns and chokers back. They always returned.

But now, the light waned. Harvest had come. The sickle blurred, its rhythmic swish a determined melody. With the grain saved, rooting out the blight came easily, and the worker twisted the weeds and brambles upon themselves, leaving the grain for his second trip. He hoisted the bundled mess, and with a strong flit of his wings, condemned it to the bonfire.

The road ambled passively, and because it rose and fell with the hills and followed them around, we could never see too far into the distance. Sometimes our progress was marked by the office of the hours, rung by a faint, far off church bell, the direction vague through the muting of forest or dale. Wary of soldiers that may be Fulgaud's or other lords', we avoided *villae*, skirting wide even their outlying farms. We stopped for the night and camped off the road.

As had become our habit on our trek across Spain, Egilolf set to kindling a fire for the evening while I gathered wood. Under his dependable woodcraft, a small dinner fire flared to life. Egilolf prepared to bake our loaves, and I broke apart the collected deadfall into manageable fuel for our fire-ring blaze.

"As this is the start of a new venture, I would like to change our routine," I began. "Rather than your usual spy-wary word hoarding, which I endured the whole road north through Hispania, I propose a more lively passage of the evenings."

Egilolf paused, a carefully selected forked branch in hand, poised to add it at just such an angle to increase the airflow and steady the heat on his improvised flat rock oven. "What swirls your mind?"

"Two months have passed of sun rising, casting itself down on us, and fading away while we came north. We have spoken of this plan and that road's chance of bandits. We have quibbled over supplies, and for what our *deniers* should dwindle away. But beyond a vague impression of a campaigner's past, I know little of you. I propose an exchange around the safety of the fireside in these gloaming hours, an exchange of stories of our youths. Or failing that, stories of our own making." I had attempted such an exchange the first morning out of Cordoba but had been rebuked that a proper scout never let his attention wander in his forays. Though I had grown used to long bouts of silent contemplation in my years under Benedictine rule, Egilolf's oral asceticism was beginning to exceed my tolerance.

He shrugged, which I knew for rejection. But having set another two shortened tree limbs delicately into their proper places in the fire, he shrugged again and gave a small smile. "What's to tell? Born not far from Lemouicensis, in my mother's native *villa*. My father…from what Mother told, his army passed through on its way from Lotharingia to the Marches. He was either slain or otherwise failed to return for marriage."

I could read which of those options his mother believed and with which the village had lashed at him.

"Before I came of age, one of the *villa* headmen named me first for the next levy." He prodded a charcoaled log back toward the fire's reach.

"And?"

"You know what they say." He chuckled, "Or, as a monk, maybe you don't. 'Join the army. See the world through your feet.'" I gave him a quizzical look, which he answered: "I marched the four cardinals. A lot."

This being the most detail in one sitting I had heard yet, I sought to keep him talking. "For which army?"

He scoffed. "All of them, probably. Anyone that claimed Charles' *imperator* title. One year, you'd start under some young Charles. While I was out scouting, he'd yield to his brother. Or to his second cousin. My fellows and I would be transferred or subsumed. Only to have our unit to be split months later in some betrayal."

"Sounds like Louis the Pious' sons," I agreed. "And grandsons. How fares your mother?"

"With the Lord now, as the priests say." He smiled to himself. "Better off. Holy enough to be the patroness of Dorrat, but that town doesn't deserve her."

"So. That answers why you never returned home. What led you from wandering soldier into relic hunter?"

It took a special snare to catch this wildling unaware. "No," he said, with a cryptic smile that did not reach his eyes. "Your turn. What led you to monkhood?"

My firewood piles complete, I inched my bundles of sticks and twigs to a handier position and sidled closer to the fire. The bread had finished browning, and though it was the flatbread of the road's way, it had a faint savor to it. Ah, the seasoning of hunger!

I allowed myself to recall the day, years short of manhood, when my father packed me off to the monastery. "Because Jacob I loved, but Esau I hated," I answered.

Egilolf frowned at this.

"My father. I was the second son, and he had no desire to split the family land. Not that there's as much to the ancestral holdings as my father would have you believe. But I am not a monk." Egilolf pointed to my robe and the fairly permanent ink stains on my right hand. "Not yet. I was somewhere past my novitiate, by years, and not close enough to priesthood by calling. I would have taken the books and left the Holy Orders if they would have let me." The thought recalled a debate with Brother Angius, lightly heated as only a strong friendship could endure without a trace of strain, on the issue of my apathy in the study of theology, as he tried to pull my face out of another historical work.

"What took you to Spain?" he asked innocently enough.

I matched his earlier tone. "No. Turn for turn." I unfurled my bedroll and curled into it for the night.

The next day Egilolf attempted to teach me a method of alternating walking with trotting, which he swore would allow us to cover more ground for the same effort. Twisting my ankle after a few hundred yards of attempt, I promptly gave up and told him I was in no real hurry. My ambivalence to the art of navigating the land kept me from hearing most of his response about calculating speeds and distances, how many days it would be to Pictauensis, and the offset heading from Nantes. Between miles of forest, we passed a thin scattering of homes and fields and were chastised by the occasional dog.

Shortly after the sun passed its zenith, I stepped off the trail to do as all men must, into the woods by the edge of a black wheat field. When I finished, I tramped back toward the trail and saw a crude eye carved in the tree with a leather-braided cord tied tight around the limb above it. From the cord dangled a clay amulet, about half the size of my palm. Facing me was a simple cross pressed into the clay surface. I flipped the amulet over. The obverse bore an outline of a female with overly large breasts.

"A ward?" Egilolf suddenly spoke beside me, and I jumped back as though I was a child caught prying. I had not heard him approach at all, but when he spoke, he was less than five feet from me.

"It seems to be both a ward against evil spirits and a fertility blessing. See?" I showed him the feminine figure. "I have not seen their like since I was a child, before I first entered the monastery. The priest of our town, having been upbraided by the bishop for being too lenient, entreated our neighbors to take down their weather ligatures. We all gathered at the church as he spoke about it. The *ligamina* looked different from this one, but I imagine the purpose was the same."

As if assessing its power, Egilolf ran a wondering hand over the cord. Its heavily cracked surface testified to age, though whether from reverence or abandonment, it would not say. "The people seek protection wherever they can." He spoke with the soft sigh of pity, without any shards of condescension. "There's much to be afraid of. To ask the people to give up their ligatures, their weavings, their wards...it asks them not to light a fire in a cold storm."

I turned the amulet back to the cross. "Our priest couldn't convince our neighbors to abandon it altogether either. I remember older men arguing back and forth with the priest. Eventually, they agreed to change their old symbols for the cross and to place their wards a little farther off the road, where the bishop wouldn't see them." I sighed. "After my first years of training at the monastery,

I thought it something of a necessary compromise with simple rustics. But now, years later…" My thoughts overlapped, like pages of parchment torn from diverse books and strewn atop one another, chaotic, a smattering of truncated phrases and ideas. I almost had an insight into the genius of bygone priests and missionaries, over the centuries slowly inching pagans closer and closer to all the ways of Christianity, rather than leaving them unreconciled, abandoned. Would other cultures on the world's fringes take generations of conversion, too?

"'*The holy cross, raised against the evil* daemons *that prowl the air,*'" Egilolf stirred my loose-leaf thoughts. "I heard a cleric sing that, a chorus as he circled our homes. After some foul miasma covered our *villa*. Between ours and the one to the south. A cross was raised high at a crossroads. If I hadn't seen other manners, in Saxony and Lombardy, but especially in Spain and Rome, I couldn't understand others' ways. But this," he flipped the amulet to show the female again. He grinned at me. "This I'm sure the Church does *not* appreciate."

"No." I took the amulet back in my hand and brushed my thumb over the cross. "But you have to encourage a replacement if you are to condemn the established means by which a fear is resisted. The fear itself has not gone away."

Egilolf and I set foot to road again, and I continued our discussion by pestering him to list the cord materials, knots, and symbols of various amulets and ligatures used in his home to protect against sickness, evil spirits, bad weather, crop blight, thievery or war.

Egilolf estimated we had covered thirty miles by the end of the second day, a feat just above typical after our exodus from Spain, and that we had covered slightly more than half the way to Pictauensis. We tucked into a narrow, treed cove between two higher hills for the evening, out of the wind. I began a small fire while Egilolf went hunting with his sling.

After dinner, he built the fire a bit higher. A fire for cooking and warmth may be universal, but something differs about it when companions gather about an open fire, as night falls, and the darkness compresses the far reach of the wild world into the meager stretch of firelight. That smallness forces even strangers to share secrets otherwise held tight, or else it ensnares a man's reflections even more tightly, and he sees nothing but the flames and his heart, while silence consumes hours.

Egilolf and I were caught in the middle of such a deep reflection, or at least I was, and Egilolf too stared silently into the flames. It is only when a man really stops, I've found, that he can assess not just the near future but the far-off fates, the possibilities of years from now, old age, and death.

Of course, when a threat prophesized from beyond the firelight, I realized death might *be* the near future.

"Move and you die," came a deep and powerful voice from the shadows behind Egilolf.

I froze.

Egilolf paused and then defied the voice by deliberately pivoting. "Peter, don't be an ass!"

The shadows paused with me, and then a great burst of laughter came from the bush, preceding a large man as he stepped into the firelight. "It's all right, men! Egilolf here,"—he swung an ax lazily— "is an old friend." At that, three other bandits emerged. Two remained cautious, hunched and shifty as the firelight shadows. The third, I realized with a start, was a woman. She stepped closer to the fire and disdainfully took our measure.

The large man, whom Egilolf called Peter, stood well over a head taller than my companion, with overly-large shoulders and a broad chest that contrasted with his narrow waist. He held a spear loosely at his side. "Everyone, this is Egilolf, my long-past war fellow," the man continued, a little too loud and too quickly, with a smile forced wide. "We were scouts together, and—"

"What is this, Peter?" Egilolf cut him off in a hard, quiet tone.

"Well..." The man dubbed Peter dropped his head and began kicking around rocks at his feet. When Egilolf didn't move or fill the silence, Peter continued. "Times are hard, you see. Our old farm fell to waste while I marched Lotharingia. After my father died. And it's dangerous to live alone outside the village anymore. And—"

"And we have families to feed," the female cut in sharply. "Families the lords can't protect, especially when we're sitting in a defenseless village." She lay hand to a short sword on her hip as though daring anyone to contradict her.

"So. A robber?" Egilolf said sadly.

His once-friend would not meet his gaze. "Wasn't my first choice. A man can only do what he knows." He dug moss off another stone with his toe. "There's families, too. The children. They need to eat."

When no one spoke, the tension mounted. I tried to lighten the mood. "At least you're robbing with less than five. The *Lex Salica*'s punishes twice as harsh for groups any larger." No one laughed with me. "Assuming, of course," I continued more soberly, "you actually survive to see a justiciar and are not hanged by those who make their own justice."

As much as I thought the advice practical, the female did not. Before I could blink, she leapt the clearing and pressed the honed point of her short sword into my neck. "You may not respect much, old monk, but you'll respect my blade. Eat your own mockery!"

"Enough, Rachel. Put it away," Peter ordered, but with a plea in his tone. "I owe my life to Egilolf, and that debt extends to his companion. For now."

She hesitated, and I flicked my eyes between the woman, Peter, and Egilolf. I did not think either of the former soldiers was close enough to stop her should she ignore the order. With a final added pressure, she removed the blade and began sheathing.

"I'm neither old nor a monk—" I quipped. But when she paused with her sword only half back in its sheath, I shut my mouth.

"Let's get their coin, then, and be gone," Rachel said, her eyes not leaving me. Odd. I never considered myself dangerous.

"We're not taking anything from these men!" Peter responded indignantly. "Didn't you hear what I said?"

"I heard one was a companion. Once. Long ago. Your obligations now are to the group." Her words carried more heat than the fire. "Our children."

Peter opened his mouth to protest, but Egilolf cut in. "Hand it over, Aristeus." Now I opened my mouth to protest, but a look from Egilolf and the vixen's hand to her sword stopped me. I dug under my tunic for my coin pouch.

"I—I'm sorry, friend. I didn't mean—" Peter began.

Egilolf cut him off with a glare. "Arduous years make men, not excuses for them. Your father taught me that."

Peter winced and kicked again at the rocks. I handed my coin pouch to the woman and only then really stopped to look at her: slight, with a taut wildness to her face and eyes, and black hair that held a glow in the firelight. As she took the bag, a softness in her touch belied the calluses of her fingers. She held my gaze, then questioned Egilolf.

"And yours?" She jiggled my pouch to make her point.

"Aristeus is a scribe. Book learned. He keeps our coin. Counts and converts better," Egilolf replied.

Rachel wasn't convinced. "What's around your neck?" Her hand went back to her sword handle.

Egilolf fumbled through the layers of tunic and undershirt. He drew out a small leather pouch. "Dust only." He shook the bag for silent confirmation.

"Whose grave dust?" she pressed. Ah, she was shrewd! I'd admire her but for her way of thrusting a blade at my throat.

Egilolf closed his hand tight around the pouch. Peter cleared his throat and frowned.

Rachel ignored him and drew her sword fully. "Whose?"

Egilolf, now truly disgusted and pained, untied the knot to the pouch's cord. "Saint Vincentius of Rome. God curse your theft."

She scoffed as she snagged the pouch from his hand, her sword arm drawn back and ready to spring if he tried anything. "And how did *you* come by it?" She retreated without waiting for an answer. Commanding the other two robbers with nothing but a dip of her head, the three stepped back into the shadows. Peter took a step after them, then stopped.

"Your wife is rather fierce," I complimented.

"Ha! Wife? Not that one. Speaks her mind too readily. Iron-hearted, though, and devoted to our children." He immediately went red, visible even in the amber firelight. "I mean, not *our* children. The group's." He held Egilolf's gaze. The fire cracked twice in the silence between them. "Will you ever come back?"

Egilolf shook his head.

"I could give up this life if you did. Rachel presses us to do something better, to give up robbing. Until the children are hungry again. Then she plans the ambush herself." His grin fell when met with the set of Egilolf's jaw. "We could try a normal life again, my wife and I, if you guarded my back. In Dorrat, I mean. People there don't trust soldiers much."

"Don't trust me, you mean. And don't pile your choices on me. My own choices are burden enough."

Still, the robber held fast, caught between fire blaze and forest gloam. "*She* hasn't convinced everyone there, you know. There are some that would still welcome you, that don't believe you're at fault."

"As I said, I've got my own burdens now." The firmness of his stance was mortared to his sad tone. "Maybe someday I'll be free to join with you, Peter. Do something both of us and your father would be proud of. But not now. And never in Dorrat. It'll never be home again." His sadness took on an edge of bitterness.

Peter opened his mouth to protest more but then shut it, nodded and only said, "God and Saint Martin keep you safe." He raised his hand in farewell, and he too stepped into the shadows, more silently than his bulk suggested possible.

Egilolf stared after him, watching him go. When he turned back to the fire, he pulled out his own coin purse from his waist belt and offered it to me. "Thanks for not fighting," he said.

"Hmph. As though I were a fighter. Your clever play on the silver at least kept us half." Egilolf sat and stared into the fire. "What's the history of that group?"

"Eh?"

I had to repeat my question.

"Don't know the group. Just Peter. We grew up together in Dorrat. It's north a day or so from Lemouicensis. Off that way," he pointed northeast, "though there's no road direct from here. Fastest is north from Lemouicensis, or east from Pictauensis."

"You fought together?"

"Rarely. Peter marched with the main warband most times. I was soon made a scout, away from camp for days at a time. But sometimes we'd scout together. Or carouse." He smiled weakly.

"I take it the female he mentioned was not the bandit girl here waving about her sword. She clearly did not recognize you."

"No, it's...someone else. Someone from Dorrat. I don't want to discuss it."

I felt I was at my scribing desk once more, deciphering the *lacunae* of old texts, those blotted, faded, or damaged words. Sometimes when I managed to fill a few gaps, it only led to more questions.

He wouldn't say another word the rest of the night. He curled inward and stared into the flames.

I woke to the unmistakable smell of acorn bread baking under the coals. I couldn't take my thoughts off the woman Rachel, which made me disagreeable. "Did we lose our food? Are we going through a famine?"

"What?" he replied, poking more coals over the dough lumps.

"Why, by God's good grace, are you baking acorn bread?"

"The acorns are free and plentiful. It'll make the abbot's food go further."

"No." My tone was patronizing. "*Peasants* bake it to make their food go further. *We* are traveling a few days to Pictauensis, last time I checked, and a few days beyond that to Father Leo's abandoned church. I see no need to subject myself to pig fodder, which you mummer up as food!"

He stirred the coals and replied, "You forget half our coin was taken last night."

I barely held back invectives against Northmen, Moors, threatening lords, relic quests, and fox-sly bandits. I had forgotten. I choked down his peasant bread before we returned to the road.

As we traveled, I kept trying to peer into the dense oak forest, scanning for bandits. I knew it to be futile, but I kept my watch anyway. The rest of the trip to Pictauensis, however, was uneventful. We overtook farmer's wagons and stepped off the road for a merchant's wains headed south, but everyone eyed each other and said nothing. I found myself wondering if they were lookouts for the bandits or spies for *Comes* Fulgaud, then realized they probably wondered the same of us.

Sometime shortly before *vespers* the following day, Pictauensis came into sight, as did an idle, whistling man lying under a linden tree by the road. The full bloom of summer crowned the tree with its scattering of yellow, starburst flowers, its heady scent attracting a swirl of bee activity. A leather harp case dangled by a cord from a low branch above the whistler. I thought it rather scout-like of me to spot an old gladius sword at his side.

The man waved a single merry hand as we approached, but he finished his tune before addressing us. "Good evening, fellow travelers!" he nearly sang in proclamation.

"Well met," I returned the greeting.

Egilolf's reply was to eye the man's sword.

"I would ask whither you went, but the last assemblage I asked such attempted to abuse me. I am Rodegar, traveler and musician. I'm bound for Pictauensis, and I would posit you are also, given that this road does not divert much from the direction you head. Shall we journey together?"

Egilolf all but glared at the musician. "Just waiting in the grass for the next passerby?"

"Not at all." The harper stretched unconcernedly. "I was resting my legs and refining a tune before traveling to a tavern to sing for a supper."

Egilolf kept scanning the area, so I copied him as though I knew the signs of an ambush. Rodegar paused expectantly.

"Sure," came Egilolf's half-grunted reply.

The harper casually swung his case onto his back. As he joined us on the road, he read his audience rightly and did not attempt to converse with us. He did keep whistling, though.

We followed Rodegar into town, past the gate and down three skewed alleys, to what he swore was the best tavern in the region. The town was much larger than Lemouicensis, large enough to boast choices of taverns, smiths, farriers, and merchants. It was still an anthill, though, to the grand breadth of Cordoba. The evening was pleasant enough that, once we reached the tavern, we sat near a window with its shutters latched open. While debating the lamb stew or roast quail, we enjoyed a round of the house red. If the tavern was rated solely on its wine and not the condition of the building, I had to agree with Rodegar. As he tossed back mouthfuls, he none too subtly kept repositioning his harp case by the edge of his seat. Following the bard's example, we, too, sought the bottom of the cups. Once they were emptied, Egilolf waved the proprietor over again, but before he arrived, a drunk from two tables over stood and hailed Rodegar in a slur thicker than the early twilight should have condoned.

"Harper! Harper!"

"Who, me?" Rodegar feigned surprise. A bit dramatic, but the rest of the audience seemed only a few cups shy of the one hailing us.

"What'll you sing for us?" The drunk expansively waved inclusion of the entire room, which had likely no more than twenty customers, the corners too dark to count.

"I sought naught but a nibbling, and later a long nap, since I spent day's length with my legs pacing the path, stopping not even for a rest since I broke my fast this morning."

The drunk thought on this a second, then seemed to register the disappointment. Then he brightened again and slurred, "What if we paid your drink?"

Rodegar was not new to his work. He feigned indifference, fatigue, poverty, and timidity at revealing a new but grand work until he bartered stew and drinks for the three of us (Egilolf and I had somehow been insinuated as his guides or servants) and lodging for the evening. He then took out the harp, stood on his chair, and began tuning while hailing the audience:

"In all of fair Francia, who has not heard the deeds of Charles Magnus, the greatest king of our great peoples? And across wide Francia, who has not heard the deeds of his mightiest fighter, the peerless Roland? And even beyond the fringes of Francia, who has not heard of that greatest battle, where great King Charles, having treated with the pagan and dissembling Moors, returned from Spain to his mighty kingdom only to find his rearguard betrayed by the vile Ganelon? His nephew and champion Roland, along with the greatest Frankish fighters, sacrificing themselves to slay the Moorish host at the high passes of Roncesvalles?"

I noted the crowd's enthusiasm dull at this oft-repeated tale.

Rodegar noticed this too. "All! All, I tell you, have heard these tales from the cradle." He swept harp and cloak as he wound through the morass of chairs and bumblers. "But who has heard of

Roland's brother warriors and their other great deeds in Hispania? Who knows the tale of Olivier, like a mighty King David, champion of the Lord, when he battled the fierce giant in whom the Moors poured all their hopes? Has no one heard the *Lay of Olivier and Fierbras?*" As Rodegar played, he strummed the same notes over and over, an almost haunting tune that seemed more harmony than melody, a counterpoint to some unknown song. He worked the crowd down to a silence as he lowered, quieted, and deepened his voice. Only the fire crackled in the corner in the pause before his beginning.

Come gather around the fire tonight
While crickets chirp 'neath pure stars bright:

A tale of glorious Frankish past,
When Charles' bold paladins, enmassed,
Quick sought to press 'gainst Sar'cen king
Who saints from Rome to Spain didst bring.

King Balon sacked and stole from Pope
Who placed in Charles, Great King, his hope.
"Counts Roland! Olivier! Abide,
Come aid me 'gainst the Moors!" he cried.

So forth went Franks, and in the van,
Count Roland, peerless knight! A man
Who sought God's glory by the sword,
Defending Francia and his lord.

Beyond the March they pressed the Moors
Right back to Saragossa's doors.
There Balon felt his periled straights:
None more than Roland Balon hates

And fears, for hundreds Roland's slain,
As reaper scythes his rows of grain.
The Moor calls loud his champion:

A fostered giant raised as son.

Fierbras, strong armed, tower'd high o'er men;
He roared a taunt 'gainst Franks, and then
He dared them fight by ones or twos.
The Franks quaked at the chall'nging news.

King Charles to Roland pled for aid.
"I'm worn," said he, "from last eve's raid."
Brave Olivier, though wounded he,
Arose from bier, answered the plea.

He donned his brother's black vizor,
Took Roland's shield, his own *Hautclere*,
And riding forth, his glaive shown bright.
He called for God to lend him might.

For hour and hour he traded blows—
Quite known was he for felling foes.
His strikes he landed but in vain,
Nor wounds at all did Fierbras gain.

"O, God on High! and Christ's Mother;
Saint Michael, pledge me as brother:
My wounds still bleed from fights before
While Fierbras' strength doth grow yet more!"

Then God and Mary heard his plea,
The Archangel could Ol'vier see.
His sword to Count he offered lend.
No earthly sword sufficed to rend.

Saint Michael taught: the giant armored,
Was daemon-shielded, couldn't be gored.
The Count took up the heav'nly glaive,
Its powers restored him, made him brave.

He smote full force the giant's helm—
Loud cheered the watching Frankish realm!—
And caved and clove it nearly through.
Down fell the giant like uproot yew.

His champion down, the Moorish king
Quick parleyed Charles, his praise to sing:
Returned the saints and gold beside
To pay the loss of Franks that died.

Count Roland praised great Olivier
Who quoth right quick whose deeds they were:
"Saint Michael, Mighty, helped me slay
The giant Fierbras on this great day,

"With succor and his sword of light
I felled the demons left and right,
And crown to toe. So I declare
'Tis best to call in foul or fair

"On God on High, and all His saints,
To fight the Demon's thrusts and feints."
Archbishop Turpin led the Mass
'Fore Charles outlaid the feast repast.

I thought the story simplistic and oversold, but Rodegar guessed
his audience rightly, for many besides the drunk stood to cheer it.
As we ate, I heard the men repeat phrases, especially Olivier
cleaving the helmet in two. I heard two comparisons to a battle the
teller had been in himself, though the foes were mostly Franks or
Lotharingians, and only once did I hear a tale that included
Northmen.

"Where and when did you come upon the tale?" I asked Rodegar
while fishing out bits of lamb from the stew.

"Ah, bits I gleaned here and fragments I found there," he evaded.
"I consider the lot I play for and fit the story to their liking. Some
of this lot held an old soldier's air. The Spanish Moors are always a

safe villain to settle upon."

"What do you mean?" Egilolf asked.

"Well, some of the tales come from Frank fighting Frank, or Aquitanian killing Burgundian. You never know whether your crowd currently hates the northern Franks, or Anjou, or the Lombardians. Perhaps they now ally. It's easier to cut cloth to fit Northmen and Moors. Or the Magyar if I'm east."

"So, to put it in rustics' words, that story is made up?" I asked.

"You don't understand the nature of stories," Rodegar huffed. "Many of the details of setting and characters don't matter. What matters is what they mean to listeners. Stories are made by a people, and in turn, *make* the people." Egilolf's puzzlement matched mine. "I've traveled amongst the Northmen at times, singing for my supper but also listening to their legends. Their sagas, too, pit a hero against a giant."

"You copied that story, didn't you?" Egilolf scoffed.

"Not at all! Their setting and characters might seem the same, but the story differs drastically. Their hero saves himself by his own might and cunning. The Northman's suppositions about his pagan gods are nearly superfluous; he acts and relies only on his own power. The Franks, though, have learned the limits of their powers and call on God and his saints to save us." He leaned across the table, desperate to convert. "Stories make a people!"

"Paid for supper and a room," laughed Egilolf. "I'm grateful."

I wished I could shrug it off as easily. Instead, I spent the night contemplating old Greek stories, the *Aeneid*, the apostles' *Acta*, and martyr passions. Perseus, the son of a god, versus Polycarp, the man of God. One a Gorgon-slaying hero commanding a winged horse, the other the bishop of Smyrna, praying for his captors and willing to die in the flames without having to be tied to the stake. What did the stories say of a people? What did they reveal about a people's God?

How different were we Christians, really, from the pagani *invaders, from our own pagan ancestors? All peoples enshrine a hero ideal, men or women more than human because of the power given to them. Were the martyrs any different? What of the unsung, the un-remembered? Eusebius' history lauded the nameless*

Christians of pagan Alexandria, sometime around the Decian persecution of the third century, who, when plague gutted the streets, markets, and inner rooms of the whole city, demonstrated the revolutionary virtue of caritas. *At best, mankind before would care for his family, and Hades would take the rest, literally. A true wonder of the world: Christians brought this new virtue, charity, by caring for all sick and burying all dead, both believers and unbelievers alike, even to the point of contracting the plague themselves. The dignity of the stranger, of the persecuting enemy even, was for the first time in human's history more important than their own lives. New heroes?*

CHAPTER 6:
WHERE MOTH AND RUSTY
NORTHMEN DESTROY, AND...

To the church of Colossae, Paul exhorted burial with Christ so to rise with him. He meant it only spiritually. Or so I thought.

The sun rose bright, and the world appeared, if not more benign, then at least more benevolent for having spent a night in warmth and safety. After a quick breaking of our fast, Egilolf and I set out upon the road, leaving our minstrel friend to glean and sow his stories.

The seven-day march from Pictauensis to Saint Philibert could not have been more different from our four to Pictauensis. The most obvious changes—rolling hills flattening to marsh and well-edged roads dwindling to weed-choked paths—were the least important. Insidiously, it took the first day to realize what was setting me on edge. In every clearing we crossed, farmers' homes moldered, where they weren't burnt to ruins. Some fields lay fallow, but most retreated before the encroaching forest. Entire *villae* lay emptied but for a phantasm of life, a door perhaps, swinging in a soulless breeze. Some decay was due to abandonment, nature, and time, but some showed elements of purposeful destruction: stone church walls black with the soot of their own burnt roofs, sarcophagi lids overturned or hammered to gravel, the remnant feet of statues ripped from walls. Not the work of a single attack, the varying states testified to cumulative destruction over lifetimes of raids and thievery. After the third day, we met no Franks at all, and Egilolf often bid me wait while he perused our flanks for Northmen.

"We'll make the church tomorrow. Or the day after," Egilolf calculated as we settled in one evening.

I could only guess that we were somewhere south of the ruins of Nantes. To avoid Northmen and bandits, Egilolf forbid any fire after we left Pictauensis, and I didn't argue. But without a fire to gaze into, I found myself searching the heavens as I lay on my bedroll. I sensed Egilolf doing the same. The moon was one night past new, and its thinnest crescent cut a weak crack in the starry mantle.

"What were you considering the night at the graveyard?" I asked. The crickets and the stream filled the silence for minutes.

Egilolf shifted. "How is heaven out there, but the saints are here too?" he marveled softly, his words as slow as the wind barely brushing the few branches overhead. "I've imagined the saints as the stars. They peer down at us, the brighter, the more powerful, the dimmer still a swirl of beauty. Or do they see from here, from their presence on Earth? Gazing out from their carried reliquaries, or sentinels from their graves? Or are they our comrades in this life's toils? Gazing up at the stars with us?"

I had never heard him speak so. My mind paired the perspective Egilolf offered to my supine resting spot. "You imagine you are dead?" I tried to joke, but the infinity of the stillness caught me mid-thought.

"Have you never wondered…?"

The celestial graveyard, the terrestrial star field. The memory of the astronomy lesson in the cemetery paired a poor mirror of the strewn stars above me with those scattered grave markers. "Gregory, the great bishop and historian of Tors, described Saint Peter's soul traveling up to join the stars at the time of his upside-down crucifixion," I recalled.

"You and your writings…. As the scribe, do you peer down on the lines and words, study their movement across the pages? Or as you think, the words are your part of the story moving through it?" The breeze stilled. "Like the saints, how can you both observe from far above and also perceive life as you live it out?"

I had no answer, and Egilolf didn't seem to expect one. Various Church Fathers and pagan writings I had copied on the topic of death came to mind. "I read somewhere that the Jews and Moors, Romans and even Franks, long before Saint Irenaeus came to our lands, feared contact with the dead. They burned the bodies or buried them far from their towns. They disdained touching a corpse, for the dead contaminated. Even Moses' law declared them unclean."

"And?"

My thoughts seemed strewn across the *aether* with the stars. Only with difficulty could I connect the points into an image and express what my mind grasped, like a vision on my periphery that if but stared at directly was then gone. "Consider us today, seeing clearly in the light of Christ and his saints. With death defeated, what have we to fear?" I leaned on my elbow and faced Egilolf, though compared to the astral brilliance, his form was indistinguishable from the close shadows. "Can you see how different we are from our pagan ancestors? What once was shunned is now honored, for death holds no terror for us." I sank back into the matted grass and looked skyward.

After a long silence, as my eyes began to droop, Egilolf responded. "That's the assurance by day. At the altar. Standing over a saint's tomb, and at the foot of the Cross." He paused. "But when I face the darkness, the void before the light, I…doubt."

We continued to stargaze until we both slept. It was not until my eyes opened to the glare of sunrise that I realized Egilolf had evaded my first question.

Perhaps because we were miles off the *Leger*, or perhaps by the grace of God, we encountered no Northmen. Somewhat after *sext* on our seventh day from Pictauensis, if we had been in a domain where the hours were kept and tolled, the game trail Egilolf lead us along opened onto a large clearing, where the last bits of scrub brush yielded to a sea of waist-high grass. A mostly un-marred church arose from this otherwise flat land. We had been following a meandering stream since early that morning, and it led directly west (as directly as a meandering stream goes) past the church.

"This is what we came for," Egilolf said more confidently than I felt. How could he be certain of his location in an unpopulated, unfamiliar, flat land?

"Apparently, that hunter at the tavern was worth talking to," I said with some uncertainty. From the outside, the church stood much like many others, though this one's roof was intact. The exterior of the rounded apse pointed east, towards us, and the short but definitive protrusions north and south marked the transept. The main doors would lie at the far west.

"Father Leo's directions were close, but the rivers have changed in a hundred years—"

"Fifty," I interjected.

"Whatever. A lifetime. Most peoples' lifetime. Regardless, a local hunter was more precise than stumbling through Northmen territory."

"Since you are sure…" I finished my sentence by striding towards the church with the renewed energy of one who first sights his destination.

"Hold," Egilolf cautioned, pulling me with him down to a crouch.

"What?"

"That church is the only building surviving for miles around. If Northmen patrol here, they'll know that. Maybe camp in it. We need to see if they're here."

I thought he meant to observe it for a few minutes, but Egilolf's scanning kept us by the clearing edge until close to *none*. Military scouting, I learned, is much like sleeping, in that you spend long hours lying very still. Yet, despite the boredom, you're supposed to keep watch. I hadn't realized I was dozing until he woke me and started forward across the grass without a word. Not sure if I should be so openly stepping into what Egilolf painted as a potential nest of berserkers, I hunched awkwardly, as if that would make me less visible in the bright afternoon sun.

His apprehension built as we reached the last hundred paces to the church and circled west to the main entrance. The tympanum arching the portal was unadorned, and though the doors were ax gouged, they too were plain, solid, and still properly set. They were closed, but the latch had long been destroyed. Egilolf cautiously pushed one of the doors inward, the hinges raising a rusty protest, and checked various angles of the interior by moving around the open doorway before deeming it safe to enter.

If the simplicity of the church's exterior conjured images of a stark fortress, the interior was the opposite. Lofty ceilings sprouted from columns and semi-circular arches alternated courses of light tan and warm red stone, a level of art and precision I would not have thought possible a monastery in exile could afford. Besides the well-ordered effect of the banded stone, the most noticeable feature of the church was the apse, raised a man's full height above the floor of the nave, bare but for the altar. A single small vertical window, not much bigger than a defense slit, pierced the east wall where a crucifix should have been. It provided the sole light in the otherwise dark hollow that contained the altar. In contrast, the ceiling over the center aisle of the nave was vaulted higher than the rest. Set with more windows, it drew the sunlight down to banish the dark of nook and corner. But of the church art, only immobile stone remained. Empty niches in the walls decried the invader's desecration.

We explored farther into the church, still wary of occupants. Taut fear banished any thought of speech. Footstep by cautious footstep, we crept to the front of the apse and studied the altar. *Accipite, et Comedite.* The words were chiseled into the border of the table.

"*Hoc est corpus meum,*" I whispered in the silence. Long and longer past were the days since holy food had been consumed here.

In the north transept, a passage opened. I peered in and saw it formed a ring hallway between the outer church wall and the wall of the apse, scribing a half-circle before returning to the south transept. Egilolf explored this ring passage, and I followed. As per Father Leo's description, halfway through the passage, at the east-most end of the church, a small doorway led west, back under the apse to a small crypt, directly under the altar. This pilgrim passage allowed an uninterrupted view of the Mass on the apse for worshippers in the nave, while filing visitors to and from the sarcophagus of Saint Philibert in the crypt. The curving hall also accessed numerous small chapels along its outer perimeter.

Confirming the church's desertion, we relaxed. We ducked into the crypt under the altar, an enclosure less than two spans square, with a pressing, low ceiling. A sole sarcophagus filled the center. As we entered this crypt, lit only by the strained light from the pilgrim passageway, Egilolf knelt to search the flooring stones. "I wish for a torch," Egilolf grumbled. "Already dark in here, and we haven't descended yet."

"At least it was easy getting in here," I said.

"That's what I told myself on my first two thefts," he replied while tapping on the stones with his knife hilt.

I had no reply, so I stood uselessly for a few minutes. Without a word, he began scraping away mortar from around a stone on the far side of the sarcophagus. He motioned me over, and I pulled out my own small blade and worked the other side of the stone.

After a few minutes of rapid progress, I asked, "Does mortar always crumble this readily?"

Egilolf grinned. "Don't know everything, after all?"

I hesitated before admitting, "Not everything is found in books."

"I'm going to quote that back someday. No, this mortar is poorly made, meant to fill cracks more than hold."

After another ten minutes of scraping and chipping, Egilolf directed me to lift with him. I thought the task would be more difficult, but as I saw, the stone was cleverly cut half as thin as the others. It rested upon two other stones under it that were part of the ceiling of the lower chamber. We stood the cover stone upright against the back of the sarcophagus, and Egilolf cautiously probed the darkness below him with his blade. When his knife struck nothing, he took one of his sling pellets and dropped it into the hole. It immediately returned the dull smack of stone on stone. "Not deep," he concluded and promptly lowered himself into the hole.

Egilolf's head was still partially protruding from the hole when his feet touched the ground. He bent to the side, and I leaned in to look.

"Step back," he said, "you're blocking my light."

I moved back to the crypt wall.

"Better. Give me a minute. Let my eyes adjust."

To fill the time, I asked, "Do you know the penalty for despoiling a *basilica*?"

"Besides a Northman's ax to the head? Is this encouragement?" His words echoed up, muted.

"I was recalling to mind our conversation with the *comes* of Lemouicensis, about the *Lex Salica Karolina*. The penalty was…one hundred fifty *deniers*, perhaps. Or maybe more?"

"He made his penalty clear."

"Yes. But that would hardly be legal of him, though."

"Who'll enforce it? Charles the Great is long gone. His dream of an empire died with him. Just took a few generations for everyone to realize." The clink of metal on stone signaled Egilolf's probing of the shadows with his knife. "Main tomb in the center of the room. Rough stone sides. No lid. Feels like a skeleton in it." Some rattling and clacking, and then, "Yes. A full skeleton, as much as I can tell." He either was not queasy at rummaging through bones or else hid it well. "Pass down the cloth."

I dug through his pack and located the silk cloth. As I lowered it into the dark hole, something brushed my hand. Startled, I dropped the cloth. "It's just me," Egilolf's growl rose from the gaping dark. "There's a crushed-wool sack in there too. Pass it down."

"What do you intend it for?" I asked.

"Rome and Spain taught me. Off the south wall down here are two niches. I've found half a skeleton in one. I'm going to help ourselves to some spare bones. We'll be ready to hand them over if someone demands our saint."

His practicality made me bite off comments about sacrilege.

A few minutes later, he passed up the silk cloth, bound shut with two leather thongs. The bones grated against themselves in the package as I stowed it in Egilolf's sack.

"All right," I called into the hole, "I secured Saint Philibert."

"You've got it wrong. The spare bones are in the silk. I'll put Philibert in the wool sack. Stop." He cut off my protest before I had half opened my mouth. "Think."

So I did. "You have put the decoy in the rich cloth. Wise."

"Exactly. Can't give someone these monk's, or scribe's, or farmer's bones wrapped in wool and expect them to bypass the silk." I sat down to wait, trying to overcome my urge to quip some reply. I heard a faint screech and moan, and for a second, I could not identify it. It was followed, however, by the clack of hard leather on stone and the harsh guttural of the barbaric north language. The church door had opened. "Northmen!" I hissed towards Egilolf's hole, breaking into an instant terror sweat. My mind fled to memories of fire, shrieks, an ax through Brother Angius's neck, a laughing triumph in unintelligible words.

"What?" he asked in far too loud a tone.

"Northmen!" I frantically whispered. This time his head popped up silently, like a badger alert for danger. We both waited and then heard the invaders' voices take a loud questioning tone, followed by its own interrogatory silence. The apse-ringing passage played oddly with the sounds, dulling some and magnifying others. One moment the Northmen sounded distant, as if still waiting at the main nave doors. The next second I swore they hovered outside the entrance to our crypt.

Egilolf had to flag my attention, so frozen was I on the sole doorway back into the pilgrim passage. He directed me with short, precise hand gestures to get our packs and join him in the sub-chamber. I hesitated at the thought of being trapped, but another echo of shod feet on stone forced my decision. Balancing stealth against speed—while wishing, not for the last time, to have some of Egilolf's scouting sense—I tossed him my pack and his and scooped up the loose diverse items that I had pulled out while locating the silk and wool. I all but dumped the last things down the hole and brushed the loose pieces of mortar in, wincing at a faint metal clank, then slid my legs into the hole. I paused, half in and half out of the home of the dead. Saint Tertullian, great Church Father and writer of Carthage, had expounded on the numerous occasions a Christian should sign himself on the forehead with the victorious Cross. He hadn't included entering a tomb in his list, but it seemed so appropriate I was struck then at its absence. Or had he included it? I tried to recall, but my thoughts were jolted when Egilolf yanked me down in the hole with him. Stunned, I rolled to my side and watched Egilolf reach back out of the hole. I bit my lip to keep from asking what he was doing and then bit it harder as he pulled the flagstone overhead and the faint light disappeared.

Rationally it made sense, and the part of my mind that venerates rationality tried to triumph over some fear-driven beast within that wanted nothing else but to claw past Egilolf and back into the light. The last slit of white disappeared with only the faintest whisper of stone, and then I sensed nothing but Egilolf struggling to silence his breathing. We lay motionlessly as the rock transmitted faint footsteps. They suddenly became louder, stone-distorted taps, unnaturally spaced out, and I pictured some overly large marauder, trying his best to move his bulk and armor with slow steps in any manner resembling stealth. The image would have made me laugh if I wasn't terrified.

Later, when I had time and energy to reflect on the ordeal, I concluded we likely waited with our dread for no more than fifteen minutes. At the time, however, when one set of footsteps seemed an immeasurable horde, and the muffled taps became more distinct, signaling what could only be one of the barbarians stepping on our hidden cover stone, time seemed infinite, even while all vast creation was reduced to me, Egilolf, the crypt, the sub-chamber, and the dreaded Northmen.

It was only after a louder, mocking tone cut across the grunting and muttering, accompanied by fading footsteps, that I realized how tightly I had been holding myself.

With no noise at all, Egilolf must have moved up next to me, for suddenly, his groping hand brushed and grabbed my forearm. His mouth was at my ear. "Don't move. Make sure there's no guard."

Imagination must be the work of the *daemons*, for it causes not only fear of the unknown but also creates fears where none may exist. Was that my own idea or something I read? I considered writing my own collection of wise sayings on a day when I was no longer creeping from tomb to crypt and beyond. *The Wisdom of Aristeus*, I imagined (see, imagination really is the work of evil, stirring up my pride). *Reflections from a Crypt* would be an appropriate subtitle, I supposed.

Thus I spent my next few hours, or perhaps the entire night, anxious over every heard or imagined sound, my mind trying to piece illusory senses into a reality. Was that the Northmen unconcernedly singing? A faint whiff of pork fat sizzling on a fire? A guard patrolling the apse ring passageway or scraping to inspect the flagstone that sounded as hollow to them as it had when it alerted Egilolf? My companion's measured breathing not only told me he was asleep but also demonstrated his relative lack of concern. How could one sleep this close to death?

After Egilolf determined most of the night had passed, he and I plotted, mouth to ear, in a whisper so light any *scriptorium*'s librarian would have approved. I say we plotted, but this was a better situation for Egilolf to plan out. So passed a maddening two days of silent dark and turbid air. We had sufficient water and food in our packs, but it was of little relief. I won't deny that, as I lay next to Saint Philibert's rough coffin, my thoughts naturally turned to death. I had previously thought Egilolf's questioning beneath the net of stars to be the closest I had come to not just envisioning but experiencing death. Lying beside a coffin, surrounded by other burial niches, in a crypt beneath a crypt, in stifling darkness and unbroken silence, however, was another reality altogether. What if this was death? Not beholding the earth from the height of stars, nor viewing from our entombed remains, but darkness and silence…terror?

Sometime after what seemed to be the second day in the tomb, however, as Egilolf scrounged through our packs for food and water, he pressed a rough woolen bundle into my hands, which clacked and shifted as I groped it. My guide spoke in a determined whisper, "Philibert, pray for us. *Kyrie eleison. Christe eleison.*"

"*Kyrie eleison,*" I joined. I wondered why it had taken days for me to seek Christ and his saints. Had I thought Him against our movement of the relics—our theft, as some would say? That He would not help because of what we were doing? Yet Father Leo had provided good reason why Saint Philibert would want to be moved, to rejoin his faithful community instead of being left in this forgotten, surrendered hole. Was there ever a more appropriate time, or place for that matter, to pray? To think not of this as an enclosing tomb stifling with fear and dreaded internment, but as a resting place, a sleeping chamber for one of Christ's saints, under His own altar?

Into what I estimated to be the fourth day, I began exploring the chamber, my boredom outweighing fear. Even horror loses impact with monotony. At least until it reasserts itself.

Most of the sub-crypt was roughly hewn to include the unlidded sarcophagus in the center where Egilolf had found Saint Philibert's remains. Many of the niches along the wall were empty, some only half dug. One seemed barely large enough for an infant. Above, below, or next to the niches were rough carvings, the work of any man with a chisel, and certainly no craftsman. Here and there, my fingers traced Latin words, or at least letters, in the dark. Much of it was indecipherable, and some seemed to be pictures of tools, perhaps to signify a trade. If I could have stood to pace it, the whole area would have been about ten paces and square. Feeling out the engravings, though, took me hours as I crawled around the crypt, exploring all sides. One name struck me, carved in larger lettering that showed perhaps no more skill than the rest, but at least more devotion and care. The name was Valerie, as best as I could make it out amidst other natural cracks in the stone. I recalled Father Leo's story of the church built over the site of this pre-existing tomb and wondered when it was built and by whom. Who was this woman, or girl, buried so close to the saint? I found no other symbols around her niche. What was her story?

Abruptly, Egilolf shifted, and I sensed him getting to his feet. "Been a day since I've heard anything. Likely moved on." His whisper belied his confidence.

"Do you know how to locate our way out?" I asked, suddenly realizing how disoriented I was from my exploration.

"Yes. Two feet off the bottom left corner of the sarcophagus," he replied. I heard him strain against the stone and then, "Come help."

I stumbled to him and confirmed he was correct, for the stone he was lifting matched the shape of our entrance stone. Its weight, however, seemed far greater, and it was all we could do to lift the stone enough for Egilolf to wedge his blade under it.

"I know it should not be possible, without a miracle, of course, but did this stone become far heavier?" I wheezed.

"Had much sleep or food these past days?" he asked.

"Good point."

What had previously seemed like dim light in Saint Philibert's real crypt above us now seemed unbearably bright, even through a small slit. Catching our breath allowed time for our eyes to adjust, and slowly, between frequent rest breaks, we shifted the stone half free from the hole. "It is hard to be quiet when exhausted," I shared. Egilolf only grunted.

It seemed to be midday, to judge by the light in the crypt. I repacked our bags while Egilolf returned the flagstone to its repose.

With a double-portion of the caution we used at our entrance, we made our way back out through the pilgrim's passage and scanned the church. A new refuse pile in the north transept was the only testament to the Northmen's encampment.

Our departure from the church seemed more mundane than the intensity of three days—Egilolf insisted it was only three—in a tomb predicted. We saw no hint of blood-thirsty Northmen nor any other sign of inhabitants as we almost strolled back east. I kept glancing back at the church for as long as it was in sight to assure myself of my memory of the hole, that pit, that holy place darker than Sheol.

"How do you know it was three days in that darkness?" I asked as we stumbled onto some semblance of a cart track.

"Had experience gauging time, waiting for the next meal. Besides," he smirked, "if I told anyone it was more, they'd think I was trying to overshadow Christ."

Now, as I write out my recollections, I realized Egilolf was right. Getting to the relics was the easy part...

CHAPTER 7:
THE BEAST FROM THE SEA

John circles in awkward silence. He had seen Jesus sad before many times. The rich youth who couldn't sell it all to the poor, the cripple at the Bethesda pool who no one had helped into the waters, the would-be disciples who turned back over Jesus' baffling commands to eat his flesh and drink his blood. But now...now Jesus weeps. Sobs. Collapsed on his knees, wind sucked from him, face in the dust, weeping. Only Mary held the courage to say what they all felt: You can heal the sick! And Martha sent warning days ago! *He catches James' eye over the crumpled form of the Son of God. His brother looks as confused as he feels.*

He scuffs the road dust until at last Jesus stands. He takes a shuddering breath. "Remove the stone." Martha makes a face and mutters about stench and decay. "No more," Jesus prophesizes. "Death itself will be unmade." He nods toward the brothers, so John puts his shoulder into it. Martha is right, *he thinks, wrinkling his nose.*

Jesus stares down the void of the tomb and in the voice that commanded the storm: "Come, Spirit, from the four winds. Come, breathe into the man." And then, as if holding a casual conversation over a cup of wine and some shared bread: "Lazarus...come out of there."

As we returned east, I reveled in the sun. The leaves were greener, the birdsong brighter, for having spent days in the tomb. We had St. Philibert, and we were heading home.

Our new freedom lasted two hours. Egilolf sighted our pursuers as we stopped to drink from a stream. We made it four hours before they caught sight of us. I reproached myself more than Egilolf's silent look did for failing to master his run-walk-run methods from weeks ago, another life ago. I don't know if it would have made the difference between capture or not, but I certainly pondered the possibility later when we were trussed like a pair of geese. God did not make the common man to run for hours on end, and I knew myself less than common at running anyway. When I was young, my father called me a runner. This wasn't what he meant.

Egilolf wasted nothing on conversation, and it was all the breath I could spare to stagger after him. The marsh-flats had given way to scrub forest and grassed clearings by the time we fled. I saw a thicker forest a mile or more off, its density offering shelter if we could but reach it.

I always imagined something glorious in the hunt, watching noble parties riding out as to a celebration and returning more triumphant than war heroes (due likely to a lack of mortal reminders that accompany battles). Acting the role of the hare or hart, however, cast a sickly light over those boyhood dreams. I was sure I could run no faster until a horn sounded at my back, a terrible cleaving of the bright afternoon. Though I had recently endured three—I still suspected four, despite Egilolf's claims—days in total darkness, the sun now became an enemy too, a furnace of fury.

A losing pursuit brings with it all the weights of grief I've felt for any loss. Denial that this was really happening—until an arrow pierced a small tree that I leaned on for breath. Anger at God, Egilolf, at the Franks of Aquitania for failing to hold back invasions of their ancestral lands, and above all, the damned, damned, thrice be-damned Northmen and their marauding ways. Pleading to Irenaeus, my patron of habit, to the Archangel, whose militant prowess seemed fitting, and above all, to Philibert, who I thought had at least as great an interest as I did in extricating ourselves from these berserkers. If their taunting calls were meant to unman me, I admit they were working.

In the midst of gasping for air and hope, Egilolf paused and let me catch up. He had stopped at a small rise overlooking a short fall to a trickle of a brook below. "We must hide the true relics," he said, peering between trees for a glimpse for our pursuers. "We cannot outrun them, but we may find some other freedom and return for Philibert." He handed me his pack and took out his sling. "I'll keep them back a bit. You hide him. Seek a fox den or a crook in a tree." I scrambled down the embankment, splashed through the brook, and frantically searched the far shore. I dug through Egilolf's pack as I went, pulling out the red silk. Red! Where was I to conceal such conspicuousness in the forest?

"The other one, you idiot!" Egilolf somehow managed to scream in a hoarse whisper.

Only then did I remember the silk held the other bones, and Saint Philibert was in the rude woolen sack. I pulled it out, spotted a gap in the roots of a twisted rowan shrub, and shoved the bundle into the unlikely reliquary, mumbling some hurried apologies while hoping Philibert assented to the necessity of my irreverent actions. "I have finished!" I called to Egilolf, and he fired off another shot of his sling before scrambling down the same slope and continuing eastward at a run. I followed, and my breath, which hinted it would return while I searched for a hiding spot, deserted me before I lost sight of the stream.

"Did you strike many of them?" I asked hopefully as we ran.

"They're at least a score. To kill one or two wouldn't help us. Just make them seek retribution. I only struck close enough to slow them." His measured breathing was irritating. "Spare your breath. Run."

The sun, cheerily oblivious to our fate, was ambling to the sea when all hope ended. That dire horn, sapping my spirit while yet urging me to greater feats, was finally answered by a call that could have been an echo were we in hillier terrain. Not half a mile onward, its repeat sounded just over the next rise. Egilolf stopped, none the worse for an entire afternoon of running. I collapsed to the mulch at my feet and considered burying myself in it. "Where to?" I managed to gasp. The forest whirled and lurched in my vision. The brambles and trees around us were too thinly spread to offer concealment, too spindly built to consider climbing.

"Best to submit. If we fight, we die. Northmen prefer slaves. Who knows what'll come?" If he felt defeated, he did not show it. He held his arms out to either side, hands open, showing no weapon. "*Kyrie eleison*," he began in a low chant. "Get up," he muttered, "or they'll think you're done for. They respect strength, despise weakness. *Christe eleison…*" I wobbled to my feet and also held my arms out, though as much for balance as to display submission.

The war party in front of us topped the rise as the others reached the gulley behind us. Whoops and triumphant cries pierced the call of their horns. One of the runtier-looking Northmen (by which I mean one still taller and broader than me) ran up behind Egilolf and struck him in the back with the flat of his sword. Egilolf collapsed to his knees. The air became thick as water around me, the sounds distorted. *A Northmen blade singing through torchlight, over screams and choking smoke. Brother Angius grasping his throat, fingers unable to keep blood from spurting along the cloister wall in overlapping arcs. Some part of my mind noted the arced blood spatter on the walls closely matched the curvature of the ceiling vault. Angius staggered to an exit he would never reach. I ran—*

"Skuli!" The call of the stoutest barbarian brought me back to the grim present. His bulk alone was imposing, but his stance and mad stare cowed even the other Northmen. I glanced at Egilolf, wondering if this word meant anything to him. One of the trailing pursuers stepped up to this presumed leader and spoke to us a mix of Frankish and Latin, the latter almost better than a rustic priest's.

"This is Arnkel, known as Skull-Crusher." Presumably, in case the translation wasn't clear, the leader pantomimed crushing a man's head between his hands while the translator continued. "He keeping this land area for Thorfinn Eirikson. What you doing here? Why is you coming to *basilica?*" His verb tenses were appalling. While the interpreter spoke, the leader Arnkel grunted a command, and two others approached us and took our bags and weapons. They began pawing through them, tossing items into piles among the decaying leaves.

Egilolf was swaying on his knees from the blow, so I spoke up. "My lord, I cannot deceive you. We did travel to the *basilica*, and obviously at great risk to ourselves, for how many Franks would brave these lands of yours?" I paused to allow the translator to catch up and to regain my breath. "I am sure my lord has heard of the power of the Franks' saints, those men and women and children of ancient times who were especially close to the one God and were granted to deal out his power. In the days of my father's father, such a saint was left at the *basilica*, hidden and nearly forgotten, when the land was abandoned due to the...ah...*visits* of the Northmen."

A great hollering broke out from the two digging through Egilolf's pack as they removed the red silk bundle. Arnkel merely snapped his fingers with astounding volume, and the two shut their mouths and hastily brought him the bundle. As Arnkel unwrapped the silk, I continued, "The power of the saint could be, perhaps, shared with—"

Arnkel cut me off with some unintelligibly barked question as the silk opened, revealing the bones. He dropped them as if holding hot coals.

"*Oss, os*...bones?" the translator stumbled onto the correct word.

"Relics," I corrected him, trying to keep a tone of authority. "The remnants of the saint on earth, the medium of his power, the link between the power of heaven and its distribution on earth."

The translator finished, but Arnkel only shifted his gaze between me and the skeletal heap.

"Since we recovered them from your lands," I added, "we could give you a gift of a portion of the relics. Along with the words for their power, of course." Every good Christian knows, certainly, the saints aren't controlled by words or rituals, but I had seen and heard enough of the Northmen and their thoroughly pagan faith to know they would see no value in relics as we saw them. But give a man access to power....

As the translation finished, Arnkel scoffed. His deprecating tone was obvious before his words were translated: "These is could being your mother's bones. You Franks are odd. Our sorceress knowing." He growled out another word, snapped his fingers toward us, and with an efficiency that bordered on routine, Egilolf and I were bound at the wrists and led back west.

A half-day's trudging (its moderate pace somehow more unbearable than our terrorizing and exhausting attempt to flee) brought us back at dusk to Saint Philibert's. High clouds, banded in rows like carded wool, blazed orange by the setting sun, casting the grass fields in an odd, deep yellow. It was as though the world were no longer lit by the sun, setting beyond Oceanus, but by a great torch preparing to consume the sky, the brush, and the very ground. Utter defeat was epitomized in spending the night back in the church, our once-concealing crypt a handful of yards away. That fear-filled darkness seemed like freedom now compared to our likely futures. Egilolf was reticent in the face of hardships, and I was left to speculate our possible fates in silence. That night lasted longer than three days.

The next morning brought a northerly march to the raider's ship, guarded and anchored along a river so wide it could only be the *Leger*. Words were spared for bantering between our captors; they directed us only by spear point. And so I found myself huddled in the middle of a longship, bound, with nothing to do but watch Francia float away as the warband-turned-crew rowed us to the sea.

By noon we made the coast, which, to my surprise, we followed south. As late afternoon approached, our craft approached another, much smaller river. An hour of hard rowing upstream brought us to the Northmen's village.

I say village rather than camp for the signs of permanence, despite the raider longships half-beached at the ready along the sandy riverbank: a half-hearted attempt at a wooden defense, more pickets than palisade; some crude shelters whose gapped stone foundation work showed more haste than skill; and a few vegetable gardens on the outskirts that threatened to be labeled fields if cultivated much farther. But it was the number of women who were cooking, tanning a deer hide, tending the gardens, or sharpening blades, and the small packs of urchins running through the place that belied the militant purpose of the camp. A few changes and this could be any *villa* outside Lemouicensis.

"One thing to hear rumors," Egilolf muttered, "another to see with your own eyes. Raiders becoming settlers."

"And still, our 'kings' peck at each other, unable to set aside the petty for the portentous."

The place was small enough, however, that the arrival of two prisoners (or slaves or sacrifices, I did not know how to classify our fate at that point) drew the entire population, who pressed around us and our captors as they marched us toward the largest building, down the shoreline. I confess I could only attempt to appear as stoic as Egilolf. The crowd jeered, the murmurings of women a backdrop to the mocking of older children pretending to be men. A few grown men slung epithets as well, their tone and laughter, despite their barbaric tongue, making their general intent clear.

The presentation before their chieftain was so typical of all such affairs in all races of men that it is not worth much description:

another bulky warrior-type, wearing the most decorated sword and wielding the cruelest of smiles, a dialogue between this chief and the returning leader, Arnkel Skull-Crusher, and a presentation of their loot. I overheard a frequent questioning of a word I had heard when Skuli mentioned *osse* at the time of our capture, some guttural braying whose repeat barely distinguished it from animal sounds.

Like most uncivilized tribes, the warrior-chief had a wise man to aid him—not a warrior but with different powers, and, in this case, not a man. The cacophony between the warriors and the chieftain suddenly gutted out like a suffocating candle as the crowd became aware of an odd figure weaving inward from its edges. The woman, her outlandish garb not hiding her obvious femininity, showed no hesitation in butting into the discussion. Even the chieftain showed her no small amount of deference.

Since Egilolf and I were left ignored on the dividing line between those in the discussion and the crowd gathered within hearing range, I surveyed the sorceress further. She was surely the one Arnkel described, for her appearance set her apart from everyone in the village. Over a dark gray shift-like dress, she wore a deep blue cloak, deeper than the blue of an unadulterated mountain lake, with a black hood thrown back on her shoulders. The inside of the hood was lined with a pure-white fur, much whiter than a sheep's. A cat's skin, perhaps. Her gloves, tucked into a belt of interlocking links of carved wood, were similarly lined and stood out brilliantly against her otherwise dark clothing. Her hair was short-cut but was so fair as to almost match the white fur. She wore tall, soft leather boots with polished brass buttons above the ankles. When she silenced a younger warrior beside her with a sneer, I glimpsed two knives on her left hip, as though she used only one at a time. One had a copper handle and a dark wood sheath, and the other, slightly longer, showed a white handle and sheath of a cream-white similar to the ivory of Father Leo's *diptych*.

She examined the relics in the silk bundle Arnkel held. He began to visibly perspire when she removed a small bone wand from her cloak, waved it over the silk, and chanted softly.

Our translator Skuli stood among the expectant and hushed periphery. The chieftain called for him and addressed us. "I seeing you Franks crazy over bones before."

I opened my mouth to respond, but a glance from Egilolf shut me up. He stood there, hands tied behind his back and surrounded by a village of Northmen, as if he was patiently waiting out a civilized court debate.

"I seeing none crazy enough to trespass into land area of Thorfinn Eirikson." A few Northmen hooted their agreement to this.

Still, Egilolf did not respond. Thorfinn shifted his attention from us to the red silk and back. "Why is these bones important?"

I'll grant Skuli some skill; he stood at the periphery of the conversation and translated without interjecting himself. If his Latin verbs didn't lack, the translation would have been transparent.

I again opened my mouth, but Egilolf spoke up first. "These relics are more than bones. May not seem more to you, but why else would anyone risk their lives for only bones? My father's father's bones may rest in lands that were once his but are now yours—let them rest. If you've been among us Franks much, you know our God has many agents. They lived great and powerful lives. They serve God even more in the afterlife." I noted that this talk of powers and afterlife began a muttering in the crowd; a few made signs against evil.

"You hold not the bones of any man. Those bones are a great saint, a powerful warrior. He lived in this land, held it in peace. He brought blessings to the people who worshipped the true God. In fear, the Franks fled the Northmen, and rightly, for they are powerful"—here, Egilolf seemed to play to the crowd, but Thorfinn and the sorceress remained unmoved—"but the Franks left behind their saint when they fled his temple. He spoke in visions to take him back to his people."

Thorfinn seemed to reply with a grunt of respect but nothing more. "Maybe the saint wants to be remembered by the people who now live in his land. Maybe he only used us to bring him to you."

Arnkel laughed at this. But the sorceress spoke, cutting off not only Arnkel, but tripping up Skuli's words as well.

"The great, uh, mighty, Ingigird demands—" He bungled a few more phrases before the sorceress cut him off. By the translator's reaction, he seemed to fear for his own soul when the sorceress's ice-blue eyes pierced him. He again attempted to translate for her. "The, eh, our wise woman, Ingigird, demands knowing whose bones."

"As I said," began Egilolf, "they're of a mighty saint who—"

"She wants the name!" interjected Skuli.

Egilolf paused. Sometimes you need a guide, a scout, a thief who's willing to dig under altars. And other times, you need a storyteller. As Deusdona's descendant told Egilolf in the crypt of Saint Vincentius, without a story, they were simply a collection of bones. And I, unseasoned gladiator, was shoved into the ring. "Long before our Great King Charles, before his father Martel, before those kings of the Merovingian line, and long before you races of the North ever came south, God sent one of his followers into this land, to teach the people to revere him, and to bring them His blessings in return." I cast around in my mind for a suitable name for this exemplar. Something credible but not already famous. "When this great follower died, God took him to heaven, but his holy power lasted in his remains, and they became the source of many miracles, healings, and protection. People considered themselves blessed if they only had to travel for weeks to reach the shrine of his burial. Many came from even farther away, and…" As I tried to switch to specifics, I was struck with an inspiration so perfect it could have been divine if it weren't a lie. "The follower, though, was not a man. She was a woman. Over her shrine was built that great church we stayed in last night. Her name was Valerie."

It was not until I had talked about burial that my mind took me back to our confinement under the altar at Saint Philibert's church, two days and a different lifetime ago, and the name I found carved there. *Let the Northmen demand some proof!*

My gloating was short-lived. Skuli stopped mid-sentence. The whole crowd gasped and stepped back. Skuli looked surprised at his own words.

Egilolf raised a puzzled eyebrow to me. I shrugged back as the murmuring grew louder, even Chief Thorfinn edging away. Only Ingigird stepped forward, her wand raised defensively over the red silk bundle that Arnkel found too horrific to even risk dropping.

The repeated word of the crowd's murmurs became clear as Skuli hesitantly asked, "Valkyrie? She was Valkyrie?"

"Yes, Valerie."

"Valkyrie?"

It took both of us repeating the unfamiliar words, accompanied by further gasps from the crowd, before I realized we were not, after all, saying the same thing. Egilolf unhelpfully pointed out the word *valkyrie* obviously held a great significance for them.

I never learned how to fight with weapons, but I have always had a decent supply of bright ideas. Perhaps this one was even mine and not divinely prompted. *Saint Irenaeus, send me Christ's grace to overcome my pride.*

"I think we may be speaking of the same thing," I dissembled. "Who is this Valkyrie?"

Disconcerted, Skuli forgot his translating role and answered me directly. "The maidens of Odin. They deciding men's fates, and carrying souls to Valhalla, to heaven, if they earning it."

Odin I had heard of, the Northmen's chief god. His valkyries, apparently, were some sort of divine intermediary. I confess my purposes at that moment were more self-centered on survival, and only later was I able to justify my actions with the wisdom of Pope Gregory the Great: paganism cannot usually be cut out all at once, but only through slow steps, keeping familiar forms and with a new Christian purpose.

"Saint Valkyrie," I continued in a louder voice, while Skuli resumed his translation, "also called Saint Valerie, had great foreknowledge, granted to her by God our Father. She aids His followers not only at the hour of their death but at all times in this life."

"*Kyrie eleison!*" Egilolf swore. Yes, it's a prayer, but he swore it.

This produced a lengthier exchange between the leadership, settled by some decisive commands and an even more emphatic gesture from Ingigird toward the bones. The crowd backed away with shaking heads and averted gazes. She then addressed us through Skuli. "You claiming much for weak Frankish captive. If these bones being of Valkyrie, or have power, how you using them?"

Fortunately, I had rather too much experience with pompous

bishops and librarians in charge of arcane works locked away in *scriptoria*—all who kept secrets for power while sending others to do anything resembling danger or work. "I don't know," I replied, mostly truthfully, for I had never had any saint provide me with a miracle. "Those who know, the bishop and his priests at Pictauensis, sent us to recover the relics. As a lowly monk, I was taught only enough to recognize her name carved in the stone and how to properly transport her remains."

The sorceress nodded at this explanation, so I added, "If you wish it, I could return to Pictauensis to send someone to show you their power. The bishop there would want at least half of the relics in exchange for lending you his priest."

Perhaps there was a chance at freedom in all this...

The chieftain laughed, but he offered a fourth part of the relics before Ingigird cut him off. She began a quiet chant, and the crowd went silent, motionless in the presence of unknown powers.

"I singing a spell-weaving tonight, under the first stars, and then we knowing if you speak truth." Her hand dropped to the not-quite ivory knife at her waist before she added, "Or lie." She then strutted off without another word, the crowd parting a respectful, fearful distance. Chief Thorfinn grunted an agreement, and Egilolf and I were taken and bound to stakes at the edge of the clearing in front of the hall.

Attempting to plot an escape with Egilolf was impossible while it remained daylight, for every time I opened my mouth, some impudent child took delight in hurling a clod of dirt, aimed at my head no less. But as dusk spread a beautiful sunset, all Creation praising God but rather indifferent to our plight, the children were called off by parents as everyone built a bonfire and prepared meals.

"Have you worked out a plan of escape yet?" I asked Egilolf hopefully, my head down to avoid more dirt in my mouth, though we had been ignored for the better part of an hour.

"Heh. So far, my plans have been to pray to Philibert. And the Virgin Mother. If he wants his bones somewhere other than a forest bole until Judgment Day, he needs to aid us. Nice work with the

Valerie name." He dared to raise his head toward me. "Odd chance it put the fear of a Northern angel in them."

"It was a rather fortuitous coincidence. I keep trying to think of some way to put that to our advantage, but I do not see any. That witch is going to come dance around the fire or something, call up *daemons* likely as not, and then plant that white dagger in our hearts when she discovers she is holding the bones of some long-lost Merovingian grandmother."

After cooking their meals around family fires, the clansman brought their dinner to a circle around the new-lit bonfire. One of the Northmen tuned a lute of sorts and began singing a light tune, which most of the group joined on the chorus between mouthfuls of dinner and drink. "Reminds me of my village's saint feasts," Egilolf commented wistfully.

For a moment, pleasant memories of home crowded out the painful, and I longed for it. "What are we even doing here?" I asked the sky. "What am *I* doing here? I should have gone on to some other monastery, some place where they needed a scribe, anywhere but beyond the borders of Francia. Our last effort, down in Spain, seemed much simpler." I kicked at the dirt. "Prideful. That is what it is—what I am. My confessor used to beat that word into my head every time I met with him, but I just could not see it in myself, I guess." I snorted a laugh at the irony of that. What proud man sees his own pride? Is that not the sin of it?

Egilolf didn't reply, but he was watching, interested.

"I wanted to be someone known, some remembered writer, like Prudentius. Someone that other scribes would think of and marvel at as they copied my works. If I am honest with God—and now seems a prudent time to be—I begrudged being a mere scribe for Him. I did not want to be another brother monk, spending his life copying out the Scriptures and the Fathers from decaying parchment to new, my name only an addendum to the copiers' list. That is why I delayed taking the monastic vows for so long. Did you know I had finally resigned myself to them? The ceremony was pending when the Northmen descended on us." I thought again of my second home, the *scriptorium*, all the works I copied obediently and read eagerly.

"I wanted to be remembered for the works I created, Egilolf. I wanted my work to have lasting meaning and purpose. When I happened upon you in Cordoba and knew you would need stories written of the saints and why we moved their relics, I thought that would be my opportunity."

The bonfire was in full blaze now. The sunset was fiercer to the west but graying already overhead.

Egilolf took a few minutes to reply. "I can't read or write. Only compare signs. I've never touched the Scriptures or a book of the Gospels. Like everyone but the priest, I listen. I imagine." He shifted in his bonds, with no effect but perhaps the relief of cramping muscles. I attempted the same, but my arms ached worse. "Maybe God has other plans for you than a copier, but have you thought what would happen if no one copied? If all monasteries burned, and no one made new books? I've seen the size of libraries. People say those are small against the libraries of Rome. Or Constantinople." He shook his head at the unfathomable vastness of the world. "No one can know all those stories. That singer Rodegar we met, working to gather the stories of Franks, Northmen, and Moors, can't memorize them all. If no one copied, they wouldn't last.

"Who remembers names, anyway? I've never heard of Prudentius before, no matter how great or famous you think he is. Everyone knows Charles the Great. But who was his father or his father's father? Of the Roman Emperors, I can only name Augustus because his name is in Christ's birth story and Constantine because he ended the persecutions. I don't ask of the wives, or chief servants, or generals to these emperors. Who were the emperors? Who can name a simple handful, these men that ruled the entire world?"

"Well, *entire world* may not be quite scholarly accurate—agh! What'd you kick me for?"

"As your new confessor, I help you combat pride," he smirked. "You know a lot, it seems, though I've never traveled with a scribe before; but you let everyone know that you know more than them. It's endearing when it's not annoying."

I grinned back. Some part of my mind still screamed we needed to escape this mess, but the rest was resigned and contemplative.

Egilolf faced the bonfire again. "Maybe it's better to tell the great stories rather than make something new."

"Well said, friend," murmured a voice behind us in our native Frankish tongue. I twisted but was bound too tightly to the stake to see the speaker. "Hold still! I cannot help you now. We must await the right window. Don't let it be known that you know me."

And then the voice was gone before I even *could* know the stranger that spoke like a fellow Frank. I might witness a miracle, after all, and then remembered that I had not even prayed yet.

With the firmament subdued, the sole light now raged from the bonfire. Singing had joined with dancing for an hour when a new singer began a tune from the far side of the fire. When he began singing, I recognized the Frank who had spoken at our backs. "That voice…" questioned Egilolf.

"Yes. It's familiar." The singer remained obscured by the fire, but my curiosity paused as he drew me into his song.

> Somewhere westward, lies the mourning
>   Somewhere north, the raven's caw
> Mirrored shards, burst from doorway
>   Fell to block the paths I saw
>
> Somewhere eastward waits a kindling
>   Somewhere south the promised land
> Always pilgrim onward, onward
>   Seek to stave hope's reprimand
>
> Somewhere homeward sought the heart's gaze
>   Somewhere back, before, before
> Torn and battered, remnants scattered
>   From four winds whose folly bore
>
> Somewhere westward, lied the rainbow
>   Somewhere brighter, swore the sun
> One more summit, or deeper cavern
>   Just find a path and you're begun

The crowd paused, oblivious to the meaning of the Frankish words but perhaps mesmerized by the cadence and tune.

"Somewhere in that song was the sense I tried to convey," I faltered. "There is some alluring lie that the next adventure, the next opportunity, the next...*something*, I suppose, that gains me satisfaction, the final satisfaction that endures." The stars watched us now. "That allows me to endure."

Egilolf only mumbled a response, so I asked, "What of you? I already admitted I only came seeking this fool quest out of pride. What makes you seek relics time upon time? Why not lift up the white flag, head off somewhere with your friend Peter and return to a real life?"

The barbaric crowd was getting rowdy again. A group of them lugged a raised seat toward the fire ring.

"Was it too boring, the farming life? Even scouting has to be better than risking all for forgotten bones." I was rambling, my mind fending off thoughts of how the night would end.

Egilolf, to my surprise, replied. "You know a lot about some bits of the world, Aristeus. Important people. Important ideas. You don't know much about other parts of life, parts so real they can't be spoken. The military. Heh. You're right that I'm a better scout than thief. Yeah, I'll say it. We've used other words, but I stole relics in Rome. And Cordoba. I've become a thief.

"You ever think this isn't my choice? You gripe that your pride got you into this. At least you have the choice to back out. Peter...ah, Peter. He doesn't know the full story either. I... I'm sorry I dragged you down with me." Egilolf paused so long I thought he wouldn't speak more, but suddenly he continued. "I can't go back. Not to my town, not to my old life. Definitely not now. Maybe not ever. Something happened. I wrestle with the sin of it, but what else could I have done? The chaplain declared my absolution, even said it wasn't a sin. Still, I felt God's eyes turned from me. I demanded a penance. The chaplain placed one upon me. That's why I seek relics. So God might love me again."

As I thought how to question him further, the mob fell silent as their sorceress, repetitive syllables spurting from her lips, wove a path through them to the high seat, placed on a crude dais. If this eldritch figure consorted with *daemons* tonight, it would seal our fate. The darkened sky confined our world to the flickering fire-shadows of Northmen and the sorceress Ingigird, whose muttering became a low moaning, a strained breathing. The bonfire's fierce blaze overpowered any view of the stars. She ascended the dais and arranged herself on the raised seat amidst gestures of her wand and the ivory-colored knife. She ceased all noise as she sunk into the chair. She crossed the wand and knife in front of her chest. A song rose then, a solo voice soon joined by another. Two young women emerged in cadence from the crowd, slowly stepping up to position the high seat between them, their airy, a-tonal chant rising with them.

Ingigird suddenly leapt out of the chair, screaming a harsh torrent and waving her wand and knife about as though fending off unseen *daemons*. Even Thorfinn and Arnkel leapt back. Half the crowd went so far as to retreat well away from the sorcerous display, only to hastily draw back to the fire's security against the dark.

The sorceress's barrage and battle continued. Without taking my sight off it, I asked Egilolf, "Do you think she is faking it?"

"Huh?"

"The bonfire, the chair, the songs, knife, wand, yelling—is she faking it? Is the pageantry only for show? Has she already decided our fate, and this is all for Chief Thorfinn and the crowd, or is she really battling with some *daemon* for a vision of the future?"

"We're dead either way," he replied hollowly. Our anonymous would-be savior had disappeared with nothing but an odd song. An obscure form of aid, if that was how he meant it.

"I would rather not cross paths with some power of the air or earth before the end. I hope she's faking it." My mouth was dry.

A trembling child brought forth the red silk bundle, all but tossing it in front of Ingigird. Wand and knife slashed the air as the sorceress began a feinting, weaving duel with the void above the relics. The song of the other women had ended. The sorceress's words became singular, all shouted, with an edge of desperation. I wondered if even the Northmen knew what she was saying. The child knelt, curling into her own bundle beside the red silk, her face pressed into the dirt.

Like a hart shot and chased to exhaustion, its gasps professing the near end, the sorceress's protesting cries began to dull, convulsed, and devolved into a spatter of words. With a final burst, she writhed and murmured again, paused, and finally ended. Through this waning, her contorted figure collapsed on herself to become a huddled form indistinguishable from the child or the bundle. Only the fire dared shift or snap the silence.

Chief Eirikson was the first to brave the unknown, speaking out perhaps as much to end the dread as to see if his witch-woman survived. He risked three steps forward. "Ingigird?" In the collectively held breath of all, it was impossible to say whether he whispered this or shouted.

The child seemed to have gone unconscious from fear, but the sorceress slowly unfolded and stood. Without a word, she returned to the raised seat. Her poise conveyed a relief. Becoming again more Thorfinn than Chief Eirikson, the leader sheepishly stepped back to the herd.

The sorceress gazed over the whole crowd and spoke. The Frankish singer reappeared behind my post and translated in soft undertones, not overpowering the woman's rhetorical display, so that it seemed I understood her directly. "A great being came at my calling, a spirit of earth, a servant of the gods, surely, by his power."

I glanced at Egilolf but couldn't read his expression. The singer was out of my view.

"The earth-god knew of the red-bundled bones before I even spoke. He was wroth because of them. He said he and his brethren would curse us for possessing them. His maw gaped wide! He breathed a consuming fire and doom!" She all but shouted this. She gazed up at the stars, and the sight of them stilled her. Quieter, still transfixed by the vast sky, she added, "Then came a woman of light, bright as the sun, descending as a star. She stood before the earth-god. She trembled not. The fire from the earth did not singe her, and she shielded me from the earth's rage. The woman of light smiled upon the bones, and the earth-god cowered."

Only the heathen could be confused by so clear a delineation between *daemons* of the Deceiver and messengers of God Almighty.

But, as befit pagan barbarians, confused they were. No sooner had Ingigird finished her recollection than the whole village broke out in uproar, and I needed no translator to perceive arguments slung back and forth. I heard not a few mentions of *valkyrie*. A Viking chief and sorceress, it seemed, had not the authority a Frankish lord or bishop in determining God's will.

"Who are you?" I asked of the Frank singer at my back.

"Patience," he said, though I could not tell whether he answered or exhorted. He retreated once more.

As the debate went on, it coalesced into a backing of Chief Eirikson against those supporting the Skull-Crusher. These two were head to head, shouting and posturing. A physical confrontation looked inevitable when the voice of the singer called out. No longer beyond the fire but beside it, the singer was recognizable instantly. I wondered why I could not place his voice earlier.

"Chief Thorfinn Eirikson," the bard Rodegar hailed the fighters. In Pictauensis, I had thought him boasting in his claims to pass among Northmen camps, but perhaps all peoples need stories enough to set aside fear of the stranger. He continued in their barbaric tongue until the chief called for his translator. Once Skuli was present, Rodegar switched to Frankish.

"I knew this one in Pictauensis," Rodegar began, pointing to me. He slowly spun to address the whole crowd. "He is Aristeus, monk of the Christian God. Beside him is his good guide. Why would such a pair wander deep in wastelands long held by men of the North, only to unbury useless bones?" He let the thought sink into everyone's mind. "You've heard the Christian God uses his most staunch servants in this life and the next, and that their remains, charred or not, are the channels of His power."

Arnkel and the sorceress replied, and Skuli didn't translate. The dialogue sank back into the barbaric tongue, and I lost most of the following conversation, with Skuli only relaying fragments. I gathered Rodegar sought to convince the camp to keep the relics in exchange for letting us go. He named Saint Martin, Saints Marcellinus and Peter, and others, presumably providing examples of their power. Egilolf pointed out that Chief Eirikson seemed to be siding more with Rodegar, against Ingigird and Arnkel.

Egilolf broke the debate: "Chief Thorfinn!" He called again, drawing the crowd's attention while Skuli translated. "Your sorceress's story is of *daemon* and saint. Hate against light—fear of relics against blessing their use. We brought them from the old church north of here. We wouldn't risk your land but for the relics.

"When Arnkel Skull-Crusher caught us, we offered your tribe some of the relics and their words of power. Arnkel wisely knew they could be some ancestor's bones. He brought them to your sorceress Ingigird for a trial. And she has tested them. Not one, but two powerful beings, confirmed these are no farmer's bones.

"We are simple relic-hunters. We gathered them for the bishop of Pictauensis. We offer a share of the relics, and I will ask the bishop to send you priests to show you how to talk through the saint and seek God's power."

When Skuli finished translating this, the crowd didn't jeer but listened. As did the chief.

Egilolf continued, "I haven't been to your North lands. Can't say what gods are there. But I've been all through the lands of Franks. I've seen crops grow, and harvests fail, healing and births, and much death, wars, plagues, and famines. God's saints give power to His people here. If you want to be part of this land, you should bind yourself to the powers of this land, instead of challenging them."

This last drew more nods, and I saw Egilolf with new eyes. "When did you become a missionary to the Northmen?"

"Had a few hours tied to this post. I thought what might sway me if I were them, invaders to a strange land."

"Well, may God smite them for appealing to false relics and fictitious saints, but only after we're well on our way from here."

It took more debate, a night's sleep, and still more debate, but finally, Thorfinn gathered the village and declared that he would accept an additional power of this land for his people and send us to Pictauensis to bring back priests. "But," he added with a chuckle, "I is keeping all relics. They are being price bargain of your lives." Skuli's speech recalled to me a novice into whose skull I once tried to beat Latin, but I resisted the urge to provide the translator with grammar lessons and tried less successfully to hide my relief at our release. We were cut free and pointed in the direction of Pictauensis. Rodegar followed us as far as the village fence.

"Our thanks," I told him.

"I sought to show the value of relics, but your mistrustful friend made them see the benefit of the gods of this land. Don't scowl at me! It wasn't you, brother monk, but this scout that spoke what I envisioned but couldn't voice. We Franks don't see the saints as gods. We know them as intercessors and patrons, but these Northmen may learn to love them, and through the saints, adore Christ, if they first see them as local gods." He nodded to Egilolf. "You may craft these people's stories yet."

We started across the rolling hills north of the village. Rodegar indicated the *Leger* was a day and a half's hike northeast but that he was off to Bordeaux. Egilolf was certain he could find Saint Philibert's church from the river, and from there, retrace our pursuit route to the impromptu forest shrine of the saint.

But apparently, we weren't rid of the Northmen. After less than an hour's trek, a band of them stepped from a copse. My spirit failed as the Skull-Crusher's broad form swaggering toward us.

"Thorfinn change his mind?" Egilolf hailed him. No one drew weapons, but menace dripped from their glares. Skuli ran up behind Arnkel, catching his breath while translating.

"I is reminding you," Arnkel spoke through his translator, "not all Northmen weakly like Thorfinn. We come for your land, women, gold, anything we want. We is not needing bones of your dead gods. You taking my message to your craven people cowering in their stone towers: Chief Thorfinn Eirikson not living forever. When next meet, I be stomping your skull into tiny bits."

We made it to the Leger *a few days later around* none, *though no one prayed the hours in these wastes. It took a warm afternoon's hour to find the stream where we were caught. Egilolf knew his woodcraft well. Even then, every tree grew the same, and we scoured miles upstream and down before we found Saint Philibert, waiting patiently where we had abandoned him.*

We laughed much of the next week's trudge toward Pictauensis, and I felt even more resurrected than when we had emerged from three days in the crypt. I caught myself saying a prayer of thanks to Saint Valerie, then laughing again at the invention before invoking Saint Irenaeus and the Martyrs of Lyon. And Saint Philibert, I added hastily, making the Sign of the Cross toward the relics safe again in Egilolf's pack as I followed him back toward civilization.

CHAPTER 8:
FROM ETHAM,
ACROSS THE DESERT (WITH JOSEPH)

"Civilization," of course, is meant to contrast us from the chaos and evil of the barbarians we thought we left behind.

"One victory isn't the war," Egilolf pointed out over a fire beneath which baked acorn bread. Chief Thorfinn had kept most of our kit, so we were reduced to eating foraged food once again. We had made a more lenient pace as we drew away from danger and now rested somewhat half a day from Pictauensis. "Made it back to our own lands, but…" He broke bits of twig apart and idly flipped them into the fire, piece by piece.

"Yes, despite the horrors of the recent past, the hardest decision still lies before us. Are we to be fugitives from the law if we defy *Comes* Fulgaud, or fugitives from God if you don't fulfill your penance and give the relics to Abbot Gonsindus? Or perhaps worse yet, personal betrayers of Father Leo's trust if we don't offer up Saint Philibert to him? Now I know what it felt like to be in Peter's position—the apostle, not your bandit friend—as he was confronted in the courtyard: Christ and certain death, or a betrayal worse than Judas' mere hours before."

"Already lost Aquitania as home," Egilolf spoke, again staring into the fire. "For my part, I'd rather flee the law. The *comes* reaches only so far. Certainly less than a saint." The fire crackled, but I held my breath. "My head says to hand Saint Philibert over to the abbot. Fulfill my penance. Yet I can't believe I'm meant to betray Father Leo. It's a long hope, but perhaps, just perhaps, Father Leo would give the relics to Abbot Gonsindus." He smiled up at me as if hitting on an idea. "After all, didn't the Father say his monks at Tournus think they have Saint Philibert already? They wouldn't want any new relics. Wouldn't it be better to leave the relics at Saint Martial's, where they'll be venerated more?"

"Quite a stretch of hope."

He glared.

"The more immediate question," I continued, "is whether to risk Saint Philibert at Pictauensis, whether we are willing to risk another Spanish March."

He went back to throwing twigs in the fire. "Then again, we promised the abbot first. Maybe Saint Philibert wants to be at Saint Martial's. Maybe he brought Father Leo to tell us which saint to bring to Gonsindus."

"At the very least, we need to stop for sustenance. While we were facing death across a Northmen bonfire, hunger was a much lesser need. But I am not choking down your acorn bread for another week if we can eat at the monastery here."

Egilolf stood and paced. "Does it matter?" he growled, throwing his whole stick at the fire. "Northmen don't just raid our land. They live on it. Conquer it. The Moors always press from Spain. All our lords do is fight each other."

"Food?" I countered.

"I don't think of the whole Church usually. But when I went to Rome, to Spain, to the borders of the Danes, I saw how pressed the Franks are. Imagine the days of Charles the Great! Before we couldn't fight the Northmen and Moors because we're too busy fighting ourselves?" He didn't seem to want an answer, so I didn't. I let go of my attempts to steer the conversation to food. "Can Christianity survive? Can it resist these onslaughts?"

I stopped to consider his line of thought before responding. "I have not seen the vast borders of Francia, except for Spain. But considering time and the history of the Church, this cannot seem the longest night of winter approaching. Surely to the handfuls of Christians surviving in Carthage and Alexandria, dragged by groups and scores off to games, or beheadings, or burning—must not that have seemed the end? Or when, after Constantine's Peace, that damned heretic Arius spewed his poison into the bishops and councils, and the emperors meddled with church doctrine"—I admit I likely quoted something I once read—"and Athanasius stood *contra mundum*, the only Nicaean against the Arians and those too weak to hold to the truth; or when the Visigoths and Ostrogoths broke the Roman Empire to pieces, the whole known and newly Christian world crumbling to ruin—must not each of those times have seemed the end?" I reflected on the darkest hours of the Church when a thought struck hard: the darkest hour was the beginning. "Or when Christ cried for his Father on the cross and gave up his last breath," I said softly, "while his chosen, his apostles, cowered in fear, shut up in a room before the Church was even born—must that not have seemed the end?"

We both let the fire burn.

"So," Egilolf stirred. "Food tomorrow?"

Suffice it to say Chief Thorfinn and crew had not debated retaining our *deniers*; a tavern was not going to be an option this time in the city. We agreed to play as pilgrims and seek provisions at a wayfarer-aiding church. Previously, I rushed past a description of Pictauensis since our outward journey had been one of haste, but now Pictauensis seemed a beacon guiding us home.

We should have pressed on.

Built between the confluence of two rivers that joined directly north of the city and continued toward the *Leger*, Pictauensis combined access to river trade with its natural barriers of rivers and southern cliffs, making an ideal location from which to govern not only the county of Poitou but the whole duchy of Aquitania. Or so I gleaned from Egilolf, who detailed the challenge of bringing an army to bear on the city.

The city walls, partially stone, were imposing, but the guards stood relaxed. I felt like screaming that a horde of bloody-thirsty Northmen lay a week to the west, but I read apathy in the soldiers' eyes. Instead, I asked where pilgrims could be fed, and they pointed us to the Abbey of the Holy Cross.

This was not my first admission to a convent, but though the layout of the church, cloister, and refectory should have been comforting in their familiarity, the weaker sex always made me feel nervous. A life spent without a mother and then around monks, I suppose. Egilolf, fortunately, did not trip over his own tongue when introducing us to the sisters. We attended *sext*, having missed the morning meal, and then *none* while awaiting dinner. Between services, we rested undisturbed in a chapel off the church transept.

A choir practiced in the nave, but I caught only fragments of their song. Something about a victory banner, which fit this final stage of our mission. I relaxed in the lie of temporal security offered by thick stone walls blocking out the chaos of nature and the fallen world. My senses, becalmed with soothing incense and unseen chanting, conjured visions of cherubim extolling the glories of God. A shaft of afternoon light from a high window shone on the altar over which a celestial host of glowing dust motes danced to the chanting's polyphony. Few things are as restorative as the blurred state between meditation and a nap.

"We spent days lying by an altar," Egilolf explained over dinner to the young sister serving us crow soup mixed with cabbage, radishes, and a heavy seasoning of fennel. She had asked where we came from, and Egilolf provided our agreed-upon tale. "Traveled to a shrine west of here. Near the Northmen territory." He made our days there seem a choice.

As she circled our table, her robe hinted at her female form, and I found myself thinking of the bandit who robbed us. I frowned, wondering why I thought of that vixen when the sister ladling Egilolf's trencher wasn't similar at all. First, she didn't have Rachel's long black hair, and second, she—

"Did you find what you sought?" the girl asked innocently, interrupting my reverie.

Egilolf's face clouded.

"While praying in a chapel, we overheard the choir practice a song," I interjected. "The piece intrigued me. What was it?"

"The *Vexilla Regis?*"

"The Banner of the King? Yes, that fits the parts I heard. What is its origin?"

The sister straightened and recited as though from a lesson: "In the five hundred and sixty-ninth Year of Our Lord, Bishop Fortunatus of Pictauensis wrote the *Vexilla Regis* as a triumphant processional for the arrival of the relic of the true cross from Emperor Justin of Byzantium." She went back to her task and continued in a less sermonizing tone. "That's when we were renamed the Abbey of the Holy Cross."

"There's a relic of the True Cross here?" Egilolf asked.

"Yes." She paused. "Set beneath the crucifix." She picked up Egilolf's cup again, though she had just filled it. "What did you seek, off with the Northmen?"

"Visions. Dreams of God's path for my future."

"We went to *incubate*," I explained, "to sleep with the resting saint and to pray for guidance. And it was not with the Northmen, just into the lands they control. An old grandmother in my village recalled an otherwise forgotten shrine."

"I suppose everyone seeks knowledge of the future." Still, she lingered. "Which saint? Are the relics there? I've heard some people seek out abandoned relics to recover."

"Saint Valerie." The name came easily to me.

"It's an old, small shrine," Egilolf said, "Lost in overgrowth. My thanks for the food." He finished by turning his shoulder to her and hunkering over his soup bowl.

She caught the hint and wandered to the next table.

When she was a few tables away, I nudged Egilolf. "Do you think her questioning a coincidence?"

"A nun spy?" Egilolf scoffed but stared long at her anyway. "Still, I'm glad we left Philibert in safety." She certainly didn't linger at other tables. If we hadn't spent days hiking on half meals of wild onions and acorn bread—that choking stuff should have its own cross-reference in a book of penances—the crow soup would have seemed watery and bland. Instead, it tasted like manna.

"I hoped for a second serving," Egilolf said wryly, "but this doesn't seem to be that kind of abbey." The serving girl had not brought the pot around again, and most pilgrims were already filing out. "Still, you can only try." He rose and headed off to the kitchens. I savored my last bites, and he returned a few minutes later, his bowl still empty. I finished my soaked rye trencher bread, and we headed toward the guest dormitory.

Beyond the main door stood an older, more self-assured nun than the youth that served us. "A word, my sons." The command was so maternal; its tone belied the stern face issuing it. She beckoned us down the passage without checking whether we trailed behind.

When we followed her to the abbotess' study, my suspicions were confirmed. Egilolf raised an eyebrow at me, mirroring my unspoken questions of how and why we came to the attention of the abbotess herself. An abbey guard across the hall waited too nonchalantly to be accidental. She closed the door and took the only seat, an unpainted though intricately carved chair with a high back next to a small writing desk, which was filled with a stack of letters and a few bound codices.

She studied us in silence long beyond my point of comfort and then studied us some more. "Did you find what you sought?" The same face as earlier, now without any hint of maternal concern.

"Food and rest. For body and soul," Egilolf began. "Our thanks for the hospitality of—"

"Don't play the fool to me!" she cut him off. I had never understood before how the Church under the Patriarch in Byzantium could envision the mild and loving Mother of God as the terrorizing general of the Heavenly Army. I could now.

"Mother, we—"

"No one pilgrims among the Northmen when they could *incubate* at Martin's tomb in Tors or a hundred other places in civilized territory. I've had word from my…contacts…in Lemouicensis of a pair of relic hunters, matching your descriptions exactly. Men who boasted—boasted!—of martyrs stolen from their resting places in Spain and beyond." A squint in Egilolf's direction closed his mouth again. "And now you come here. After a sojourn through the desolation of the barbarians, yet empty-handed. So I ask, did you find what you sought? Or do you seek some easier-picked fruit?"

"Knew the girl was a spy," Egilolf muttered.

For my part, I wondered who in Lemouicensis had sent her our descriptions. We glanced at each other, and Egilolf squared himself as if for trial. "Abbott Gonsindus sent us to find more relics. To join Martial at his abbey. We searched old churches in Northmen lands. Abandoned churches. Those saints will never return otherwise. We found church ruins near the *Leger*. Found relics under the altar. The inscription, read by Brother Aristeus, named her Valerie. Hadn't heard of her, but she had to be a saint, buried in such a position of honor.

"No sooner had we got her relics than we were caught by a band of savage Northmen." Egilolf paused to shake his head. "Truly barbarian. Couldn't believe we went all that way for old bones, as they saw it. Their sorceress did a ritual over them. We saw nothing, but she said she saw a woman of light fight a demon. They set us free, but kept the relics. Their chief, Thorfinn Eirikson, seemed open to hearing from a priest."

The abbotess pressed her lips together. Her eyes darted between us.

"A priest to show them about the saint," Egilolf tacked on.

"What they deserve is an army storming them," I exclaimed, "to crush them back into the ocean!"

The abbess recoiled.

"And, and to recover the holy remains, of course…" The thought of those murderers receiving any grace! I pressed my hands together and exhaled slowly, trying to calm myself.

She scrutinized us both, her face unreadable. "Tomorrow after *prime*, you will accompany me to see the bishop. We will see what he makes of this...tale. Which reminds me, if you're in the mood for an interesting story yet tonight, ask any of the sisters about the last wretch who tried to steal our relic of the Cross. A hint. Boils." Her turning to the writing table seemed all the dismissal we would get, so we let ourselves out.

The guard still lounged outside the door, and one was always in sight in every corridor back to the pilgrim guesthouse. I'm sure one loitered around the privy when I stumbled there during the night. Perhaps the abbess doubted the efficacy of her story of the botched relic theft.

I held my tongue until we settled into our pallets for the night. "In the defense of our lives, it is a small matter to lie to some barbarians. Dissembling to an abbotess or a bishop tomorrow is far worse. *Saint Valerie?*"

Egilolf untied his belt and empty scrip, the only items returned by the Northmen, and stowed them under the hood of his cloak. He lay his head on this meager pillow and pulled the cloak over himself. "That sorceress saw...something." He yawned. "A saint? An angel? The Virgin Mother? Maybe Valerie was a saint. Maybe, as Rodegar said, God's starting them on the narrow path to Christ. My penance is enough to worry about. Why add more to it?"

"Why add more indeed?" I huffed and rolled into my own cloak.

Why do we dream of danger long after we are safe? All those nights in marsh and forest, in Northmen territory, but it wasn't until I slept in the Abbey of the Holy Cross that my dreams filled with the Skull-Crusher, and *Comes* Fulgaud, one grasping each of my arms, dragging me to a bonfire over which Father Leo burned, while he held Saint Philibert's skull in the *Hodegetria* pose, his cries overpowered by Ingigird's mournful chanting, and the sparks of the fire rising to mingle with the vast, twinkling graveyard of heaven. As they threw me onto the fire, I woke.

As commanded, Egilolf and I set off for the bishop's residence shortly after *prime* flanked by a set of guards. The abbotess must have sent word ahead. We were in and out of his quarters in the handful of minutes it took to explain the tale that Egilolf had locked us into the previous evening. His Excellency, Bishop Hecfroi, promptly marched us off to the *dux's* great hall, upon the southern heights of the city.

The hall was much alike to others I had seen: mostly wooden walls and soot-blackened roof, a few high windows letting in sufficient light on bright days, and with a flagstone floor and stone foundation. Most of this lord's construction expenses went to the outer walls and tower forts.

Ranulf, the second of his name, *Dux* of Aquitania, *Comes* of Poitou, and probably able to claim any number of other titles, was one of those few men who could convey, with but a moment in his august presence, that he cared nothing for you and expected his command obeyed as if he had brought the Law down Sinai's heights himself. He sat on a rough bench below his throne breaking his fast.

After being announced, the bishop led our party within a respectful distance. An armed, scarred man hovered over Ranulf's repast. By his stance, build, and iron gaze, he reminded me of Fulgaud's captain Sichar—a man who first drew his sword to solve problems. His graying hair marked him more senior, though, than his Lemouicensis equivalent.

"*Rex* Ranulf, I present a possible solution to the problem on the *Leger*," Hecfroi began.

I'm not sure which surprised me more: the bishop addressing Ranulf as a king, or Ranulf taking a few more bites before bothering to give his attention to a shepherd of the Church. I meant to quietly mention to Egilolf my surprise at Ranulf's address, but merely turning toward him generated a glare from the guard captain. We were kept waiting for close to a minute.

Finally, Ranulf put down the remnants of a roasted lark. "Since when did you become interested in a *solution* to the Northmen problem?" Before Hecfroi could open his mouth, Ranulf continued. "Yes, you've sent your chaplains and given your blessings, but unless you've come to offer your guards...?" He paused just long enough for Hecfroi to grimace. "Then I must *ask* you to keep to the court schedule. And not interrupt my meals."

"Your Highness," Hecfroi began again, in the same cajoling tone, "the solution I propose does not involve massed troops. Tensions run high with both *Dux* Rudolf and *Rex* Odo, and either of those problems may require your soldiers. Brother Aristeus and his guide Egilolf here have returned from their ventures to the coastal wastes, trying to reclaim relics for the church. They have relayed—"

"Relic thieves?" Ranulf interrupted, his eyes on Hecfroi.

His guard captain, however, assessed us while the fingers of his right hand flexed. I wondered if Egilolf was trying as hard as I to recall the shortest path out of the king's hall, his fort, and the entire town.

"Not thieves, Your Highness. Someone who risks his life to recover saints from once-Christian lands should not be confused with cheats and dissemblers who steal from churches where saints are properly venerated." The bishop smoothed his robe with both hands. "As these men told me, though they recovered relics of a once-forgotten saint, they were ambushed by Thorfinn Eirikson's band. Most miraculously, however, they were not killed outright, and the Northmen have accepted the relics as something holy after witnessing a battle of the saint against a *daemon* in the center of their camp."

At these words, Ranulf leaned forward and studied me and Egilolf for the first time.

Also, for the first time, the captain seemed interested in more than protecting his lord from us. "You have been there, to Thorfinn Eirikson's camp? May God damn that pagan to the lowest levels of hell." He puckered as if to spit. "Could you find it again? Was it north or south of the *Leger*? How many ships? That Skull-Crusher whoreson was sorely wounded when we last met. Meaty hands, likes to tell everyone his name. No chance he's dead?"

Egilolf answered for us in a quick, clipped tone. "Captured us three hours march due south of Nantes, your Highness. By boat down the *Leger*, south along the coast for half a day, south of Herius, to the mouth of another river. Two hours upriver. Camp on the north side. Two days march southwest of Nantes, on the right path through the lowlands. Twenty longboats on the bank. Signs of twice that beached at one point. Twenty ships means fifteen hundred men. Only half that were in the village. Women and children roughly equaled the number of men. Village was growing roots: stone foundations, wooden palisade, small fields." He paused. "Oh, and we met that Skull-Crusher mongrel. Uh, your Highness."

The *dux*, or *rex* rather, studied Egilolf, barely glanced at me, and returned his gaze to Egilolf. "A proper scout's report. Who did you serve under and where?"

"Lord Carloman, West Francia. Until '84. Then the third King Charles, until Arnulf's revolt in '87. Pressed into service for various campaigns. I've lost track of all of them. Your Highness."

Dux Ranulf shrugged. "Worry not, soldier. I don't hold a soldier's service to his lord against him. Sounds like most of that was not against me, anyway. Twenty ships, though. Are you sure? No, that question was not fair. A scout of your years would be sure."

Ranulf and his captain shared a calculating glance, and I wondered how soon they would visit a map and re-draw campaign plans. "What drew you to the *Leger* marshes?" Bishop Hecfroi opened his mouth, but Ranulf raised his palm, cutting him off. "Specifically, scout Egilolf."

"More relics from Saint Philibert's abandoned church at Dee, Your Highness. Heard from an old priest that though Philibert was taken to Tournus years ago, his reliquary was built over an older crypt. We sought older relics, forgotten saints. Hoped to rescue them back to Christian lands."

Bishop Hecfroi broke in. "Your Highness, it is the recovery of relics, and the Northmen's snatching of them, that leads to my proposal."

"Very well, Your Grace. Your proposal." Ranulf leaned back and picked at the remnants of eggs on his platter.

"Aristeus and his scout indeed were led by a saint, whether they realized it beforehand or not, to the very *locus* where the remains of the virginal Saint Valerie lay undisturbed. Envision the glories of heavenly light and the scents of incense as they came to the holy site! Imagine the rapture of opening the grave, lifting out those sacred remains! Would that I have been so blessed as to—"

Ranulf cut him off with a raised hand. Recounting to myself our discussion that morning with the bishop, and with the abbotess the evening prior, I was fairly certain we had not mentioned any virginal status of Saint Valerie. I began reflecting on church assumptions about saints' lives, but Ranulf had continued immediately: "I'm listening, Hecfroi, but not enough for a sermon. Your point?"

The bishop, managing to appear both humbled and annoyed, continued, "Very well, Ranulf. As I initially said, before you were sidetracked into boat counts and camp locations, Thorfinn Eirikson did something quite unusual. When he captured these two, he did not kill them outright. Instead, he kept the relics and seemed to be considering what their holy power means. If we sent a mission, with my legate and a small band of your guards to ensure his safety, we could build a church, call the Northmen to Mass, teach them to reverence the saints, and show them the narrow way to Christ. What would it mean for Aquitania if the west was no longer a border to be defended, but one held by converted allies?"

The guard captain and Ranulf both appeared apathetic to the bishop's oration until his well-pointed question. Again they exchanged glances, and now I could sense a sharper eagerness to review their maps and plans.

"Your plan has merit. Perhaps it would be worth discussing further, Your Grace," *Rex* Ranulf declared. "Over dinner, if you would be my guest."

"I am honored, Your Highness," the bishop responded graciously. "Until this evening." He withdrew, but as we followed him out, the *rex* commanded, "Of course, Hecfroi, you'll hold onto these two. If nothing else, I'm in need of more soldiers at Thoucars." It was not a question.

Hecfroi ushered us outside and pointed us back towards his cathedral. "When, and by what causes, did the *dux* of Aquitania become a king?" I asked, curious.

The bishop huffed his derision and sputtered, "All of two seasons ago. Right after he heard Rudolf of Burgundy declared himself a king, and Odo in West Francia, and—well, nearly everyone made himself king with the death of Charles the third, who had no heir, and no one has thrown support for his young nephew Charles. The Fourth, I mean. The whole kingdom—well, the third part of it that was Francia—is splintering. Have you not heard?"

"Your Grace, we've been mostly in Hispania this past spring, and rumors being—"

I was cut off by the martial approach and imperious gesture of a young man, armed more decoratively than the average guard but barely old enough to have a real sword. "I would have word, Your Grace, with my father's two...visitors." His sword hilt and pommel were gilt with silver filigree, and his cloak's vivid blue bore no stain. He smiled, but thinly, and it emphasized a gaunt paleness to his face.

"Of course, my lord." Hecfroi nodded to the newcomer and stood by until the youth motioned us to follow and held back the bishop with the same open palm gesture the *rex* used so effectively. We followed to a courtyard beside the great hall.

"I am Ranulf, the third of my name. I heard the bishop's...proposal...to my father, but no one asked the necessary question." Before he could add more, another man hailed us across the courtyard, approaching with long, quick strides.

"Scheming again, *brother*?" This one was a handful of years older than the young lord Ranulf, nearly of an age with me and Egilolf but with darker hair. His cloak was undyed and his sword plain. His boots had certainly seen hard use. His nose and ears declared him and the young lord both offspring of the *rex*, but whereas young

Ranulf's face was thin and sallow, the older brother's bespoke vitality and an iron ambition.

"Ebalus, I don't scheme. I seek to learn. About *all* of my father's kingdom."

"*Our* father's kingdom." The older brother Ebalus addressed Egilolf. "Well, man, I don't know what use you find for a cleric on the road, but I heard your report on the Northmen's camp. I have my own ideas about ending the Thorfinn problem, and a church mission might be good cover for it. I need a man who knows the camp layout and has a strong stomach. Might you be such a man, for the right reward?"

"Ebalus! What you're suggesting—"

"No one wins wars by preening." Ebalus sneered at his half-brother.

"There are strengths beyond bashing everyone's head in," young Ranulf replied, with a sharp strength I would not have suspected of him, "and solutions beyond a blade." A not-subtle cough interrupted the fraternal dispute, and Bishop Hecfroi lowered his crozier to shield us from the siblings. A good shepherd.

"Young lords, I must take these, your *father's* servants, and prepare them physically and spiritually for the trials our Lord and Father has set before them. His plan, and likely your father's too, is to see them as guides and ambassadors of our mission to the coast for the conversion of the Northmen *pagani.*"

Before either lordling could respond, the bishop herded us, with open arm and shepherd's staff, back toward the valley that promised more than a wan shadow of death.

Another duplicity, another burden. With the novelty of Saint Valerie firmly ensconced in ecclesial and lay leaders' minds, and Egilolf's insistence on delivering Saint Philibert to someone in Lemouicensis without coughing up his secret in Pictauensis, our options became more grim with each bell tolling the hours. Back at the guesthouse at the Holy Cross Abbey, I voiced my doubts privately to Egilolf that Arnkel or Ingigird would welcome a mission, guarded or not. Egilolf agreed but pointed out the bishop and king neither asked for nor would likely consider our opinions. Caught between king, son, and bastard son seemed even worse. The only option survivable was to slip from the abbey, collect Saint Philibert's relics, and scuttle our way to Lemouicensis, and whatever heavens-decreed fate awaited us there.

Many trials Saint Paul endured in fulfilling God's will. His epistles list whippings, beatings, and imprisonments, and I don't doubt suffering produces perseverance, and perseverance, hope. But at least once, the apostle slipped away, lowered by a basket from a window, much like Joshua's spies at Jericho. Even Our Lord Jesus Christ walked off through the crowd seeking to throw him over a cliff. Having received no heavenly vision to the contrary, Egilolf and I agreed to emulate these Biblical exemplars.

In the abbey guesthouse, the plan had seemed straightforward: hoard food from the refectory at dinner, await the full dark of *matins*, hop the abbey's perimeter wall, and then scale the city wall at the low ground to the east. We would then ford the river and make all haste to Lemouicensis. After picking up Saint Philibert, of course. Egilolf made it sound easy. I swiped extra rye bread at dinner, Adelhard's ratios to Corbie be damned.

We did have to overcome the ubiquitous guard, so Egilolf put me to the task of distracting him while he planned. "Just talk about something no one else knows. Something interesting," Egilolf suggested. He paced in our windowless guesthouse room. I did not know what he would accomplish with such efforts, but I followed his direction. Outside the guesthouse, the yard was lit only by the guard's torch. I entered this glow and casually struck up a conversation, discoursing on Prudentius' least known work, the *Dittochaeon*. I fought to keep pride from my tone as I related how this collection of four-lined poems were written not just to be inscribed under church paintings of biblical history as they claimed, but how I had uncovered a catechetical purpose to them by contrasting the modeled Scripture passage to the poems' details.

"For instance," I told the guard, who had since taken a seat and was peering intently at the ground, a pose I often take myself when focusing on a complex recitation, "Prudentius includes Abraham's purchase of a cave in which to bury his wife Sarah, itself a lesser story of Genesis mostly intended to establish Israel's long-standing right to the land before their slavery, exodus, and reclamation. But Prudentius describes the burial of Sarah's 'holy ashes' in a 'suitable resting place,' descriptions not found in Genesis. Thus he clearly points to a lesson—a lesson for the early Church about how to properly bury, and not distribute, the remains of any Christian. And then considering the Elijah poem—" A soft snore broke my concentration. I gave the now-sleeping guard an indignant scowl and was preparing a most suitable tongue-lashing when Egilolf's hand stole over my mouth. He motioned me to silently follow him toward the wall.

Once we were safely out of earshot, he said, "Knew you'd talk him to sleep." Before I could protest, he scaled the wall and dropped over the far side.

Escaping the abbatial wall, an easy eight-foot clamber, left me triumphant and soothed my annoyance that Egilolf had planned— planned!—on my exegesis putting the guard to sleep. Rustics!

We slinked through the city's back streets, cut back and forth as if laid by a drunkard, for the main road through town was too exposed. A light wind portended a cool, refreshing journey. Then we rounded a corner and faced the city walls. My neck craned to follow their height, for they rose more than thrice the abbatial walls. Boosting each other clearly wouldn't suffice, and seeking the guard's ladder risked finding the guard.

"Have to chance the cliffs," Egilolf muttered, probably to himself, but I couldn't help responding.

"Cliffs? Your plans described nothing about cliffs. Some moderate wading and swimming I can accomplish and even a bit of wall scaling but not cliffs."

Egilolf pulled me back into an alley little more than a gap between houses. I had to turn my shoulders to slide through. He lowered his voice. "The walls are much lower on the south edge of the city. They stand over some short cliffs. Steep hills, really. I thought to try this east wall first because it's closest to the abbey and the river, and the terrain is lowest, but their walls are highest here. I don't see how we can climb it. It's our—"

"Heyya!" A nasal whine split the night's silence from the other side of the rough planking that served as wall to the house I was wedged against. "You skulkers outside my walls best move before I call the guard!"

Egilolf pushed me back out into the roadway and thrust a handful of his cloak at me. "Hold on and follow!" he hissed, dashing into the night. Not fast enough to suit the tenant, apparently. Behind us, the nasal voice began screeching for the night watch. Egilolf led me on a whirlwind chase, the half-moon cutting between thin wisps of cloud as fast as we darted from shadow to alley to shadow again. Citizens' cries of "thieves!" and "invaders!"—even a few of "Northmen!"—split the night, but the guards knew better than to announce their positions. Torches and heavy breathing gave us only seconds of notice, though reflections and echoes confused safe directions. Once, we rounded a corner only to surprise our pursuers, and Egilolf nearly impaled himself on a startled blade. He reacted faster, knocking aside a guard before dashing up a moonlit street, then slanting through a back garden as the moon winked out under a heavy cloud. So frantic was death's argent-light pursuit of us, I cannot now order the events aright. Sometime after tripping over a full privy bucket, and perhaps before I tore my tunic on a splintering fence rail, we vaulted up a rain barrel and onto the low roof of a tanner's shop, dropping to lie still and stifle our own labored breaths with fistfuls of our cloaks. I cannot recall what detail led a searching citizen to suspect our rooftop concealment, but I thank Saint Paul, and whoever may be the patron of escapees that it was a shopkeeper and not one of the guards. More than once, Egilolf decried the lack of an aqueduct.

Again like the clouds riding the winds around the moon we ran, and I would have questioned Egilolf's choice of running up a hill if I could have spared the breath. Suddenly, a long rake in the clouds aligned with the moon, illuminating the city wall fifty paces ahead. At chest height, it was more a jump than a climb. Egilolf urged me on, then sprinted even faster and vaulted the wall seconds ahead of me. I went to do the same but slipped as I leapt, smashed my shin against the lip, and rotated headfirst over the wall. Egilolf's form rolling down a steep slope gave perspective among the moon-shadowed ruts, and I barely grasped the upper edge with my right hand long enough to swing my feet under me. I dropped as a guard commanded me to halt. I hit the dirt, ran, stumbled, rolled, and ran again down the uneven slope. An unidentifiable buzzing sound past my head revealed itself as an arrow when it chipped off a rock toward which I had grabbed to steady my descent.

Somewhere past the bottom of the hill, still running and very winded, I felt the disorientation of my foot reaching for ground not there. A jarring impact followed before I realized my face was inexplicably pressed to the dirt. For a few seconds, the scrapes to my face felt the worst of my injuries, but even as Egilolf ran back to me, demanding in a hissing whisper that I rise, a firestorm of pain exploded from somewhere below my right knee and proceeded out my mouth as a wail fit for a soul tormented in hell.

I confess now, rationally back in my own mind, the pain of my fracture seemed worse than anything else in life, briefly even worse than the possibility of dying from guards' arrows. I vaguely remember images of the rest of that night: Egilolf tying a gag, cut from his own sleeve, into my mouth when I couldn't stop shrieking; him carrying me on his own shoulders, like a sack of grain, long enough that the throb of blood in my down-turned head became as agitating as the throb in my leg; my companion tying long sticks to my lower leg and muttering about hedge doctors being so far off any regular path. A crude litter on a stony path jolted me perpetually back into consciousness despite my fatigue. Egilolf never did tell me how we crossed the river, but I don't recall near drowning, so I suspect a stolen raft.

In the foothills somewhere east and south of Pictauensis, Egilolf brought me by late morning to a deep glen, not directly far from a village but on a path rough and ephemeral enough that it could not be followed without purpose and foreknowledge. Though the woods we came through were thick and dark, the glen was cleared of trees and glassy. The glen was more arrow-pointed than bowled, narrowing to a short waterfall at the back. The edge mixed broken slopes and cliffs to make the refuge impenetrable except from the narrow downstream outlet to the forest. It seemed a haven walled off from all the world except the warming sun overhead. Set partially under an overhanging, short cliff along the northern curve of the glen was a haphazard hut, more akin to a beaver's den of sticks than a crofter's home of hewn beams.

"Thank Philibert, the old man's still alive," Egilolf sighed as he set my litter down before the hut.

A breeze stirred, and I first smelled lavender, followed by a heady mixture of sage, peony, parsley, fennel, and other scents too exotic to name. For a moment, I forgot my pain. "What is this place that conceals the fragrances too exotic to name?" I marveled.

In reply, Egilolf pointed to the far side of the hut. In the strong, midday sun were a half-dozen racks on which were drying a cacophonic vision of plant stalks, roots, flowers, seed clusters, bales, leaves, and fibers.

How I missed it can only be attributed to the pain in my leg. Besides what I had identified by smell, I saw roses, thyme, rue, borage, anise, pennyroyal—overwhelmed, I sank back onto my litter.

"Old Master?" Egilolf called out. "Old Master?" He muttered quickly to me, "This *herburgium* is well-respected in these parts. But he's even more particular than you. Call him Old Master. Be polite. Don't question *anything*." The stress in Egilolf's last command was sharp despite his whisper.

A hide-covered door swung open, revealing Egilolf's healer. I wondered whether unkempt appearances drove a man into becoming a hermit or that a reclusive man often decided appearances no longer mattered. Regardless, the man who emerged was clearly old, as Egilolf had named him, though he strode to us with a straight back and steady step. It was his hair, I decided, which gave him a forest's wildness, stiffly askew in all directions. An oiled sheen made the black parts so vivid that the gray struck me first as patches of missing hair. I was especially glad to note his eyes shone clear—and sane—that latter distinction calming some of my nerves of being taken to a hedge-healer. Cracked and tanned, his face showed years of hard weathering. He should have been dressed in camel-hair clothing and eating locusts and honey while submerging the repentant in the Jordan.

"You didn't try to set it before splinting, did you?" he accused Egilolf. "Last arm break that came to me had been shoved and pulled three different ways before his fool friends decided his arm wasn't healing itself. Cut too many internal bloodways with their thrashing about. Waited too long. Awful mess. God awful." The way he said God was not an invocation. "No," he continued before Egilolf could answer, "your friend would be feverish, delusional, or screaming in pain if you had. What can you pay with?"

Egilolf again began opening his mouth, no doubt to apologize for our poverty, but the *herburgium* cut him off again. "I expected as much. 'Old Master, save our brother, but we can't pay!' 'Old Master, you must heal my daughter, but I never stopped to consider that you're a man that needs to eat too and buy his fine ingredients, and—' No one thinks anymore. No one." His exasperated sigh was likely more pronounced than Jesus' decrying the perverse and unbelieving generation. "Get him inside. I've got chores and herb gathering I'll have you do as a start on your payment, and we'll barter the rest later." He strode back toward his hut, leaving Egilolf to haul me in.

The crude home was barely large enough for two beds at the back, a stone fireplace at the front, and a small table with three mortars and a pestle on it beneath shelves, baskets, jars, and amphorae dangling in chaos to match the haphazard stick walls. Surprisingly, the old man was gentle as he helped me up and into the bed closer to the fire, which he stoked. He examined my leg as he undid the splint, begrudgingly complimenting Egilolf's work. I got my first good look at my leg; a distinct bulge on my shin coincided with my pain.

"I'd offer you a mixture of crushed pearl and lavender—pearls help with healing blood flows, and lavender calms the melancholic airs, allowing faster healing—but you've already said you can't pay. Fortunately, this can be done without any medicine. Unfortunately," and here he cast a wicked smile at me, which belied his words, "this is going to hurt a lot."

"We can—" Egilolf began again, but the Old Master cut him off yet again.

"No use arguing. I don't begrudge the poor being poor. Just don't expect a lord's worth of healing for rustics' wages."

"I am hardly one of the village rustics—" I began before I gasped in pain, Egilolf nudging my leg.

"Sorry. Wanted to see if the bone broke skin," he said and shot me a warning glance.

"Hold your friend down hard by his forearms," the Old Master instructed Egilolf. He knelt down by my bed and began probing my leg. "Lay across his chest if you must. I'll probe the leg first to determine the bones' positions. Then I'll pull it into place. Now, I find that a story often helps distract the mind, and since a story's free but a pearl is beyond your price, I doubt you'll object."

He began the story without chancing dissent. "I'll give you warning, though," the Old Master began, "some don't care for my stories. No one can explain why, except one farrier likened them to misshaped iron. Once in my youth, I took to traveling pilgrimage paths, seeking lost *medica* knowledge in unused corners of monastery libraries. Not all knowledge is collected at the great libraries, and you'd be surprised what can be found in the dusty fringes of a wayward abbey. Assuming you could even read it, of course." Egilolf gripped my forearms tighter before I could protest.

"Once over dinner at one of these places—off in Lotharingia, perhaps, or Mercia—I met a man who relayed a tale. It begins like this—with your mind's eye, see an idyllic pastoral scene, a flock of sheep contentedly grazing a verdant meadow under an azure sky, fenced-in safely by low hills that ascend to something that could be called mountains by anyone who has not traveled the passes from Burgundy to Lombardy. A village lies within sight down the valley, and the sun, of course, is neither stingy nor extreme in its radiance this auspicious morning.

"Our character is a youth old enough that his parents thought him capable with a few sheep but foolish enough that no one would yet consider him a man. He was not, of course, vigilant in fulfilling his duties, but like most immature fellows thought work beneath him, and so he was spending his day alternating between griping at his lot and wool-gathering about wine and the blacksmith's daughter.

"Bored, the youth pondered a local story, common enough to many locales, of rich robbers caught and hung without divulging where they secreted their hoard. Everyone is assured robbers actually amass a hoard. Of the various legends, the youth concluded the story of an undiscovered cave in the southern forest the most likely. Without qualms over abandoning his charges, he set off for the southern hills and made the forest shortly after the *sext* bell. He searched and searched, but as the afternoon wore on, he could not bring himself to admit he was neither more clever nor more lucky than all past generations.

"Only a youth can be more stubborn than logic, and so he unreasonably kept searching past the time he could return to the flock before dark, then past the time he could get back to the village before dark, then past the dusking hours themselves. Now, a forest is no place to be in the dark, alone, unarmed, without path or shelter. Perhaps it is only when a young man exceeds himself, and realizes it, that he starts on the path of prudence that will lead to manhood. Hopefully, not too late. Regardless," he paused only to glare at my interrupting winces at his continued probing, "the youth became quite lost. Nocturnal animals stalked his periphery.

"He was on the verge of crying for divine intervention when lo!, a girl appeared, stepping from a screen of fallen tree and vines. Her dress was white enough that, in the otherwise shadowed forest, he could see her clearly, and he was surprised to find someone more beautiful than the blacksmith's daughter.

"'Are you lost?' called the girl with a laugh that couldn't be mocking if only because her face was so beautiful.

"'Yes,' the youth admitted, momentarily grateful for the shadows that hid his heated face. 'Do you know the way home?'

"'Yes, I can take you home. Follow me.' He realized he must have become even more disoriented than he thought, for she led him away from where he suspected the village lay. Though he jogged and then ran, he could not catch up to her enough to ask more of where they went, and he never gave any thought of not following her.

"The girl in white stopped at the base of a small hill, not far from a brook that babbled gaily, defying the gloom of the night forest. 'You must pass through,' she said simply, pointing to the hill. The youth saw only darkness until the girl stepped forward and outlined with a hand a stone portal all but hidden in the hillside.

"'Are you sure?' the youth questioned, 'The path I followed earlier seemed broader.' He thought again of dinner with wine and maybe a late visit by the blacksmith's house. The girl in white only pointed at the portal, so the youth crept forward, stooping to pass in. He soon fumbled in near-complete darkness, through layers of dirt and carpets of old, moldering leaves. Underneath, he felt sharp, pointy objects and saw they glowed pale white against the dark, much like the girl's dress. *Bones?* he wondered. He took two steps more, then could not bring himself further.

"'Have you brought me to a tomb?' the youth cried, blinking back tears. 'Will you trust me?' the girl replied from the mouth of the tunnel, 'To reach home, you must pass through.' Barely reassured, the youth pressed on, now forced to his knees by the lowering ceiling. As his hands recoiled from cobwebs, spongy fungi, and the occasional crawling thing, he thought back to his 'toil' in the sun and repented his foolishness that led to the forest."

The story was rather banal, and I caught Egilolf rolling his eyes, but I must admit the Old Master's voice was soothing, a chant that took my mind elsewhere, certainly off the fracture of my leg.

"As the youth crawled, an overwhelming stench arose, a mixture of decaying matter and his own body's fear. He saw nothing before him. Looking back, he barely made out the doorway. But he knew retreating out the door would still leave him lost. Stuck, he called out again. 'Will you help me?'

"'Of course,' said the girl, suddenly at his side. 'I but waited for you to ask.' She took his hand, and together they pressed forward."

Pain shot through my leg, worse than when I first broke it. I screamed aloud for God, the Virgin Mother, Saint Irenaeus, and the whole host of heaven.

"There!" exclaimed the Old Master, who set to splinting my straightened leg.

"Years later," he continued his story over my whimpering, "the youth who grew into a man in the tunnel tended the shrine, aiding weary pilgrims at the terminus of their journey. And every night, he watched the sunset fall to forest-dark, followed the cleansed passage into the shrine, and consumed the bread crusts and dregs of wine left by the pilgrims. Then he curled up at the foot of the altar, wrapped his arms about the simple reliquary, and spent the night sharing dreams with the beautiful girl in white."

He drifted to a small hum as he checked his splinting work. In the pain of setting my leg, I thought I had missed part of the story until Egilolf spoke up. "That's it? What happened in the tunnel? Did he ever get home? You can't skip over the best part!"

The old man remained intent on his work.

"It seems a hole gapes in the middle of your story," I tried to subtly remind him. Perhaps his mind wasn't all there? But the pulsing pain in my leg tore at my thoughts. "You skipped the main conflict. Everyone knows a classic story. Even ancient Greek plays. Everyone knows you have to describe and resolve a trial. Before the end."

I thought the old man would huff and rage, but he didn't. "First, you must admit it did distract you from the pain, whatever you think of my stories. Your welcome, by the by," he grimaced. "Second, I assert every story has a hole, especially stories that are true. Pieces get lost to the wayside, and what gets found may not be what the finder thinks important. You can never assume the motives of the teller are the ones the listeners desire. Not even a child's tale is told for only the idleness of amusement."

"No wonder everyone says your stories are cracked," Egilolf sputtered.

"Oh, come now!" the Old Master stood at last, not angry but lecturing. "You," he pointed at me, "claim to not be one of the rustics, and your ink-stained thumb labels you a copyist at least. Can you only copy others' works, or do you have a mind in there too?" He began tapping annoyingly on my head. "Is a text with *lacunae* useless? Can you not deduce what happened, what the boy discovered at the tunnel's end, the true identity of the girl? For that matter, did you stop to question the holes before the story or after—why had the boy grown up shiftless and self-centered?—did he ever tire of dreaming with the girl's relics and leave her shrine to be forgotten once more?" He paused to let his questions take root. "Every story is full of holes. They start with holes and end with them. They are punctuated throughout with bits the listener wants, but the teller doesn't know, finds irrelevant, or assumes they are easy to deduce."

Egilolf grumbled something about a simple saint's tale gone wrong. "I'll split your firewood," he finally said, heading for the door. "Know a bard that crafts stories. I should send him your way." Soon the rhythm of chopping wood lulled me toward sleep.

The old man turned back to my leg at Egilolf's exit, checked his work, and then began muttering. I first thought him upset at our deprecations of his tale, but a rhythm to the mutterings alerted me. "Are you casting some *incantatio*?" I tried to sit up, but the Old Master was stronger than he seemed and pushed my chest back down to the bed with one hand. His muttering didn't stutter or slow. "Isidore of Seville wrote a condemning piece on *magica* for healing, which forces me to ask—are you a real doctor or some charlatan? True healing does not rely on magic. Moreover, Rabanus Maurus, Archbishop of Mainz—ahh! What are you—ahh!"

"Bite your cheek, and I won't have to compress your leg so." He gave a fey grin. "I'm not invoking *daemons*, nor any necromancy, geomancy, aeromancy, or whatever you fear I'm doing. If you had listened, I was praying over your leg for the healing aid of Saint Foy. She's always quick to aid me. Now, lie still, close your eyes, and recite the prayers of the hours until I return. A calm and hopeful spirit heals better, and you, copyist, are taut with suspicion." He left. I grant him that at least the prayers caused me to drift off to sleep.

I napped the afternoon and ate some of the Old Master's soup as night fell. He had sworn that one of the best remedies for any illness was chicken soup, a curative found in the *Vita* of Saint Benedict of Aniane. Or so he claimed; he did not have a copy of the text, so I had to rely on his word. But full and warmed, I hobbled outside the hut on rickety but lightweight crutches Egilolf had fashioned while I slept. I sat to wait for Egilolf, who was hauling water buckets and gazed at the stars appearing in the firmament. Lavender was still the strongest among the drying racks' swirling tangle of scents. The stars whirled with them, or perhaps I was lightheaded. The dark spaces of the night sky between the bright pinpoints became the holes in our stories: Egilolf's and mine, Rodegar's stories of the warriors Roland and Olivier, even the story of Saint Perfectus' martyrdom, isolated from any details of his life. Voids. Was anyone's story ever complete, all-encompassing? Once considered, could anyone stop realizing their entire life has a hole in its story, a hole they've been seeking to fill?

The slosh of water in the bucket alerted me. Egilolf set his burden down and folded himself up next to me, also gazing upward at the starfield filling the darkening expanse. "Somewhere westward, lied the mourning; somewhere eastward, swore the sun…" he began.

"Torn and battered, remnants scattered—I cannot remember the rest, but you are right: Rodegar and the old man would talk an astrolabe of circles around each other discussing stories and their meanings."

"Figured I'd find you looking at the stars," Egilolf quipped. "Keep that up, and you'll go mad as the Old Master. Knowledgeable and useful, maybe. But mad."

The next morning broke with low clouds and a light drizzle. "Just enough to make the road treacherous. Not enough that we should delay," Egilolf asserted.

I agreed we didn't want to risk *Rex* Ranulf's men flushing us if they hunted. We decided I would wait out the morning while he retrieved Saint Philibert's remains, stashed away outside Pictauensis. He seemed to take as a challenge my doubt that he could return before *sext*. I idled my morning eating a buckwheat porridge mixed with what the Old Master assured me was a partridge a *colonus* had brought him.

All must have gone smoothly because, though *sext* passed without him, he was back admittedly well before *none*. He had seen some of Ranulf's men patrolling, so we decided to continue through forest paths and try to clear the *Vinhana* before nightfall. Egilolf reassured me that normally such a distance would have been easy in the remaining half-day, but I fatigued quickly on the crutches, not to mention the blisters I chafed under my arms within a few hours. Eventually, retaining the full sleeves to my undershirt seemed less important than the pain under my arms, and I cut some makeshift padding. Egilolf joked about God rewarding suffering. My body felt too pitiful to muster anything firmer than a glare.

I had decried any necessity of Egilolf building a crude litter, but as dusk fell, I admitted to myself, even if not to Egilolf yet, I would need it the following day. My blisters were becoming that severe. We didn't reach the *Vinhana* until well after dark, but Egilolf appreciated the concealment and forded the river carrying me. Perhaps the nightly rain and morning fog did keep us from the *Rex*'s men, but I griped to Saint Irenaeus, Saint Philibert, and even Saint Martial—we were nearing his *locus*, after all—for the rain to stop.

After a few hours of dragging me along the roadway in a litter of pine poles and interwoven boughs, he pulled me to an abandoned horse shed. Half the roof still held, and though the thatch smelled aged with mold, it wasn't leaking. He set me in the dry corner facing the open doorway. "Can't carry you, or even drag you, here to Lemouicensis. I'll be back with help shortly," he said and ducked back out the doorway.

At first, I hoped by "shortly" he meant a half-hour trip to the nearest village or farm hold, but as the sun passed its zenith, I considered how best to lecture Egilolf on precision.

I dozed off...and woke to a caress of my brow. Usually, an unexpected touch while sleeping startles me, but this occasion was...indescribable, even at this writing. To wake to a woman's touch—I have nothing to compare it to.

Long black hair, glowing in the afternoon sun streaming through the opened roof, hid her face in shadows. "Time to rise, monk," she mocked softly, and I recognized Rachel, the bandit-companion of Egilolf's comrade Peter, leaning over me. "Your companion's been telling us of your exploits. Lords, saints, Northmen, and crypts. A good storyteller, that one. How much is true?" I started to sit up, but Rachel didn't draw back. I stopped myself with inches between us. I felt warmth from her face, her breath. It took no imagination to notice a scent in her hair, a blend of laurel and rose. "Blushing?" she asked.

I thought—whatever I thought or felt, it was interrupted by Egilolf's quip, "Still abed?" as he stuck his head in the door. I could have praised him as savior or cursed him as intruder. Instead, I sat dumbstruck while Rachel arose, smirked at me, and stepped to the door.

Egilolf blocked her way.

"Move aside," she ordered.

"Give me back my relic of Saint Vincentius," he countered.

"You came and asked for our help. If anything, I should be asking for payment."

Egilolf glowered. "I asked for Peter's help. You, I could do without." They stared at each other until Peter called indistinctly from outside. Egilolf stepped aside at last, but his jaw was locked as he watched her go.

Miles and hours in the litter down the road—only able to see where I had come from, unable to turn my neck to glimpse Rachel as she ranged ahead of us—left me too much time to contemplate our exchange in the ruined shed. Peter and Egilolf took turns dragging the litter or worked together carrying me over puddled ruts and rocky inclines. The rain had stopped after a good soaking. Peter was laughing, recounting war stories, and rekindling the better memories of his youth when he and Egilolf weren't singing bawdy soldier songs. All that seemed distant to the memory of a smile and the scent of laurel and rose.

We set up camp outside a small crossroads chapel. I saw no other buildings, or even evidence of ruins, in any direction. Peter talked of hunting, and Egilolf joked of hunting for a crypt as he followed Peter to the range for our dinner. That left me awkwardly alone with Rachel. I opened my mouth once, twice to speak but turned away when she stopped her camp chores to listen. I felt heat in my face but it wasn't from a fever. I pulled out my crutches and hobbled away to the chapel.

The wayfarers' chapel, like at many a crossroads, had likely been kept up by a sole monk, his whole life devoted to the building and his ministrations to pilgrims and the other road-weary. The walls were uncut, stacked stone without mortar, chinked once with mud now more missing than present. The roof braces were half-hewn, more log than beam, but the east end still supported a tile roof, the clay so lichen-cracked that they were more green than brown. At the west end, above my head as I entered the nave, the tile was long gone. A close examination of the dirt floor showed tile shards succumbing to the dirt, remnants of a collapse never quite swept clear. Even the thatched straw replacement was crumbling back to the dust of the earth, those parts that yet clung to the beams. As sporadic as the missing chinks in the walls, but with much larger gaps, entire sections of the roof gaped. Amber clouds announcing day's end drifted in and out of visibility through the holes.

The tile shards, random in their shape and array—here a small cluster left together, there but three pieces showing within a span—recalled briefly the ruined mosaic floor of my childhood home. That floor had so many pieces gone, I could never tell the original scene beyond a face here, an animal paw or a grapevine motif there. "A Roman noble's home!" my father always spoke proudly, as though we were better than the other freeholders on the *villa* manse by virtue of owning the last crumbled sign of another age's glory.

What sort of dung heap age did we live in now that we gloried in the dog scraps of a greater civilization? The golden age of Constantine and Theodosius, the silver of the empire of the Great Charles, the bronze of his pious son Louis…and now a brittle age of clay. Only fit for shard flooring, if that.

I surveyed the rest of the chapel. The empty doorway faced the setting sun. Opposite, the altar was pitched, one set of legs crumbled. Broken, like me. Despite ruin, its very smallness held a privacy, an isolation from the world and its demands.

I shuffled forward and knelt on my good leg. Unable to put my fears into words, I crossed myself and began reciting aloud, though quietly to match the enclosure, what I recalled of Prudentius' *Liber Cathemerinon*, starting with his prayer for the evening meal.

—hic draco perfidus indocile
virginis inlicit ingeium,
ut socium laesuada virum
mandere cogeret ex vetitie,
ipsa pari peritura modo…

—conscia culpa Deum pavitans
sede pia procul exigitur
innuba femina quae fuerat,

coniugis excipit imperium,
foedera tristia iussa pati.

auctor et ipse doli coluber
plectitur inprobus, ut mulier
colla trilinguia calce terat
sic coluber muliebre solum
suspicit atque virum mulier —

Then the Serpent's guileful hate
Would not innocency spare:
Bade the maiden urge her mate
With the fruit his lips to sate,
Nor 'scaped she the self-same snare…

Far they both in terror fled
Thrust from dwelling of the pure:
She who erst had dwelt unwed
Subject to her spouse was led,
Bidden Hymen's bonds endure.

On the Serpent, too, His seal
God hath set, Who guile abhorred,
Doomed in triple neck to feel
Impress of the woman's heel,
Fearing her, who feared her lord—

"A woman *subject* to her spouse?" The tone would have pulled down the roof if it weren't already a ruin. I hobbled up from kneeling, pulling on the altar for stability. Before I could turn, Rachel continued, "You fault a woman for man's sin? I suppose I shouldn't be surprised, you having lived in a monastery your whole life."

My mouth opened and closed and, in the continued absence of ideas on what to say, opened and closed again.

"From Peter's praise of your companion and Egilolf's recounting of your contributions through your trials, I had higher hopes for you."

"It's Prudentius!" I finally burst out. As if that explained anything. "His prayers of the hours. Before meat. The prayer before eating meat, I mean. Since we were going to eat soon. Presumably. I—" Why couldn't I speak? Rose and laurel swirling my head! "Let me begin again. That passage refers to Genesis and the Fall, the temptation of the woman by the serpent, and the man by the woman—"

"I understood enough," she countered, "especially the last bit about the serpent under the woman, as the woman is under the man."

"I—I cannot…" It was Prudentius! Questioning his ancient acclaim felt like questioning…everything. "Get away from me. Please." My voice was hoarse, and some large part of my mind asked the other what, in all levels of hell, I could possibly be thinking.

Was it fortunate she stayed?

"Why? Why do you fear women?" For once, I heard no sarcasm.

"Women are a path to sin. Eve was the first corrupted." That, and I had never really talked to one. Not even my mother, who died in my infancy.

Rachel began gliding toward me with a sway to her hips that was not there before.

I took a step back.

"The *weaker* sex, correct? That's what you're taught in your monastery?"

I backed into the altar. I scanned both sides of the church. Why were the windows so small in here? Why did the entire chapel seem no bigger than a cupboard? Like a mouse hypnotized by a snake, I had to stare back at her face. I had no choice.

She stopped a hand's-breadth from me. "Do you fear because if I take your hand, like this, and place it here on my hip, you know without a doubt, that you have no more control? That how far this encounter goes depends on my say?"

My throat turned dry. My whole body shook. With fear? With anticipation? Rose and laurels! The sun behind her glowed in her rich, black hair, like a nimbus of holiness.

"So who is the weaker sex now? Is it the woman who lacks the self-control?"

I couldn't answer, nor, it seems, take my hand off the warm, firm, but soft flesh I felt under her tunic.

"It took a fallen heavenly power to tempt the woman, but only a fellow human to tempt the man." She leaned in with a lascivious, wild grin, and though I'd like to say I resisted, I did not. That nimbus about her could not be one of holiness, I decided. It wasn't a question of if I could resist or not. At that point, I did not want to. Just before her lips touched mine, with her dark eyes lit with some glory, piercing through me completely, she turned abruptly and all but skipped to the ruin of the doorway. There she glanced back. Again that smile, mocking now. "Who is weaker?"

I sank to a knee as she swayed out of sight. "Wait!" I called out. She stepped back into the doorway, a silhouette to the evening sun. "That's not how it ends." Some part of my mind beheld itself babbling and was helpless. "You only heard a portion and that the harshest. For man and woman." She didn't respond, but she didn't leave either. I knew not where my rudder steered. "The rest is beautiful. The Second Man, the inviolate Maid, the worthy Virgin who crushes the serpent. A petition that God sustain our bodies. God's glowing life, his breath which restores dead flesh. The living body, after slumber in a spice-scented tomb, re-joined to the living soul. As Christ leads us to the shining stars." I could only sputter phrases.

She paused.

"I don't know if that's meant to be endearing, romantic, or haughty."

I hobbled a few steps closer and again caught that glint in her dark gaze. "It's like your eyes. The stars. The glory of the *lux aeterna*, strewn across the expanse of *aether*."

"Not what a girl expects to hear quoted…"

My mind caught up to what my tongue said, and, blushing profusely, I tried to dash back to the sanctuary of the broken altar. Blinding pain shot up my leg—how had I forgotten it was broken?—and I found myself sprawled on the flagstones, prostrate before the altar.

Rachel hovered over me again as she rolled me onto my back.

"Careful, poet-scribe, or you'll break it again." Her wry tone belied her sparkling eyes as she helped me to my feet and the campfire.

Back to safer shores, we idled about our childhoods, home life, antics of siblings, once-held aspirations we outgrew. She recounted an older brother sent to a monastery who amused himself during home visits by teaching her rudimentary Latin. She spoke ardently of a wish, a fantasy, to read and write. She smiled when describing Peter's crew but waved off my inquiries about robberies she had planned. "For the children," was all she answered. "The night we met, you said the penalty doubled for more than five robbers. You quote old poets like everyone knows them. Have you been reading your whole life?"

I smiled at her topic change but did not mind. "My father got rid of me when I was twelve. I studied grammar and letters for four years before I was allowed to copy. Brother Angius selected my first work, Saint Paul's *Epistle to Philemon*. The shortest work possible, in case I was a disaster. He chastised me for taking three times too long; I kept re-reading it, fascinated by the message, instead of copying the letters."

Under her questioning, I recounted meeting Egilolf and our flight from Cordoba with Saint Perfectus. Anything not difficult to discuss but which kept her talking was a fair topic. She asked about my past before Spain, and I talked only of copying texts in the monastery. I asked about her life that led up to banditry, but she suddenly had to tend to the fire.

At some point, Peter and Egilolf returned with game. I know I ate food, but not what kind. Everything seemed ethereal that night, gloriously so. It had little to do with the patchwork light of the waning moon rising through the elm branches overhead.

Easy enough now to see myself bewitched, not by some succubus seeking to damn my soul, but by an array of beauty I had not found before in human form. I learned that day that not all revelations of God's majesty are found in logic, philosophy, or books.

Usually, the last span of a return journey seems the fastest, but...

As we rejoined the road the following morning, I hoped to continue conversing, but Rachel scouted ahead. Her reticence was offset by Peter and Egilolf discussing the inevitability of *Rex* Ranulf recruiting soldiers to resist *Dux* Odo in West Francia or *Rex* Rudolf in Burgundy. Or was it *Rex* Odo and *Dux* Rudolf now?

"If not north or east, he'll need more west. He talked of Thoucars. If rumors around Pictauensis were true, he's building small counties as a shield between him and the coast."

"Between him and this Chief Thorfinn?" Peter asked.

"Between him and the whole Northmen nation. They're building villages now, not just raiding bases. Women and crops. Children even. The width of Aquitania will be theirs if nothing's done." Egilolf booted a rock off the roadway to emphasize his disgust.

It was likely still before *terce*, when we came to another crossroads, deserted but for a gallows cage. We must have passed it on our way to Pictauensis. Unremarkable then, it now contained a wretch fast turning skeletal. A small sign below his cage displayed his crime: *furta.* Even illiterate rustics could recognize some life-ending symbols.

The skeleton stirred behind his bars, shifting the cage with a clank of chains. "Mercy..." his rasp dried up. "Mer..." Rachel poured him a few mouthfuls from her water skin. "God bless you," his voice now a consistent scrape. "Free me, I beg you. I'm wrongly accused."

Egilolf stepped up to the cage.

I cautioned, "The *Lex Salica Karolina* fines heavily anyone who removes a man alive from the gallows."

Egilolf waved a dismissive hand.

"It's a much lesser penalty to remove them once dead, of course," I continued, "but, God help me, I cannot recall the different amounts."

Peter considered me oddly.

Egilolf only barked a short laugh. "Aristeus, only you would worry about not recalling what most have never known. I only wondered what the man stole. Whether anyone will help us if *Comes* Fulgaud makes this our fate."

"Well," I reflected, "the penalty for robbing a dead body is twice as severe as freeing someone from the gallows. But the kin can also petition for the grave robbers' death. Most would not risk aiding the condemned."

Egilolf stared at the thief, who stared back from sunken eyes.

"I don't see that being the nature of our problem, however, since the law was written regarding robbing the body, whereas we only took remains, and for a holy purpose..." I trailed off as the thief's hollow gaze swung to fix on me with new interest. "Perhaps we'd best continue?" I offered.

Rachel gave the condemned man another swig, and we continued on our way.

"The gallows resurrect our unresolved question," I ventured once we were a few bends and dips from the crossroads. I was attempting a long and longer hour on my crutches. "The count, the abbot, the priest."

"Why don't you dole out parts to each?" Peter questioned. "They'll all be happy."

"They'd all be furious," Egilolf cut in. "Fulgaud wants something unique. And complete. Abbot Gonsindus will too. Pilgrims won't divert from Conques for a third of a saint. Father Leo...the man's devoted his life to Philibert. It'd be condemnation all around."

"Perhaps the logical approach would be to ask which penalty would be most severe?" I reasoned. "Before Pictauensis, you pointed out Fulgaud's reach is shorter than a saint's. Though it'd be less than ideal, we could seek out another saint for Abbott Gonsindus and for Fulgaud."

Egilolf scowled.

"Perhaps in Brittany," I continued. "There's only one Saint Philibert, and he really belongs in Tournus."

"Aristeus, we couldn't get to the coast without getting caught by

Northmen. How do you think we'd make it past them?" He sighed heavily. "I'd rather risk Lombardy. Even Cordoba again. Plenty of saints resting forgotten in mosques that once were churches."

"Are we resolved to submit Saint Philibert to Father Leo then?" I asked. I admit, it did feel the truest choice, if not the most prudent.

"Riders!" Rachel hissed, pointing north at a dust cloud over the last rise. A small knot, perhaps half a dozen, pressed hard in our direction from behind. All appeared armed and wearing helmets. Rachel and Peter, without debate or farewell, slipped off behind the nearest trees and kept on until I was only still imagining I could see that flowing black hair beyond two fir trees. Egilolf trailed the litter while I hobbled on a few more steps. As the horses approached, we took a few steps off the road so as not to be trampled, but the horses slowed.

"Where are the others?" demanded the foremost soldier, his speech slow. I suspected him to be dim-witted. In addition to his helmet, he worn a leather jerkin and already had a fist on his sword.

"Who?" Egilolf asked, spinning around as if searching the area. The man was much faster than he appeared. The flat of his sword came whistling through the air where Egilolf's head had been. Egilolf was even faster, stepping forward and within the arc of the sword.

"Stop. Please, stop," a terse monotone sheared better than the guard's sword. The speaker emerged through the line of guards. It was hard to say whether he commanded Egilolf or his own guard. He was dressed in a brown monastic robe. "No violence is necessary. Not if they carry what we want."

"We're poor travelers," Egilolf protested. "Pilgrims, really. Nothing of value. Not even a few coins." He shook his scrip.

"Save your soul from deceit, my son." This, though the speaker was no more than a handful of years older than us. Suddenly I recognized him as Saint Martial's prior, the one who had debated bread allocations with the abbot. "The pair of you were commissioned, as it were, by Abbot Gonsindus, and we're not bandits. I'm Father Ageric, the abbot's prior and emissary."

It was all I could do not to glance at Egilolf. My turn to make a story, I guessed.

"We know Abbot Gonsindus and are bound his direction. Indeed, he sent us out, though we are returning empty ha—"

"Lie again, my son, and your penance will be severe," the priest cut me off. "Your caution in Pictauensis was prudence, but between the abbot's sources there and the caged thief a mile back, I know you're carrying relics. Be at peace"—and here he shared a toothed smile—"for you are truly among sheep again and have escaped the wolves. Abbot Gonsindus sent us out to shepherd you and our holy relics back in safety." He finished on a grand note, as though proclaiming himself our savior. His guards, however, circled around us.

"Can't be too cautious," Egilolf replied. "Have you a sign you're from Saint Martial's?"

The priest dug around in his pack while most of the guards relaxed. The dim-witted guard, though, kept his sword at hand and seemed disappointed he wasn't swinging it. He scanned the tree line furiously. "A letter of authorization," the prior said as he produced a small scroll with a flourish. "This is the abbot's signature here," he pointed patronizingly to the bottom lines. Egilolf studied at it dubiously, but I could see the signature did spell out the abbot's name. "'Fear not!' our Savior told his disciples. I haven't come to take the relics from you. Keep them safely, and you can give them yourselves to the abbot tomorrow."

"Tomorrow?" Egilolf's surprise mirrored mine.

"Of course! A saint, coming to his new home, needs a proper welcome. It would be unfit for the abbey, even the abbot himself, to wait on the saint as though he were greater. No, my sons, we have all come out to greet our new patron and bring him with all proper reverence and celebration to his dwelling." His smile suddenly twisted into question. "Who is it? Who have you brought us?"

Too late to pretend we carried nothing, Egilolf and I locked eyes, and somehow I knew he also was thinking of Father Leo. I was the first to turn back to the mounted priest. "A quick correction is in order, Father. The saint to whom God led us is not the warrior-king Abbot Gonsindus asked for. We were led, instead, to a holy virgin of antiquity, buried under the altar of a forgotten church, in a forgotten land."

"Her name?"

"Saint Valerie."

Without other options, we continued on the road, now accompanied by a shield wall of Father Ageric's guard. When we were alone, Egilolf badgered me about lying to the priest—as if he was not the one who lied to the abbess in Pictauensis! But I pointed out Abbot Gonsindus, not wanting a female saint, would send us off again, leaving us free to return Saint Philibert's remains to Father Leo.

One benefit to Father Ageric's confining presence was the use of his horse to pull my litter, and we made better time toward Lemouicensis. The sun beamed almost too strongly, yesterday's dampness rising in a humid sheen of wavering light over the fields we passed. A "growing day," as the old gardener at my abbey would have said. Was it really only two years ago, that night of burning and Northmen swords, the start of my drifting life? The sun belied the turbulent thoughts of my monastic past, the uncertain future. Some breeze, I swear, carried a rose scent to me, but I doubted Rachel would join our way again.

We met with Abbot Gonsindus' entourage as the *vespers* bells rang over the hills' long shadows. The prayers were perhaps a shade rushed as the abbot had vowed to speak with us as soon as the hours were kept. He invited us to dinner, and not even Father Ageric joined us in the confines of the farmer's house the abbot had blessed by commandeering for the night. One guard at the door secured our privacy. The abbot treated us to a repast of a venison haunch in a sauce of garlic and shallots, though the bread was Moorish buckwheat. The meal was scarcely cleared, however, before he stood.

"I prayed daily for you for God's favor. 'Seek, and you shall find!' I would have thrown open your sack on the road myself to venerate the relics you found, but holiness must be kept holy. Besides, a procession will ease our return to Saint Martial's. Fulgaud would go to many lengths, not all of them of pure motive, to lay hold of your relics. Surprised? I know most of what goes on in Lemouicensis and beyond! As though Fulgaud could detain you without me discerning his purpose. A fox, that one." He dug through Egilolf's bag in a manner as rambling as his speech. "Come, tell me the story. Where did you find him? Who is he? What became of my silk?" This last came abruptly as the woolen wrappings around the bones fell open.

"Northmen took the silk, Father Abbot," Egilolf began. "This journey wasn't easy." He kept mostly plumb to truth, only omitting any mention of Father Leo or Saint Philibert. I swear he picked up some storytelling tricks from Rodegar: a dream led us to an abandoned church, deep in Northmen territory; we pried under the stone in the crypt under the altar, seeking a sub-crypt; we found relics directly under the altar—obviously a saint—and I read the inscription: Valerie.

"Valerie?" the abbot interrupted. "A female?"

"Yes, and when the Northmen sorceress conjured a *daemon*—" Egilolf tried to continue.

"I wanted a saint-king. These dark times need a warrior's strength, a king's protecting goodness. I was very specific!" He ran his hand over his tonsured scalp, hissing between his teeth.

"But, Father Abbot, she certainly is a saint because in the sorceress's duel—"

"I even shared my table with you! My venison, my spices!"

"God's ways are not our—" I tried to soothe the man.

"Get out! Get out!" He brushed wool bundle, relics and all, off the table in one sharp sweep of his arm, and only Egilolf's quick reactions spared them from the dirt floor. "Take your merchant's wife's bones with you! No one's heard of your saint, and no one will care. No one will believe in a saint they haven't heard of."

Egilolf and I scrambled out the door. Once outside, he gave a quick grin in the fading light. "You were right, Aristeus. Tomorrow, to Father Leo." We laid out our cloaks in some leaves and duff we scraped together under the spread of a linden tree. Almost home, if Lemouicensis was home. Almost done with this careening runaway ride.

The stars were coming out, mostly in the east, but spreading west as the last daylight ended, like brothers at *matins* lighting candles shared from a few to all, and like the tongues of fire spreading from the apostles to Jerusalem, to the Gentiles and beyond. The Pentecost of the *aether...*

If either of us had noticed the abbot's guard missing, we would have pressed on in the night.

Waking to a crowd hemming you in isn't the worst way to greet a new day, but it's not the best. I caught only murmured snatches of "Where is it?" and "Are you sure?" I elbowed Egilolf only to see he was already awake. A hulking form pushed through those milling and pointed. "That's them. I'm sure of it." It was the dim-witted guard who swung his sword at Egilolf yesterday. "We're out here to keep safe the relics they're bringing home. A holy virgin, they said."

"Where is she?"

"What's her name?"

"Can we see her?"

Once we stood, the crowd soon pressed us against the linden's trunk. "Abbot Gonsindus sent them himself and prayed for their success. I heard him say it last night, as he had them to dinner," the lumbering sword-swinger kept on as though he were an evangelist.

"Did you manage to overhear the end of our conversing, also?" I asked wryly, but the man pressed on.

"That's why I left so quickly and spent the night gathering up the villages around," he explained to the crowd.

"How do you know she's a saint?" a dubious female called out.

"Ask them. They said she fought off a *daemon* brought up by a Northmen's sorceress! I heard them! Saint Valerie, they named her."

"Blessed Valerie!" a farmer knelt. "Pray for us!" He produced a bit of a coin and pressed it into my hand. "Blessed Valerie!" a bent old woman picked up the refrain, offering a small basket of hazelnuts.

"Sorry, Father Leo," Egilolf muttered.

Despite our pleas, the guard summoned Abbot Gonsindus. By the time of his arrival, the pile of gifts had overflowed our hands and spilled over the tree roots like a skirt—some coins, baskets of foodstuffs, and a bleating lamb. Amidst the invocations of the rustics, the abbot's agitation of last evening seemed miraculously soothed.

He quickly gave orders to arrange everyone for *prime* and pulled me aside long enough to say, "God's ways, as you said, brother." He presided over the prayers and promised the crowd Saint Valerie would be interred suitably at Saint Martial's. Abbot Gonsindus produced an ebony wood box, inlaid with gold, in which he placed the relics. He produced small ribbons of red silk to stream from it, and my litter became the platform on which to raise it aloft. He then demanded we escort the remains back with him as witnesses of Saint Valerie's efficacy. At least he promised to pay us upon arrival. He ordered Father Ageric to arrange the necessary escort for relics, which just happened to include his guards in a wide circle around us.

The sun was a few hours into the sky, so our southeasterly road pointed us directly into its rays as the procession was organized. The attending monks chanted psalms in plainsong, and Father Ageric arranged each monk to his assigned task until the column's order reflected the divine plan. For the unity of the Godhead, one monk held aloft a cross worked with silver; for the two natures of Christ, two brothers followed, casting holy water over the crowd and the ground the relics were to pass over; for the Trinity, three brothers swung brass censers, wafting the aromas of incense over road dust and sun-warmed earth; for the four virtues, four musicians with ivory trumpets announced the procession to the whole countryside after every hymn. In the midst of the trumpeters, a priest carried a codex of the four Gospels. Behind this, my litter-turned-bier was carried on the shoulders of seven monks. Behind rode the abbot amidst the remaining brothers. Few others rode, though I was given a horse on account of my leg. As the procession began, Gonsindus blessed the crowd and then dismissed them.

Only they didn't disperse.

Behind and before us, the villagers milled, and as we set off, their numbers only grew. Everyone from miles off must have hastened to us, and the crowd waxed with the sun. Soon the roadway was lined with people as far as its turns were visible, the road itself teeming with farmers, woodcutters, an ironworker still holding his implements, mothers nursing, maids weaving garlands or strewing passersby with flowers of all colors. Children, catching the crowd's mood, if not purpose, dashed in and out of the procession, laughing. Hour after hour, people joined the pilgrimage, swam in the stream of the road, stepped back out to the bank of the roadside under a shade tree to share their eagerness with a friend or stranger, or to start a spontaneous picnic. They then joined the throng again when a new antiphon broke out. Mixed through the mass of souls was something like the expectation of a bard's arrival, the glee of children watching a fool in his tumbling acts, the solemnity of an Easter vigil, and the gaiety of a wedding feast.

I spoke as much to myself as to Egilolf, "This procession is a blessing! A glimpse of the glory of Christianity in its golden age! Prudentius" —Egilolf made a mocking comment under his breath, which I ignored— "wrote sweeping poems, so vivid you could see the scene as you read: the anniversary celebration of the martyr Hippolytus, where Romans and other races blend together without distinction, where blood makes no difference as plebeian and patrician bump shoulders freely in the crowd, and men, women and even children are all equal in the great procession to his *sub-terra* tomb and the memorial church raised over it, overflowing their capacity. Gentile or Jew, slave or free, woman or man—never more!" My companion raised an eyebrow.

"Can you imagine it, Egilolf? The whole world united under one ruler, the Church and Emperor Theodosius once and for all had anathematized Arian's heresy, paganism was swept out of the public fountains of Rome." The crowd continued its hymn. "The sack of the Eternal City was a decade away or more in the unthinkable future. Such a brief triumph before the world resumed its crumbling under new waves of pagans, stranger heresies, more contentious bishops. Such a glorious but brief triumph." I sighed heavily.

We continued until the afternoon sun was upon our backs, one hymn finishing as another spontaneously began further back in the crowd, the disjointed timing of the meandering sections not dampening the fervency of the people. The pace of crowd and monks slowed, hurried, or stopped at the whim of many wills. We had not made many miles as *vespers* approached, and Abbot Gonsindus announced he would hold Mass. The nearest chapel was too small for the throng, so they spilled over into the fallow field.

After the service, Egilolf and I wandered the camp, seeking food from the scattered cook fires springing up around the chapel. Well, truthfully, Egilolf wandered, whereas I hobbled on my crutches, taking the most direct line from fire to fire. My leg ached fiercely, which Egilolf took as a sign of rapid healing.

We lingered by a less-reverent group who all enjoyed their revelry. Someone had brought wine, and with a shepherd's flute, set of pipes, and an old man keeping rhythm on a pail, many of the younger men were swinging girls about rather lustily.

The day's joy did not touch Egilolf's face as we sat to our supper. "What's gnawed your happy root?" I asked. I pointed to the dancers and revelers for contrast.

"Is this it?" he said, his tone as melancholic as his face. He sounded resigned. "All our effort, the Northmen bondage, running from Ranulf and his bishop—was it all just for this? For some new saint to end up in the abbot's hold, by happenstance more than design? What of the old priest and his devotion?"

I didn't want to consider it, despite Egilolf's questions. "Perhaps this is God's will."

Egilolf flushed. "That's not what you said last night!"

"We, feeble children of God, have done what we could," I spat back. "We've asked, we've prayed, we did what we thought best." I stood, feeling the need to pace, but only took two steps with my crutches. I motioned to the whole encampment as I spun back toward him. "Now, this has come along instead, and we can sulk over it or consider this a blessing." He almost seemed convinced for a brief moment, but I hesitated. "The rest is up to Him." I slumped back into my makeshift seat.

"But have we done all we can? Or should?" Egilolf poked at his meal.

Loud acclaims from the other side of the field drew groups of the impromptu pilgrimage together. Soon everyone was streaming from all sides toward a tightening cluster. I stood to follow and pulled at my companion's shoulder to rouse him as well.

At the edge of the cook fires, Father Ageric stood on a small mound next to a rough and gouged worktable on which the ebony reliquary sat, alone but for a solitary tallow candle. The small mound raised the reliquary above the field of people but not much more than a man's height.

"What's the commotion?" Egilolf asked an older lad sitting on the shoulders of another fellow.

"Some blind boy from Mortemart prayed for Saint Valerie's blessing and was healed!" The lad waved his hands toward the reliquary. "They say he can see his ma's face now for the first time."

The fellow beneath reddened and staggered as he worked to hold his burden aright. "He's called the people for repentance—the priest—I mean."

Egilolf leaned into me and whispered, "A wonder that 'Saint Valerie' could heal a wound."

"You are forgetting," I countered, but still under my breath, "it is really Saint Philibert there in the reliquary. Even if they do not know the true identity, it is nevertheless a real saint, with real relics."

Egilolf remained dubious.

"Look, it's old Magneric!" the lad grabbed my shoulder and pointed toward the mound, off-balancing his companion even more. Why this should be surprising, I didn't know, but the local crowd apparently also saw the magnitude of this act, for whispers and pointing fingers rippled through the press of bodies. Slowly a bent man hobbled forward, leaning heavily on a staff. He almost fell, attempting the short rise of the mound and grumbled over having to be helped up. Once at the table, he rested his right hand on the ebony box and raised his left to the crowd, waiting for silence.

"I would have this witnessed by all here today," he began in a firmer voice than I would have thought possible from this frail figure. "My brother and sons and their wives and children all joined the celebration today, and they dragged me along with them. A glorious day for the recovery of a saint of ours, and I felt youth flow through me again, even if but for the duration of the hymns' refrains." The crowd resumed its murmur of side conversation. "But that was not my miracle today!" he boomed, snapping everyone's attention back. "As the celebration continued, I went to clap on the back of the man next to me, to encourage and cheer him—and found it was Ragnemod himself!"

Gasps throughout the crowd, but Egilolf and I shrugged at each other.

"I am not sure who was more startled. Yesterday I would have pulled my dagger. But today!—today, we stopped, Ragnemod and I, while others slipped around us and the trumpets blasted. The Holy Cross caught a beam of sunlight, and I smelled scents more astonishing than the incense that had already passed on.

"I know Saint Valerie was watching us in that moment, and I knew what must be done. For my part, my kin's feud with Ragnemod is ended, any past grievances forgiven and forgotten, even unto the memory of my eldest in his grave and the infant in Matild's womb. On the relics of Saint Valerie, I swear it!"

Even in the dimming evening light, I could see the consternation break out in the face of the younger man who helped Magneric up to the table. His features confirmed him as the old man's son. Rapid but hushed chatter broke throughout the crowd, and the lad beside me slipped down from his friend's shoulders, saying, "I'd never have thought it."

Magneric stood still on the mound, his hand unmoving from the ebony box, as though seeking anyone to defy him. Movement through the crowd caused more excitement until another aged man, gray-haired against Magneric's baldness but otherwise dressed alike, stepped to the base of the mound.

The crowd whispered, "Ragnemod!" He paused before Magneric, his face a stone, then extended his right hand. Magneric reached down to him and, grasping forearms, pulled him up. Still gripping arms, they together faced the group. "I too," Ragnemod declared, "end my feud with Magneric. Any past grievances are forgiven and forgotten, even unto the memory of my father in his grave and the grandchildren I hope to see." He placed his left hand on the ebony box. "On the relics of Saint Valerie, I swear it!"

Stunned silence erupted into cheers greater than any I heard along the road today. The procession continued over the next few days, all at the pace of an infant's crawl, and every evening brought more miracles—an old woman who heard *daemons* in her head was exorcised and had them silenced, a thief who stole a new scythe came forward and returned it, though he was uncaught—but the miracle I recalled the most, the one that astonished the crowd beyond all reason, was the forgiveness of that long, ugly, murderous feud that had continued for more generations than anyone remembered.

Even chaos becomes familiar with enough time, so to us, the procession had become routine by the fourth day. We were moving, however, into new lands, closer to other villages where rumor outpaced us and enticed others to join. For them, the celebration was new. Without thought, without order or logic, without schedules or plans, new people joined our procession continuously, sometimes in twos or fives, sometimes a village whole. As we moved beyond homes and hamlets, people left the festivity to return to obligations of hearth and field. Never a break nor total ending, our stream along the roadway ebbed and flowed with the hours.

Every place the relics stopped for the evening became a new shrine, if only a cross to mark Saint Valerie's resting place. The procession did not keep, however, to our main road back to Saint Martial's. Abbot Gonsindus took the procession through as many local byways as he could reach while still drawing toward his abbey.

When we followed the fork toward the village of Dorrat, Egilolf became withdrawn, almost sullen. I did not connect this behavior to our course change until we approached the village, by which time it was too late to ask him privately. Every village, to include this one, swelled the crowd as we drew close enough for the crippled, young, and old to join in.

Whether due to my entreaties to Saint Philibert's relics one night, or the Old Master's healing art, or a combination of both, my leg had grown strong enough to test some of the days alongside Egilolf and my horse, a slow hobble aided by crutches. Attempting to draw Egilolf from his melancholy, I was discoursing on Justin Martyr, that great second-century philosopher who, like Saint Augustine, found the logic of philosophy alone unsustainable and had surpassed it when he found its fulfillment in Christ. "Did you know," I expounded, "he was the first Christian to write to the pagan emperor, to educate him on our practices so as to dispel rumors and forestall persecutions? He was the first to document details of the Mass: gathering on the morning of the first day of the week, reading Scriptures, and the writings of the apostles. Imagine it! Christianity so new there was no New Testament, just a collection of letters and memoirs of the apostles. And after the readings, the priest declares, 'Hearts aloft,' and we all respond, 'We lift them up to the Lord.' Can you believe it? Not only the structure of the Mass but its very words unchanged all the way down to our sorry age. And then, of course, the Eucharist. All this spelled out in detail for the emperor to clear up misconceptions…"

I halted. Egilolf had stopped a few steps before, moonstruck in daylight, staring at the side of the road. At *someone* on the side of the road. Dressed like every farmer's wife in the area, she was a woman of middle years, young enough she could not be a grandmother but old enough a few worries of life etched her face. Perhaps more than a few. She seemed familiar, almost. Her auburn hair shone in the sun and flowed in a breeze, making her beautiful but for her stony face. She returned Egilolf's gaze, but her face quickly passed from startled wide eyes to a mien of drawn brows and bared teeth, a silent snarl as she fumbled at her waist for a small skinning knife.

"Egilolf!" I warned, and both seemed to wake from a spell. I grabbed his arm and pulled him away—not an easy feat for a man with a mending leg—while Egilolf kept glancing back with hollow eyes. Even as the crowd swarmed back around us, I saw the woman glaring.

Once she was left safely behind, I ventured, "Who was that woman?"

Egilolf ignored me. A hundred paces down the road, and again a few hundred after that, he stopped in the stream of people, frozen in shock or concentration. I had to tug him along by his belt.

As we neared the far end of the village, a *colonus* joined us, calling for Egilolf by name as he strode to catch up. He was older, but not stooped, and bore the smoked metal scent of a farrier. We three stopped under the shade of an ash, stepping out of that river of sanctimony. Once he closed with us, though, he wore the dumbfounded gape of a man who caught a fish too large to land. "Egilolf…eh…where've you been? I mean…" His mouth opened and closed again without comment, as if he now were the caught fish. "You still in the campaigns then?"

Egilolf gave a shake of his head.

"I figured. Most of the village call-up has returned. But I thought maybe you'd have seen *her* boy. He finished his fostering. Old enough now that he joined up with the *comes*, they say." If he expected Egilolf to share more at this, he was mistaken. Again, his lips flapped.

Egilolf didn't help fill the struggling silence. He studied the ground at his feet.

"I'm Aristeus," I introduced myself, more to fill the awkward moment than from any necessity. "Egilolf's companion of these past treacherously filled months. Did you know we were the ones to recover the new saint's relics?"

The fish-mouthed smith ignored me, his attention spent on trying to issue words. "I've tended the grave."

This brought Egilolf up sharply.

"Not his, your mother's," the farrier continued.

Even that did not rouse much more than a half-mumbled reply that may have been a thanks or a protest.

"This is still your home too, boy," the farrier finished, his last volley spent.

Egilolf grasped his arm, in gratitude, or solidarity, or farewell, I couldn't tell.

"Regardless of what the widow says, there's plenty that would welcome you."

Egilolf wordlessly stepped into the flow of the pilgrimage river and walked stiffly away. I glanced between the two, the *colonus* struggling yet for the right words. At last, I hobbled to catch up, leaving the man, his village, and his questions behind.

Egilolf didn't acknowledge anything the rest of the day. I thought dinner might break his withdrawal, but he only grunted his thanks and stared into the fire. That night, when Father Ageric set up the reliquary for all to see and venerate, I hauled Egilolf along to break him from his silent fire-gazing.

"Who was that woman to you?" I asked for the hundredth time. By this time, I didn't expect an answer but desperately retried past failures.

He stopped for several moments without response. He faced the ebony relic box, visible over the heads of the crowd. "Some things can't be reconciled," he sighed. Then he wandered into the dark.

After seven days passing through hamlets in the hills, meandering north and east and north again, we finally turned south toward Lemouicensis. It likely wasn't coincidence that Abbot Gonsindus's approach brought us in from the north, as far from the *comes'* fort as possible without coming across the river from the east. Egilolf remained taciturn for a few days to the point I considered dragging him up to the reliquary one evening to request Saint Valerie dispel his melancholic air. This only proved how distracted I had become with Egilolf and how enmeshed with the abbot's procession—they were Saint Philibert's relics, of course. Perhaps my prayers were heard anyway since his disposition slowly improved. I dared not ask him further for fear he'd succumb to dark moods once more.

As we proceeded through town, we passed close enough to the fort to see an unarmored man upon the high tower. His stiff grip of the parapet conveyed his menace. I pointed him out to Egilolf, whose low grunt of "Fulgaud!" reminded me of the severity of our dilemma more viscerally than had our prior debates. Surely such an informed man knew the procession's meaning and who had precipitated it. Though his guards lined the street, perhaps because the jubilant crowd swelled larger with the town's populace, Fulgaud and his soldiers only watched and fumed as we reached the abbey gates.

As the tower announced *Comes* Fulgaud, so my sight of the abbatial refectory recalled our meeting with Father Leo. The first produced fear, the second guilt, and I am not certain which was stronger. I saw nothing of the old priest, however, and the column of argent Cross, candles, and monks into the church was

triumphant and undisturbed. As the reliquary neared the nave
doors, both flung wide, a chorus broke out from within, echoing
across the abbey grounds. Abbot Gonsindus had outdone himself
apparently and had a song hastily prepared for the occasion. Each
verse of the antiphon was sung by half of the choir, split by the nave
aisle. As one half of the choir finished a verse, ending with "joy!"
the other side took up the new verse, their rejoicing pronounced in
the call and answer.

> With joy! We rise to greet the morn
> The glory of the Lord bursts forth
> He chases out all dark and fear
> All creatures now reflect our joy
>
> With joy! The hills and trees ascend
> Now joining with our rising hymn
> Quick carry, hymns, our hearts aloft
> May we, with morn, in Him rejoice.
>
> Rejoice! Rejoice! Saint Martial lend
> Your aid this day in all our toil
> With nature as our form and field
> We fill our tasks with grateful joy
>
> With joy! Rejoice! Saint Valerie shield
> Us from all Evil's wiles and snares;
> Now grant the Savior's holy blood
> And body to our souls with joy!

As the hymn rose through the columns to echo off the domed
roof, the refrains rose in fervor. The monks bore the reliquary at a
solemn pace but with upturned, alight faces. Raised high on my
makeshift litter, they carried it to the altar amidst wafts of incense
from the censers. The mid-afternoon sun burnished the paving
stones of the aisle and the robed men filing through perfumed
glowing clouds, leaving the chorus under shadows of columned
arches, their joyful voices disembodied as though truly sung by an

ethereal, heavenly host. Egilolf and I pressed our way through the door with the following crowd, spilling into the nave and halting in rapt awe at the impassioned, mingled senses.

"When the new Jerusalem descends, and God dwells among his people..." I intoned.

"Maybe Philibert took it out of our hands," Egilolf suggested. "No choice but for him to remain under Gonsindus."

Were there questions yet written across his brow?

The church held as much glory as man could muster, but if this was God's will, I suspected that my companion sought passage to Tarshish.

After the ceremonies, Abbot Gonsindus was true to his word. Taking us to his residence, he gave us enough coin to keep us housed and fed for near half a year. We thanked him for the hefty reward, but I could tell by the tightness in Egilolf's grin that it didn't sit right with him either.

CHAPTER 11:
THE PRICE OF THE POTTER'S FIELD

Jesus sits on a lone rock by the seashore, surrounded by sand, grilling a breakfast of fish to the tune of soft waves. Sunlight has recently broken strong through the clouds, banishing the last vestiges of dark. Jesus looks west, across the sea, as though he sees to the world's end. Or to its center, Rome. "Peter, do my will." The man sitting beside him on the rock cannot bring himself to look into his Lord's eyes, much less follow his gaze. The other disciples shuffle aimlessly a few paces away, just close enough to overhear without risking Jesus addressing their failures too.

"Lord, you know I'll do your will, if you but show it to me."

Jesus flips the fish over on the grate to sear the other side. He prods the fish with a thin rod of iron, and the silence grows. He looks west again. "Peter, do my will."

If shame kept Peter's eyes down, exasperation raised them. "Lord! Show it to me and I'll do it!"

Jesus pulls the fish onto a platter, cuts off their heads, and offers the first to Peter.

"Peter, do my will."

Though Egilolf and I kept a guilty eye out for Father Leo, we saw no sign of him that first evening, not at the hours, nor the refectory, nor the guesthouse. "Perhaps he left," speculated Egilolf. "Perhaps he died." His casual attitude toward life's grim possibilities, perhaps from his soldiering past, grated.

"It would make your penance easier," I reproached. Then, as quickly, I corrected myself. "No, that was not fair. Sorry." I sighed. "But I spoke truly when I said it would make this mess easier."

What wasn't making anything easier was *Comes* Fulgaud. Egilolf and I circled inside the abbatial wall after our repast, only to see thick patrols of Fulgaud's guards too leisurely marching their rounds not to be intentionally stalking the abbey. "Does he seek us or the relics?" I sighed.

"Both," answered Egilolf gloomily.

A silhouette figure paced Fulgaud's watchtower, though whether he was a guard or the *comes*, I couldn't tell at this distance. The sinking sun advanced the northwest hills' shadows from the fort, across the town, and steadily toward the abbey. "If Father Leo isn't here, we should move on. Quickly."

"I have significant doubts Fulgaud's captain will let us go that easily."

"Oh, I imagine it'll be like our Pictauensis departure." I felt lightheaded, and Egilolf smirked. "Without the broken leg, of course."

"I do not think I am quite up to running streets and vaulting walls."

"You're walking on it already. You'll be yourself in a week. We hole up here until then."

Or so we thought. No sooner had we set this course and left the wall, we were summoned to Abbot Gonsindus's residence.

It was unchanged but for more parchment stacked on the desk, where the abbot sanded a letter. While we waited, I perused his books, noticing a new codex, *De Trinitate*. "Augustine's, or Hilary's?" I asked. Gonsindus grimaced while still focusing on his desk, ignoring us and the question. Egilolf and I stood in silence until, at last, the abbot turned in his seat.

"Captain Sichar has made apparent the lengths he'll go to get Saint Valerie's relics. He came bashing at our gate not an hour ago, after our throng of rustic followers dispersed to their homes, of course. Christ Himself alone knows what that man's problems are. Perpetual scowl." He grimaced again. "Fulgaud demands the relics and you. Sichar insinuated he'd be content with just you.

"I planned to have my librarian write out a *translatio* account, but it might be better coming from you"—he pointed to me—"if you haven't forgotten how to write. It seems many days most of my monks have." His pressed lips expressed more distaste at this thought than the idea of Fulgaud at his gates. He spun back to his desk and sharpened a quill. "Father Ageric thinks we can keep Saint Valerie if we turn you two over to Fulgaud." Egilolf's protest was forestalled by the abbot's raised hand. "You two got me into this morass, encouraging those rustics with tales of your Saint Valerie." I felt like adding he had been quick to capitalize on the people's faith, but the man was already debating handing us over to Fulgaud. "Now it's left to—"

"You can't be serious!" Egilolf yelled. "After we risked our lives to bring her relics to you, after you led the procession through all the surrounding countryside, you're throwing us to the wolves at your door?"

The door exploded open behind us, and not one, but two, guards stuck their heads in the door, only to be held back by a wave of Gonsindus's hand.

"Have you asked Saint Valerie?" Egilolf cut in. "What she wants, I mean?"

"I'm not seeking advice on holy matters from a peasant and a once-scribe! Sichar confirmed you two were told, explicitly, that Fulgaud needed some relics. Rather than bring this disaster on my head, you could have been decent enough to get a second set of relics for him before returning to me. I'm not risking him storming my walls, pulling me to my knees before him, and carting off the relics along with whatever else his soldiers loot. You, scribe, stay here until you write out the *translatio*. Maybe by that time, Fulgaud will have been satisfied with this thief, and you can leave in peace."

The guards grabbed Egilolf's arms, and his eyes went wide. They dragged him to the door as he protested, his boots trying to dig into the flooring. His arms uselessly strained against the larger guards. "We followed your holy orders! You're a liar—" A fist to his nose cut his argument off.

The whole scene seemed surreal, a passing vision for which I was not truly present. The spray of blood, Egilolf's mangled grunts and shouts, the guards' struggle to hold him while wedging the three of them through the narrow doorway all became a cacophonous maelstrom in my head.

I spat dirt clods from my mouth and struggled to a knee. My oldest brother stood over me and probably debated whether it was worth his effort to beat me down again. Maybe I could reach the forest before him... "Big mouth, but not a fighter, that one," he laughed. "Nah, he's a runner," my father agreed.

"Aristeus!" Egilolf's last cry as he disappeared out the doorway brought me back.

I rounded on the abbot. "Your Grace. Our reward. I'll pay it all back and gladly. Just let us go!"

Another guard stepped into the doorway, eyeing me as though I could actually put up any resistance. He blocked my only exit. I realized my hands were clenched. "Please, your Grace. We have done nothing wrong. We did as you asked."

Abbot Gonsindus had gone back to writing and ignored me again until his next line was complete. He didn't face me but instead addressed the stone wall before him. "You, scribe, will write out the *translatio*, as I've directed. Your payment is already forfeit. Your companion—guide or thief or whatever he is—will be kept here until you finish your task, as incentive. After that, we'll see. I may be merciful." The abbot ordered the guard, "Take the scribe to a cell and bolt him in. In the morning, take him straight to the *scriptorium*." The guard stepped up behind me, grabbed my arm, and ripped my coin pouch off my belt before depositing it on the abbot's desk. "And get someone in here to wipe up the blood." The abbot bent back over his letter.

The guard's crushing grip on my arms didn't abate during the march to my banishment to the cells, as though he expected me to fight.

I spent the early night hours between *compline* and *matins* pacing, trying to pray, and replaying the nightmare of the abbot's office in my mind. If I could go back, I would do it differently. I would fight the guards, enough to free Egilolf, and we'd both make a run for it. I could see myself punching the closer guard, and in his stunned surprise, drawing his dagger to swipe at the other's hands or face.

I knelt to pray for God's wisdom and aid, and my mind wandered to images of pushing the one guard into the other, yelling at Egilolf to save himself while I blocked the doorway and faced both guards down myself. But every time, I woke from these reveries and saw myself for what I was. My brother and father were both right.

I was tired enough to lie down after *matins* rang but not weary enough to sleep. I lost count of my tosses and turns on the mat when I heard a voice, faint but holding the authority of age. "Aristeus, Aristeus."

Speak, Lord, your servant listens, I thought.

"Aristeus, are you in there?" the voice whispered.

My mind finally placed the voice. "Father Leo?" I whispered back. I sat up and fumbled to the door, brushing my fingers along stone and wood until I found it. Silence. I knelt and peered through the crack at the base. "Father Leo?" I called again. A quiet hushing command was the only reply, followed by a waft of chrism oil, of all things. *But the sacristy was all the way across the cloister*, I thought. I assumed I was confused, yet the scent was unmistakable. A muffled pop followed, and suddenly my cell door swung open to a darkness only slightly less black than my cell. The chrism oil smell was stronger. A hand in the shadows of a sleeve grabbed my own, and a robed figure guided me past the *cellulae* of the monks' dormitory. Not knowing what else to do, I followed.

Under the darkest shadows of the cloister edges, we crept, and then through the refectory, my fear discerning an abbey guard's form in every shadow. I followed the figure around the exterior of the church and into the graveyard. The moon was a day past new, and starlight alone illuminated the outlines of buildings around. Downward, the ground revealed only a deeper darkness, so we tripped and stumbled through a series of small grave markers before the man pulled me to a knee in the grass with him. Only then did he close his face to mine and speak.

"Aristeus, you are well, yes?" The old priest's face and voice were discernable enough now.

Was I well? I thought to myself. *You removed me from a prison, and my friend remains there now, and you ask if I'm well?*

Father Leo continued, however, without awaiting my reply. "When you first approached Saint Martial's, with your triumphal procession, crowds, and story about this supposed Saint Valerie, I planned to denounce you by asking how your thirty pieces of silver would be spent. A pair of modern-day Judases! What else should I have expected from relic thieves, I asked myself."

"I—"

"I said *planned*," he cut me off, covering my mouth with his trembling hand. The heady spice of the baptism oil became cloying; the priest's hand was smeared heavily with it. "I changed my mind.

Or God opened my eyes. I talked with some guards, loosened Ageric up with wine. The relics of this supposed Saint Valerie everyone's babbling about are really my Philibert's, yes?"

I nodded, realized he couldn't see that, and muttered yes. I explained the trouble while we, under the dark heavens, acted like murderous conspirators. We moved to a nearby gravestone, short but broad enough for Father Leo to sit. I told him everything: the second bones from the lower crypt, the Northmen, the flight from Pictauensis, Father Ageric's "escort," the *comes'* wrath, the duplicity of Gonsindus.

"Simple enough then," the old man said. "We get your thief friend out, he steals the relics back from Gonsindus, and we all run off before he or the *comes* are any wiser."

"I do not think Egilolf will agree. It undoes the fulfillment of his penance."

"You had this debate on the road! You both agreed to bring Saint Philibert to me!" he hissed in exasperation.

"We had, once, Egilolf believed it all—Ageric, the procession, the installment of the relics at the church here—as a sign of Philibert's will."

The old priest cringed. "To be venerated as someone else, forgotten for who he truly is? This is a saint we speak of, not some debt miraculously paid off. You see, it could not possibly be the saint's will, yes?"

"Well," I conceded, "The abbot's betrayal may have swayed Egilolf's mind back."

Father Leo sighed heavily. "Gonsindus isn't a monster. Just a sinner, weak-willed, and willing to give up one man for the peace of many. I can't see that as Philibert's will, though, either."

"How can we know Philibert's will? How can we know God's will at all, with any certainty?" My words were sharp and hot. "There is no passage in Isaiah or the Letter of Saint Paul to the Church in Some Greek City telling Egilolf and me what to do with Saint Philibert's bones amidst three competing masters. We were staring down Cerberus with only one bone to feed him!" I was quivering with all my unanswered questions, ready to yell and shout. I stood and cautiously paced around the gravestone Father Leo sat on. "We thought claiming the bones as Saint Valerie's would lose Gonsindus' interest or gain us some time. Instead, hundreds and thousands flocked to see her. Miracles happened nightly! Healings, and forgiveness, burdens laid down. How could that not seem like God's will?" My feet stopped when I ran out of words, and I sat on the grass.

Father Leo didn't respond, and the silence drew on. Weary, I lay on my back. "If the saints are up there, Father, in the *aether*, watching everything, why is it so hard to find what we must do? The doing alone is sufficiently hard."

More silence, not even broken by a breeze. Father Leo pulled back his hood and also gazed upward. "If you were them, in the glory of heaven, would you want to recall this mess of a place, the squabbles of sinful man? What would compel someone to forego the beatific vision and reach a hand back to aid those self-twisted in sin? You would rather attend eternally the glory of God, yes? We get angry with God and his saints for not aiding us—no, don't deny it, we've all shaken our fists at heaven as Job did—as though they owe us anything. As though we're owed an explanation. And yet, un-owed, undeserved, the saints do reach back, they do listen, intercede, and partake in Christ's work for us. Just as He chose to leave eternal perfection with the Father to join the mud and muck of our sin, to aid us and intercede for us."

The stars transfixed, the only light of the night, of all Creation in those dark hours, stayed in immutable perfection overhead. The rest of the world faded. Somewhere as possibly far off as heaven, a single, high, clear bell rang. Then a closer bell rang in the tower of the abbey church.

"It is *lauds* already," I said.

"Yes. Whatever else, we must thank God for this day." As the bell rang again, Father Leo pulled up his hood. "You and Egilolf know Saint Philibert deserves his rightful name and resting place. That is why I freed you and will free him. But you're right that if you steal back Saint Philibert now, they'll forever pursue you. I'll return to Tournus to collect the false relics there and bring them back to Lemouicensis. But I may need your aid in exchanging them for Philibert's relics. In the meantime, you could do as you said Egilolf once suggested and seek out other relics with which to appease Gonsindus. Or Fulgaud. I will meet you at Saint Martial's bridge, starting on the second Sunday after the Dormition of the Blessed Virgin. I will watch for you each evening after *compline*. If you secure other relics, we'll put them in Philibert's place. If not, the bones from Tournus will have to do. Come, we must get your friend from his cell before dawn breaks."

Cells. Guards. The strewn stars became visions of Egilolf's blood spraying from his mouth across the expanse. "How did you get me out?" I asked. "What did you do about the guards?" For all my fantasies, my mouth went dry now at the thought of facing armed men, even to free Egilolf. Another thought came to mind, and I rolled up onto my elbow. "I read about a prison break once. I cannot remember where—but you go to the cell, tell the guard you come to hear his confession. I mean, I cannot remember where I read this. Anyway, have Egilolf tie you up, and he wears your robes out." I may have been babbling a bit at this point. "In the morning, the guards come for him, only to find you tied up." I was up and pacing.

"There are none."

"What? Of course, there will be a confession. I just—I cannot remember where I read…nor the details…"

"There are no guards. Gonsindus had you bolted into cells," he cut in, "but his guards all patrol the walls. You see, Fulgaud is his main fear, yes?"

I tried not to gasp too loudly in relief.

Father Leo made to rise, and I grabbed his arm and hand to help him. "But Ageric sleeps at the east end of the dormitory. It's best to pass through the refectory and cloister."

"Now, who's the master thief?" I shook my head. "One final question, Father. Why do you smell of chrism oil?"

"It greases the locks and hinges. And it was readily available in the sacristy," he said with a short laugh. "The saints won't do all your work."

Father Leo was correct. Extracting my compatriot from his cell was not difficult. Unfortunately, he had no plan after that. As he told me, he was a priest, not some skulking thief used to slinking about in the night. Unlike Pictauensis, I could not blindly follow Egilolf. Escaping over the walls was going to be difficult since the guards were there in force. Egilolf was of no help. His face was a mass of bruises, his left eye swollen completely shut. At least one tooth had been knocked loose, and not only did he wince when he spoke, but his mumbling was nearly unintelligible.

"We have got to get over those walls," I repeated uselessly as we returned to the graveyard to plan. "Think, think, think," I commanded myself. Egilolf slumped over one of the tombstones. "Rahab, the prostitute, hid two spies under flax on the roof of the wall of Jericho. We could hide until you are better, Egilolf, and maybe then flee. Or…ah! Disciples lowered the Apostle Paul over the wall in a basket to flee Ephesus. Or was it Corinth?" I couldn't picture Father Leo being strong enough to lower us. He was attending to Egilolf. It was clear from Egilolf's condition if anyone was going to get us over the abbey walls, it had to be me. But no historically applicable example came to mind.

"Polycarp was warned of the mob hungry for his flesh to be burnt and fled to a farm outside Smyrna. But he did not have walls to deal with. Ah! King David's wife Michal propped a dummy idol in his bed and let him down through a window. We really should have left some formed shape in your cell in case they check in on you. We could return and prop up some hay or an old robe." I shook my head clear. "But still, we have no ally to lower us." Was I treading in circles as I thought, or was it my mind reeling? My monologue was leading me nowhere. "God is not sending an earthquake to release us like Paul and Silas, I dare bet." *Saint Irenaeus, aid me against my doubts.* The east sky was noticeably lighter. How was it so easy to flee from our cells but so difficult to escape the walls?

"Perhaps it is time to entreat Saint Philibert, yes?" Father Leo asked. He had produced a rag from within his robe and daubed Egilolf's face. It was alarming to realize it was light enough I could easily see him moving.

"Of course. I have been praying to all the saints since you opened my cell." Well, I would have been praying if I had had a moment to think.

"Not here in the graveyard," Father Leo countered. "You must entreat Saint Philibert directly."

We would be cut off in the church, of course, with no exit. Possibly some side chapel would conceal us for the day, and we could flee when night fell again. Certainly, we couldn't stay outdoors any longer; the sun, though not yet risen, was forcing the stars' retreat. I could see the dark silhouettes of guards patrolling the perimeter, even at this distance. I sighed and nodded.

The priest continued, "I'll be missed if I'm not back to the dormitory soon. I will find you in the church tonight and spend the day praying for God's intervention."

Father Leo helped me guide Egilolf back to the cloister. I led him to the south transept doorway and into the church. I kept anticipating the bell for *prime* and the train of brothers and novices who would stumble from the dormitory, through these same doors and into the church. I knew I had become too accustomed to the ways of deceit and falsehood when the shadows and dark corners of a church felt like a blessing. Egilolf and I slipped from column to column. I had not seen where Gonsindus laid Saint Philibert's bones, but the best guess was the crypt of Saint Martial, the most honored part of the church save the altar.

Unlike Saint Philibert's church at Dee, Saint Martial's had no easy pilgrim's pathway to its crypt. I hunted around the folds of the columns and buttresses by the tabernacle before I found the small doorway behind the choral area, near the north end of the apse. I didn't hesitate to take two tapers from the candelabra, and then we descended into the holy abode of the dead.

Like the campfire at night, my thoughts curled around the finite reaches of my weak taper. Crypts. The bowels of a church. The deepest innards secreted away. In darker ages, did we fear our dead and keep ourselves from having to see them? Is that why we buried bodies deep in the earth? Now we at least interred in the Church, the proximity of holiness, yet sealed in darkness beneath the altar. Would men one day again, like the Romans, take to burying their dead far outside the city, far from the Church, as though by not seeing the gravesites daily, they could deny death, foil it if it were but ignored? Is the dark of our burials the deepness of fear, the triumph of evil, or is it the soft, mute enveloping of repose? And the saints…why are they buried differently? Why do we sometimes entomb our saints under the altar and at other times carry them about in golden cases, in crystal phylacteries, in silken pouches? Prudentius, with his complex meter, memorialized and glorified the Church's dilemma to keep the holy *corpus* whole or to share the body's parts out as personal conduits of God's power.

The ancient poet's vision sprang forth in my mind's eye: *the great bishop Fructuosus of Tarragona, along with his deacons—an hour before, promising his sheep that in death he would still tend them and all the Church, East to West—was now refined and purified to ashes, still glowing, and blackened bone fragments, some half charcoal. Despite the persecution of the day, some Christians risk the hatred lingering in the abandoned amphitheater as night falls. Doused with a libation of wine, the holy ashes are seized, caressed, and carried off, each husband, widow, servant, or slave vowing to find a salvific way to carry their precious bishop close at heart. But contrary to this good intention, blessed Fructuous appears that night in the dreams of those who possess him, beyond death in the white garments of heaven, admonishing all to return his scattered parts to burial under the altar. Let the body be one, as Christ's Body is one, and the Church is one, and the Triune God is One.*

Those hidden bowels, loosened and opened, bursting with the filth of death, or pouring out the glory of resurrection…

Even brief, cautious steps down into the crypt, while my whole world was reduced to the sphere of candlelight, were long enough for Prudentius' verbal tapestry to flit through my mind before Egilolf's grunt brought me back to the all-too-concerning present.

Some years past the age of naiveté, though not so old that others would assume him bitter and broken, Egilolf groped forward in the wan light of a taper. Stooping despite the sufficient ceiling, his burdens were hard to determine. His sharp nose had been broken, and his fair hair was splattered with blood. The layers of dust and the stale, dank air declared every living body foreign to this crypt. From the niche-filled walls to the solid stone sarcophagi at the center, the place boldly whispered a forbidding peace. Though the abbot had brought Saint Philibert here yesterday, the musty air and silence felt like there had been no visitor here, not for an age.

The mocking repeats of life...

This time, Egilolf was not alone. I took his wrist and towed him along to kneel before the interred, gathered, and complete remains of Saint Martial in his stone bed, the ebony reliquary of Saint Philibert resting atop the sarcophagus. The bells of *prime* murmured overhead, dulled through a span of stone and earth. We knelt, and I followed Egilolf's example, pressing my forehead to the cool, marbled edge. "All the holy saints, pray for us. Saint Martial, pray for us. Saint Philibert, pray for us. Saint Irenaeus, pray for us..." My litany continued in a whispered reverberation, and my unabsorbed mind added of its own accord, "Saint Valerie, pray for us." I heard Egilolf shift, and I opened my eyes. For a handful of heartbeats, the darkness was a repose, and the saints really had but fallen asleep, *spiritu et corpus*. Then my small flame, having devoured the body of my candle without residue of ash or bone, flickered, dimmed, guttered...and the darkness again threatened fear and the vacuum of evil nothingness. My feeble flame continued to waver, ready to yield its last breath at each wisp of air.

"Aristeus." Egilolf tugged at my sleeve, and I rose with him, the battered and blind man now leading. He led me behind the sarcophagus to one of the many niches along the wall opposite the stairs. I heard his sleeves waving back and forth, fingertips whispering over stone or earth, bone or dust. He waved his hands slowly, hovering them over crudely chiseled letters.

"What are you hoping to accomplish?" I asked.

In response, he only grabbed the taper from my fingers and held it near the wall, moving it slowly past each niche.

"I suppose we could hide in them if the abbot thinks to search for us here," I ventured, "but only if it's empty. I am not sidling up to some skull."

He shushed me. Slowly, deliberately, he continued to move the candle past each niche, from one end to the other. Like stacked bunks in a guesthouse, each excavated hole appeared carved from the earth and then lined with stone where possible, one niche directly above the other. The walls of this crypt were not built up, stone upon stone over a foundation, but carved out, a hollowing from the earth. Suddenly, the candle guttered again and nearly went out. My alarm was countered by the joy on Egilolf's face, a grin cracked with pain. "Draft," he muttered, and then I realized—a small stream of air blew between stones at the back of the niche. He pried at the identified gap, working loose a large flat stone. The last of our light showed an emptiness the taper could not fill.

Tunnel is too magnanimous a word for the enlarged rat warren into which I was sure we were crawling. The occasional beam to support the roof did little to discourage my fear of suffocating in a collapse, especially as the wood felt crumbly with rot.

Egilolf dove in, convinced this was some sort of secret exit, built for times of chaos, war, pillage, or abandonment by God. Times like ours, I suppose.

After an eternal minute of crawling on my stomach, with arms overhead and wriggling like the banished serpent of Eden, I doubted this was meant to be a tunnel for the use of man. It felt more like a device designed to inculcate permanent claustrophobia in even the most agoraphobic.

Ignoring his battered face and swollen eye, Egilolf didn't hesitate to lead. Otherwise, I may not have gone into the tunnel even if Gonsindus' guards descended to the crypt. Or even if Arnkel the Skull-Crusher charged with axe in hand. Writhing an inch-worm progress, I continued my prayers to the saints until a few clods in my mouth changed that plan. When I was not more than twice my body length into the hole, I backed myself out until my feet were in the niche again, to reassure myself I could return. Crossing myself twice, I penetrated the earth deeper. In hindsight, a trinity of cross-signs would have been better.

With little to do but squirm forward, my mind wandered again. If the crypt had been the bowels of the church, was this the tubular entrails? Did that make us the expelled waste? As long as we were eventually expelled, I would be grateful. Egilolf remained silent, but the sound of his constant shimmying and scraping lent me courage for a time.

I'm sure we had been inching forward for at least a quarter-hour when, scrabbling at another rotting post for leverage, it pulled free in my hand. Dirt rained on my head, and the now-unsupported crossbeam sagged, pressing on my elbow. The thought of all the spans of earth overhead bearing down, a hair's breadth away from burying me.... I couldn't breathe! "O, God! O, God! O, God!" I began yelling, as if by the force of my shouts, I could enlarge the breathing room collapsing around my head. My own blind groping had killed me.

I felt a strong pressure on my hand, crushing. The next beam was collapsing! But then the force was yanking and pulling, and I felt my face scraping against the rocks even as my shoulder threatened to separate from its socket. First, my hand, then elbow, then the crown of my head broke free, and at last, the viscera of the earth birthed me once more into the purest air of a dank cellar. As Egilolf extracted me, my panic subsided, and my chant of terror turned to grateful psalms with the fervency only matched by those just escaping death. "O, God! O, God. O…" My eucharistic gasps faded, and Egilolf pulled my legs clear.

"Reminds me of another cleric who chanted the same!" he quipped.

I couldn't help but laugh. When panic and relief subsided, I pushed myself up to kneeling, the wooden log ceiling too low to stand.

"I had pulled myself clear when I heard you beg and beg," he chortled.

"I was not beg—" I cut off my own protest. "Well, perhaps I was." I took in more deep breaths. "Where are we?"

"Beneath a stable by the smell. Can't see a door." I had forgotten Egilolf's swollen eyes. To be doubly blind in those earthen bowels—I shuddered again. The light in the cellar was bright only in comparison to the earth-dousing darkness of the tunnel. I assessed the room as much with my hands as my eyes. The uneven floor was dirt, as were the walls, sloped back at an angle. The edge between floor and wall was lined with stone to prevent a wall collapse. One of these stones Egilolf had pushed aside at the tunnel's end. The post I had pulled on in the tunnel had been but a pace from this cellar. The cellar's former purpose was undeterminable since nothing was stored in it currently. Probing the ceiling earned me a splintery rebuke three times, but with no other alternatives, I continued until I felt the outline of a trapdoor. With

Egilolf's assistance, I shifted the planks up and aside, then cautiously stood aright, my head and shoulders protruding from the opening.

"I feel reborn. And I will be damned if I ever enter some hole in the ground again." Twice entombed with Saint Philibert and twice rebirthed. The Alexandrian theologian Origen posited truly, the old foreshadows the new.

As to the building's purpose, Egilolf was correct, and we were indeed in a small hostelry containing some half-dozen horses. The question was—as I pulled myself up to the stable floor and offered Egilolf a hand—"Do you think God's plan might have allowed us to make it outside the abbey?"

"We should be. Tunnel led north, the shortest direction to the walls. Why build a tunnel but escape? Poke your head out the door. See where we are. Then we decide if we run or await nightfall."

I followed his suggestion and crept to the stable door. I found a few knotholes and some gapped slats and was able to piece together that we had indeed made it outside the walls. The bright light of a new sun cast long shadows of homes onto a street.

"We seem to be somewhere outside the abbey walls but still in town. Perhaps an inn?" Something had to explain the stables. I sighed as much in disbelief as in relief. Had we escaped without following a Scriptural form, without some divine guidance? Who would have thought to pass *under* the walls? I plowed my brain, overturning turf of long-forgotten exegeses, but I could think of no parallels in the Holy Word to what we had just done. "Like Jonah, spat out onto dry land once again." It was more a tangential comparison than a true parallel. I peered back through the slats, watching the glory of a simple straw roof as the morning light washed it gold. If the sun never set again, I would not despair of its unending rays.

"Hardly three days in a leviathan this time! A briefer passage through the fish guts." Egilolf came up to the wall and tried to peer out with his slightly better eye. "Too late. Some folk up and about. Guards will spot us for sure."

"So we wait for night. And then what next?" I asked.

Egilolf exhaled long and hard, and his shoulders drooped. "I aim to leave, Aristeus. Father Leo's a good man, but what happened to Philibert is out of our control. I fulfilled my penance. I think. Brought this abbey a saint. To keep meddling now...well, I see what comes of it." He headed back to the cellar. "Better to head off. Think about a new life." He lowered himself carefully, feeling for the ground beneath.

"*Agricola* Egilolf, is that it? After all this, you turn farmer?" I joked, but my words seemed to hit the walls like a mud clod, slumping to the ground. I recalled Father Leo, earnest, desperate almost, when he set us to task and drew out his maps in the abbey garden. His voice was drawn tight as a bowstring when he called me a modern Judas. A man as old as anyone could be, without even his fellow brothers to support him, yet he risked his life to free us, all for Saint Philibert's sake. *Lord, what is your will? Give us a sign!* I prayed.

I thought I had been silent, but Egilolf responded, "There will be no sign, Aristeus. Not in the stars, nor the *sortes*. Not incubating for dreams at the altars. If God, or Philibert, or anyone wanted us to succeed, we would have by now." His head disappeared into the cellar. He called from the hole, "No sign."

You perverse and unbelieving generation. No sign will be given but the sign of Jonah! I put my head in my hands and shuffled toward the hole. *Lord, we believe! Help us overcome our unbelief!*

And then the stable door swung wide, the near-blinding light of the risen sun in my eyes as I spun toward the hinges' groan. Carrying saddlebags and blocking our only exit stood Captain Sichar and two of his guards. Out of the entrails, into the cesspit.

Though the source escapes me, I read once about some pagani *belief from strange lands of the utter east, beyond even Persia somehow: life ends only to begin the same broken, sin-reft existence on earth again. Not ever anew, just always again, without hope and without change. For once, I understood the source of that sentiment. In the same hall of the same fort, with Egilolf and I standing in the very spots, a span of indistinguishable weeks later,* Comes Fulgaud *paced. The only difference was his demeanor, which was, unsurprisingly, decidedly for the worse.*

CHAPTER 12:
YOU SHALL KNOW THE TRUTH,
AND SOME TRUTH...

But that I could don Patience's impenetrable cuirass, for I surely faced Wrath, all as Prudentius envisioned her, complete with mouth-foaming, darts for eyes, and shot through with blood and gall, ready to wield both pike and javelin. In the Psychomachia, *Patience withstood all blows from the battle until Wrath wore herself out and threw herself down on her own spear point. The suitability of Patience's model against Fulgaud, though, seemed dubious....*

"Hang them." The dismissive hand wave cut itself off. "No, the gallows." The *comes* stormed over to a window, surveying the town. "Outside the west wall, down the abbey road. Give Gonsindus a good view."

Egilolf raised his hands to entreat him a fifth time. Or maybe the sixth. "My lord, there's been a mistake."

"Your face tells me that much, thief. As did the procession of *my* relics, going right through *my* town, past *my* fort, but *not* to my chapel. Seems Gonsindus didn't like being double-crossed either. Flay them alive!"

The *comes* screaming my pending future, the hefty guard at my back twisting my arms in his grip, the flickering torchlight beyond Fulgaud which left his face in shadows, all seemed a repeat of the Northmen's camp, though now Fulgaud was the all-too-present *daemon*, and we had lost our saint.

I contemplated the state of my own soul, whether our actions with Saint Philibert were a mortal sin or a salvific act of righteousness, and whether God or the saints had the least bit of influence on our terminus in this chamber pot. I vaguely heard Fulgaud continue to vacillate on the specific end to our temporal existence. "You told everyone in Pictauensis your Saint Valerie was taken by the Northmen, didn't you?"

I was suddenly and painfully aware that instead of pacing and ranting, Fulgaud was right in my face, peering into my eyes, an accusing finger somewhere on the periphery of my vision. I hesitated.

"Don't lie now, cleric! Not minutes before your eternal judgment!"

"Ah, I…" I glanced at Egilolf for support, but the *comes'* hand shot up around my chin, his thumb and forefingers locking onto my jaw to keep my sight on his hellish gaze. His lesser fingers pressed a none-too-gentle threat on one side of my neck.

"You can't even lie convincingly! Not a true clergyman, I wager, just a pretender in robes. Our bishop's lowest man dissembles better than you. Another sin before judgment. Don't keep piling them up. You told everyone, from the abbess to the *dux* himself, this Saint Valerie was taken by the Northmen. And yet here she is, in my town. But not my chapel! So which is it?"

His thumb slipped from the jawbone down to the other side of my neck and pressed. My sight blackened into a night of swirling stars. I envisioned the martyr Marcellus, a Roman centurion tearing down his own battle standard and refusing to fight in a pagan army any longer, beheaded; Saint Conon's stake-pierced feet as he was forced to run before a chariot until his death; Saint Irenaeus' writing of my own Lyons' first forty martyrs, stretched apart on the rack, burned with hot plates in their privates, flayed to the organs with metal claws.

The truth…

What is truth? Pontius Pilate himself once asked.

"We buried the relics outside Pictauensis and told that story while we got food and rest. So no one would question why we were empty-handed. We never met any Northmen. Else I do not think we would have survived," I spat this out as Fulgaud crushed tighter on both jaw and throat.

Fulgaud laughed, his hand loosened, and my head fell free. I glanced to Egilolf, also twisted up by a guard, and he mouthed something I couldn't make—"FOOL!" Fulgaud's hand slammed back into my throat, not even bothering with chin and jaw. The guard twisted up on my arm even more, and my shoulder threatened to snap as my feet left the ground. "You told that self-made *rex* Ranulf your saint was taken by the Northmen in exchange for your lives, and you told Gonsindus she fought off their *daemon*. I told you

I stay alive by knowing things. The story of the *daemon* fight caused villages to flock to a procession with nightly miracles. If that much is true, then you met the Northmen. What did you leave them in exchange?"

Would he kill us if I told the truth? Was it better to hold Saint Philibert's secret? Is truth always right? Was I to be martyred for my faith or a complicit thief seeking to avoid my fate—God alone knew.

Habib the Deacon beheaded in Edessa;

Saint Vincent sunk in the sea;

Bishop Fructuosus and his two deacons bound in the fire like Shadrach, Meshach, and Abednego;

Bishop Ignatius of Antioch ground like Eucharistic wheat between the teeth of lions—

Christianus sum, but as one stillborn.

"A second saint," I gasped.

"No! You swore never to tell them of the cache!" Egilolf howled.

Fulgaud spun from me, and though I could breathe again, my mind swirled, wondering what Egilolf was talking about. "You betrayed us, Aristeus! That was to be our second share."

"What do you mean, thief?" Fulgaud questioned, hand poised over Egilolf in the same manner it had threatened me.

For my part, I would have fallen but for the guard still grabbing my wrists. My freed throat could not draw in enough air.

Egilolf was jerked higher onto his toes by his guard as the *comes* loomed. Puzzlingly, my comrade pressed his lips together, though that crushing hand moving to his throat opened his mouth again. "All right! No point to keep quiet now, curse this weak scribe."

Fulgaud withdrew his hand and motioned for the guard to lower Egilolf. He shot me another scathing glare and then glared defiantly at Fulgaud.

"We found another saint. Probably. Missing some parts. Lying in the same grave as Valerie. Not enough to bring to you, but maybe enough to sell to a *villa*. Or a byway priest. When the Northmen ran us down, we needed some reason why we dared their territory. We hid Valerie and most of the other bones but kept some. Didn't think they'd do much, but praise God they had power when that sorceress called upon the darkness of hell. The scribe said something about a second saint, or maybe Valerie's power transferred to someone else's bones. They did lie in her tomb with her for many centuries. Don't know why they worked. But they did." He shook his head, and still, Fulgaud's hand hovered inches from Egilolf's throat. "Northmen kept those bones because of their power. After we picked up Valerie and the rest again, we went to Pictauensis. Stashed the remaining bones along the *Vinhana*."

"Why not bring them back as well?" Fulgaud pressed.

"Weren't enough. Half a body to begin with, even before the Northmen took their share. We figured they've got some power, obviously, but you wanted a full saint. We left the extra fragments behind. Planned to return later to sell them. Then the abbot waylaid us on the road, that Ageric of his and some guards. Diverted Valerie into his own keeping. Now we've got nothing but those relics pieces."

Though his feet had been let back down to the ground, as had mine, Egilolf seemed to hang in balance, like an immutable statue. Fulgaud considered Egilolf with suspicion, then glanced around at his guards, calculating. I could almost see him weighing his unbelief against his soldiers' faith. As long as his people thought it real—

He strode back to me, eyes locking with mine. "You're a lettered scribe." It wasn't a question. "Perhaps you had time to read some other inscriptions on the tomb of this Saint Valerie, the name of her co-sleeper in death. Perhaps you've heard that name elsewhere in the histories, enough to piece together a *vita*." Still, no questions. I didn't know what he wanted me to say, other than he clearly didn't want me to disagree. He stared at me for several more seconds in silence, then strode back to his table at the front of the room.

"Sichar and my guards will take you to this cache, this temporary burial site, as it were, to recover these saint's bones. That will give you, scribe, time to contemplate and recall everything you've read in your *scriptorium* of this saint's life, death, burials, miracles, and so forth, and write it all down. You'll return the saint to me, and together with my chaplain, we will listen to who this saint was and decide whether he belongs in the altar of my chapel." To his captain, he added, "And stay afar of Pictauensis. I've had word this morning

Ranulf has died, possibly of poison. Ebalus has declared himself the new *dux et rex*. Against the younger Ranulf's claim. I will not get embroiled in that bastard's power grab until I see how strong the younger Ranulf is." He waved his hand dismissively.

The guards prodded us to the door, Captain Sichar following, when Fulgaud halted us: "Oh, and Sichar, if they can't find this cache, and have proven themselves liars, flay them. And then hang them. In a cage."

Fulgaud's hand about my throat or not, truth was elusive. Egilolf's ploy saved us for a few days longer, and at night on the road, I whispered vain hopes of escape and flight, surrounded though we were by mounted guards. Egilolf could have managed it alone, even with his healing eye, but my leg ached with any sustained pace.

Egilolf never once mentioned abandoning me, though, despite failing him at the abbot's office. Still, as we marched, he scanned the horizon wistfully.

But even if we had some other bones secreted away somewhere, anywhere, I could barely keep separate the overlapping stories to Fulgaud from the lies to Gonsindus, the truth to Father Leo from our claims in Pictauensis. Egilolf thought little of the option of praying for the appearance of a second body of Saint Valerie, or Philibert, even after my explanation that I had read of just such a miracle in a translatio *somewhere. His idea was to dig at a roadside chapel and hope to find some bones. Mine was to run off in the night. The only truth we knew was that we were grasping for wheat but clutching chaff. And that was even before the morass of Pictauensis sucked us in again.*

CHAPTER 13:
THE CORDS OF DEATH ENTANGLED MY SOUL

Captain Sichar was a blunt man. He told us he'd allow no more than a day along the Vinhana *for us to find our lost relics before he flayed and hanged us. I suspect he stopped short of denouncing us as liars only out of respect for his lord; he surely had the ropes measured and knots threaded already. But perhaps because he was just such an unimaginative workhorse, he put no question to us and left us to our own conversations while we traveled. Small comfort, that.*

"That guard again," Egilolf muttered. Once death passed over us on the first day along the road, our thoughts wandered to more mundane matters, mankind's constitution not suitable for contemplating death, no matter how impending, each hour. A rough half of Sichar's score of guards were mounted, while the poorer remainder shuffled along with us in the dust behind. Since mid-morning, a *colonus* trailed us with his handcart, its woven baskets bursting with first fruits for market minus a gift to Sichar exchanged for the escort's security.

Egilolf, periodically helping when my healing leg burned sore again, flicked his eyes towards the laden trudging fellow a few paces ahead on our left flank. As far as I could see, the guard's only distinguishing feature was his nervousness—he kept shifting his spear grip—but that was likely due to his young age.

"What of him?" I offered while attempting to remain in reveries of some happier time. Cordoba, perhaps, or illuminating my favorite copy of—

"It's that same blond youth. The one who seemed familiar when we first left Fulgaud's grasp."

I made to joke that his right eye was likely distorted, but I regarded the young warrior first. "Heyya, boy, what's your name? My companion ponders your semblance—" This time, I was cut off by Egilolf's sharp elbow to my ribs.

The youth turned all the same. The lack of weight behind his eyes matched his easy face and thin attempts at a beard; it was likely this summer only that he was cut loose from his mother's heartstrings.

That clear grace of youth lasted but a second, twisting to more scowl than sneer, the gruff tone obviously an effort. "What does it matter, to you or him? Two thieves out to find us treasure. Or else, more likely, a rope." To his mocking, he added disdain. "One a scout, no less. My father always named them cowards, too scared to march into the real fray. Leastwise, he did until—leave me be!" He added the energy of youth to his step and passed up his comrades on the pretense of offering water along the line.

"Touchy and haughty: the omens of youth, or nobility, right?" My smirk disappeared as I saw Egilolf. "What is with you? You are as white as, well, as I probably was with Fulgaud's fingers around my throat!" Egilolf stared after the young guard. "What is it? Who is he?"

"It can't be…" he rasped faintly, or perhaps I imagined it, for when I asked him again, he shook himself, denied anything wrong, and became petulant and distraught at my further questioning. I finally dropped the matter, though it tumbled in my mind.

None was not far off on the second day, by sun's gauge, when I took it upon myself to break Egilolf's silence. "I was most worried in Cordoba, you know, about being mixed up with the theft of a saint. I wondered if you were some grubber out for coins. Had you really some holy purpose in mind? I half-doubted you'd extricate yourself from the city alive with Saint Perfectus."

Egilolf gave me the slightest of glances.

I continued, "Oh, not from the Moors. I doubted they'd care two bits if you stole from Christians in their city. Nor were cathedral guards my worry. I have read of true saint thefts, when the saint did not want to leave and took his revenge: monks paralyzed until they repented, desiccated holy bodies suddenly leaving blood trails that led straight to the perpetrator, tumors of the brains or eyes. The archdeacon of Turin was struck stone dead for taking but the littlest joint of the Baptist's finger, and that just in the days of King Louis the Pious, not some long-ago story! I half-expected Perfectus himself to strike you down. That is why I agreed to await you outside the city."

Egilolf had no response, though whether it was his current indifference or dismay at my long-ago callousness, I couldn't scry.

"I had my doubts, too, when you disappeared into the sub-crypt at Saint Philibert's old church. I swore to myself I would not join you, but a Northman at the door quickly changed that priority!" I received the briefest smile and, uncertain whether I was cheering him or blathering to the air, fell silent again.

Ah-roo! Ah-roo, ah-roo! A horn, singing like a hunting horn but with a small grating buzz, called from the north. A horseman galloped at us from the tree line a few hundred paces from that direction, and he covered half that distance before I recognized him as one of Sichar's men, scouting ahead. Sichar raised a hand for the column to halt and rode his horse ahead, but the scout's report was panicked and loud when he reined in his horse: "A half-century of armed men march south. Sounded the war horn when they spotted me. Got but a glimpse, yet I'd swear it was Aquitania's colors."

Sichar twisted in the saddle to face us. "Little alarm then. Still, form ranks. As a precaution."

The mounted scout joined the rest of the horsemen to form a broad front that filled the road from ditch to ditch, two lines deep, and those on foot formed up similarly behind.

I strained to catch any sight of the company coming from the woods ahead, then noticed Egilolf eyeing the tree line closest at our right side. On our left and at our backs, only open meadow stretched over hills.

I felt I had time to chant any number of litanies, though it was probably only a few minutes until the other company emerged, the first horses quickly pulling into a line at the sight of Sichar's formation. They closed at a walk, their leader recognizable by his gray hair and unyielding mien as Garbart of Pictauensis.

"A battle of two captains," I murmured to Egilolf. "Perhaps they will do us the favor of killing each other, leaving us free to wander off."

"More like we'll be trampled in the fight. Or questioned after we're already run through."

"You're a hope-killer."

Garbart's crew stopped within ten paces. All the soldiers sought not to be the first to reach for any weapons, while still keeping hands near if needed. It made for an odd sort of dance, everyone's eyes locked hard on someone opposite, hands acting as if disembodied and of their own will, now flickering toward a hilt, now skirting away.

"Sichar. What are you doing out this way? We heard rumors of some force coming, seeking to support the rebel brother to our king."

Sichar laughed. Or grunted. "Which brother is the rebel? Which the king? We've heard a few rumors ourselves to that end." He waved his left hand dismissively as his right was coiled motionless like a snake near his sword grip.

"Don't play the fool. *Rex* Ebalus sent his messengers. They'll have reached your *comes*. I ask again—what are you doing out this way? And with such a force?"

Sichar's horse whickered, and its rider adopted a friendly, mocking tone. "This? This is hardly what I'd consider an invasion force, if that's what your lord fears. And we've heard only rumors of petty squabbles between Ranulf's son and the bastard. No, old man, you won't believe me when I tell you the truth. We're out relic-hunting, of all things. Or rather, putting these relic hunters to the lie before I flay and hang them."

Garbart sat up in surprise and stepped his horse to the side as he peered between Sichar's ranks. His eyebrows raised when he caught sight of us. "Well. I thought to call you a liar, but I know those two. Claimed all their relics were taken by the Northmen."

Sichar scowled, and I read our deaths in his eyes. Sometimes the future isn't all that hard to know.

"Still, *Rex* Ebalus and I have use for the scout. How about we escort you all back to Pictauensis and sort it out there? As guests, of course." His iron gaze, much less his hand going to his hilt, cut off any shred of question in his words.

"*Daemons* take you first," Sichar grated, his hand also going to his sword. Both captain's men followed, but no weapons were drawn. Yet.

"Prepare to run," Egilolf whispered.

I glanced at my leg.

"Be reasonable," Garbart countered. "We're double your strength. Give up your weapons, come drink with us for a few days.

Let our lords bicker it out."

Sichar didn't pause a second before replying. "I was hostage once. And swore never to be again. We'll ride out, and as you said, leave it to the lords." The new *rex*'s captain surveyed the Lemouicensis soldiers in front of him. Per Egilolf, he was likely assessing their desperation or resolve.

Garbart refocused on Sichar: "No. You'll put up your weapons and come with—"

Sichar didn't even voice a command. One second, Garbart was issuing his decree like an old Roman imperator, and the next, Sichar's sword was flickering toward his head. And then chaos descended, like a waterspout flinging at random the storm-wrecked contents of a Northmen's longship: men, blades, horse, blood, mud, curses, exclamations, cries for divine mercy.

Egilolf grabbed my arm and began dragging me east, but my eyes stayed fixed on the bloody lodestone of pandemonium. I tried to watch where I placed my feet as I hobbled. The peonies. Small wild roses. The tree line might as well have been the horizon. *A pealing clash of metal, and I'm glancing back over my shoulder, darting eyes hunting for the roaring, horned barbarian stalking me through flame and smoke, the church bell a polyphonic discord to axes pinging stone after sinking through flesh, the cloister now only so many pillars of fire by night. My leg on fire.* My leg!

"Aristeus!" Egilolf screamed at me, pulling at me.

He had likely slapped my face as it stung fiercely. But not as fiercely as my throbbing leg. We were only halfway across the meadow. "My leg!"

"Keep moving!" He ducked his head under my arm, and half carried me as we hobbled disjointedly toward the tree line.

Riders quickly overtook us. Side by side with Egilolf, I felt more than heard his sigh of resignation. He stopped dragging me and raised both hands, open and outward. Leaning on him to keep the weight off my sore leg, I followed his example. We faced a half-dozen ring of mounted men whose faces gave no indication of why they hadn't run us down. Riders and fugitives alike stared, caught breaths, and probably wondered as I: *did that just really happen?*

As tatters of Fulgaud's force fled back south, Garbart trotted his horse over to us, stone-faced, not even glancing at his sword as he wiped it clean. He nudged his horse through the circle of his men until he loomed over us. "Relic thieves." He spat. "A happy day running across you two again." He wasn't the least bit happy. "I'll be blunt. I don't care about your old bones. But you," he pointed to Egilolf, "are going to lead us to Thorfinn Eirikson's camp." He guided his horse westward and called over his shoulder, "Bring the scribe as surety."

And so that afternoon, we marched on, still on the same road, still heading toward Pictauensis, and still under guard, just under different captors. And perhaps without the immediate requirement to find additional relics, though with the added burden of burning pain in my leg.

As for the skirmish, six of Garbart's men were wounded, one killed. Sichar escaped with all but three of his men, one captured and two corpses tossed to the ditch. The captured one was the now not-so-haughty youth, his hands bound like ours. *You fool, this very night, your life is forfeit.*

The sun, the wind, and the rest of the world continued undisturbed, oblivious to us shuffling down the road as we were able. When evening fell, and the light streamed golden through bough and leaf, we passed by the ruined chapel where Rachel confronted me some odd lifetime ago. I counted back the days— only twelve? Where was she now? Running free across the forest, or starving to spare a meal for a bandit camp child? Watching us now from a tree bole? Wishing to rob the farmer, who was still following us, having had to offer an obligatory gift to Garbart, his new escort?

Near nightfall, my leg was so sore the soldiers untied me for balance, and when we made camp, they didn't bother to re-bind me. They had seen my attempt to run off once already. Our camp was a clearing amidst tree clumps, one low hill, and a thin valley east of the road. A simple place where I learned what my books could never teach.

In my past, when I copied martyr stories from every century of Rome, I imagined the glory of Christ's grace strengthening me beyond my human frailty, beyond my fear: Justin Martyr, both of his *Apologia* to Emperor Antoninus Pius unheeded, scourged by whips alongside his philosopher companions before beheading; Saint Pothinus, bishop of Lyons, immediate predecessor to my beloved Irenaeus, beaten by an enraged mob despite his nine decades of wisdom, dying of his wounds in jail two days later; in Alexandria, the young virgin Potamiaena coated with boiling pitch, from feet to head, who appeared after death in a dream to Basilides, the one guard who had been merciful to her, converting him and causing him to profess his faith and receive the Eucharist before he too was beheaded. In Pergamum, the city that once boasted the greatest library in the world, Saints Carpus and Papylus, after refusing to sacrifice to *daemons*, were scraped with claws, their skin at first flayed in neat parallels before the backstroke made the Greek *chi*, a repeated pattern of the great Cross marking at their sides, back, legs, stomach—before blood besmeared it all, and pieces of flesh began shredding off. Even more disturbing, the story of Saint Lawrence, deacon of Rome under bishop Xystus, roasted alive on a fixed spit during the second persecution of Emperor Valerian; fortified by Christ's grace, he felt no pain and directed the proconsul to flip the spit over, for he was half done, and to taste and compare his raw and roasted sides.

I had once daydreamed that the recollection of these stories would gird me in the needed hour with courage beyond even my father's expectations. But none of the stories prepared me for what I saw that night. The written word has little comparison to reality. Brutality in war, in contest, in the hunt, is of survival. Though the whole war, battle, or campaign be just or unjust, determined before or later by Saint Augustine's criteria, the fight, the struggle—that crucial minute, second, pause in time—is about only survival. But torture—torture has no necessity, no contest. Only the emotionless application of pain to a fellow son of God, as cold as an engorged moon clinging to the last still hours of a night's snow-bitter watch.

I'd rather not explain, but my story deserves it. No, demands it.

The dinner fire was barely begun when Garbart started in on the youth. He gave up his name at the second blow, his illusions of courage likely beaten senseless too. Ennodius. A few heated blades pressed to the arm, waived over the inside of his thighs, and the young warrior wept for the lie that was the glory of war. Saint Lawrence's martyrdom never mentioned the *smell* of burning flesh. Words can't convey it. The youth told everything he knew of Fulgaud's strength, positions, and intents, which, for a common soldier, was little more than I could deduce from my own brief visit with the *comes*. Yes, Fulgaud was rejecting Ebalus' claim for Pictauensis and all Aquitania, as *dux* or *rex*. No, he knew nothing of the location of the younger Ranulf. Yes, he had been on some sort of scouting mission, heading for the *Vinhana*, but east of Pictauensis. No, he didn't know why the two of us were along, but he knew us as prisoners and thieves. No, he didn't know of any other force out from Lemouicensis' garrison. No, he didn't know of any alliances with Rudolf of Burgundy! Nor *Rex* Odo of Paris! He didn't even know where Burgundy was! No, he didn't know! By God, and Saint Martial, and Saint Peter, and the Blessed Virgin herself, he didn't! Somewhere in the sobbing litany of saints, his screams became unintelligible, though I can still hear them clear in my head.

I was hobbling between the dinner stew pot and Egilolf, trying to categorize the effectiveness of various blockages of the ears, trying to shut out the sizzle of flesh between screams. I returned to my trussed-up companion. "I thought Fulgaud's tactics with me severe," I whispered to Egilolf. Any melancholic acceptance of our fate I felt I had embraced that afternoon showed itself as dross in the more imminent face of torture and death.

"I would kill him…" Egilolf whispered hoarsely, his eyes fixed across the fire on the very scene I averted.

"If you were but free and armed?"

"If my conscience could bear it."

"Why would a once-soldier—"

More than firelight writhed red in his eyes.

After a thin barley and onion soup, I was trussed up again and left with my companion. Like the dinner fire left to smolder out once its purpose was served, Ennodius' screams abated to a dull whimpering, and then he too was tied and dumped upon us. It was sadly difficult to attempt to comfort the suffering youth while shifting him off us, all while bound hand and foot. I am sure I wounded him further, but eventually, I was comfortable enough for fatigue to win out over misery.

I tried to sleep but kept waking from dreams of my father. As much as I tried to change my thoughts, to alter the dream in my half-waking state, I could not, and I tossed between cruel mocking dreams and the painful plight of reality. A sharp and sharper jab woke me fully. The stars had shifted more than my fatigue would indicate possible. Egilolf squirmed against my back in his sleep, and I endeavored to roll from my side without waking Ennodius, whose feet were propped over my ankles. My companion's hands, however, seemed entwined with the cords around my wrists, and his elbow was intent on cracking the ribs along my spine. I twisted harder.

"Lie still," Egilolf grated lowly. "I almost—"

Though my back was now aching from his elbow digging into it, I concentrated on feeling what he was doing. The elbow to my back was leverage, and the entwined fingers probed the knots at my wrists. I tried to spread my hands to give him room to work. "No. Together." His terse commands puzzled me, but when I clasped my hands tight to each other, I felt a slight give in the rope, and Egilolf's manipulations quickened. Soon my hands were free, and I returned the favor. He cupped a hand to my ear and whispered, "Thought they'd get lazy with your binding. I was right. Valerie may get us out of this mess yet. Work on your legs. I'll free the young guard."

Now free, I saw Ennodius again for what he was—not a fellow captive, but a once-captor, possibly the one that would have hanged us when we failed to locate another set of relics. The safe shadows of the tree line beckoned. My leg throbbed. I was in no condition to aid someone and had no obligation to help my former captor.

I shot Egilolf a glare, which he probably missed in the low light of coals and stars. I cupped my own hand to his ear. "We need to leave now! As much as I feel for his torture, I am not beholden to any who pledged loyalty to Fulgaud. We need to leave this whole mess behind, Saint Valerie or no. We cannot risk ourselves for someone that hours ago was our own captor."

Egilolf's struggle with Ennodius's knots continued.

"We will be lucky to escape ourselves; we cannot possibly with him."

Egilolf kept his hands busy on the ropes but whispered back, "He comes. I'll explain later."

Ennodius was by now conscious enough to realize we were helping, and he remained blessedly silent. Or perhaps his hours of crying had dried his mouth and swollen his tongue. Egilolf gave me directions to carry Ennodius toward a far copse of trees away from camp, indistinct at the edge of firelight, but I pointed to my leg. Hobbling there myself was about all I could bear. With an agitated sigh, he agreed with me.

Following the second plan, I half-dragged and crawled to the darkened rallying point on my own while Egilolf slunk away around the sleeping forms ringing the fire. The former scout's cautious pace was an art form, and I lost sight of him when he was but a handful of paces from Ennodius' unmoved body. If there was a watch, patrolling or posted, I couldn't see him.

Once at the copse, I waited for what my mind thought was half the night, though the stars chided a half-hour at best. I kept watching the fire and didn't hear Egilolf approach from behind until his hand slipped over my mouth to prevent my shouting my alarm. His mouth at my ear, he explained, "I'll drag Ennodius to you. Then we'll make for two horses I tied up. Directly south." He cut off my protest. "He comes."

I gazed upward and found the northern star for reference. We had come somewhat more south than east in our retreat from the camp thus far. At Egilolf's direction, I tried to rub life into my sore leg while invoking Saint Irenaeus's aid. The scout slipped again into shadow, and though he should have been silhouetted to me as he returned toward the fire, I could only fitfully follow him as he crawled between shadows cast by taller grass tufts. I strained against the dark, searching for the horses, and I confess I debated abandoning Egilolf and his Samaritan virtues.

I had lost sight of my companion for what seemed the other half of the night before I caught a shadow move. Egilolf, part dragging and part guiding his limp burden, was already most of the way back to my position.

A second movement flickered on the left edge of my vision, but when I turned to stare at it directly, I saw nothing. I turned back to where I had last seen Egilolf and again saw a peripheral shift. One of Garbart's men was slowly pacing his way around the fire, his gaze outward into the dark. He shouldn't have been able to see me behind my trees, but I froze anyway, not even daring to breathe. The guard kept to his deliberate encircling. He was headed toward Egilolf's path.

My God, shatter the teeth of my enemies! I prayed and then cursed Egilolf for his insistence on saving Fulgaud's soldier. We would all be caught.

I grabbed up the stoutest branch before me, the length and thickness of my forearm. I scanned south to the horses. *"Not a fighter,"* my father's voice mocked. Images of the past churned in my mind: running from my brother's fist, then from the smoke of my raided monastery. I thought of Saint Philibert's church and the flight from the Northmen, Egilolf encouraging me past what I thought were my limits. The dash through the streets and rooftops of Pictauensis, a broken leg, and Egilolf coming back to carry me to safety through the night.

The guard, still unaware, patrolled closer to my friend. I cocked my arm back. Should I throw it to strike the guard? Charge him? Toss it far off to distract him? Stay silent? Less than one in a hundred men of this land—farmer, mason, soldier, lord, smith, whatever the profession—had both the ability to read and the access to all forms of ancient knowledge I had once held in my hands. Even fewer had spent near a decade copying it. All that high, lofty knowledge of the world and the otherworld, and none of it worth straw in that minute. Would I help Egilolf or only hinder him? Was he lying in the grass, willing me to throw this knobby wooden shaft as distraction, or more strongly willing me not to move or do anything else foolish?

My indecision cast lots for me. I saw a second silhouette rise from behind the guard's. Egilolf's arm shot over the guard's shoulder and around his throat as another boxed his temple. Some twist of the legs caused both to crumple rather silently to the ground. I hobbled forward, still grasping my branch. The guard was grunting hard, his hands flailing between Egilolf's arm at his throat and his own sword belt. "Ennodius, run for the horses. South!" Egilolf managed to whisper between soft, deep gasps for air. I helped Ennodius rise and pointed him in the right direction. By some miracle, none of the soldiers had yet awoken.

"Strike! His head!" Egilolf gasped louder now. The guard was hoarsely wheezing himself. I swung my branch overhead, but the thrashing pair rolled unexpectedly, and I thumped the ground. Realizing a broad swing was as likely to strike Egilolf as the guard, I knelt over the fray and punched the butt-end of my makeshift stave down onto the side of the guard's skull.

It caved with a sick crackling, like dry bark crumpling inward on a soft-rotted tree core. *Brother Aethelmar's head had made a similar, though stronger sound, with an odd soft echo across the cloister, heard distinctly in some slice of otherwise silence, between the bell clangs and the sword clashes and fire-eaten beams squealing as they caved in when the Northmen's maul met Aethelmar's skull—*

"Again!" Egilolf demanded.

I began retching horribly.

Of course, we were captured. My hesitation allowed the commotion to continue until Garbart's cohort awoke to it. Egilolf flung his guard to the dirt, grabbed my still-purging form, and for the second time in a day, we, still broken, tried to flee an immediate pursuit. We made it but a few paces.

I think the only reason they didn't kill us outright was Garbart's demand to know what happened. We huddled back around the fire, brought back to a roaring blaze. The night watch, who his lamenting fellows named Rudericus, was laid out on a layer of bedrolls closest to the fire's warmth. He was muttering nonsense and couldn't be woken. My only relief was to see he still breathed.

Any gloating or anger I could have felt that Egilolf ignored my prediction about the waste of saving Ennodius was crushed under my frantic horror. That sick crackling…

Egilolf gave a plausible story that Ennodius had wormed loose, freed us, and brought down the now-poor form of Rudericus before slipping off into the night. Egilolf pointed out that only Ennodius' arms and head had been seared, and that unlike me, his legs were fully functioning, thus enabling him to escape ahead of us. I only half-heard this, and stared into the fire, willing myself not to weep at my failure of nerve or at the vision again and again in front of me of those panic-bulging eyes, the cudgel-branch burrowing into hair, then flesh, then bone...

I tried to pull myself from my own well of horror. Sitting on a log before us, Garbart pretended to consider Egilolf's tale. I say pretended because the man was far too shrewd to buy it. I believe he weighed the potential loss of one guard against the loss of a guide to the Northmen's camp and weighed whether the rest of his guard really believed Egilolf's story and would demand satisfaction. If they chose to kill us, would they crush our own skulls? Would I hear my own bones crackle, with the mush sound of—did I describe my mind as a well of horror? No, a well is deep, but still. Mine was the eddied cauldron below the cataracts, stirring captured muddy debris over and over, caught between thrashing river rapids.

Egilolf, too, must have gauged Garbart's silence, for he added, "The lords have many wants of us. I hold it against neither's guard. As proof, I'll guide you to a healer nearby. For your man Rudericus here."

"Who's that?" Garbart asked, curiosity and suspicion vying in his tone.

"Most around here have heard of him. Few know the path to his home. A *herburgium*. Goes by Old Master."

Garbart remained encamped until daylight, with both of us trussed up again with an extra measure of rope. I kept my back to Egilolf and would not face him, even when my arms went numb. As dawn broke beautiful to belie the evils of the night, we were led to a small brook and untied to drink and relieve ourselves.

I knelt in the dirt by the stream and cupped water into my mouth. In the rippled surface, Egilolf's head flickered. Seeking me. I kept my eyes on the water. Egilolf reached out a hand, and I shrank as though from a cuffing from my father.

Instead, he grabbed my chin, firmly but almost tenderly, and raised it. Where I expected disgust—or at least disappointment—there was only grave sorrow on his face. "Forgive me, friend."

My mouth opened in question.

"Forgive me that I asked you."

"You did not leave me behind in Pictauensis. It was right not to leave the youth," I conceded, though my throat felt as if I ate sand.

"No, not that. Forgive me that I asked you to kill someone when I would not."

Egilolf persuaded Garbart to only bring himself and two others to carry Rudericus. The remaining soldiers, anxious at the mention of a *herburgium*, clamored quickly to set up a camp near the *Vinhana* and avoid any contact with the spirit world. The two volunteers were likely the unconscious man's closest fellows, and hope vied against fear in all their words and expressions the farther we hiked. I went along so my leg could be re-examined. The twist of hills and hart paths we followed lost me and the litter carriers, but probably not Garbart. His reptilian gaze absorbed every detail.

Half a day later, we emerged from thick forest into the hidden glen. The Old Master was seated on a bowled log and was busy wrapping ligatures of rosewood bark to crosses cut of beech wood. He was soft-chanting a repeat phrase that sounded like a psalm, but I could not make out all the words. Some did not sound like Latin at all. Egilolf and Garbart approached him while I remained with the soldiers at forest's edge. Garbart had already stripped Rudericus of his boots and belt knife, and these, along with a small satchel of flour, were offered and bartered over. All this I heard through a murmuring at a distance.

Suddenly, the crazed healer sprang up and shouted, "Prepare! Prepare the way!" He strode long paces towards the door of his hut, ignoring all others, then, as unexpectedly, he raised a forbidding hand to the pursuing captain. "No! Not you. Away!"

Garbart paused with a rare expression of confusion.

The Old Master, meanwhile, strode on again to his door, announcing almost as an afterthought, "Bring the wounded man.

And the scribe. No other!" He ducked through the doorway. For better or worse, he had remembered me.

I stood over the same bed in which I was once treated, watching the steady breathing of the man whose head I had crushed. The old man tinkered in a corner, sorting through a box of leather-wrapped vials. To divert myself, I scanned the shelves of the opposite wall. Myrrh, incense, ambergris, rose petals, camphor, sandalwood leaves, aloe wood, musk, dragon's blood, mummy— "Mummy?"

"What?" The old man's head popped up from his digging and sorting. "Oh, that. Yes. Useful for stopping bleeding. Especially of the lungs, for a bloody cough. But expensive. Far too expensive for the likes of you."

"But where do you get it? You did not really dig up some corpse, did you?"

"Of course not. Not me. And not just any corpse. It comes from ancient tombs, when bodies are embalmed with the correct spices. It is a hot and dry confection of the second degree. And it can't be just any scraped remnants of a wrapped-up mummy. Most of the body is a whitish, opaque powder. Crumbles easily. Useless. No, the true mummy essence must be collected near the brain and spine. It's a black, thick substance. Awful smelling." He poked his head back into the corners of another box.

Was I intrigued or appalled? "How do you possibly know such a thing?" I caught my deprecation and added, "I mean, out here, so far from civilization."

He grabbed a bottle, popped the plug, and lightly waved it under his nose. "Ah!" he stood triumphantly. "You don't think I lived here my whole life, did you? Born out of the waterfall, clay and the blessing of some sprite? Heh. I studied in Rome once and passed a few years in Messina. Met with a few Moorish doctors, some Byzantine apothecaries. I learned the trade of noble medicine. All set up to live in the palace of Pictauensis, I was. Perhaps even at Aachen with the great kings." He crossed over to the soldier, knelt beside him, and drew out a small knife. "Hold his head while I cut back this mess of hair."

I knelt beside him and willed myself to lay hold of the man I nearly killed. May still have killed. I put my hands along each side of his jaw.

"No, no. Not like that. Get a good grip. Back of the head, around the other temple. If he wakes as I'm cutting, I don't want to lose my finger or slice off his ear. I'd have a time explaining that to his captain."

I did as he instructed.

The Old Master, after lightly probing the impacted area, began shaving Rudericus' scalp.

"So how was it you ended up here instead of Aachen?" I asked anything to take the conversation away from dismemberment.

"Too much *realgar*. In small doses, a wonderful syrup for diseases of the womb. I was very specific when I prescribed it to Ranulf's third cousin's daughter. Hardly my fault they ended up using two weeks' supply in as many days. Killed her, they did. Had to flee for my life." His fingers probed the wound gently. "Now I live out here, middle of nowhere, where no one's heard of the properties of mummy, much less can afford it." He sighed heavily. "And you? How did you end up here, not once but twice?"

Now there was a question with short and long answers. But if I thought back to first causes, the truth was: "Too much wandering, I suppose. My home was lost to Northmen a few years back, and I've drifted around since."

"Seeking to fill the hole in your story, hmm?" He shaved the hair very finely around the wound, then prodded it in a way that made my stomach curdle.

"In truth, that of my companion's." With the false safety of hut walls blocking out the threat of Garbart and his soldiers, my mind caught up to the questions developing in it. "A military scout reluctant to kill? Some imagined moral tie to a young, tortured soldier who was our captor hours before? I cannot make any sense of it. He is bound with a severe and unusual penance. We met a woman he refuses to mention but who hates him enough to kill him." I shook my head. "What are you doing for him?"

"This hapless fellow has the blessing of some saint, for sure. The tissue moves and grates a bit. The skull is cracked, but what few know is that the skull has two layers, and only the first is fractured. The inner layer is intact, so not all may be lost. But you must first understand the hole in your own story. A sick doctor heals no one. Your own mind's cracks are beyond my healing."

He pointed to various shelves. "Grab up that padding and that binding strap." He took the linen wad from me and produced the vial he had earlier scrounged. "The blood of Venus! You've heard of it?"

I shook my head. "The planet or the pagan goddess?"

"Neither. There are actually two varieties. The common, which is all I have available, is a boiled-out extract from an herb. It's root more specifically. Comes from beyond Persia by Saracen caravans to Byzantium. Or maybe to Tripoli and on to Palermo. I've read the more powerful, purer version, at a cost to ruin most small lords, requires a blending with the blood of a virgin when the moon is in Virgo and the sun in Pisces. But I don't believe much in the healing power of the stars. A lot of charlatan nonsense, from what I've seen." He poured about a spoonful onto the wad then held it to Rudericus' head. "Now, bind it with the strap. Tightly, so it won't come loose, but don't crush his skull further." I did as directed, and Rudericus began stirring and muttering again.

"Lastly, to remove any evil spirits that cloud his mind, we'll affix an amulet." He stirred through a wicker basket of undiscernible scraps. He held up for my examination a small clay disk, baked with a hole at the top, through which ran a thin leather thong. The thing was crude and clearly handmade, likely by the Old Master himself out of streambed clay. The Cross was furrowed into one side, and on the other was printed *Medica Christus Salvus*.

I raised a questioning eye.

"The healing of Christ saves. At least, that's what I meant." He shrugged and tied the thong into the strap over Rudericus' bandage. "My Latin's hazy, but this fellow's is less clear. Who will know better? Besides, it's the intent and the prayer bound with it, that'll heal him." He stood and crossed to the door. "Or not. As Christ wills it."

We spent the night in the Old Master's clearing, hobbled again and separated from each other. I dreamt of my home and the cellar nearby descending into the ground, my brother poised above that stale darkness, daring me to enter, taunting. He pushed me, and I tumbled down the rough cut slope, finding myself in a harsh crypt where crumbling dirt walls slid me toward a cracked sarcophagus, it's lid ajar. As I stood, I shrank, or else the sarcophagus grew, even as it sank into the earth and became a vast crater. The lid cracked in two and fell into the gaping maw of earth, and into it poured a libation of kings, and Northmen, and abbots. Last, most oddly, in toppled Rachel, weeping for the loss of me, weeping and refusing to be comforted.

CHAPTER 14:
HOW LONG SHALL HE PUT UP WITH US?

It would have been ironic if, upon our return to Pictauensis, it was a cloudless, sunny day heavy with the glory of mid-summer. My heart and mind, though, were in such turmoil that I cannot now recall much of those next days. Except our audience before Ebalus. As memorable as Fulgaud, that one.

The lure of eternal rest had crossed my mind on the road, but when we stepped back before the throne of the King of Aquitania, now occupied by *Rex* Ebalus, a dread of punishment accompanied by visions of Garbart's torture of Ennodius swam again in my mind. This late morning, though, our fate was apparently going to drag its feet, as the new ruler decreed other matters of justice first.

Egilolf and I stood tied at the back of the great hall under guard while Garbart, with a respectful nod to his lord, took his place next to the throne.

A rather haggard crone, not inclined to self-care, or more likely just dragged forth from some mudhole dungeon, hunched before Ebalus, who appeared deep in thought or just plain stumped. Her black, stringy hair clung to a covering of patchwork skins that seemed more shift than dress. It was her only garment and hung to her knees, leaving legs and feet bare. Lest anyone assume this a pleasant, enticing sight, I would note she was covered in mud, or grease, or worse, into which was stuck bits of twigs and leaves. She mimed the part of a storm-battered finch, exaggerated by her thin arms and knobby elbows protruding at awkward angles and twitching unexpectedly as she twisted her hands together before her.

The guard beside her held a spear against her ribs and a knuckle-white grip on the woman's arm, even while he awkwardly leaned his shoulders and head away, as though to distance himself from her as much as possible. Egilolf raised a meaningful eyebrow towards this, probably because neither of us seemed as feared as this wisp of a woman. Our own guard kept his weapons sheathed and slouched against a wooden pillar.

A smattering of merchant and warriors, *fideles* and adherents, hovered along the columns, caught between the safety of the peripheral shadows and the morbidly curious maelstrom swirling at the hall's center. The trial continued despite our interruption.

"My lord," the guard next to the bird-woman stammered, "we searched her hut, the marsh around, and even a small cave hollowed out nearby. We didn't find a sign of anyone but her and the…the…the child." His voice became hoarse. "If it was still a child…"

Ebalus stared at her, almost with fascination, though his hand inched closer to his own sword. "What do you say for yourself, woman?"

Before the avian woman could speak, however, the nervous guard jerked his spear point up to her throat. "What if she casts some hex? I've told her that if she opened her mouth, I'd cut her throat." The woman had not moved or even shied from the blade. Garbart's only response was to raise a clenched fist at the guard, and he, evidently more afraid of his captain than of malevolent forces, removed his hand, though he continued to cast quick, doubtful glances between her and the *rex*. A murmur of concern went up from the timid purveyors.

The king had to repeat his question.

The woman spoke with her head cast down. "As I told your soldiers, my lord, I sent the girl out early to bring in wood for the morning baking. I heard a rumble and ran out to find the woodpile toppled onto her. Her head must have been hit, for she would not wake. I brought her inside and then restacked all the wood."

"And then?"

"I don't know what you mean, my lord." She raised her face to her questioner.

"The rest of the day?"

"That was mostly all that happened. I…I went about my day, I suppose. Baking, tending the garden, mending my neighbors' clothes, as I do."

"And how was your daughter?"

"What?"

"I would assume you kept checking on her?"

"Oh, of course, my lord. I kept expecting her to wake, but instead, she began vomiting some hours later."

"Only vomiting?" Whatever Ebalus was, he seemed a shrewd man, his questions calculated.

The woman's gaze fell again toward her feet. "Between bouts of vomiting, her breath did start gasping, and her whole body would stiffen, right down to her fists, as though she were dreaming, a dream of fighting someone."

"And that was all? Anything else you did for her? Any other change in her?"

"No, my lord. I went to bed, woke in the morning, and found she had passed in the night."

The guard beside her interjected, disgust overpowering the fear in his voice. "That cannot be all! She didn't even tell her neighbors, and the body was tossed on the muck heap, covered in old straw."

A hard glance from Garbart silenced the soldier once more.

Behind Egilolf and I, our own guard had gone still, as a field mouse hopes to sham the falcon.

The new king continued. "What of this report from your neighbor that you were harsher to this dead child than the younger? That she was your husband's, but not yours?"

"My Chramsind is a good man! The girl was his daughter by his first marriage before his wife died in labor. Despite her faults, she was no bast—" She must have remembered who she was speaking to, for she cut herself off.

"But you struck her more often and cursed her for being lazy?" the king pressed.

"My own Mathilda has passed her second year and is already a sweet angel. But the girl had four years and was stubborn and unruly, despite my discipline. Once Chramsind left for the summer campaign, she grew even wilder."

The king had been leaning forward, as though it were him and the woman alone over the supper table. Now he sat back and looked to the rafters, as though Solomon's wisdom were writ on the roof beams. "Tell me again of the bite marks," Ebalus instructed the guard. "Omit no detail."

After a nervous swallow and a sidelong glance at the woman, the guard fixed his eyes on his lord. "I've never seen the like, my lord." His voice came out a whisper and tightened as he spoke. "We had her neighbor wash off the mucking mess and straw to prepare the child for burial, like any good soul would do…and we started seeing these marks. Up the arms, on the hands…one on the ankle…both cheeks. At first, I thought some animal had been at her, but the skin was not broke, only deep—deeply bruised." His voice seized completely, and he crossed himself. "But the bite mark was not complete, my lord. There were gaps in the arcs, with a lower canine missing and the opposite front tooth too. It wasn't until I asked her again why she would have tossed the body out on the dung heap, why she never called for any help, why she—I saw, my lord, I saw her missing teeth."

Murmurs rumored among the *fideles*, gasps that spoke of shock, and low gratings that spoke of dark and darker plans.

At least one in the crowd was bold enough to name what we all dreaded: *strix*.

"Woman, open your mouth," Ebalus ordered.

As though it would help, the woman curled inward and clamped her mouth shut, her jaw muscles taut with effort.

Ebalus pointed Garbart forward. "Pry it open, if need be, but don't injure her teeth."

The captain drew a dirk as he strode to her, and I expected him to threaten her with it. Instead, he grabbed her nose with his free hand. The woman twisted her head to break the grasp but could not.

"Hold her neck," he ordered the guard at her side. "Stiffly." He complied.

When her breath ran out, she opened her mouth to suck in a short breath, but Garbart was faster. In he thrust the dirk. I thought he meant to kill her, but he only pried it between her teeth. With a twist that angled the blade, her mouth went wide. "It's as your man says, Ebalus. She's missing her left upper front tooth." He withdrew the blade. "And her lower right canine."

The woman fell to her knees and started sobbing.

Now the crowd spoke it openly, harrowed with fear: "*Strix.*"

"A child-eater…"

Some gave the sign against evil, some the sign of the Cross. A few did both. Our guard took a half-step back, as if to avoid even the possibility of contact. The woman's guard had already retreated six paces.

A *strix* was a sorceress of the worst kind, powered by eating the very flesh of her victims. I had read about such in the penalties of the *Lex Karolinus*, but to come across one, to be in the same room as one—I'd rather have faced the sorceress Ingigird again. At least her *daemon* power seemed of the elemental world. The crowd's fears bred on themselves.

"Burn her."

"Send for the bishop."

Two or three of that war-bold crowd near trampled each other in their haste for the door. Ebalus, meanwhile, conferred with Garbart and motioned forward two others from his *fideles*. They huddled in discussion around his high seat. Everyone else held a collective breath as tight as the woman's a minute ago.

The *rex* was still in debate when the door to the great hall flung open. Past Egilolf's side strode Bishop Hecfroi, his crozier held in two hands across his body, the butt of it forward, like the Archangel preparing to spike the groveling Serpent. Two grim-faced clerics flanked him, one holding up the Cross as though a shield.

"I am innocent! I did nothing wrong! She just died. I did nothing." The woman beseeched the *episcopus*, like a killdeer faking its own wounding to distract would-be predators.

"Silence, woman," the bishop said. The clerics murmured a chant between them, taking up the guard's position at either side of her, the Cross aloft, unwavering. "My...king," the bishop addressed Ebalus as though the title stuck in his teeth, "I offer my counsel also, if you would consent to listen."

Ebalus gave a nod.

"I would not, my lord, risk her gaining death at this time."

The crowd murmured, echoing my own thoughts, surely. If this woman did not deserve death, who did?

The bishop ignored the crowd and explained, "Can you say what bargains she struck in exchange for the life of the young innocent? Perhaps this woman would only reappear as a haunting shade or malevolent evil on this land."

The *strix's* guard kept his spear point up, as though he were still guarding her from his retreated position, halfway across the hall.

"You propose?" questioned Ebalus.

"Give her to my guard and priests. I will see her escorted to the convent at Tors, where she'll be held and exorcised. They have practice in this form of redemption. The evil in this woman is not her own but of some *daemon* working through her. Perhaps the soul of this once-daughter of God may yet be spared. But send this evil out of your lands, to never return in this life or the next."

The king discussed this among his companions, as did the knots of whisperers. After some minutes, Ebalus nodded sharply to the bishop. "Good riddance."

The *strix* began to shriek, a piercing cry that plunged into gibbering phrases, amidst which I only heard her pleading for her other daughter.

Ignoring her, Ebalus continued, "Give the remaining child to the care of whoever will have her until her father comes home. And, bishop, please be so good as to see to the cleansing and burial of the other, and the exorcising of the house and all those she touched."

Hecfroi inclined his head to the king, then directed his own priests. "Bind and gag her, but do not otherwise injure her," he commanded, re-gripping his crozier. His two clerics, with the reluctant aid of the guard, proceeded to do so. "Keep her watched in a cell until my return."

Her hands were tied with a leather thong, her elbows protruding oddly, and once more, she was little more than a pitiable wretch. Only after she was dragged off, her muffled cry disappearing into the wide world, did everyone in the room relax.

"As for these two, your Highness—" the bishop dipped his staff in our direction.

Ebalus held up his hand to pause Hecfroi and held a whispered discussion with Garbart, presumably for the latter's report. "What's your interest in them, bishop?" Ebalus asked.

"Besides my concern for the peril of their souls, having taken in the hospitality of the church and abbey before slipping off in the night like thieves when they were last here, they are linked, I'm told, to the problem in Lemouicensis."

"The reports that Fulgaud throws support to my brother?"

"No, sire, the problem of Fulgaud and the abbey of Saint Martial. I hear the *comes* is besieging the abbey in his own town over relics these two men delivered to the abbey instead of to him."

Ebalus blew a thin stream of air from his lips and waved a deflecting hand.

I snuck a glance at Egilolf, but he too seemed at a loss for how best to escape this snare.

"Garbart and I have already discussed the options for the kingdom. Only two matters concern me: the support of the lords for me over my renegade brother and the security of the kingdom of Aquitania. I don't care what these two did with some bones they dug up. But that scout's knowledge of the Northmen"—he pointed at Egilolf—"that I do care about."

"Your Highness," Hecfroi gritted, both desperate and angry, "where the relics of a newly recovered saint lie will matter greatly for the future of Lim—"

"I said I don't care!" interrupted Ebalus, rising from his chair to tower over the bishop. "I've long wanted to throw back the Northmen incursions on the coast but thought I'd need all the lords' fealty and support first. But now I have the means to strike the Northmen by surprise with a smaller, accurate force, rather than thrash around blindly with a force large enough to scare them up from the brush. Once we beat down that threat, the other lords of Aquitania will recognize what their eyes should long have told them: I am the stronger of their two potential rulers. Only I can bring them peace. Against Northmen, Moors, or Rudolf of Burgundy, or *anyone* who would threaten my kingdom!" He stared straight at Hecfroi.

The bishop managed a respectful nod without bowing. "Very well, your Highness," he said, in conciliation, "but forget not the needs and aid of the Church in your stratagems. If you are going to resume your late father's plans for the Northmen, I would remind you these two relayed how the barbarians had kept relics of some saint and sought religious instruction. I will need to question them shortly about these two separate sets of relics and why they kept quiet about the one, but imagine, my lord, baptizing these heathens! If you were to subdue this threat by enfolding them into the kingdom of God, imagine how your name would read in the annals of Aquitania for such a glorious and holy feat!"

Ebalus wasn't impressed. "Keep your ideas of heavenly glory, Hecfroi. But I'll agree to this much—you give me two score of your guard, and I'll let you convert any survivors."

Garbart smirked at the mention of survivors.

For the first time since our entrance, someone addressed us. "What have you to say, scout?" The new *rex* offered an open hand. "It seems you and your companion have cost me a man, but I'll spare your life for your service on this raid."

Egilolf stood erect, as a soldier braces, and met the *rex*'s gaze. "Northmen spared my life. They could have killed me or sold me off. Would be dishonorable to repay them with betrayal."

The *rex* wasn't the least bit upset by this. He nodded toward his captain, and Garbart simply drew his sword, approached me, and began pressing his blade into my neck. Fortunately for me, Egilolf immediately deflated and spat out, "Fine." The *rex* nodded, and our fate, it seemed, was decided for us once again.

Damnable planets.

The bishop's quarters off the cathedral of Pictauensis were a pleasantly kept place, with finer furnishings and wine than Abbot Gonsindus's room at Saint Martial's. Or so I assume about the wine; the room we saw briefly as we met with Bishop Hecfroi, explaining to him the bones we gave to the Northmen had been found in the crypt next to Saint Valerie's remains. I relayed how we had just doubled the use of her name when the Northmen took them from us. Another fractured truth.

Satisfied, the bishop sent us off to a cell for the afternoon and night, sufficiently guarded by one of Ebalus' men, without even a pallet. I spent the afternoon trying to recall which story we had told to whom about which bones—and with which name. Egilolf sat morosely before the window, unresponsive to my few questions.

Dinner in the refectory provided a surprise and not in the soup of barley and pork cuts. "The Return of the Relic Hunters!" a cheery voice announced to a tune. I glanced up from our corner table, where our guard kept an easier eye on us. Wending through tables and servers was none other than Rodegar, harp case slung across his back and sword still at his side. "What an epic title," he continued as he reached our table and clapped us on our backs. "Now you need to supply the story that goes with it."

My spirits rose to see the jovial bard again, and Egilolf's face, too, opened with the first broad smile I had seen in days.

Between bites, I relayed our travel to Lemouicensis, the relic processions, and how we ended up torn between Father Leo, the abbot, and the *comes*. I had planned to only recount the somewhat salvific capture by Garbart's men on our way to finding new relics, but somehow over the second half of my bowl, in the presence of a trusted, listening person, and against the backdrop hum and clatter of others at dinner, I found myself spilling out details of the horrible escape, of nearly killing the guard Rudericus (I found I could not think of him without recalling his name), and our attempts to heal him at the *herburgium's* glen.

"Then, to top that, we watched the questioning and sentence of a *strix* in Ebalus' court today. In a bizarre turn, the bishop showed up and hauled her off to a convent at Tors."

"Likely to spare her from death," Egilolf pointed out.

Rodegar replied, "Yes, I've heard of him having similar sympathies before. He gave a sermon once that anyone so potent in powers dark must have been lured into possession, and any faults are less the person's and more those of the evil entwined in her soul. He'd rather return the soul to salvation, if possible."

"All the same," I rejoined between spoonfuls, "the *Lex Salica Karolina* specifically penalizes with death those that carry copper pots for the brewing of malefic potions. I would say the demarcation seems rather blurred for one such as the Old Master."

"Bite your cheek," Egilolf commanded. "You want Rudericus to live, don't you?"

"Of course! I'm just saying that given the poultices and incantations, should one of his charges die under his care, what prevents that man's relative from claiming the old man one of the *malefici?*"

"Ah, but is it the actions that are evil, or the intent, or must it be both to be sin?" countered Rodegar. He was smiling and seemed rather off-hand about the whole topic.

Egilolf was in earnest. "Here's a question: can harming someone be needful but still a sin?" He stabbed at a pork bite floating in his bowl. "What of killing someone?" He paused for a long drink and stared at the fire. Rodegar and I waited to the point I wanted another bite or sip myself, but I dared not disrupt this infrequent divulgence by one so secretive. Finally, he continued, "When is *needed* truly needed? Not convenient, or easy, but the only choice? Who decides? Was there no other way?" He caught himself out of his reverie and cut a thin smile. "Like this matter of the Northmen camp…" I was certain he had been about to speak of something else. He gazed into the fire.

Rodegar appeared puzzled by Egilolf's last statement, so I clarified. "*Rex* Ebalus means to use Egilolf as guide to go crush the Northmen camp where you found us. For my part, I hope he succeeds." I thought again of my abbey burning, my brothers slaughtered. "May he shatter them in the day of his wrath."

Egilolf spun from the fire, and his eyes bore into me. His tone was sharp and sharper. "Who will do the killing, Aristeus? You?" He slew each word he spoke. "It's all well to let someone else kill, very well to think of the enemy as evil, some monster against decent men and without salvation! But give them a face, or worse, a name. Or a child."

At nearby tables, eyes watched us. Whether Egilolf noticed or not, I don't know, but he quieted before continuing. "I heard a priest say Satan used to be the chief angel Lucifer before he fell from heaven like lightning for his pride. We talk of Saint Michael the Archangel as chief over the heavenly army. That means Michael was at first the right hand of Lucifer. The two together led the legions."

He trailed off and faced the hearth fire again, but his mouth was set and kept twitching. He raised his cup twice but set it down again without drinking. At last, still staring into the fireplace, he sang a melancholic tune:

"Did you weep at the loss of Lucifer?
Did you cry as you pierced his side?
He had betrayed the King, and he deserved to die,
But did you whisper, to your brother, 'goodbye'?

Did you reel at the order in disbelief?
Wonder as you gird your sword?
Did you pause as you led forth the host of heaven,
And pity the waste of the Fall?"

He said no more the rest of the night. I kept his solitude for my own, and at some point, Rodegar left us for a merrier crowd.

The longer I stared into the flames, the more the flickering shadows cast on the firebrick became the snakes of darkness, suspended over the lake of bubbling, fiery mire which Saint Peter foresaw in his Apocalypse: the eternal judgment for murderers. Fitfully between the snap of flames shimmered the face of Rudericus.

I first considered the above to encompass all the pertinent events for Pictauensis, but as I began scribing the next chapter, I concluded that despite the personal nature of the following passages, I could not explain my subsequent aberrant actions at the Northmen's camp without retreating a step or two and adding this peripheral note.

"The adventurous scribe persists, I see," a feminine voice purred behind me. Wonder smote with the scent of laurel, and before I could rise, a small hand used my shoulder as a crutch. Rachel lowered herself to sit by my side on an impromptu root seat along the boot-churned trail. After a few days' preparation, Ebalus' warband had set out and was a morning's march west of Pictauensis. Though Egilolf was under close watch, I was left free to set my own more moderate pace-and-rest stops.

"Where? How? I thought—" This bandit woman had a way of stealing coherency from me. I unstopped my water bladder to cover my clumsiness but managed to drop the cork into the dust. In my haste to recover it, I dropped the bladder. She laughed, and I almost dropped it all again to hear her continue.

"The new *rex* is raising armies, just as your scout-friend said. Peter's band joined up for what they call honest work." She took the water from me and drank deeply. My eyes were drawn to her lips. There was something enticing in how she pressed the water bag to them. "And where does that leave me? A camp follower, for now, I suppose. Heading as far as the supply camp at Thoucars."

"Oh?" I couldn't see her as a washerwoman.

My tone must have conveyed as much, for her eyes flashed, a spear-fork of lightning. "Don't think that leaves me as some weakling to take advantage of, monk." A short dirk glinted in her hand from nowhere and disappeared as quickly. "I thought to keep up Peter's exploits, lead a small band of the women myself while the men returned to playing war." She sighed. "The other camp women only laughed and followed their husbands."

"So why do you follow the warband? Why do you not settle down somewhere? Find...something else to do," I finished lamely, uncertain what else she could do.

"That simple, is it? If so, why haven't you settled back down somewhere, found 'something else' to do? At least you can read and write. You could join any monastery. Why you haven't remains the mystery."

I opened my mouth to say what I'm not sure, but she pressed on.

"You've never thought of it, have you? The options open to a widow? Peter took pity and bullied his band into taking me in for the sake of my children."

Now I did interject: "You have children?"

She shut her eyes, hard and harder. "Had. Lost them both to Saint Anthony's fire. I stayed with Peter because the group was willing to keep me, and there were other children to worry about feeding."

"Saint Anthony's fire? My God, I am sorry." That disease was of both body and mind, producing excessive heat in the flesh before corruption and nightmare visions amidst great pain. I had seen no catalog of worst ways to die, but it must have ranked near the top.

She stood quickly and fled behind wagons as they creaked along the road ruts.

Not knowing what to say, I followed her nonetheless and caught up to her. She pulled up her hood though the late morning sun was hot. "So you stayed for the sake of the other children then? But now, I assume, they are following with the camp...and you..."

Beside me trekked a woman who served children but was denied them. Following the opposite road from us wept another woman, bound for a convent, who had sacrificed a child from her own selfishness. To say all creation groans with the pain of evil was one of Saint Paul's vastest understatements.

Rachel didn't reply for a hundred paces, and I pretended not to notice as she dried her eyes. "I'll linger on, I suppose. Sell Saint Vincentius' grave dust bit by bit, if I can. But it'd be a strange *villa* willing to take in an unknown woman. And I'm sure even a recluse monk like you knows what assumptions go with a solitary woman in town." Her expression turned grim. "At least one without children or not old enough to be a grandmother."

Harlot. Witch. A refuse heap for others' fears. Nothing I wanted to voice.

Trying to find the right words was harder than scrying the heavens. Neither were subjects taught at my old monastery. I tried to imagine Brother Angius expounding on *Three Theorems for Discourse with the Other Sex*—

"What's so funny?" she accused, suspicion in her eyes despite her tears.

"I—I, I do not know what to say, and the thought came unbidden that if I had only had lessons on how to speak to a woman…" I could see she didn't follow my humor. "Never mind. I suppose a convent is out of the question?"

She glared but then sighed. "I've been trying to come up with anything else, but that may be my lot. Not everyone runs to a life of singing and quiet contemplation." A few more hundred paces of mind-scrambling silence when she continued, "You didn't answer me earlier. Why haven't you found another monastery?"

"I—I don't want to." Would I ever be able to form a full thought around this woman without sounding the idiot?

"Sure, you'd rather troop up roads and down, torn between Northmen and lords and abbots. As if I believe that!"

"I have my reasons!" I grated. She seemed taken aback, and I realized I had shouted at her. I dropped my tone and feigned apathy. "Just drop the matter, I ask you."

We shared a small lunch together, and by the mundane exchanges of food, water, and petty insights about a cluster of wrens flitting about for crumbs, we managed to reach a semblance of normalcy, each the wiser perhaps on what wounds not to probe.

"I've seen the bishop himself has joined this army," Rachel commented. "Are the rumors true that he doesn't come to bless the warriors but to convert the Northmen?" We had started out the afternoon's journey, and from a rise in the road, I could see the uplifted cross close to the front of the column.

"He and Ebalus are at odds over a suitable disposition for the

Northmen," I explained, recounting the exchanges in Ebalus' hall. "I think it a fool's path. That barbaric race will never convert. Their gods and sorcerers, their whole way of life is naught but of plundering and death." I all but spat out this last bit and cut myself short. I glanced away and pretended to study the sun trying to stream through the upper branches, struggling to reach the forest floor.

"That's not true at all," Rachel protested. "Haven't *you*, of all people, heard of Anskar, the first missionary to the far North?"

"What do you mean, me 'of all people?'"

"You know everything. Or think you do," she laughed.

"He was the first bishop there too. Archbishop," I corrected myself. "His *vita* was authored by his successor, Rimbert, and it was around the second decade of this century—" Her jab to my ribs abruptly stopped me.

"Someday, I may want you to teach me, but not today." She smirked. "My point is his mission was successful."

Now it was my turn to laugh. "What success? They tried to kill him. More than tried for his fellow priest."

"Aren't you the one always spouting about the glory of the martyrs? That's what Egilolf says."

I grabbed her arm and pulled her aside as carts of supplies continued to roll past. "I have seen violent death staring me down!" I hissed, pulling her face close to mine. "Anyone that readily welcomes it is—is a maniac!" I let go of her and pushed her back by the arm, moving to step past her and back on the road.

Instead, she blocked me and pulled me close. "So have many. Faced their own death, I mean. You think it makes you different? You think it excuses you? Some of the Northmen converted. Why should these not be different?"

"What do you care!" I barely kept myself from shouting in her face. "A few years ago, their fleet sailed upriver to Paris, burning and plundering as they went, taking slaves and silver. Why should these barbarians not be different?" Now I did push past her, then stopped and spun back. "And why do you care so much whether some Northmen live or die?"

The carts now were strung out along the roadway. We had lagged to the last stragglers before the rearguard. I hurried to catch up to the one ahead, but she matched my pace. "Why do you hate them so?" If she had still been angry, I may have been able to keep moving and leave her behind. Instead, her soft question snared me.

I tried to remain calm. I really did. I stormed back to her yet again, but once I spoke the first word, the rest poured forth, like a breached dike. "They're barbarians. Ignorant. Unthinking! You can't expect Hecfroi to sit down for a theological debate with a man who calls himself Skull-Crusher! Justin Martyr doesn't get to have a *Dialogue with Trypho the Barbaric Northman!*"

"What?" she puzzled.

"The *Dialogue with Trypho the Jew.* Second century, Roman philosopher and a Jew named Trypho." I bit each word. "They have this quite civilized exchange about—"

"Don't think you're superior to me because you can quote some old book." She glared. "There's always been fighting, and somewhere, there always will be, whether it's some Emperor Charles, or his second nephew Charles, or this kinglet in Lombard, or the Moors, or in my home, to the east, to the north. My father died in wars. I assume. They sent him off with the army to Lotharingia, and he never came back. My mother never heard from him again. Two of my brothers are gone, too. And now, likely Peter. And Egilolf. And—and you." She was trying to keep back tears. "And then what becomes of the rest of us? What becomes of the children? What of the Northmen children?"

Her torrent continued as mine had. "What if these Northmen would convert, become allies in time, and secure the western coast? Why fight if there's another way? If we can't see that, how are we different from the barbarians?" She wrung her hands fiercely around the end of her braid, her eyes now defiant, daring me to challenge her yet again.

I didn't know what to say and was still considering all she said. When I didn't respond right away, she threw up her hands and yelled, "God take you all!" She stomped off toward the carts, and this time didn't come back.

I stood there dumbstruck, watching her go down the road. Peter stepped from the brush behind me. "Said she had a fiery spirit."

"I was thinking good riddance myself," I agreed.

"Oh, sure," he snorted. "That's why you're staring after her so hard." He grabbed my shoulder and guided me back into the stragglers shambling along behind a lamed ox.

At camp that evening, I kept an eye out for Rachel—just so she didn't release another volley about peace with the Northmen—but I didn't see her again the rest of the campaign.

We waited two days in Pictauensis as Garbart completed his preparations, and all the while Egilolf was kept under close watch. He spent the hours praying or sighing, refusing to speak of the contentions of his spirit. Even setting out on the trail failed to burnish his mood. A spark of his usual self returned when he grumbled on the third day how much more slowly an army moved than even a hay wagon, but the eight days toward the coast were largely unbearable. We dropped the wagon train and followers at Thoucars, and the army continued at a quicker pace towards the marsh plains.

On the third day out from the supply camp at Thoucars, Garbart had Egilolf and I draw out separate maps of the area around the Northmen's camp. Egilolf's was formed in dirt, complete with hills, rivers, streams, and pathways he recalled. Mine was quill to parchment, scraped down from a Psalter, the darkened neumes hardest to scrape clean and left like pox-marks across the land I drew. A palimpsest of the land, as it were. Much like war. Though I could recall little compared to the intricate replica Egilolf molded, apparently mine matched his well enough that Garbart knew Egilolf not to be lying.

Ebalus called a council of war as evening closed to *vespers*, though we had left any hint of bells far behind. He gathered his men around Egilolf's earthen map. Why Egilolf and I were demanded, I was not initially sure. Regardless of what he named this meeting, the *rex* asked little counsel of his *fideles*, instead rapidly directing leaders of a raiding party, a main line, a reserve with the extra supplies. Positions, movements, signals. Commands and rally points. I'm sure it made more sense to the soldiers.

"And lastly…" the new *rex* concluded, motioning toward Garbart. That iron presence stepped forward.

"All that's for the main battle on the morning after tomorrow," he addressed the warband leaders. "But in the night, we shall ensure these marauders cannot retreat to return another day. I will lead a raid to hole their ships. I have my own selected men, and with us will go our scout Egilolf, who has been to this camp before and who drew out this map you see before you."

Egilolf's grimace said this was news also to him.

Garbart's eyes fixed on my companion. "His scribe friend comes too. As surety for the scout's performance. That's all. Rest up tomorrow and sharpen your blades." Garbart stepped back.

My mouth opened and closed as uselessly as the doubting Zechariah's must have.

Egilolf dragged me from the council and off to our pallets, my thoughts a churning swirl. "No use in protesting," Egilolf muttered. "If God or Philibert or anyone wanted a different result, they've sure not shown it." His words were resigned, but his tone belied this. "We're pushed here by fate, Aristeus. Fate, or God's will, or what have you. We fought it. Tried to do what we thought right. But in the end, what difference has it made?" He hunched his shoulders as though shifting a heavy pack. "Our course is as fixed as the stars'."

I tried to sleep. I had come upon an ancient scribbling once, more wandering thoughts than true poem, which mirrored my thoughts on God setting us to a task only to withdraw the aid needed to accomplish it.

With wife and child, encumbered fugitive
He crosses moon-cold wastes
Flee to Egypt?
An angel said so.
But my son is The Lord Saves!
An angel said so.

Joshua,
Seven times round, and solid walls crumble
Leads the people to Paradise.
But we must flee; abandoned?

You have the power to warn us, but still we flee?

Where is the salvation, the Promise?
God, are you With Us?

Full of grace, and nothing is impossible…
Words I cry to remember
A ninth-month journey, a cave, some straw
A light for revelation to the Gentiles,
And glory to your people Israel.
But a sword will pierce your own soul too
'Dear woman, here is your son.'
But I want my *own* son.

Did Job's wife have it right?
I am the handmaid of the Lord.
May it be done to me…

Did I even want to fight this fate or destiny or will placed upon us? Certainly, I wanted to be far from the fighting proper. I was neither scout nor raider. But I wanted to be close enough to watch the destruction of those accursed barbarians. *Rachel just doesn't know,* I thought, images of burning walls and blood-warmed swords flashing again to mind. And yet, a skull caving like a rotted tree, and curious children mingling around the posts Egilolf and I were lashed to in the Northmen's camp and Hecfroi's dreams of converting new Christians and raising churches.

"*And who will do the killing, Aristeus? You?*"

As I lay on my back as the dark night went silent, positioned as if for my eternal repose, the immutable stars arced overhead and…what? What was it those stars did? Affixed the future? Described it? Left it unchangeable? Watched our sad hopes with mocking? The moon had not yet risen, leaving a brilliant, unanswering astral graveyard overhead.

The whole army was allowed to sleep late the following morning, but I was still up with the sun. Egilolf was already baking bread. I mumbled my thanks when he offered me a small loaf. I sat beside him, and we silently watched the small cook fire consume its thin branches. My first bite was sour, bringing a sad smile to my face. Acorn bread. I ate it gladly and thought of what memory dissembled to be a simpler time, somewhere in this same stretch of lands abandoned to ravaging Northmen. Neither of us had anything to say.

Around *none*, Ebalus gathered the soldiers and addressed them from the height of a cart. His mail armor held off-colored links indicating repair, and the shield resting against his leg showed notches and a gouge. The only sign this was their king, and not another veteran soldier, was a thin, gold band added to his helmet. The *rex* gave a rousing speech about not driving the Northmen back to the sea but slaughtering everyone and reclaiming all of Aquitania. He hefted his spear as if he would lead the charge himself. Perhaps he would.

When finished, Ebalus called on Bishop Hecfroi to provide a blessing. The bishop clambered onto the cart beside Ebalus and held his crosier aloft:

"To you, O Lord, I lift up my soul;
in you, I trust, O my God.
Do not let me be put to shame,
nor let my enemies triumph over me…"

The Twenty-Fifth Psalm. An interesting choice, not just a battle-cry plea. I watched for the *rex's* response.

"No one whose hope is in you will ever be put to shame,
but they will be put to shame who are treacherous without excuse."

Yes, there was the king's raised eyebrow and a glance of doubt. As the Psalm continued, the bishop recited from memory the words of King David, the warrior zealous for God but too blood-stained to raise a temple. "Remember not the sins of my youth…he instructs sinners in his way; he guides the humble in what is right…forgive my iniquity, for it is great…the Lord confides in those who fear him…" The present king seemed apoplectic about these less-than-martial phrases, and mollified only somewhat as Hecfroi concluded:

"See how my enemies have increased and how fiercely they hate me!
Guard my life and rescue me; let me not be put to shame,
for I take refuge in you.
May integrity and uprightness protect me,
because my hope is in you.

Redeem Israel, O God, from all their troubles!"

Hecfroi led the Amen and the *Deo Gratia* before addressing the crowd: "God is ready to lend aid in the defense of our land, but if after the Psalm today anyone knows his need to examine his conscience"—here the bishop scanned the crowd but ignored the *rex*—"then let him seek out any of the priests scattered around the periphery to hear your confession. May God's mercy be upon us all."

As night fell, Garbart gathered his score of hand-picked men, assigned one of them to guard over me at the rear of the column, and set off with Egilolf at the head. Mail was left behind, and all wore dark clothes. Shields and spear also were left, with only the short *seax* sword bound at the hip. We headed southwest and, by Egilolf's estimate, were but a few leagues from the Northmen's camp. He thought we would likely reach it sometime before *lauds*, with a few hours of darkness to spare.

As Egilolf had explained, Thorfinn's camp lay almost due south of Saint Philibert's church at Dee, on the north side of a small river, where it bent its southern course westward. This offered the river as protection to the camp from both the south and east. From the war council, I had a vague idea Ebalus was bringing the main army around from the north to pin the Northmen against the corner of the river. Typically, the Northmen would flee by ship if so pinched, hence our raid to cut off retreat. Garbart's men carried coracles slung between each pair, though the small boats measured large enough for one man only. The plan was to float across the river by night, the barely-waxing moon allowing such stealth. We would hole as many ships as possible before floating downstream and rejoining the army from the west. It seemed a foolproof plan to me until Egilolf grumbled about plans never surviving an hour past war council.

It was obvious on our trek I was the only one unaccustomed to stumbling about in the woods at night; obvious because I *was* the only one stumbling. All others managed somehow to glide like shadows, each reaching out to touch the shoulder of his comrade every ten paces, the whole column stopping to find stragglers if this contact wasn't maintained. Even re-writing the same line repeatedly does not make a night stretch to eternity as readily as this slow trekking method.

At least the land was relatively flat. Dawn was not even hinting when we, at last, reached a river. Egilolf had spoken before about deliberately offsetting the destination, in this case about planning to arrive north of the camp, so that once the river was reached, we knew for sure to follow it south and not wonder in which direction the Northmen's camp lay. I hoped and prayed, though truthfully as one tossed by wind on sea waves, to not have to cross the river with the raiders. I wasn't, therefore, terribly surprised when my weak faith allowed them to force me to a coracle alongside a taciturn shadow, who only whispered, "A whimper and I'll cut your throat."

What did shock me was that no one got into the small boats, but rather the pairs going out swam alongside, holding the coracle between them for buoyancy. Though my father never mocked me for it, I was not much a better swimmer than runner.

The wind brushed lightly, so the only waves came from my frantic paddling, but I still silently cried for Jesus to save me. Such is the way of my little faith. Until that moment, I had never really appreciated the strength of the Apostle Peter's faith when he stepped out onto heaving waters. My whole body shook, and not from the river. I would have prayed aloud, but the warning of the soldier floating on the other side of the coracle was ever-present amongst my eddying fears.

Perhaps He had not fully abandoned us, for after dark, eternal minutes, I at last touched the sandy streambed on the far shore, and felt my guard must have reached the same, for he angled the raft to float down the west bank of the river.

As I said, for late summer, the water was not cold, but our efforts to maintain silence hindered our pace. I estimated an hour passed before the silhouettes of squared edges stood out in contrast to the hints of low tree branches. Long ships. Their unique design had enabled the forefathers of these raiders to begin their encroachment on Francia when Charles Martel was still but a palace steward under the last, weak Merovingian king. The thought of sinking this fleet was rather...satisfying.

The tall peak of Thorfinn's hall was clear against the starlight, and the glow of a few banked fires gave a sense of proximity and depth to the village spilled out on the field in front of these ships.

If Garbart had planned a method of distributing us evenly along the beached ships, I didn't know it, and implementing any such plan would have been near impossible. Instead, we all bobbed into one another and exchanged signals mostly by pushing others on toward the next ship downstream. We were likely doubling up on some ships needlessly and accidentally skipping over some in the assumption others had them in hand.

Working an auger, in theory, is very easy. With a cross-shaped handle for torque and a straight shaft tapering into a spiraling, spoon-like twist, it bites off pieces of wood like a small hand plane moving in an orbit much akin to Archimedes' screw. The whole tool is crafted, of course, from iron for strength. Friezes and mosaics showing Roman construction, though, have the gall to put smiles on the carpenters' faces, probably because they weren't working at night, from a bobbing raft, with hands and auger below the waterline. Of all the times when a curse or the sharp invocation of Saint Irenaeus was called for, I couldn't, for fear of the cluster of barbarians a few score paces away.

The wood was very tough—oak for all I could tell, for I obviously hadn't followed Christ into the carpentry trade—but it was only as thick as the first joint of my thumb. When the first hole gave way, a satisfying, low gurgle began murmuring its protest within the boat.

We worked hard to put several holes into the first ship, then, at my guard's direction, floated downstream to another.

Where was Egilolf in all this? He had led us unerringly to Garbart's target, but where were his thoughts? Did they wander in the eddies with mine?

The soft breeze of the past hours that had been stirring the water ceased.

A scuff of boot tripping on rock brought me to a halt. One of the Northmen was much closer than I had thought, carrying a torch on his patrol, scrying the dark expanse of water in our direction. Perhaps the boring had been louder than it seemed to me. Rachel's yearnings again came to mind, and inwardly I laughed. What could I do? Cry alarm to the sentry, force Garbart's band to flee in the night while risking capture or an arrow in the back, all for the hope Bishop Hecfroi could treat with the Northmen tomorrow, that the Northmen would listen, that the Northmen would yield to Christian civilization, and become allies? Too many hopes. *Christianus sum...but I am not a martyr.*

I held my breath as the sentry waved the torch back and forth. By his silhouette, I saw him make a sharp motion, and a small blip near me indicated a pebble thrown into the water. The next one skipped off my head. I bit my tongue against several curses and kept half-floating. The sentry stooped for something at his feet, keeping an eye toward the water, and my guard pushed our raft to deeper currents.

Then a seraph must have broken the Seventh Seal, for brimstone struck me square in the forehead. I yelped. The sentry began screaming, and the chaos of hell broke out across the land. The sentry's guttural bray began echoing, intermixed with cries to flee, and the raft began pulling me away from the ships, away from the shallows of the shore. I kicked at the water to stay with it. The raft jerked in my hand, and I struggled to grip tighter. It jerked again, my hand caught nothing but water, and I sank like a stone. A mouthful of water brought back visions of my brother holding me under the pond beyond the north rye field when I was but eight. The chaos of fighting was reduced to the sole need for air. Perhaps I managed to kick off the riverbed, for I briefly resurfaced. Gasping,

I sensed a blurring of ink-sky and dark waters and cries triumphant and desperate all about. I lost all direction. I saw the stars falling into the sea. Or were those fire arrows? I had lost track of anyone else around me—my guard, Garbart, Egilolf, anyone—and my vision was darkening, my thrashing growing weaker. I dragged myself into the shallows, feebly clawing the sandy shoreline. The taste of blood filled my mouth, likely associated with my throbbing forehead. As my head touched sand, I vomited out a stomach's hold of water and wondered that I could see it mingle with the blood and flow down the thin beach to the waterline, inches away. With a last heave of effort, I rolled over to my back. Torchlight everywhere, just above me, obscured the stars, and an odd accent questioned, "The scribe?"

It may not have been the same pole, nor even the same cords, but they sure felt like it. Dawn woke me to pain and the realization I was again bound, in the Northmen village, as if awaiting another duel between Saint Valerie and the *daemon*. The sunlight was breaking thin shafts through short brush across the river, but it hadn't yet cleared the treetops. The light seemed blinding. I tried to speak and instead coughed forth a dry hissing. The buzz of a locust swarm burned through my ears, as if they were crawling all through me, devouring the inside of my entire head. I was vaguely aware that the Northmen camp was frantically active, with most of the village heading towards the ships. Some of the longships listed heavily in the river and were ignored, dying war comrades left behind in a panicked retreat. It took a few minutes to accept I somehow lived through the chaos of the river, but as to why I was spared, and for what worse end, I did not want to question.

Delusions, dreams, apparitions. Something of the sort flickered across the fragments of my consciousness as the sun became a furnace. *Polycarp stood in a consuming pyre, unbound, kept to the stake by his devotion alone.* Or was that another stake-burned martyr? How frail the faith of our modern age. "God above," I mangled, "it seems I've failed everyone, and I was not even sure what You wanted me to do. Even now, I cannot ask as the martyrs did, that You uphold me to see my martyrdom through. I have and will accomplish nothing. Let Your Will be finished with me..." Fire, sword, beatings—I knew I could bear none of these. If I could but lie in peace, like Saint Valerie's bones in the crypt of Saint Martial. Now there was a saint! Martial left the civilized world in the golden age of Rome to come to this once-barbaric land. Are we now any better than when he first came to Aquitania? Have we carried his salt and light farther? And Valerie, her past unknown, maybe a convert of Saint Martial's, buried in an old shrine that grew to the church of Saint Philibert. It was fitting then that she now lay in peace with Saint Martial.

My head swam again, and somewhere Joshua, son of Nun, commanded the sun to stand still and beat down on me. Some water touched my lips, and I licked it eagerly, only to taste my own blood, running unfelt over my eyes from that continual throbbing on my forehead. *Pace requiem*, Valerie. But the thought seemed wrong. I felt like I was fighting to resurface in the river again, to think clearly. It was Philibert there, in the abbey of Saint Martial. Wasn't it? Valerie was...here. The thought was so surprising, I caught myself seeking her among the women and children fleeing with bundles and baskets to the ships.

"If you...hope for...the *rex*," a crusted voice wheezed right behind me, "the Franks will come...from the north."

My vision spun worse when I twisted hard to see the speaker.

"But it will...make no difference.... We are...already dead. Damnable Northmen." As though this was too much, the voice devolved into labored breaths.

"Who?" I questioned.

"A...dead man." A deep rasp. "Nothing more." The reply was thinner than before. It did not sound like Egilolf, but who could tell through the strain? One of Garbart's raiders, most likely.

A commotion escalated above the din by the ships and drew closer to me. One called out in broken Latin as the group stopped before me. "The bone hunters. Chief Thorfinn is angering at your faithless return." Skuli, the translator, stood before me with the chief and a few others. My heart sank further to see the Skull-Crusher among them.

"Faithless?" I spoke, pondering if my soul's dilemma was really so exposed. Had I muttered more in my addled state? A cuff to the head left me reeling once more, my vision surreal, adrift it seemed from my head.

Angry North words spewed out in reply. "You is promising peace and priests for your goddess. You hinting at hope of appeasing the gods of this land area." More garbled sounds followed before Skuli's Latin continued. "You is bringing an army. Like thieves, you is slinking about at night, destroying our ships. Your death will being measured to your treachery."

God, please, not drowning, I prayed. *And not fire. Saint Fructuosus, please no. Nor flaying.* Martyr stories whirled through my mind, fiery chariots of thought too ephemeral to solidly grasp. "*Christianus sum…*" I began, but then my throat went dry and all other words stuck in them. The wretch behind me wheezed.

"Before you die, Thorfinn would be knowing if your soul fears death enough not to lie. Who leading the separate camp, at west end? Are they allies, or not, that they be remaining apart?"

"Who? I do not—" My head lolled about as gravity and my will contested over its movement. Iron hands locked about my skull and wrenched it over my left shoulder, sinews popping somewhere in my neck. I strained to focus my eyes. Beyond the thin northern palisade, a mass of soldiers formed up, the mocking hope of *Rex Ebalus* too far removed to save me. They formed atop a slight rise even the greatest tale-teller could not name as a hill. Separated by a weak notch in the crest of this rise, another group split from Aquitania's army. The morning was too calm to stream out any banners. "I'm not sure…"

"Bish…" wheezed the soldier captured with me and who thought himself dead.

I indistinctly made out the staff of one mounted man. Did the staff curl?

It could have been the crosier of Hecfroi. "It is the Bishop of Pictauensis. Named Hecfroi." The smallest glint of a thought flashed across my mind. Surely the leviathan spat Jonah back onto the road to Nineveh, the same road he fled. "He is the one I spoke of before." I fought the dual labor of forming clear thoughts and intelligible words. "He is the high priest, as you might say. The one who can provide priests and show you the power of Saint Valerie and the Christian God. He has come with *Rex* Ebalus but opposes him over their purpose here." I paused as much to focus my energy as to allow translation. "He would willingly show you that power and seek out a peace between our peoples, if such is possible."

After some translation and what sounded like an argument between Thorfinn and Arnkel, Skuli spoke, "Your betrayal not being forgotten. But some of families will be dying surely if it coming to fighting. How would we treating with bishop?"

Part of my mind wondered if I could tactfully insert some grammar lessons in our dialogue; Skuli's speech was becoming quite painful.

"Raise a parley flag close to his lines. The bishop has enough independence from the king to delay any fighting long enough to talk." I didn't believe such a thing truly possible, but perhaps my inevitable death could forge something Rachel—and God—could be proud of.

The Northmen leadership hurried off, discussing, but one swung back. Arnkel Skull-Crusher stepped up, his face suddenly snapping into focus. His grin and drawn dagger loosed any carefully bound thought. Then he struck me in the head. Hard.

The details of the following hour are pieced together, like a Moorish mosaic, with fragments chipped later from the memory of Egilolf over shared cups and pressed atop my own recollected shards. Waved to parley, Hecfroi's envoy approached the Northmen's pickets, and after a short exchange with Chief Thorfinn, the bishop's entire entourage stepped forward. Thorfinn and some of his closest warriors matched this move, and two small squads, each a rough score of warriors, soon faced the other in close proximity, their respective main forces behind them grumbling darkly.

One particularly brutish Northman, though tame compared to the Skull-Crusher, cut me from my post and dragged me to the center of the unlikely discussion, throwing me like refuse on a midden heap, while the yet-grinning Arnkel pressed a heavy-shod boot on my head. That part, I recall.

As bishop met chieftain, each side did as warriors do. As roosters, bull elk, and most other male animals will do, truthfully: staring, glaring, and exaggerated chest-puffing. Hecfroi had the brothers chant a psalm—the twenty-fifth, perhaps, though Egilolf could not recall—and hold the cross aloft. Ingigird, not to be outshone, waved her staff around, chanted arcane words, moaned and wailed, threw down bones to read signs (this may have been Egilolf's own flourish), and muttered deprecations about the whole affair to Chief Thorfinn. Jeers and the clattering of spear haft on shield, both behind me in the Northmen's village and before me in Ebalus' army on the far rise, swirled around like a periphery of a less-than-heavenly host.

Egilolf remembered little of the exchange, formalized and repeated through interpreters in both parties. Hecfroi had extended a peace on behalf of the Church and the *Dux*—no *Rex*—of Aquitania. If Egilolf had been less concerned for my fate across the negotiating field, he might have heard more than that this peace was to include a cessation of fighting, an exchange of hostages, land given to Thorfinn up to a day's journey from the coast of Oceanus, a requirement of the Church to send priests to teach Northmen youth in the ways of the relics, saints, and God Almighty, and of course, the need for Thorfinn to place his hands within Ebalus' own, to become his vassal. Thorfinn seemed to be ready to accept, but the more Bishop Hecfroi spoke, the quicker Arnkel Skull-Crusher paced and fumed.

At last, the torrent exploded, with Arnkel spewing forth his full fury—at his own chief. Here my own memory lent a few parts, and I wished for the first time, and hopefully last, that I knew the grating language of these barbarians. Regardless, Arnkel's displeasure was clear. He yelled, waved his arms about, and pressed his face into Thorfinn's. The older leader stood as unmovable stone, and Arnkel responded as fury usually does, devolving into shoving, smacking and cuffing the head and neck. With Arnkel's attention diverted, I had enough presence of mind to scramble out of the way, crawling to the foot of the Cross, planted firmly next to Hecfroi, as I escaped the rising storm.

Like opposing arbiters, Hecfroi and Ingigird stood facing each other, at cross angle to the contenders. At a small break in the cuffing and taunting, Arnkel stepped back, drew his ax, and issued what was clearly some formal challenge. The Northmen crowd all gasped and fell to buzzing among themselves. Thorfinn replied, at least in action, drawing his own sword. Ingigird began intoning, and—

"Your Grace," a terse yet melodious voice broke the storm. "You should be aware, the one challenging Chief Thorfinn claimed his right to lead the clan. The two are to battle between themselves. The challenger calls the people to cast down Thorfinn for considering our God and abandoning their own."

I managed to swing my head upward at the voice. It was Rodegar, the carefree minstrel persona gone, a dole face surveying the impending fight. "Most importantly, it sounds like their sorceress has thrown her support with the usurper."

Thorfinn himself addressed the crowd, though briefly.

Rodegar continued his translation. "The chief is calling to his people that in these foreign fields, their new home, they should learn to appease the gods here too."

Arnkel brayed some response to cut off Thorfinn and swung his ax menacingly. His massive shoulders rippled, and the large ax moved lightly in his arms.

With a sharp cry, the chief leapt toward his challenger. Sword and ax rang peal after peal, faster than any five bells could toll in most earnest ringing, and the two circled each other, now pressing, now retreating, barely dodging, urged on by the crowd, or mocked and jeered. Arnkel was clearly the stronger and younger, but either Thorfinn's sword length gave him the advantage of distance, or he knew his craft better.

A hand fell on my shoulder, startling me. "We'd best remove you to the rear of the line," Rodegar warned me. "You are in no condition to contend."

"Contend?" I managed to reply dumbly. He put hands under my arms and hauled me to my feet. I wavered, and a second pair of hands steadied me. Egilolf supported my right side.

"This parley could conclude any second. As soon as they kill each other, they will descend on the bishop," Rodegar explained. Egilolf nodded.

"Barbarians," I concurred. The enemy seemed all too close, and I realized how true Rodegar's assessment was. I, not a warrior, to begin with, stood unarmed at the front edge between two packs of yearning weapons. My knees shook, and I let them draw me back through the ranks. A sharp peal of weapons and gasps from both crowds of warriors swung my head back toward the contest. My view was narrowed by the rows of guards I had already passed, so I caught only a glimpse of Thorfinn pressing the Skull-Crusher back. They passed out of my windowed gap between the helmets. That view now framed a single Northman warrior across the parley field. His lack of facial hair marked him youngest among his fellows.

What will become of the Northmen children? Rachel's words thrust into my gut.

I halted. Egilolf took this for an impending collapse and adjusted his grip under my arms. I shrugged him off, Rodegar also, and turned back to the field. I hesitated. Swords and spears and a pack of brutal, agitated Northmen stood forty paces away. Two of them were attempting to kill each other as I wrestled within myself. Common sense and memories tugged me to the rear of the formation. Toward safety. Toward sanity.

Aren't you the one always spouting about the glory of the martyrs? Were Rachel's words a spear point at my throat or a guiding hand round my arm? A man never tells a female to be a woman, to step into her role, to shoulder her motherly duty, or any other duty—but how often must a woman make the man!

Justin Martyr doesn't get to have a Dialogue with Trypho the Northman.
Or does he?

In the duel, Thorfinn kept up his sharp battle cry, and at the third or fourth utterance, it pressed my memory. "Valerie! Valerie!" The Northman chief was invoking the saint. An invented saint. Egilolf's and my lies from weeks and months ago would get this man killed and crush any of Hecfroi's hopes of conversion.

And what did I hope? Rachel's face was before me, her faceless children somewhere at the back of the barbarian village crowd.

Should Arnkel win, surely Ebalus would storm down and bleed this scourge into the Frankish soil.

And should Thorfinn win?

I knew what Rachel wanted. I knew what the bishop hoped for. The smoke of my flaming home sprang to mind. *Brother Angius' throat poured out its offering of blood. My father's laugh mocked me down into the dust.* The clouds spun about me overhead, and the image of the smooth-cheeked Northman boy-playing-soldier across the parley grounds doubled as my vision blurred. What of God's will? Dared I hope? The sorceress herself had seen a spirit come to fight her *daemon.* All the rescues of me and Egilolf, from the threats of execution, from pursuers, from the bowels of the earthen grave itself—were they chance, or miracles?

Christianus sum…

"Your Grace!" I called out. I took a step and was halted. I had to shrug off Egilolf's grip again. I jostled back through the episcopal guard toward the crosier, though my eyes were fixed on the Northman youth. "Bishop Hecfroi!" I stumbled through the last rank and fell to my knees before him. If fighting broke out now, I had no strength left to avoid it.

"Your Grace…" I called again or tried to. My voice came as a dry hiss. I struggled to use the stave of the cross to pull myself to my feet. "Your Grace…."

This time Hecfroi heard. As he turned, he recoiled from the drowned and mangled rat I was.

I gave him no chance to cut me off. "Aid Thorfinn. Call on God Almighty, all his saints, and especially Valerie. Loudly, in front of the barbarian people. Throw your weight behind him."

Hecfroi recoiled further. "This Valerie of yours! You said these were not her bones, that they were just another's, that the real relics were carried to Lemouicensis. Would you mock God, my son?"

"Your Grace," I rushed on, "we made a tale. The relics carried to Lemouicensis were those of another saint, Philibert's remains, if you will believe it." The bishop's glare said he did not. "The bones here, those were the remains of Valerie. And regardless of how we obtained them, or the various stories we told of her, she was surely a real person, with real remains. And those remains, brought here to this camp, they had their own influence on these people. Their sorceress described her coming in glory to fight a *daemon*. To them, she is real. They hold split right now, debating and wondering, not if she is real, but if she is more powerful than their gods."

Hecfroi surveyed the crowd, past the contest that swept back and forth.

I pressed, "She can be God's grace to them, by their faith, if not by ours. If she or Thorfinn fail, this battle between Ebalus and their army is inevitable anyway. But should she aid Thorfinn and carry the day…"

I could see Hecfroi calculating, weighing possibilities, perhaps praying for the far sight of the angels.

Don't we all?

He faced the fight again, the Northmen warriors, and their villagers beyond them. He raised both hands, outstretched, like Moses upholding the Israelite strength through his own upraised arms…or as Christ Himself sacrificing all. Victory in battle or victory through sacrifice, the old foreshadows the new. The *episcopus*, shepherd of the church, inheritor of the authority of the apostles, cried out with a loud voice, "God the Father, Christ our King, Spirit of Power, all his saints, and Saint Valerie, come to our aid today! Saint Valerie, be Chief Thorfinn's strong arm! Saint Valerie, be his shield and bulwark! Saint Valerie…" The whole lot of Northmen began muttering and pointing, even retreating a few cautious steps away from this invocation.

The contestants battled on. Ingigird, opposing the bishop, raised her own chant and wail, drawing symbols in the air with her staff, and then also with her whale-ivory knife. I felt we should have been atop Mount Carmel, Elijah and God against Baal's four hundred.

But no pillar of fire descended. No bolt of lightning speared. No wild animals came, driven by God's power to aid Thorfinn. The sun did not stand still in the sky. If anything, Thorfinn was flagging, his breathing heavier. Even I, never trained with weapons, could see he no longer pressed the attack. He barely deflected Arnkel's blows.

Not without cause did the Great Charles proscribe the sale or gifting of Frankish swords to Northmen or others outside his empire, for our iron is stronger, or stronger forged. Perhaps the angle was wrong, or Thorfinn could no longer deflect the might of Arnkel's cleaving, but at last a clash of ax against the chief's blade caused a rending snap, twisting the ear to hear it, as though a *daemon* decried its shattering punishment in the eternal fire. Thorfinn, the great Northmen leader, stumbled under the impact, and Arnkel slapped the broken hilt from his hand.

Thorfinn stood unarmed and stunned against the wild fury of the Skull-Crusher. Some of the Northmen villagers hooted, others moaned crestfallen, and many glances went to the praying bishop, still standing in the universal *orans* posture, arms outstretched wide. His prayers to heaven were not to be heard that day.

The contempt clear on his face, Arnkel used the flat of his ax blade to knock Thorfinn to the ground, and the weaponless man could only dodge part of the stroke. Arnkel hailed the crowd, some of whom cheered. He called upon Ingigird, who pulled from a leather pouch a scrap of red, bright as the blood running down Thorfinn's face.

"Your Grace, we might wish to withdraw," Rodegar put in tactfully. The bishop's guards around us inched backward in agreement.

Arnkel addressed his village with what could only be a victory paean, and then he drew from Ingigird's red silk bundle what I knew he must: a skull glowing in the morning light with the opaqueness of antiquity.

Only human, after all.

Lord, have mercy, I thought. *Valerie...* The new chief, ending his speech with a roar, threw the skull to the ground, and then, true to his name, brought his boot down upon it and smote it into an eruption of fragments.

Thorfinn, lying there in a pitiable daze, reached out a feeble hand to the shards of skull, what should have been the most valued relic of the saint Valerie, if she ever had been. Arnkel laughed in his triumph, raised his ax high over Thorfinn's neck, and roared what was presumably a mocking joke to the crowd, for many laughed.

Thorfinn's hand reached to Arnkel's calf, and I thought he pled for his life. Ah, Pride, you tempt us all. For it was then, when Arnkel's ax was raised in triumph, and his victory certain, that the miracle occurred. Thorfinn's hand flashed again, and again, at the hamstring, and as the Skull-Crusher's legs buckled, Thorfinn's hand plunged to his opponent's lower back—the kidney. Rising to his knees, now matching Arnkel's crumbled height, Thorfinn paused. The words of the bishop, the gyrations of the sorceress, the mutterings of the crowd, the circling birds overhead, even the very wind all stilled, a muting gasp. In that instant, it was clear: Arnkel's ax tumbled, his body wracked in surprised agony, and Thorfinn's hand lifted high a small short blade of gleaming white—a jawbone, snapped to a piercing, jagged point. The broken skull of Saint Valerie herself a weapon. Thorfinn plunged it deep into the neck of that prideful one that had sought to overthrow his lord.

When he drew it forth, the entire reservoir of blood in the fallen man sprayed out, following that fragment, the holy bone. The Skull-Crusher's corpse toppled to the dust, and Thorfinn, too weak to rise beyond his knees, raised the shard high. "Valerie!" he shouted. Again, "Valerie!" And then the crowd took up the victory cry.

"God Almighty…" gasped the bishop.

Rodegar adjusted his harp strap on his shoulder. "Your Grace, you may want to start Thorfinn's salvific conversion with the stories of Samson."

Not a martyr after all—not even a confessor—but I could, perhaps, lay claim to saving the Northmen from destruction. If nothing else, I claim this—I was there the day the barbarian horde met the Cross and knelt.

What would Rachel think?

The peace was sworn, and all were amazed and rejoiced that day. All, that is, but some of the Northmen who refused to follow Christ, hailed Ingigird as their leader, and fled with her back to sea aboard a longship. And Garbart, too—I swear he wept for the loss of full battle and slaughter of the Northmen. As part of the accord, Bishop Hecfroi demanded the relics of Saint Valerie, though he acceded to Thorfinn's counterclaim to the fragments of the skull. After a day of feasting, oath swearing, and still some wary glances between opposing warriors, Ebalus and his army marched back to Pictauensis with a new vassal on his western flank and a fledgling mission for the bishop's diocese. For our part in the successful outcome of the campaign, Egilolf and I were given our freedom. Yet in that heady triumph, still, the horizon showed one last (God, let it be the last) storm menacing.

James the Apostle wrote of the uncertain man, without faith or conviction, tossed to and fro like a rudderless ship at the whim of every wave. My mind found certain parallels between this and the trackless routes and wagon ruts Egilolf and I followed now for the fourth time, back to Lemouicensis.

Before we struck camp, we spoke to Bishop Hecfroi, now the keeper of the remaining relics of Saint Valerie, minus her head, about the final truth I had revealed on the contest field. I could hardly blame his reluctance to believe what was now our third—or fourth?—story to him, but he did agree that if the bones venerated at Saint Martial's abbey as Saint Valerie were actually Saint Philibert, then they needed to be returned to the monks at Tournus, in all haste. All *subtle* haste. In the end, we had to swear some rather terrifying oaths on the relics of Saint Valerie, and, for added assurance, on the relic of the True Cross at the abbey in Pictauensis. Bishop Hecfroi, at least, was certain that Valerie was a saint, no matter how unconventional our methods may have been in finding, recovering, and establishing her.

"If nothing else, I've learned a saint may use even a thief and scribe to restore herself," Hecfroi addressed us personally over his dinner. "Take her, then, and go exchange her with Saint Philibert, with my blessing and hers. But tell no one of this…mix-up. Let's not confuse those of weaker faith with needless complexity."

Egilolf nodded his thanks and retrieved Saint Valerie's remnants from him. I bowed to receive the bishop's silent blessing.

"But," he added, "you should go with speed and the stealth of Joshua's spies. *Comes* Fulgaud has openly declared for the young Charles as *rex* of all Francia and resists Ebalus' claim of kingship. Ebalus' brother is reportedly banding with this Charles also. With a warband disappointed they could not prove themselves against the Northmen, Ebalus may be quick to sway Fulgaud's mind, by swords first and later by words with any survivors."

We left the bishop's residence with Valerie's relics, not in a silk cloth, nor in an ornate box, but bound by a simple wool wrapping. Lacking elsewhere to go for the night, we returned to the pilgrim house at the Abbey of the Holy Cross. We made sure to avoid the abbess. Our table companions that evening were a carpenter and his two sons, the down on the elder's cheeks yet dewy. The father spoke little beyond a greeting, but the older youth shared, with the unmatched enthusiasm of youth, of their pilgrimage thus far, particularly their veneration at Saint Martin of Tors.

Egilolf politely kept up the exchange for both of us, but my mind wandered. Or rather, though it didn't follow the conversation, it kept sliding into one thought: Rachel. Egilolf's elbow to my rib was the first notice I had missed something.

"What?"

"You should find her. Tell her how it went. Make a plan for after. After Lemouicensis, I mean." Egilolf slurped his soup between phrases.

"Who are you talking about?"

"The woman. The one you're nearly betrothed to."

"I do not know what you are referring to," I protested, to Egilolf, to God—probably to myself. "I…I was planning to swear myself to God. Back, back at—"

"I don't doubt it. Wouldn't tell you to cross an oath. If you made one. You didn't. Maybe God calls you now not to some book but to the woman."

"Stop calling her 'the woman,'" I growled. "Her name is Rachel."
I stabbed at a small loaf.

"That's my point. This whole mess may be over soon. You should dream of beyond."

"And what is your dream of beyond?" I retorted.

He didn't mock. He didn't dodge my comment with a joke. He didn't even grimace or frown. He just paused. The idea had only now struck him.

At Egilolf's urging, I circled the army's camp the next morning after *terce* was sung. I meandered among cooks, menders, and washerwomen but only succeeded in getting crude comments slung at my back, suggestive questions as to why I lingered among the women.

"Maybe she's still at Thoucars," Egilolf suggested.

I sighed.

That afternoon we idled through town, occasionally piecing together the frenetic route of our midnight escape months ago. All lanes and passageways bustled with the chaos of an army preparing for war, as though market and fair and parade were all flung together. Despite the peace with the Northmen, most gossip murmured of the *strix* and bitten child. As we approached the east gate, we saw a gleeman on the street corner. I've found that street performers hold little sacred, this one no exception. With puppets and props, he reenacted his suppositions of the arcane child-eater, now babbling to mock her speech, now casting inane household items into a battered cauldron to ape her malefic acts. Town children encircled the show, rapt as though spellbound. He bobbed his head and crooked his arms askew, tossed about his wild hair, and issued a hissing squawk as his bird-woman parody devoured a rag doll.

"Except the voice, a good likeness," Egilolf commented.

The gleeman's actions did evoke the fumbling awkwardness of the thin woman condemned in Ebalus' hall. His twitching recalled another image: Ingigird, the sorceress, with her wave and twist of staff and knife seeking to counter the prayerful Bishop Hecfroi.

We continued down the lane, but the juxtaposed images of the two women lingered. Their illusions now safely stripped, both seemed frail and almost pathetic in their stature, perhaps for the smallness of their worlds. They seemed caught, if not by a legion, then at least by a cohort of their own confining demons. The *strix* at least was bound for the convent of Tors, for exorcism and a narrow salvific hope. But for Ingigird, retreating to barbaric wastelands, where was hope? Was her chance for eternal forgiveness forever gone?

"What churns your mind?" Egilolf broke into my mental wandering. As I opened my mouth, he directed, "Give me the brief version."

"What is the blasphemy against the Holy Spirit, that unforgivable sin? Is anything more evil than leading an entire people away from the Lord? Or consorting with *daemons* by killing innocents? Better a millstone around the neck than to lead these little ones astray."

"Maybe it's killing at all, innocents or not."

I paused in the street, the milling crowd flowing around us. "Peace, peace, they cry! Now, who wants to become a monk?" I grinned. He half-matched it. "No, I think not. There will always be war and rumors of war, but even the saint-killer Saul became an apostle, and he called himself the worst of sinners."

He abandoned his smile. "There is no peace."

Heeding the episcopal warning, Egilolf and I left Pictauensis the following day. Despite the bishop's dire talk, our travel was pleasant, for the days had cooled somewhat as harvest approached, and we traveled openly, at least while in Pictauensis's range of influence. Once east of the *Vinhana*, we paralleled the road, close enough to move quickly into the brush, in case Fulgaud's scouts swept near.

When we came within a day's travel of Saint Martial's abbey, we stopped for the afternoon to rest in anticipation of completing our journey at night. We moved into the forest south of the road and reached the *Vinhana* again, downstream of Lemouicensis, before *none*. Egilolf dozed off easily, but I lay beside the sluggish river, under leaves skittish of the breeze, and tried not to think of Rachel, aglow in the evening sun at that roadside chapel…

Egilolf woke me as the waxing moon cleared the tops of fir trees up the river. A dream had left a pleasant feeling, if not a distinct memory. Thin clouds drifted east, and we followed the riverbank against the water's flow. We were one hour from town by Egilolf's reckoning, which I now knew meant we were exactly one hour from town. He was an excellent scout. My companion handed me a cake of acorn bread to munch as we hiked. Perhaps it was made from better acorns, for it didn't taste as bitter as before.

Gonsindus was satisfied with Saint Valerie, and now Father Leo would have Saint Philibert once more. But *Comes* Fulgaud.... A tracker might see my boot tracks even and measured, but my own thoughts were as tossed about as our antiphonal trekking back and forth across Aquitania had been these past three months. I mentioned as much to Egilolf, but he just shrugged. "We should have some faith. Look how far Valerie's brought us. Little more couldn't hurt much worse."

"Unless it kills us."

By the time we reached Lemouicensis, the clouds raced themselves on some far-above wind, casting swift-rushing moon shadows. The night around us, though, was still, so still that the few ripples of the slow-moving river downstream of the town seemed an affront.

As promised, Father Leo awaited us by the west end of the bridge, cowl thrown back and leaning hard on a staff, as though he awaited some holy calling to cross that ink-dark stream before him. Our path along the river had skirted the town and abbey. Egilolf told him of our tumultuous voyage through the mire of Northmen beliefs, of drownings in rivers and deceits, and of jaw-bone victories.

"It's really her, then? Your Saint Valerie, yes?" the priest asked, eager beyond his years.

"Well, half of her," Egilolf mocked. "Minus a head. Doubt Gonsindus will include the real tale of that in the *Acta*."

"Let me see!" the old man demanded.

I spread across the ground the dark gray woolen cloth in which we had wrapped the bones. I trusted Egilolf to keep a sharp eye on the town, especially the fort and abbey. The bridge lay close to both. The moon shadows slid away, and the bones appeared to glow in the eldritch light. "A hand. Ribs, yes? And the pelvis and right leg. It's all here."

"Maybe you did not hear, Father," I cautioned.

"No, no, I heard you. I know not if it is coincidence or the provision of God Almighty Himself, but the bones I took from Tournus seem to be the other half of this body."

"What?" Egilolf's head snapped toward the priest.

"You recall when I was a youth, we switched Philibert's remains in the crypt for some in the lower crypt, yes? When I returned to Tournus and gathered what the monks there thought to be Saint Philibert, I remarked it was an incomplete skeleton. I began wondering. And now, seeing the other remains you've brought confirms my suspicions. Abbot Gonsindus and Saint Martial's abbey shall have all of Saint Valerie, as they should!" The old man exhaled heavily, and I checked if he was just relieved or expiring.

"That worried?" Egilolf questioned.

"It weighed on my conscience, this hunting and sneaking, this moving of relics without the church's knowledge. I didn't doubt the rightness of recovering Philibert—that was always affixed in my mind. But the dissembling, this…*creation* of Saint Valerie I doubted. But now, with her remains all here—"

"But the head," Egilolf interjected.

Father Leo waved him off. "The saint will be in her proper *locus*." He smiled. "As will Saint Philibert."

"If we get Valerie into Saint Martial's crypt. And Philibert out."

"That's the easy part," the old priest said. "I have trusted access to the whole monastery."

"It's fulfilled then," breathed Egilolf, like a sigh with no relief.

Father Leo raised an eyebrow.

"My penance. Near enough once you swap them."

Father Leo wrapped the bones back up in the cloth and pulled himself erect with his staff. He faced Egilolf squarely. "Yet, you sound…unsure," the priest probed.

The doubts rippled over the once-soldier's face, wrenching his mouth violently. "Thought it would feel more definite," Egilolf sputtered, "Thought that my burden would feel lifted. A greater relief."

Father Leo crossed himself, and then Egilolf, as though preparing a prayer. "You anticipated the blessing of grace at the end of your penance, yes?"

Egilolf looked at me for support.

The old man continued, "God's grace you already received, at the confessional. You've been seeing your penance wrong this whole time. It was not a payment required to obtain grace but more like a fertilizer to encourage its growth in you."

Egilolf barked a cynical laugh. "It was a dung-heap sort of task."

Father Leo leaned into Egilolf's face. "Perhaps you could see the purpose better if you had angelic vision. But trust for the present season. You see now, God's grace will work to restore you if you let it, yes?"

Egilolf shook his head. "Father, my thanks for all you've done, back to when you first pointed us to Philibert. But this penance was to heal something within me. That much was promised. The priest said…" He spun away, his eyes locked on the gurgling river. His voice returned, hollowly, "'A great work it would be, to help a saint be found again. Sometimes a saint wants to be remembered.'" I barely heard the last bit. "But now…"

He picked up his bedroll and kit and gazed at the moon. He stepped toward the bridge, Roman-built, most likely, its stone unshakeable. Across the river, away from the abbey, the path led to a dark forest and high and higher hills beyond, mostly shadows in the moonlight against the night sky. "Now I don't know where to go. Or what to do. If that penance didn't restore anything, nothing will."

Father Leo swung from him to me. "What, you think you two are done?"

I pointed at the bundle in his hands. "You have Saint Valerie. You are known and welcome in the abbey. You stroll in and swap the bones. Like you said, that's the easy part."

Egilolf looked as confused as I felt.

"Did you need an escort to Tournus, Father?"

"Don't patronize me, young man. The problem's not the journey, but here. The bones themselves are insufficient. You promised Abbot Gonsindus their story. Now you must write the *translatio*, yes?"

It was my turn to scoff. "To what end? Abbot Gonsindus knows the tale well enough. We told it to him right before he threw us into locked cells. It would be more than fair to leave him to write his own story."

Egilolf nodded in agreement and stepped to the bridge.

Father Leo's staff swung quickly to block his way. "You know why the story is needed," Father Leo pressed. "Without it, without it written down and read aloud on her feast day, without copies sent to other libraries, it becomes some fireside yarn, changed to the teller's liking. Within a generation, it will be altered. Within two, it'll become irrelevant, and within three Saint Valerie will be forgotten." Father Leo jabbed his staff at my shins to cut me off even before I realized I had opened my mouth to protest. "Everyone here knows you two were the ones to find her, the ones to recover her from the grasp of the Northmen. What will they say if Abbot Gonsindus writes it out himself after you two disappeared on him? The rustics will take up some tale that you were true thieves, slinking off before the bones were recognized a fraud."

Egilolf turned back, half-facing the old priest again, yet leaning toward the bridge.

And I? Part of me did want to see this through, properly, if only to stand clearer in the sight of God and Saint Valerie. And Rachel, perhaps. The other part of me envisioned the abbey cells, the crypt, the earthen tunnel bowels, and Fulgaud's promises to flay us. And hang us.

"The abbot and the *comes*," I countered. "It is not safe."

"What of Fulgaud?" Egilolf echoed, scanning the town and the tower fort above it.

Father Leo continued. "I explained the whole problem to the abbot earlier. Well, most of the problem. He thinks you left to recover the rest of Saint Valerie from the Northmen, and he promised to pray her aid for you. As for Fulgaud, he's called his soldiers off from the abbey. Rumors have eddied on breeze and stream of *Rex* Ebalus marching, coming here to press his royal claim. From the little I've heard, Fulgaud is anticipating the new-named Burgundian king to support him instead. If the young Charles and Ebalus' half-brother don't get here in time. It may be a race to see whose support arrives first. But either way, you see his attention is off the abbey, yes?"

I questioned my companion with a glance.

"Your choice. I'll follow you," Egilolf said, his tone unreadable.

"There is no logical reason to risk both of us. What would you stay for?" I asked.

"Make sure you get the story right," he chuckled. "That bard said I knew how to tell a tale."

I admit sometimes I've pretended to debate my options when already I knew what was needed and just didn't want to do it. With reluctance, I finally nodded. Contrary to his spoken ambivalence, Egilolf seemed satisfied with this. In hindsight, I wondered if, despite Father Leo's words, he thought his internal torment was yet awaiting some final step, some last work to obtain his peace.

Father Leo escorted us through the town and abbatial walls, directly to the *scriptorium*. There I slept the night soundly, maybe for the home-coming familiarity of the smell of vellum and ink. We woke the next day around *terce* to a meal of rye bread and game-bird stew, brought to us so our work would be uninterrupted. We had the building's second floor to ourselves to secure our isolation.

How many times on our journey had I considered the earlier steps difficult until faced with my current task? I learned that a parchment will hold up only so many times to scraping and re-writing. It felt sacrilegious but I had to consign the first ruined sheet to the fire for all the holes I wore in it. For that was the day Egilolf and I found it had been easy to create a story without truth and also easy to tell all events as they actually occurred, whether they had made any rational sense or not. But for the life of us (and despite Father Leo's assurances, I was *not* sure Abbot Gonsindus wouldn't make it a capital issue if we couldn't produce a masterful *translatio*), we struggled to relate what was relevant, parsing the necessary from the obscuring, the needed truth from convolutions that would keep a rustic listener from the heart-knowledge needed for faith.

The day wore on, the sunbeam through the window passing across my writing desk, illuminating my parchment for a few hours, then moving out of reach. Egilolf paced the room, as though he could scout the path to a proper story if he were but free of these confining walls. My second parchment was nigh opaque in patches, portending another sentencing to the flames. Our snare was the half-stories and lies, told in Pictauensis, mutated before Abbot Gonsindus, and altered once again before *Comes* Fulgaud. Could anyone really understand our demands as we had felt them?

"What if we dropped mention of Pictauensis?" Egilolf picked up our third argument.

"Then it makes no sense as to how and why we returned to the Northman camp," I reminded, gritting my teeth. "As we rehashed, well before *none* tolled, we cannot omit the Northmen, for it was the whole Valerie versus Valkyrie mess that led to the sorceress, which is when we first knew she was a saint."

"Suspected. Suspected she was a saint."

How was it that actual danger was less agitating between us than writing about it? To cover my ire, I stood and stretched the cramps from my hand and back. Through the window, I watched the shadow of the hills stretch over the streets of Lemouicensis. From this second floor, most of the town and countryside were visible, except directly north where the church rose even higher. Our elevation provided the illusion of far sight.

Egilolf paused his pacing. "What if we—"

But I never learned what he thought he had struck upon. Though it was barely past *vespers*, church bells rang an alarm. Before they ebbed, horns sounded, dire and triumphant, like the breaking of the seven seals but bearing no hope of a New Jerusalem.

Ebalus had arrived. From the northwest, his army poured down the roadway and began to invest the town, Fulgaud's tower, and the abbey.

Why my dread? For once, being held in the monastery was a blessing, a haven. Ebalus' concern would only be with Fulgaud. Hecfroi would see to it Ebalus left the abbey and town unmolested.

And yet....

"Your friend Peter is likely out there," I mentioned, not sure why I said it. Or not willing to admit it.

"For sure," Egilolf replied, his pacing stopped. "Him. The whole army." He moved to the window also, standing behind me. "The camp followers." My back was to him, but I felt the grin.

"Fair enough," I matched him. "Do you think we could reach her and flee?" Or should I just finish the *translatio* and be done? What could I do to spare Rachel's life when I couldn't save my own?

I recalled that one best evening at the ruined chapel along the road, kneeling at the altar and reciting Prudentius with Rachel standing in the western nave doorway. Backlit by the evening sun, her wind-blown hair had glowed as with a holy aura—

And in that thought, far easier than writing, the pieces fit.

"I can prevent this war."

Egilolf cocked his head.

"No, truly," I turned to him. "We need to find Rachel. And a spear. And Peter and a white robe."

If I couldn't write that day, I definitely couldn't that night. *Compline* rang, and I smiled at the sheer boldness of my plan. By the deepest night hours of *matins*, I would have recalled Egilolf to the *scriptorium* if I but could have reached him, certain I was needlessly sentencing us to death. How could one man scout into an entire war camp and find one soldier and one washerwoman? Now it was my turn to pace around my writing desk, biding time, anticipating possible failures and successes. Most of my plan hinged on Egilolf's preparations through the night, which left me time to finish the *translatio*. Supposedly. I couldn't keep my mind to the task.

As the sleep-eyed chorus stumbled from dormitory to church and murmured *lauds*, I struck upon another great detail to my plan and was so emboldened that I myself crept out to enact it. With the monks in the church, the sacristy would be opened for the vestments. My skill at sneaking was meager beside Egilolf's, but it was sufficient to skulk through the dormitory and the hall toward the south transept. The chorus called from the church, their song clear through the open transept door. But rather than enter the church, I stopped short. In the same hall, a side door to the sacristy opened. For the office of the hours, it was unsecured, as I had anticipated.

Vestments, candles, silver plates, cups, and holders, I rummaged through the shelves quickly and came at last to what I sought. In a cypress wood box, I found the dark resin shavings of frankincense, the scent of paradise. With a short prayer, I pilfered—borrowed for God's service, if I may—half the contents of the box, crumbling the shavings into a scrap of cloth I tore from an old, moth-worn vestment. I passed this into my scrip and prepared to return to the *scriptorium*, when I thought better of it.

I took with me a small candle and filed into the church. I pulled my hood up and shuffled to join the chorus—a latecomer not an uncommon sight at this early hour. I lit my candle off a brother monk's. Once the prayers were all sung, I hung back in the shadows, trying to keep my light hidden as the others filed out, until the church was empty but for me and God. Then I passed to the north side of the apse and down the narrow stairwell into the crypt of Saint Martial.

The air seemed closer than before, likely from the collapse of our former escape route, but the more notable difference was the addition of a new sarcophagus, awkwardly pressed into the space south of Saint Martial's own sarcophagus and the niches in the wall. I could have returned to the *scriptorium* to debate and worry and pace. But it was time for prayer to be a by-thought no longer. I knelt at Saint Martial's sarcophagus first, dripping some wax to the stone floor and setting my candle into it. I pressed my forehead to the rim of the lid, my downward gaze catching shadows candle-flickering over the relief carvings. The *vita* of Saint Martial was writ in stone into the side of his sarcophagus: his easy life among the safety of the Roman empire, his long journey to savage Gaul, the preaching and miracles, and lastly, tied to tree pole and following the model of Christ, his questioning and death. With each flicker of the candle, the relief shadows moved, as though the carvings were animated stone puppets, reenacting their scenes again and again.

I had meant to pray, but my thoughts have always easily been scattered. To what extent had Martial's sacrifice changed anything? Was it a veneer, this Christianity brought to the Roman and Celtic people of Gaul, adapted in form only as the people mingled with Goths and blended into Franks? Had Anskar's mission to the Northmen that Rachel told of seemed as futile as Martial's must have to his own family and followers? Would any crack or worn seam in the rites of pagan Odin and Tyr admit the small mustard seed that might grow into the Church, grow to break apart those rites and the bloody passions that went with them? Would Francia ever see the day when Saint Martial's example pointed to Christ's and brought complete conversion, that neighbor might no longer slay neighbor, and wars might cease between one stronghold and the next?

I stood, pried my candle from its paving stone, and circled to Saint Valerie. Once again, I set my candle and knelt, but this sarcophagus was new, its roughhewn stone not even carved with any pattern, much less scenes from her life and death. Perhaps that was why the abbot was so desperate for the story. Without one, what was her place among the people? Without the story of Saint Martial, what was the Frankish people's place in the Church from distant Rome? Rodegar's words echoed in my mind: "Stories are made by a people, and in turn *make* a people." What stories of Saint Valerie would shape the people into the image of Christ? Was Abbot Gonsindus correct once to say the people needed a saintly warrior-king, a Frankish King David to beckon warriors and kings alike to seek God with the intensity of the Psalms? Or did they need a once-virgin, just leaving the carefree days of childhood for devotion to husband or Christ, soul and body, a virgin who like the Roman Agnus defied the limits of her society and stood tougher than most men of the day, all for the love of her eternal Bridegroom? Did Aquitania need the story that God's saints were also the near-child women, emboldened to resist the dictates of men for the passion of God, with the quick reminder that God's protection and power, not lightly to be crossed, extended to these little-but-not-frail ones too?

Here I had come to pray for God's aid in the next hours and aid for writing, yet my thoughts were strewn across ages, and stories, and peoples. "Saint Irenaeus, pray for us. Saint Martin, pray for us.

Saint Martial, pray for us." My hand passed over the scars of hewing chisel marks, the side of Saint Valerie's tomb a blank slate. In the sarcophagus housing her body on Earth, even as her soul was in heaven, her remains were the channel that might bring the power of God here today. "Saint Valerie, pray for us."

What story could I—needed I—make of her?

My candle burned out. *Prime* surely approached, and my double-minded doubt returned twelvefold. Before orator and chorus arrived, I stole back up the stairs from the crypt and fumbled across the apse to the altar. I knelt there for a final blessing and felt the altar cloth still unfurled across it, not returned to the safety of the sacristy. I laughed at the tongue-whipping some acolyte would receive when this lapse was discovered. With a final Amen, I stood and groped toward the north transept. It was time to enact the plan.

The first doorway in this alcove led east to stairs winding up to the bell tower. But a second door was set across from this bell tower entrance, a narrow and short doorway which seemed an afterthought to the building design, perhaps to allow easy access to the abbot's quarters. I unbarred it and put my hand to the cold iron of the latch. My heart beat harder than when I was lashed to the stake in Thorfinn's camp. "I have a wild plan, but with your beauty and aid, it may work," I thought I might say to her. I rehearsed its delivery once more. I was sure I could say it without stammering. Fairly sure, at least. I took a deep breath and pushed on the handle.

Andrew and Nathaniel find the twinned disciple first, in an inn so crowded it has no room for these two messengers. Didymus holds a cup before him, from which he will not drink. He fears the centurions. He fears the Judas option, too. "Come and see, Thomas!" the sent ones urge. But Didymus knows hope unfulfilled is dangerous. As he follows them to Peter and the others, he beats to death his hope with an iron rod, though he stops short of draping it in scarlet. Andrew darts them into a small alley, up a twisting flight, to a darkened upper room. All of them are there, even the women. Mary's face is clothed with the sun. No surprise; it has been so since that third morning. Peter's face hints now too of the eternal: "We have seen him!" Didymus' hope was already a mangled corpse, but he pummels it a few more times, just to make sure. "Unless I see his riven heart, I will not believe it broke for me."

The handle held fast. I pushed again, harder, with no better result. Because the doorway was dark and darker, I swept its frame with my hands—no locks, no other bolts but the one I already pulled. I leaned against the door, hard. Nothing. Fighting panic, I groped at the hinges and felt the unmistakable sharp crumbles of thick rust. Add some moths, and I had a parable for the making.

I considered the main nave door to the west and rejected it. With the dormitory providing the monks ready access through the south transept, the main doors would be barred and locked for the night. A bird had begun its song outside, a sure sign the bell-ringer would be coming from the dormitory any minute.

"Saint Irenaeus," I yelped and threw my whole weight hard against the door, raising a dull thud that echoed off the vaulted arches.

"Aristeus?" called a voice faintly at the door. Rose and laurel, from sound alone!

"Rachel, wait there!" I urged as loudly as I dared. Sheer stubbornness made me try the door handle again, my skin grating against the rough metal. "Irenaeus and all the saints!" I muttered, a groan as much as a curse. I raised my eyes to heaven to plead and caught sight of the transept window, a shade lighter than the walls with the first hint of morning. High over the door, it was well beyond my reach, and yet…

I dashed back to the altar, blocking out Rachel's continuing questions at the door, certain now I heard a shuffling from the direction of the dormitory. With desperation that masqueraded as insight, I grabbed up the altar cloth and bolted to the bell tower stairwell. I took these three to a step, and in my hurry, I nearly passed my last hope—the bell tower window, normally a narrow slit to limit arrows, but damaged and cracked wider. *A long time since war threatened here*, Egilolf had said on that star-pondered night, a full season that felt a lifetime ago. Hopefully, the gap was wide enough for a slender woman to pass through.

"Rachel!" I called quietly out the opening, noting I could not quite fit the marred width. I spun the altar cloth into a length like a cord, slightly longer than the span of my arms, and lowered it out the window.

"Lower!" Her sharp command still carried a flowered edge, somehow.

I knelt on the steps and stretched my arm through the opening, pressing my body as far out as I could. I was rewarded with a sharp tug that would have yanked the cloth free of my grip if I hadn't already wound it once around my wrist.

Within seconds, Rachel's face appeared in the window, the morning's deep blue lighting her face far better than the dim inside the stairwell. As planned, she wore Father Leo's robe, her disguise for entering the abbey. Seeing her eyes and that slight smile on her face—I was never more certain of my choices for the future.

"I thought the strong warrior was supposed to climb up and rescue the maid?" she quipped.

Her full weight was still borne by my one arm, pulled through the window hole and awkwardly pressed over the rough edge of the sill, but I knew enough to bite my tongue on any comment about a woman's weight. A matched grin seemed the safest reply. I extended my other hand to offer her a higher handhold.

First, she passed in the shaft of a common spear, where it clattered freely down a few steps before the stairwell's curve caught it. It was a squeezing passage through the broken slit frame, even for her slight build, but once her arms and head were through, I was able to work myself to standing. I switched my grip to under her arms, uncomfortably aware of how close that put them to her chest—how could I think such things in this time-desperate moment? God, this woman drove all rational thought from me!—and with that leverage was able to pull her through. Her waist and legs came free faster than I expected, causing me to trip. We ended in a heap on the stairwell, her body atop mine. Rachel's face smirked into a wicked grin that I knew would precede a friendly but assertive mocking.

The bell struck loudly overhead, however, sparing me the comment. *Prime!* Even now, the monks sang as they filed into the church. "Come quick!" I urged, flailing to stand before grabbing her hand, snatching up the spear, and tugging her up the stairs. Another circle brought us to the bell chamber, the ringing nearly deafening now as the bell-ringer below kept a steady pace at the rope.

The windows to the four cardinal directions were much larger than the arrow slits below to allow the bell's peals to carry. To the east, low clouds were fiery orange with the foreshadow of full sunrise. To the west, a few last stars defied the loss of night as though claiming the right to witness this portentous hour. Also to the west—two columns of armed men scuttled across the approaches, one bending northward, uphill toward Fulgaud's tower and gate, the other reaching the edge of town before hooking to the tower's flank. The bell slowed and stopped its ringing, spent at last. From below, chanted psalms arose, majestic and powerful with the praise of morning.

"Thank God, we are just in time."

"For what?" questioned Rachel.

"No time to explain. Doff Father Leo's robe and—"

"You just said we had time—"

I cut her off, desperate enough to grasp her robe and tug it upward. She grabbed my hands, fighting them away from her waist. "All that waits until marriage! If you wanted a view of the battle, or something else, this was rather an extreme way to go about it."

"Did Egilolf not tell you the plan?" I gaped. "You do have a white robe on under this, do you not?" My cheeks felt bright enough to match the sunrise clouds.

"He's a bit terse. He said nothing of wearing the white robe, only that I was to take it and a spear to you at the north transept door before dawn." She reached under the priest's robe and brought out a white bundle.

"Put it on quickly!" I ordered. Surprisingly she obeyed, without question or even comment. She threw it on over Father Leo's robe, but his brown cloth stuck out below the white, and its hood bulged out the back of the neck. "You will have to take off Father's robe first." I scanned westward, as much to watch the spreading fight at *Comes* Fulgaud's tower as to give her privacy. "No comment," I cut off the jibe I felt her readying. "Hurry, or we will miss it."

"Miss what? The battle? Yes, yes, I'm hurrying." Her voice came muffled through layers of robes. "I'm ready."

The sun was not up yet, but even in the half-minute it took her to change, the sky had lightened considerably. She was radiant, dressed in all white.

Around me, the world stopped. "Who is this that appears like the dawn, fair as the moon, bright as the sun, majestic as the stars in procession?" The phrases spilled from my mouth before I realized I had said them.

"It's not every man that'll quote old poems for you," she quipped. All the same, she was blushing.

My head came back to me, and with it, the panic of time. "Take the spear," I directed. "Head out on the roof, over the nave, and be ready to cast it down when I give the signal."

"Signal? Wait—out on the roof?"

"You will be more visible. Do not question. We have no time." I pushed her to the west window ledge, the roof ridge but a span below it. The sunrise clouds had quickly lost their orange and were losing their yellow. The sun would be up in a minute at best. The clash of swords, shouts of defiance, and screams of agony rose from the direction of Fulgaud's tower. In the waxing light, the wooden wall around the tower swarmed like a disturbed anthill. "Trust me, please."

She glanced at the roof pitch. "What's the use of being a bandit girl if you don't take some risk?" She swung her feet over the window ledge and dropped. I handed her the spear. Light on her feet, she quick-stepped the transept ridgeline to the intersection with the nave ridge, then followed it out to the west end of the church. My own Saint Perpetua, stepping into the gladiator's ring…

Egilolf's tale, told later in a saner moment, was more harrowing than mine. As per our plan, once he pilfered a white robe and spear, located Rachel, and pointed her to the transept door, he hid himself away in the last shadows of a barrel next to a small weaver's hut, less than a hundred paces downhill from Fulgaud's fort, prepared for what lay ahead, or so he thought. My plan called for him to announce the miracle and draw all the fighters' attention toward it. Peter had scrounged for a signal horn. But do any of us know all, truly *all*, that we'll be called upon to do, this day or the next?

As he recalled it later, sitting by ourselves at the end of the dinner table, revelry swirling around us, leaving us untouched: "Did I hide out of cowardice? No. It was not my fight. There was no need to risk anything. Also, I swore an oath to God to never kill again. Not after…" His head hung, and his voice trembled. "It's a terrible thing to kill, Aristeus. More terrible if you know the person, their family. Terrible when there's not even the illusion of battle honor, when you have to kill someone to stop the blood rage of their murderous plans. Where's the justice in that? What becomes of that soul, killed in the midst of their sin? There can be no hope of salvation. How great is my part in their eternal damnation?"

"Whoever he was, he chose his actions. No one can claim the fates or planets made them sin."

"But what if I killed him needlessly? What if in the last minute, that last instant, he changed, or would have changed, would have stayed his hand, but now he's damned for eternity because I took that chance from him?"

"Was that part of your penance?"

"No. And yes." To my confusion, he added, "Not a part the priest added. My own resolution. My own…atonement." He sighed.

"Such as I had hoped it to be. But outside Fulgaud's gate…"

Before the battle, he waited in the morning shadows tucked behind the barrel. The house was a squat frame, leaning with age, and the roof needed patching. The small garden before it, though, was ordered and clear of weeds. The front door faced the town below, defined by the abbey walls, the church tower rising above all but the treetops across the far river.

The tramping of many feet weighed with weapons and purpose spoke of the final approach of Ebalus' columns on the other side of the house, closing the last distance to the fort.

Just await the miracle, Egilolf had told himself. His blood quickened anyway, a response trained by a score of past soul-searching moments before an attack, those stomach-clenched minutes waiting behind a wooden wall or sod berm he hoped he and his comrades had built high enough. His hand twitched to grip a spear. Part of his mind brought up past battles, old training, narrow gates of chance that had barely kept him from death's broad path. *Like the siege of Paris in '85, when he and Peter had shared a last worried grin before the sallying strike against the Northmen supplies. Like that vile and viler night, in Dorrat, the soldiers all home on leave…that infinite pause while the blade hovered over the unprotected back of a comrade swearing he'd kill his wife…*

The tempo of feet picked up a quick step, then following some bellow, broke to a run. Ebalus' men were charging. He didn't have to fight, Egilolf reminded himself, trying to force his heart to slow. Not today. *Never again will I kill*, he reaffirmed. *Await the miracle*. Battles cries, wails, the discordant notes of iron dulling iron. The battle was fully engaged at Fulgaud's fort.

Egilolf stood from behind his barrel, the sky too light for its shadow to hide him any longer. The eastern sky strained, the horizon unable to contain the sun much longer. A brief sally of some of Fulgaud's men, jumping down from un-assaulted portions of the wall push back the near breach, was quickly failing. Ebalus' second column had caught the sally unaware. A few of Fulgaud's stragglers attempted to flee the crush between the two arms of Ebalus' men by running toward the dubious safety of the village. Egilolf sank back into the corner between hut and barrel as the last fleeing man was run down paces past the weaver's hut, a spear through his back. The spear's owner pulled it free and turned to join the battle once more, his comrades already heading back up the hill, when a small cry of fear broke the chaos of battle sounds.

The sound caught the attention of both Egilolf and the soldier, for it came not from the battle, raging a hundred paces up the hill, but from directly inside the weaver's house. It was undoubtedly feminine. Egilolf watched, a sick dread growing, as the soldier hesitated, gauging the distance to the battle, how it fared, whether he would be missed. He ran to the hut door and would have seen Egilolf but perhaps for his fixation on its occupant.

The woman grunted in desperation, struggling to shut the door and drop the bar in place.

"Come on, lass, let me in!" the soldier laughed, prying at the door, his fingers wedging in cracks. "It won't hurt if you lay easy!" He put a foot to the wall and heaved, yanking the door outward, the woman hauled with it.

She shrieked again, a pitiable wail like a bird with a broken wing, making its last hops to elude the fox.

The soldier dragged her easily into the house. A second later, a toddler was tossed out the door, rolling in the dust, too stunned to do anything but cry in the mud.

I will not fight. I will not kill. Never again, Egilolf repeated to himself. Through the cracked shutters and the listing door, the woman shrieked louder, heard by none over the sound of battle. None but Egilolf. A fleshy smack cut the cry short, likely a fist to the face. *Just await the miracle.*

"God Almighty, Saint Martial…and Saint Valerie," he began to pray. "Step in. Aid us today. The battle. The woman in there. Give her strength for what she's facing." *Was it something like Aristeus' martyrs for a woman to bear such?* Egilolf heard the tearing of clothes, the weeping…or was the last his imagination? He shut it out and watched the battle. He had tried once to be God's justice, and that had led to disaster, guilt, and an unhelpful penance.

Sometimes a saint wants to be remembered.

The incongruous thought jarred him. What of Valerie's memory? What if someone had fought to save her? What if Valerie's story called others to the sword of justice? Egilolf searched for the last stars, but they had all faded. The *diptych* images swam before his eyes: Saint Michael spearing the serpent—*did you weep at the loss of Lucifer?*—and the Holy Mother's face, blurring with the face of the widow of Dorrat, a widow because of him. *God almost damned me once; He will surely damn me forever if I break my vow.*

He glanced toward the abbey, toward the rooftop of the church. *Almost,* he thought. *Almost. Await the miracle.* He twisted the signal horn in his hands, brought it to his lips. Paused. A motion caught his eye, the child attempting to rise from the dust, largely unhurt, at least outwardly. But the toddler stared at him, his eyes deadened by the malevolence that had suddenly befallen him.

Just await the— "Oh hell," he spat out. He dashed to the door and flung it open.

The scene was no surprise. The woman was flung on the floor, not even on the furs and bedrolls, but on the dirt by the firepit, sprawled on her back. The soldier was atop her, struggling to pin her legs wide. He didn't notice Egilolf. Something in the way his back was turned…*that twice-vile night, his enraged comrade drawing blade and swearing to kill her….* Time had slowed or sped before, in the worst intensity of thrust and dodge and smoke and screams that had been every thick battle. But now, his vision constricted to the soldier, the woman, the dirt floor—was the house really that small, he later thought, not more than an arm's span across?—time did not merely slow. It stopped. Some part of his mind stepped aside itself, calculating, in a world as bound as Joshua's sun before Gibeon. With the soldier's back to him, he could strike and kill him. A spear lay on the floor beside the soldier, a knife at his waist. He was larger, stronger than Egilolf, more recently trained and fit. If he challenged the soldier, and they fought equally, he may not win. Or the woman may not live. Was there any *added* honor to a *fair* fight? Was there any honor at all to killing? *I vowed to never kill again.* It was not too late to close the door.

Defend the orphan and widow, came a voice, long lost to his memory. His father's? The Almighty Father's? His mind whirled, the uneven battle raging not at Fulgaud's gate, nor in the confines of a weaver's hut, but far removed, in his thoughts…*Eloi, eloi…*

Then he saw her face. Fear, pain, need, terror. Bulging eyes, whimpering mouth, loss and shame and loathing retching itself from crevasses of the soul, out every wrinkle, from every pore.

All this in less than a second since he threw open the door. Perhaps there was a matched silence in the heavens for half an hour. The soldier's head was just starting to turn as he caught the reaction of the woman beneath him.

Egilolf leapt onto the man's back, driving him down onto the woman. He drew the dagger from the soldier's belt in the same motion. As the soldier's air was knocked from him, Egilolf began plunging the blade, deep and deeper, through the base of the neck. Again and again, for certainty, between the ribs, seeking the heart.

Paralyzed by the first stroke, the soldier lay still atop the woman; aorta and esophagus cut by the second, he began gushing blood from his mouth onto the victim beneath him.

Egilolf stood over them, his stomach lurching, the knife held stiffly at this side. The woman's shrieks returned with a frantic flailing of limbs.

Egilolf threw off the corpse, brushed aside the woman's thrashing arms, and tried to calm her. Yet on and on, she shrieked, spastic now, and only began to subside to a sobbing when Egilolf backed off, all but tripping through the doorway. He had enough presence of mind to grab the corpse and drag it out with him. He threw it next to Fulgaud's fallen man, the runner who had brought war's horror to the town.

Egilolf caught sight of the child. Dazed, perhaps as much as the toddler, he prodded the lad toward the doorway, then staggered a few paces from the hut and dared to raise his face to heaven. *What have I done?* The world did not pause now, and yet diverse parts of his mind continued to question each other, clambering, pulling, writhing like the *daemonic* Legion in a holy day parable play. *You saved her. You damned yourself. Justice. Be merciful, as your heavenly Father is. Those who have no sword should sell their cloak to buy one. All who draw the sword shall die. The poor are plundered, and the needy groan. A sword will pierce your own soul, too.*

A shaft of light pierced the mist across the river, through trees and the air thick with battle, and lit the abbey bell tower, radiant and triumphant. He went to raise the signal horn to his lips and realized he had dropped it somewhere. And then he saw the angel of God…

I have seen with my own eyes the likeness of the coming of the Last Day. Three seconds after Rachel reached the nave ridgeline, the sun breached the treetops east of the river, lit a halo of low fog rising off the water, and pierced through a small gap a shaft of brilliance that none can match but the dawn. The town still held to weak shadows, but that shaft reached the highest rooftop, the church, setting alight that avenging female, her white robe glowing as it billowed to a slight breeze. The dazzling snow and blazing fire of John's Apocalypse were a close second to this. High over her head, she raised the spear, no fumbling, timid maid but a warrior ready to pierce her enemies through. I hastily drew forth the incense from my scrip and tossed the powder to the breeze. Such a powerful aroma, even a whiff caught by anyone in the monastery or town, could not be mistaken for anything but the scent of heaven.

The blast of a horn echoed off the trees across the river, cascading to the town and the embattled hill. The horn repeated its own call, a rising sound to drown the battle din. Slowly at first, but with a gathering power, stillness settled across the valley of Lemouicensis, the Pale Horse reined in, as warriors' heads turned and arms wielding sword and spear lowered, uncertain. Then fingers pointed, and shouts of surprise and alarm sounded from the tower fort.

In the town, a new chant arose, spreading up the hill to the fort like a wildfire, neither paean or psalm, but the overwhelmed cry of adulation, a much lesser repeat of the seraphim transfixed by the full glory of God Almighty enthroned: "Valerie! Valerie! Saint Valerie!"

So caught up was I in the intensity of the chants, the horn, and the blazing sun-shafted light, I missed the opportune moment. Perhaps Rachel had read my intent, or the mass invocation of the crowd spread across the valley indeed brought God's grace. Regardless, Rachel worked her own timing and grasped her spear flat overhead with both hands. With a deliberateness that left no gap for doubt, she struck it down over her raised knee, snapping it. The crack of that shaft caught a pause in the cacophony below.

I studied first the fort's gate, where Egilolf was supposed to be, ready to interpret Saint Valerie's demand for peace for any too dull to see it. His role in all this was to announce the miracle, to make sure there was no misinterpretation. I didn't see him, but—

I glanced at the fort for a moment, yet when I swiveled back to the ridge, Rachel—spear, robe, halo, and all—were gone!

I cannot say what I thought in that second, or if I thought at all. Did I consider a new Assumption, my angel called up like the Queen of Heaven, clothed with the sun, the stars at her feet? Was it blasphemous to even think so?

My eye caught a frantic thrashing at the south edge of the nave roof. Rachel had fallen toward the cloister and barely clung to the eave. I sprinted down the bell tower stairs, tripping on narrow curves and glancing off walls in my haste. Before the monk chorus could wonder at my crashing entrance into the north transept, I had flown across the church width, out the south transept door, down the hall, and out to the cloister. On the south wall of the church nave, which was the north wall of the cloister, Rachel hung in an indecorous twist of limbs and white robe, only one hand grasping the rim of a column. I ran under her even as she slipped free, and I more broke her fall than truly caught her.

"Father Leo's robe!" she cried as she rolled off me and struggled to untangle herself. "Do you have it?" Unremembered, it was still in my hand, and I tossed it over her shoulders, tugging the hood to cover her head as feet came slapping flagstones from the church.

"To your knees," I hissed as I pulled her down with me to a posture I hope resembled awe and reverence, facing us both towards the church wall from which she had fallen.

"What is this?" a voice behind us called. Inwardly, I groaned. Father Ageric. If my miracle wasn't picked apart now, it would be, well, a miracle. Rising to face him, I kept my hand on Rachel's shoulder to hold her bowed and facing the church.

"A miracle, Father! Do you hear the battle?"

"No," he gruffly began. "I've—"

We had an audience of other monks now, and perhaps therein lay my salvation. I cut him off. "Exactly! An apparition! The most holy and blessed Saint Valerie appeared just now on the church roof, over her own crypt, with a warning to the war-bent parties beyond these walls to cease their fight." The monks all followed my pointing finger to the empty roof, but the prior kept his eyes fixed on me. The man wouldn't be taken for a fool. And yet, he was calculating. Probably to the penny, he could figure what such a miracle would bring in pilgrims' donations.

"Your scout friend should best stay here then, in veneration. But you, scribe, should come to tell the abbot." He turned back to the dormitory portico. He motioned to the rest of the monks. "Come, all of you. To the abbot."

It was not surprising that Rachel, with her bandit past, made good her escape. The peace held, yielding a parley and eventually a treaty, with Fulgaud placing his hands in Ebalus' after all, in exchange for promises of support for the young Charles, perhaps next rex *of Francia. Ebalus' brother, the third Ranulf, was to be given the comital rights to Pictauensis and enfeoffed to his brother, so I later heard.*

Rachel had peace, as did Lemouicensis, and even Saint Martial's abbey. As for Saint Valerie, before the combined efforts of Gonsindus, Hecfroi, and Lemouicensis' bishop Anselm, Fulgaud withdrew any claims to her remains. Who, after all, could gainsay such a sign over the church that held her relics?

As for Egilolf—well, there is peace, and then there is peace.

CHAPTER 19:
DAVID'S BLOODY HANDS

Jesus puts away the towel and washbowl, now full of dirty water. "In my Father's house are many rooms. I've prepared one for each of you." Peter can bear knowing he understands at best half of what his Savior means. Jesus leads him, barefooted, from the entryway into the next room. He pauses at the doorway and motions Peter inward. "I will not leave you as orphans."

Leave? Peter wonders.

"My peace I leave you, my peace I give to you." The room is a banquet hall, and the feast is laid around the Passover lamb.

Peter eagerly steps in.

"But I have not come to bring peace, but a sword." The door swings shut with the clang of iron, the rattle of prison chains...

And Peter wakes from this dream to the chill, stone walls of a holding cell— solid rock melded to iron rods. He stands and tries to stretch out the scars from years of scourgings, stonings, and beatings for the Name. One of Rome's Christians had brought an ewer of clean water in the night. Peter considers washing his whole body but contents himself with his feet. He steps to the window and watches the stars fade before the sun on his last day on this earth.

Peace but also a sword...

Some of the younger warriors, perhaps from both Ebalus and Fulgaud's armies, were disappointed in the sudden end to the battle, practically before it started. The monks, villagers, and older warriors, though, were grateful for the passing of the crisis without much blood. The warbands from both sides withdrew until the peace was sworn, but the townspeople waited not at all to storm the gate of Saint Martial, as eager as they had been at Saint Valerie's receptive procession, yearning to venerate her relics, offer thanks, and hope Abbot Gonsindus would contribute to their impromptu feast from the monastery's storehouses.

As it was early harvest season and this region at least had been spared famine, plague, army—mostly!—or other apocalyptic equine disasters in the past few years, food was plentiful. Before *terce*, tables were dashed together into the roadways approaching the monastery gate to create a common feasting area. By *none*, the monastery bakery was handing out fresh bread beneath the hot sun, town wives were setting out hastily made stews, and, though rumor could but barely have reached them already, outlying rustics were arriving for the celebration.

The lack of fasting, decorations for the tomb, or even a tale of Saint Valerie's life to read—my agony at the thought of sitting down to that prodigious work had only grown during my furtive activities—all made for a strange feast day, but who could return to the monotony of toil after witnessing such a miracle?

As the preparations began in town, I was led to the abbot's study. My meeting with the abbot was preceded by a discussion, behind closed doors, between only Gonsindus and Ageric. The tumult of waiting in the hall outside his study, doubled for the memory of Egilolf's thrashing and my cowardice the last time here, was all wasted. If Gonsindus was not as simoniacal as Ageric, he nevertheless knew the upkeep costs of his abbey. Our discussion was not much longer than his command: "Scribe Aristeus, the averted battle outside notwithstanding, you must still complete a…suitable…*translatio* of Saint Valerie. If you are also able to include the start of her *acta*, beginning with today's wondrous sign, well, I'm sure the abbey could see fit to sustain you for your additional efforts." Unlike the previous meetings, this time he was concerned enough to give me his full focus, his writing implements untouched on his desk. He had more pressing concerns than the distribution of bread this day. "I recommend you revisit other saints' lives for examples of what information to include; Saint Foy of Conques comes to mind. A copy of her *vita* is held in the library. Holding to certain…"

He seemed to struggle for the word, so I supplied it: "Truths, Father?"

"No. Certain *forms*, I was going to say." He tried to suppress his annoyance and failed. "Yes, holding to time-tested *forms* helps ensure a writer covers all that is necessary without wasting a listener's attention on details not exemplary, details that don't beckon the flock to reform. Too much deviance from these forms and listeners get lost in the morass of the trivial, a temptation, however subtle, of the great Deceiver himself. So think carefully as you write."

Gonsindus' tones held their own marginalia to his words. I was being asked to write a more common, a more acceptable, story of Saint Valerie's relocation and miracles. God, through Saint Valerie, used my hands and feet to work out a miracle—the cessation of the battle—only a few hours ago, preventing further Frankish in-fighting, and yet here I was tasked again with the impossible. *The Lord gives, and the Lord takes, but some days he does more taking.* I checked myself and guiltily added, *Saint Irenaeus, pray for me.*

All the worry about writing fell away, though, when I stepped outside, into the light of day and the bustle of preparation for the feast. Egilolf and I met at the gate, and after some scouting, we found Rachel emerging from the women's quarter of the guesthouse, like any other pilgrim.

She passed on the rumor that an eager soul had located the two halves of Saint Valerie's spear, tumbled among the grasses below the north eave of the church. Before this layman got too far, the monks heard of this, claimed the relics for the people's saint, and deposited them into the sacristy for safekeeping. If a tentmate of Peter's cursed the theft of his best spear the night before battle, no one thought much of it, and the weapon of a comrade dead at the fort passed to him for replacement, did much to settle his temper.

Egilolf, of course, deserved to be told all the details of the panicked last seconds in the bell tower and the even more horrifying dash to keep Rachel from falling to the reward of a broken limb. How much he told Peter of our plan last night, beyond the need of a spear and the urging to look east for a great sign during the battle, I know not, but a scout knows to keep his military secrets, and those best kept by telling none.

We three searched the crowd for Father Leo. The talk throughout the town was the miracle, of course, with the heavenly light and the glorious beauty of the saint. I passed a group debating whether one had actually smelled the incense of heaven during the apparition. I smiled to myself. I also overheard talk that Abbot Gonsindus had already announced plans to create a statue containing Saint Valerie's remains, like Saint Foy's. Egilolf cut off my forming dissent with a strong grip to my arm and a cup of wine.

Father Leo was not to be found in the town streets, yet finding Peter in the crowd, we four managed to claim an empty table and enjoy the feast. Peter, happy to have a soldier's pay once more, tossed back his wine as though he had fought all day. Rachel and I said little but glanced at each other a lot, which drew plenty of remarks from both Egilolf and Peter to fill our lack.

Egilolf seemed glad enough at table, but in the heat of the afternoon, he and I sought a shade tree outside the abbey gate, and here a pinch of his brow revealed some of his troubles. When I inquired, he revealed his morning's dilemma at the weaver's hut and the doubts that yet plagued him. I listened but couldn't see a solution beyond allowing him to drift off into his own thoughts or perhaps a nap. I left him alone and wandered back to our table.

As the afternoon sun shifted first one then another set of tree shadows over us, requiring us to occasionally move our tables to chase them, Peter left to find Rodegar, who he said had followed the army up from Pictauensis. Rustic music had, of course, filled the crannies between the cheers and laughter throughout the day, with short dances for children, the unmarried girls bold enough to grab hold of a lad, and occasionally an old woman who gained her youth again for a minute or two.

I realized with a start that Rachel and I were left comparatively alone at our table, with music in the background threatening to reveal my total lack of dancing skill. I tried to cover with conversation. "So, how goes the washing?"

She glared and then grinned in good humor. "You mean when I'm not getting hauled up to a roof tower and getting disrobed by a mendicant monk?"

"I was not disrobing you!" Heads turned at nearby tables. I dropped my voice. "And I am not mendicant. Nor a monk, for that matter. Did you know I never took vows? The Northmen raid came weeks before my final rites." I ripped pieces off a bread loaf to keep my hands from shaking. I prayed that one day I could speak with this woman without getting nervous. "Egilolf once told me it meant the Lord had another future planned for me."

"So what are you, then? What will become of this Aristeus I keep hearing so much about?"

My first thought was of me and her, holding hands, gazing together toward…the rest of the dreamt idea was nebulous and refused to coalesce. At the table, I studied my bread. "I do not know. Find a monastery…other than this one." I shrugged. "The cells, the abbot—yes, it will be far from this one."

"You don't sound excited. And you never answered why you didn't find another monastery before all this relic hunting." She cut me off my reply. "No, I can guess. Your hatred of the Northmen is clear."

"Was," I answered.

Her brows drew together in confusion.

"It *was* clear. Now…" The image of Thorfinn holding aloft his triumphant shard of bloodied skull clashed against that of Hecfroi, leaving his missionary priests behind to baptize Northmen converts, and also clashed against a remnant horde of aches for my lost monastery.

"Is it past?" she asked softly.

"Past enough to lay down my hate. Maybe." Smoked and screaming memories lingered. "But truthfully, maybe not enough to return to the life of a monk."

"What about the life of a traveling scribe, paying your way by copying and transcribing? Maybe teaching me and others to read and write." She hesitated, which was quite unlike her. "Perhaps with a wife traveling with you?" She blushed.

I smiled at her. "That could work."

I don't know about heaven, but there was silence on earth, as far as I could tell. I think we just sat there and gazed at each other.

Rachel and I came back to the world of our feast-day dining table when Peter returned late afternoon with the bard, already tuning his harp. Slowly the crowd began to shift seats and tables to encircle him in preparation for an evening of tales. Fulgaud and Ebalus, each with their captain, men, and bishop, held to their own periphery of the communal celebration, likely for the healthy best of all as barrel upon barrel of wine were breached.

Rodegar leapt onto one of the empty barrels and began calling, "Come near, come near! Tonight I sing the tale of Olivier and his heaven-aided combat against a Magyar giant, beyond the eastern edge of the Great Charles' empire."

"*Magyar* giant?" Egilolf questioned softly, resuming his place at our table after his nap. We both chuckled to the confusion of Rachel and Peter. *Rodegar's malleable stories*, I thought.

"Lest I forget or change my mind again," Rachel addressed Egilolf, "I have something of yours." She drew out from around her neck the pouch of Saint Vincentius's grave dust. She flipped it over in her hand, smiled, and then tossed it to my companion.

He caught it with surprise. "Is that an apology?"

"No," she smirked. "My need was once greater than yours. But I'll be all right now." She took my hand, and we spun away from his astonishment and toward the strumming bard.

We listened to the story of the Great Emperor Charles' *fidelis* Olivier overcoming a Magyar giant in mysterious lands east of Lotharingia. At the end of his tale, the bard glanced our way, but the crowd pressed him to another performance before he could reach our table. "Very well," the bard conceded to the crowd. "A new tale, which recently crept out from the timbers of eastern Germania: terrifying dog-headed men discovered, and a missionary trio commissioned to convert them. I give you the *Missionis ad Cynocephali!*" His fantastical song kept the crowd's attention through all their laughter and tears.

"Nice tale!" Egilolf cheered as Rodegar strode up, fiddling with his tuning pegs. "Heard something like the giant story once before…"

"Ah, a story was a pittance for these people today. Tomorrow I'm eager to ask what and why of witnesses to this morning's miracle, so I can assemble its song."

"You didn't see it?" Peter asked. "The whole town saw it."

"Ah, I missed it, to my misfortune. I blazed trails beyond the town border, in the east woods and boles, blowing my horn. For practice." His mouth twitched with a hint of a smile. "So as not to disturb the townsfolk, you know?" He winked and ambled on, singing a line as he approached the next table.

I questioned Egilolf, who shrugged. "I added to your plan," he explained. "Would've been a shame if everyone in a pitched battle missed your sign. His horn drew all eyes. Better than mine would have."

The next hour passed in the fine idleness of a feast day, all of us complaining of stuffed stomachs and yet finding room for another sip or bite. Peter and Egilolf spent the time talking of Ebalus' plans to reclaim land near Thoucars, to give soldiers land not only to guard but also to own and farm. Somewhere between staring into Rachel's eyes and blushing at suggestive comments by Peter, I heard them toss about the merits of turning their hands to a farming life.

Dusk was yet an hour or two off when, quite full of meat pies, breads (not acorn, praise God!), and even some roasted rabbit, I suggested we all make our way to the church for a thanksgiving prayer to Christ and Saint Valerie. It seemed a fitting conclusion. Peter readily agreed, his eagerness bolstered by a cup in each hand. The abbey gate was thrown open, and we passed through unchecked, any guard having long since joined the feast. As we passed into the church, the din of the crowd outside faded. It was not with somber awe but sated near-drowsiness that we all ambled, more than processed, to the apse. The wheat-gold sun of late afternoon cast its beam onto the altar, and I raised my hands—

"Mother!" a voice called from behind. "Here he is! Come! The man that saved me!" We four turned, and I saw, silhouetted by the light outside the west door, a young man drawing into that golden silence a woman.

To my right, Egilolf sighed, and perhaps only I heard the groan in it, something of the wailing of the caught-unaware sinner whose oil has run out before the dawn. The youth, however, hastened with a dance to his stride hampered only by a slight limp. "I saw you! I saw you at the feast, good man, and have come to thank you!" He pointed at Egilolf with his right hand even as he pulled his mother with his left.

Then I recognized them. Both. Egilolf, it seemed, already had. The young man was the tortured soldier Ennodius, Fulgaud's guard, who Egilolf risked all to save when we were captured by Garbart. The young man who Egilolf had been so desperate to free, who he found familiar at our first departure from the *comes'* fort.

And the woman.

For a brief second, I did not recognize her, so happy and carefree she was in the presence of her son. But as her eyes followed the son's gesture toward Egilolf, her face contorted, and memory erupted like a boil: the hateful widow of Dorrat, who almost drew her knife against him on the roadway of Saint Valerie's procession. It would have been fitting, almost heavenly ordained, if the young warrior stood in a shaft of light while the woman remained in shadow, such contrast split their faces: his alight with the relief of salvation, in the presence of his terrestrial savior, hers twisted with a furious hate, more the bringer of damnation than any recoil from its proximity. Her breath immediately switched to a rasping, frenetic struggle. I checked to see if she reached for her belt knife yet again. She did not move, but I could have sworn the sharp crack of a backhanded face echoed through the vaults. Something of her shock and pain—with denial, perhaps—recalled to me the visage of the child-eating *strix*.

Egilolf tensed to flee, like a startled deer. He began to turn away from the woman, away from the confused son, torn between his fading joy and his mother's torment. But my companion halted himself and faced the woman squarely, shoulders strong set but not defiant.

He spoke first.

"You know what he said. What he was coming to do." Before she could reply, he added, "I'm not the only one who heard it."

"He said it before. He had his fits, his flares, and then they'd pass."

"Not this time." Egilolf's voice was soft, but firm, an iron rod set to guide, not to strike. "He thought you betrayed his bed. We told him it was a malicious rumor, but he wouldn't believe otherwise. Stormed home with his knife held low. At the ready. Said he would cut out your cheater's heart."

"You didn't have to! You could have, have—see what came of it! What we've become, what we've fallen to. All because of you!"

Egilolf's restraint did little to settle the woman.

"What—" I ventured.

"Stay out of my life! Mine and my son's! You have taken enough of it!" Her scream degenerated into a wail that collapsed into a sobbing mess. "You have taken…"

"I saved you. Saved your son," Egilolf countered, yet his iron quivered with a creeping doubt and a shadow of fear.

The woman bolted up, back to her feet, plunging both hands towards Egilolf as though to bury daggers in his chest. The son and Peter both intercepted her, trying to pull her back without injuring her, while she railed, "He wouldn't have needed saving! My son wouldn't have had to be a soldier! But for you!" She screamed louder, "But for you!"

Rachel took a step toward the woman, then paused, her outstretched hand hesitating. She withdrew it awkwardly. The youth's face was now as tumultuous as a spring flurry, changing temperament by the minute: agony, questioning, wonder, indecision.

The woman's surge of strength spent, she collapsed once again, this time held up by her son.

"I—" the son started. "What I mean—" He took two steps backward, half-dragging his mother, his face now transfixed with confusion. "It was you? You killed my—" Another stuttering of steps backward, and then, "But then? Why did you?"

As if he knew there was no answer, or he could not face it, he stopped. He cradled the wracked form of his mother and staggered to the door. There he paused, as though to come back, but instead, the two passed out of the church.

Silence reigned again, but the afternoon sun was waning, and the serenity of before had fled or had been shattered. No one moved. Did everyone else burn to ask the youth's questions?

Egilolf faced Peter first, but I saw no trace of questions on the bandit-soldier's face.

"Someone's called a storm, eh?" Peter's joke dried up in the first two words.

"Go. Please." Egilolf's stoic iron was gone, rusted to exhausted shards.

Peter questioned, "But—"

"I know I have your friendship. Despite all." He waved his hand with the fatigue of futility.

We stayed.

"Please," Egilolf repeated. "I ask you all to leave. I would be alone for the hour."

"Alone?" I asked.

"Well, I have God." He tilted his head toward the altar. "And my failures. Neither will leave me."

We withdrew, but only as far as the door. Outside, I motioned Rachel and Peter to await me and slipped back into the nave.

My intention was not to spy nor to intrude, but to be present, close enough if Egilolf had need. He seemed to face the hardest struggle in our travels yet. Whatever had passed between him and the woman, he had borne it for a personal eternity.

I stayed in the shadows of the north colonnade, shifting silently from column to column, up to the transept. Egilolf knelt before the altar, his lips murmuring a prayer heard only by God. He paused, and I thought by the cock of his head, he had detected me. But he leaned his ear south, toward the dormitory.

A few seconds passed, still in silence as far as I could tell, but then I too heard the shuffle of approaching, unsteady feet. Father Leo entered. His path took him straight to the altar. He knelt beside Egilolf, sharing the stillness for drawn-out minutes, until at last Egilolf bowed his head and joined him.

The old priest raised his head, crossed himself before the altar, and opened his eyes. Focused on the altar and crucifix, he began: "The miracle of the four companions cutting open the roof to bypass the crowd, hoping Jesus would heal their crippled friend— the miracle is not that a born cripple takes up his mat and walks, but that Jesus forgives his sins. It baffles the Pharisees. It baffles our world today, if anyone would attempt to understand it. Do our sins create a greater debt to those we sin against, or to God?"

Father Leo remained facing the altar.

Egilolf himself did not reply.

"You have seen more of the evil of this world than most, yes? That much I knew from your past as a soldier." Again a pause, and no reply. "The men you killed. Justified by Augustine's treatises or not, you bear it heavily."

Egilolf's glance told his surprise.

"I have borne many people's confessions and have been His

assurance of forgiveness," the old priest explained. "You are not the first who begged forgiveness for a killing the *dux* ruled justified. Feeling guilt does not mean you are truly guilty. Yet you sought a penance…"

So thin was his voice I could barely hear him, though we were enshrouded in the silence of the church.

Father Leo turned to Egilolf, wincing as he shifted on old knees. "What was the purpose of your penance? Did you think to *earn* God's forgiveness?"

Egilolf buried his face in his hands.

"You see now the cripple did not *do* anything for Christ to redeem him, yes?" The question reverberated in the silence.

"But I…" Egilolf's voice was hoarse. It trembled. "I killed a soldier. Not in a war. From my own town. Maybe without need. I— I don't know." Now his words tumbled out. "I am certain of what he meant to do, what he said, as he headed for her. Should I have challenged him? He had a wife and son. My thought was to spare her. What if I was wrong? What if it didn't have to happen?" He twisted as though fending off restraints. "I felt, no matter what they said—the commander, the tribune, my friends, the priest—I, I was certain God could not, would not, set his eyes upon me anymore. That I was forever damned…" Egilolf slumped over his own knees, head to the ground, his body wracking in silent sobs.

Father Leo held the silence for three minutes. He then probed, "Perhaps you needed forgiveness for what you did. Perhaps not. There is no harm, right or wrong, to put it all upon God's altar and seek His offered restoration, yes?"

"But it didn't work. The woman still hates. My heart is still cut…like a hollow in the deep earth, too cavernous to fill. I swore to never kill again. But today, again, the need was great. Maybe. Should I abandon soldiering, or does God call me back to killing as more punishment? The penance…didn't work."

"Your penance?" the priest sounded surprised, "No, it didn't *work*, as you say. Not as you thought, no. You misunderstood it from the start. It was not the four friend's work of cutting open the roof, nor the cripple's struggle to rise, if he attempted such a thing, that *earned* Christ's healing. He never earned it. But he did *seek* it."

The sun was setting outside. The church dimmed. Father Leo, unhurried, drew a taper from his robe and exited the nave. He returned a minute later with the candle lit and continued as though there had been no interruption. "Could your penance have been not a punishment, but an opportunity, the chance for you to turn your soul toward His grace? The grace of conversion is not an instant. Or rather, it is, and also it is not. The servant told to work in the dairy and convert milk to butter—is she done and back in a minute? A farmer who sows a field—does he judge a week sufficient for growth? If some land does not yield, he does not scorch the rest as waste, yes?

"Now think this: Christ took upon himself all the evil of all men at all times...and still forgave them. Just as you cannot control another's willingness to reconcile, neither can that person prevent God's willingness. His grace is already offered, no matter how unworthy you think you are. The purpose of the penance wasn't to *earn* grace. Still less was it to change the woman's heart. Yes, I saw the whole exchange from the transept. Her heart is God's to reconcile; you have done what you could. So you see now your penance was to put you on the path of acceptance, yes?"

I was fascinated with Father Leo's sermon and wished for parchment to write it all down, but as neither had noticed me, the old priest continued without pause.

"You've fought Moors and Northmen and your own countrymen in Lotharingia. Much has been to fight back evil. And evil encompasses more than war. It's found in simple villages, corrupt priests, husbands' mistreatment of wives, the abuse of the poor, and abandonment of children to slavers or the cold. I've heard confessions from every role in society, *comes* to soldier, *colonus* to slave. All see some evil. But when you've waded through it too long—perhaps especially in the fight of it—its ways infect your mind, waking or dreaming. You fear it has become you, yes? In battling it, you no longer distinguish yourself from the evil you fight." He handed the taper to Egilolf, then pulled something else from his robe. In the small light of the candle, all I saw was a white object. I took cautious steps closer.

"The *diptych*," the priest continued.

Egilolf only glanced.

"No, look closely. Study the expression, the posture. The Mother, pointing to her Son. Michael the Archangel, trampling evil."

Egilolf brushed the image with two fingers, lingering. "Mary's face here is like—like the woman. As I remembered her when we grew up together. Before her marriage darkened." His voice lightened. "Maybe it's better to remember her this way."

"These portraits are not happenstance. The battle is real, as is the evil. The battle may even be noble, if you fight evil. Other warriors have pondered the Scriptures on this. The Great Charles himself had his scholars compile every Word of God on the subject of swords, for the answers are not easy. Is the defense of others not holy? If so, why did defending the kingdom make David, the man who sought God's heart, unworthy to raise His temple? I should not think it condemnation. Maybe there remains, even in this noble task, a caution, a strong caution, to killing in the name of God or justice. A caution so strong that it wears the visage of rebuke. Why? Because the archangel was made first for the trumpet, not the sword.

"Give me your finger." From anyone but this priest, Egilolf would have resisted. But he did not hesitate when Father Leo brought out a small blade from his robes and made a prick in the fingertip. He squeezed out drops of blood onto the *diptych*.

I crept closer, within an arms-breadth behind them.

"You still have that grave dust around your neck? Give it here."

Egilolf's mouth worked, perhaps to tell Father the story of the theft and recent return of Saint Vincentius, but instead, he wordlessly handed over the pouch.

The priest shook out some ashes onto the *diptych*, then swirled the blood and ash together. His shaking forefinger made a mess across the serpent's body, and suddenly the carved *daemon* seemed alive and sinister.

"The Deceiver's last trick is to lock your thoughts onto the battle, to see only the contest against sin, whether it's in the fallen world, fellow man, or your own life. Surely you know as a fighter that in the Archangel's thrust into the serpent's side, much blood must spray back over Michael's white robes." Father Leo pressed his thumb through the bloody ash. He smeared it over the radiant warrior. "Grime bespeckled is a truer portrait of this fighting angel, yes? I've survived marauder raids a time or two." Now the angel was indistinct from the sinuous enemy. The priest raised the *diptych* above Egilolf's head, forcing Egilolf's gaze upward. "But in keeping your focus only on the battle, even the battle against evil, you take your eyes off of Christ." He put one hand over the Archangel's bloody half of the *diptych*.

"That is why Saint Michael is on the left, for you to read it like a book."

Egilolf began a protest. "I can't –"

"Someday, maybe, we'll have the luxury to teach everyone to read. For now, read it like a picture series, yes? After the battle of angel and serpent on the left, the Mother follows on the right. She who all generations will call blessed points us, her other children, back to her Son. The only action is her hand, pointing us away from the world, away from the serpent, away even from Saint Michael's righteous contest. Off herself. All to Him." He paused. "It is the great purpose of the *Hodegetria*, forgotten in its commonplace repeat. Perhaps, with your gaze reaffixed properly, you will find your strength again to do His will, to take up in defense the sword you fear." He slid his hand away from Saint Michael's half, revealing the chaos of blood and ash.

Using the assistance of Egilolf's shoulder, Father Leo stood. He placed the *diptych* on the altar and angled the left half perpendicular to Egilolf's view. He left the *Hodegetria* pose square. Only the image of Mary and Child could be seen from where Egilolf knelt. The old priest took the candle from Egilolf's hand and stuck it to the altar in a drip of its own wax, beside and just in front of the ivory tablet. Father Leo shuffled out the way he came in.

The rest of the church was dark now and equally silent, the birds of the day gone to rest, the village outside perhaps continuing its celebration, but in abatement, so that I heard no strains of music. I approached and knelt beside Egilolf, in Father Leo's place.

My companion did not turn his gaze, but he smiled and grasped my forearm with a reassuring strength.

Beneath our feet, in the crypt of Saint Martial, the relics of Saint

Valerie also lay, a conduit, a nearness of presence, as she joined our prayers to hers: healing from the past, hopes and fears for the future, a seeking of His will. High above, seen faintly through the slot windows in the apse, stars appeared in the east.

Upon the altar, directly over the sarcophagi in the crypt below, directly beneath the eternal lights in the *aether* above, the candle's flame lit a small sphere, only enough to illuminate the icon. Egilolf and I—indeed, anyone entering the church—would be drawn by that small light to the image of Mary, and by her guidance, to her Son.

I left Egilolf to spend the next hours in silent contemplation. From the church, I returned to the *scriptorium*, laid out a piece of parchment, and then laid out another beside it. Atop of both, I wrote *Translatio de Sancta Valerie*. Then, without pause, I wrote on the first sheet the expected stories. The usual *miracula*. The usual? Yes, the common ones that would readily be accepted—but more so, truly understood—by a wider audience than those of us who had come to know her as well as anyone could, carrying around her bones and seeing seed fall onto the good soil of renewed hearts. Who would truly understand those stories, convoluted and personal? A courtship of ignorance, a courage found, and for Egilolf a heart-wound…well, a wound not healed, and yet a soul turned once again toward God. Even if the wound heals not in this lifetime.

None of those personal miracles I put into the version I would leave with Gonsindus. No, the abbey's version held the usual miracles: the heavenly fight against the Northmen's *daemon* and sorceress, the healings, a feud ended, the apparition that halted a battle. Those were stories that would be understood near and far, by those a hundred years from now still facing battles with countrymen and foreigners alike, still crippled with disease and close-held hurts festering into grudges.

But if for no one but myself, the company of angels, and the fuller memory of Saint Valerie, I labored all night on this, the complete but private version of her miracles.

I have just taken my last break, rubbing out a cramp in my hand. Out the east window, the stars fade to a new day. The sun rises late and later. Autumn will hold off no more.

Coming across the vegetable and herb gardens is the unmistakable form of a woman—my woman!—hair radiant in the sun, coming to pull me from this enclosed world of books, off perhaps, to distant lands together. May we make it back to see Egilolf and Peter, and this domain of Saint Valerie's again. Somehow, the scent of rose and laurel reaches me at this distance. If it is a trick of the mind, it is a very pleasing one.

I finish this as I have every great and lengthy work I copied: *Completed, thank God! This calls for some wine.*

Multitudes who sleep in the dust of the earth will awake, some to everlasting life. Those who impart wisdom will shine like the brightness of the heavens, and those who lead many to righteousness, like the stars for ever and ever.
Daniel the Prophet

Prologue:

Note 1: *"Translatio Sancta Valerie."* *Translatio*: literally, the translation (movement) of a saint's relics from one place to another. Since a saint was considered most present at his or her physical resting place, a translation was not a simple exchange of houses, but more momentous, like if the British monarch were to abandon Buckingham Palace for a new home.

Note 2: *"Pictauensis to her new home at Lemouicensis."* Modern Poitiers and Limoges, respectively. The spelling of the name is from the 12th c. *Chronicle* of Bernard of Itier, librarian at the abbey of Saint Martial. See Note 15.

Note 3: *"Saint Irenaeus, intercede for me."* Irenaeus was a late-second century bishop of Lyons, sent to Gaul from the churches in Asia Minor, who studied under Polycarp, bishop of Smyrna, who in turn had studied at the feet of the Apostle John. Upon the death of Polycarp, he wrote *Against Heresies* (also known as *On the Detection and Overthrow of Knowledge Falsely So-Called*) to help churches distinguish orthodoxy from various Gnostic ideas. This and other works of the Church Fathers can be found online at www.newadvent.org/fathers.

Note 4: *"If this was a history, I would start with the Creation."* Many medieval chronicles begin with Creation or Genesis genealogy and summarize the Bible and the Roman Empire up to the start of their present age. For instance:
Gregory of Tours, *A History of the Franks*. Trans. Earnest Brehaut. Digireads.com Publishing, 2009.
"The Russian Primary Chronicle," in *Medieval Russia's Epics, Chronicles, and Tales.* Ed. Zenkovsky, Serge. New York: Meridian, 1963.

Lewis, Andrew W., ed. and trans., *The Chronicle and Historical Notes of Bernard Itier.* Clarendon Press: Oxford, 2012.

<u>Chapter 1:</u>

Note 5: *"a carving of three youths, standing in a fire, arms raised."* For further regarding Roman Christian burial art commonly found on sarcophagi, along with possible symbolism, see Jensen, Robin M. *Understanding Early Christian Art.* New York: Routledge, 2000.

Note 6: *"A libation hole for the hungry dead."* MacMullen, Ramsay. *The Second Church: Popular Christianity A.D. 200-400.* Boston: Brill, 2009. Includes descriptions and modern, reconstructive sketches of Christian sarcophagi, libation holes, feasting with the dead, and the alignment of saints' sarcophagi directly below church altars.

Note 7: *"For a hundred years…this has been my family trade."* Einhard, biographer and courtier of Charlemagne, wrote the early 9th c. *Translation and Miracles of Marcellinus and Peter,* which describes a relic-supplying deacon named Deusdona, who, with not too much reading between the lines, appears to be a fence in the illicit relic-theft business; the work reads as a multi-stage cover up and attempt to legitimize Einhard's subordinates' theft of relics from a church in Rome to his church in Selingenstadt, Germany. Dutton, Paul Edward. Ed., trans. *Charlemagne's Courtier: The Complete Einhard.* Ontario: Broadview Press, 1998.

Note 8: *"The trader sealed the incense jar."* See Paul Freeman's *Out of the East: Spices and the Medieval Imagination* (New Haven: Yale University Press, 2008) regarding the many uses of spices, including their use in healing and denoting sacred items and rituals. Scents of heaven are also described in multiple Roman-era hagiographical works; one of the earliest is the 2nd-c. *The Martyrdom of Polycarp.*

Note 9: *"Don't fear, I'll find a suitable new locus for him."* *Locus* literally meant location, or place, and was the precise burial site of the saint, but more importantly, the point of the strongest *praesentia* (presence) of the saint. This accounts for the necessity of pilgrimage—a journey to the place where the saint's presence, and presumably power, was strongest. For further, see Brown, Peter, *The Cult of the Saints: Their Rise and Function in Latin Christianity* (Chicago: University of Chicago Press, 1981).

Chapter 2:

Note 10: *"the ideal patron for the new abbey he was building for his son."* For more on the Spanish martyrs under Moorish rule, particularly in the early and mid 9th c., see Coope, Jessica A. *The Martyrs of Cordoba: Community and Family Conflict in an Age of Mass Conversion.* Lincoln: University of Nebraska Press, 1995.

Note 11: *"the great translation of Saint Foy from Agen to Conques?"* St. Foy is also known as St. Faith. For more on the theft/translation of St. Foy's relics from Agen, and how Conques placed her relics into a statue, along with her Passion, miracles, and the *Song of St. Foy*, see Sheingorn, Pamela, trans. *The Book of Sainte Foy.* Philadelphia: The University of Pennsylvania Press, 1995

Note 12: *"the only practical one to convert the rustics."* Pope St. Gregory the Great, c. 540-604 AD. For instance, Gregory proposed removing Angles' idols, but by purifying their shrines with holy water, adding altars and relics, they could be converted to God's use. Gregory the Great. *Registrum Epistolarum.* Bk. XI, Letter 76. Translated by James Barmby, From *Nicene and Post-Nicene Fathers, Second Series,* Vol. 13. Edited by Philip Schaff and Henry Wace. Buffalo, NY: Christian Literature Publishing Co., 1898. Online: http://www.newadvent.org/fathers/360211076.htm.

Note 13: "I read of the first martyrs of Lyons." In 177 AD, according to the martyr record, numerous Christians in Lyon, Gaul, were tortured and killed for their faith by various methods, their remains burned, and their ashes thrown into the Rhone river, so that remaining Christians would not venerate the remains.

Musurillo, Herbert, ed. and trans. *The Acts of the Christian Martyrs.* Oxford: Clarendon Press, 1972.

Note 14: *"Abbot Gonsindus hunched over the desk…"* The *Chronicle of Bernard Itier*, chief librarian of St Martial's abbey in the late 12th - early 13th c., listed Gonsindus as abbot until 893, but then separately listed Fulbert as abbot from 881-887, and a second Fulbert as abbot from 887-907, demonstrating, if nothing else, the fragmented nature of post-Carolingian sources. Lewis, Andrew W., ed. and trans., *The Chronicle and Historical Notes of Bernard Itier.* Clarendon Press: Oxford, 2012.

Note 15: *"Adalhard's ratios to Corbie are well reasoned."* Abbot Adalhard did actually prescribe precise amounts of bread for distribution to pilgrims, travelers, and the poor at the gate each day, in addition to what needed to be kept for the brothers. Adalhard of Corbie, *The Statutes.* In *Carolingian Civilization: A Reader.* Ed. and trans., Paul Edward Dutton. Toronto: University of Toronto Press, 2009.

Note 16: *"Gregory, bishop and historian of Tors, had written about at least as much intrigue, plotting, and death three centuries ago."* Gregory of Tours' *History of the Franks* paints a picture of the Christianization of the nobility of Gaul in the 5th and 6th centuries, while his *Glory of the Martyrs* exemplifies the transition in hagiography from Roman antiquity to the early medieval period, which shifted from a focus on the death of the saint to the numerous miracles and power associated with their remains, and locations (singular *locus*, plural *loci*) associated with them.

Note 17: *"Who recalls the influence of the lowest planet?"* See Wetherbee, Winthrop, trans. *The Cosmographia of Bernardus Silvestris.* New York: Columbia University Press, 1973, and also Flint, Valerie I. J. *The Rise of Magic in Early Medieval Europe.* Princeton: Princeton University Press, 1991. Both works investigate the medieval struggles to reconcile "positive" portions of Greek philosophy and mythology, the "sciences" of astronomy and astrology, and their overlap with

Biblical Magi, revelations, and lists of divine powers and angelic degrees.

Chapter 3:

Note 18: *"my abbot died without telling anyone about hiding Saint Philibert."* The multiple relocations of St. Philibert's relics are recounted by Ermentarius, a monk of St-Philibert, in 863. Herius is the modern island of Noirmoutier, abandoned in 836, and Dee is now St-Philibert de Grandlieu, in turn abandoned sometime after the Northmen pillage of Nantes in 843. Historically, there is no concern that St. Philibert was actually left behind. That is my own invention, but of course, any such scandal of mixed up bones would likely have been hushed up. "The Wandering Monks of St-Philibert." Dutton, Paul Edward. Ed., trans. *Charlemagne's Courtier: The Complete Einhard*. Ontario: Broadview Press, 1998.

Note 19: *"the fight between the brothers that brought this treasure to me."* I recommend Pentcheva, Bissera V, *Icons and Power: The Mother of God in Byzantium*. University Park (Pennsylvania State Press, 2006). Her exploration of Byzantine views of the Hodegetria icon and its protection in battle also provides descriptions and pictures of diptychs and triptychs.

Chapter 4:

Note 20: *"Sichar, first fideles of Comes Fulgaud."* *Fideles*: literally, the faithful men (singular *fidelis*); the closest, most trusted companions/subordinates of a lord.

Note 21: *"the church can withhold all relics to their ends."* Patrick Geary's work *Furta Sacra: Thefts of Relics in the Central Middle Ages* (Princeton: Princeton University Press, 1978), p. 18, describes the reinstatement of a canon of the Fifth Council of Carthage (401 AD) which required relics being incorporated into all altars. I am also indebted to this work for introducing me to the medieval activities of relic thieves and showing the potential complexities of their motivations.

He persuasively argues that the authenticity of physical relics were unverifiable unless accompanied by a suitable translation story.

Note 22: *"the penalty for…despoiling the dead in a basilica."* Fischer Drew, Katherine, trans. *The Laws of the Salian Franks.* Philadelphia: University of Pennsylvania Press, 1991. This work includes 6th-century laws and the Carolingian revisions, but also gleans social and economic insight into daily life, particularly the agrarian nature and farm/village organization of society, as discoverable through legal focuses and strata.

Note 23: *"the ruins of a small chapel…dismantled for the home of a colonus across the vale." Colonus* (male), *colona* (female): a social status between a slave and free person. Its exact distinction appears uncertain, but it was likely somewhere between a free person and a slave. Dutton, Paul Edward, ed. and trans. "The Polyptyque of St-Germain-des-Pres" in *Carolingian Civilization: A Reader.* Toronto: University of Toronto Press, 2009.

Chapter 5:

Note 24: *"The ligamina looked different…"* See *The Rise of Magic in Early Medieval Europe* (cited above) for further on the practice of ligatures and the popular crossover between pagan practices and Christian beliefs, particularly the Church's method of redirecting similar actions, symbols, or places to bring about conversion.

Note 25: *"The Lay of Olivier and Fierbras."* The legends of Charlemagne's paladins are too numerous to list, and the *Song of Roland,* in which the eponymic knight dies defending the pass of Roncesvalle from a Moorish ambush, is only the most famous. Its earliest written form came about a few centuries after the deeds; the story was originally passed on, and likely altered, in the manner of oral stories. I recommend M. I. Finley's *The World of Odysseus* (New York: New York Review Books: 1954) for an assessment of the veracity of social structures and norms seen in oral translation, even if actual facts of events are altered or lost. I also recommend Julia

Creswell's *Charlemagne & The Paladins* (Oxford: Osprey Publishing, 2014). While not a historical work, it portrays the variety of Charlemagne stories and their reinvention through subsequent eras.

Chapter 6:

Note 26: *"Gregory…described Saint Peter's soul traveling up to join the stars…"* Gregory of Tours. *Glory of the Martyrs*. Trans. Raymond Van Dam. Liverpool: Liverpool University Press, 1988.

Note 27: *"Even Moses' law declared them unclean."* Cf. Peter Brown's *The Cult of the Saints: Its Rise and Function in Latin Christianity* (Chicago: The University of Chicago Press, 1981) for how extremely alien the Christian culture of contact with dead bodies and remains was from the cultures from which Christianity sprang (Judaism, Greek and Roman paganism), and his subsequent argument that therefore the cult of the saints, especially in the close contact with relics, could not be any pagan syncretism.

Note 28: *"The curving hall also accessed numerous small chapels along its outer perimeter."* Conant, Kenneth John. *Carolingian and Romanesque Architecture: 800-1200*. Baltimore: Penguin Books, 1959. This work explains the development of small corridors built up around crypts, for pilgrims' access, and particularly shows three stages of the development of the church of St. Philibert-de-Grandlieu between 814 – 847, until its abandonment in the face of Northmen invasion. This church remains to this day, with alternating-colored bands of stonework, and with apse and altar raised over the ground-level crypt. The sub-crypt is my invention, yet often churches were built over existing holy places or burial sites of saints that were subsequently forgotten.

Note 29: *"the numerous occasions a Christian should sign himself on the forehead with the victorious Cross."* Tertullian was a church writer of the early 3rd century, in Carthage, most famous now for his description that, no matter how Christians were martyred, their blood continued to be "seed" for more Christians. He describes the use of the Sign of the Cross at every step, when going in or out, when dressing in clothes and shoes, bathing, sitting at the table, lighting lamps, and in all the ordinary actions of daily life. Tertullian. *On the Crown* (De Corona), Chapter 3.

Online   http://www.newadvent.org/fathers/0304.htm.   From *Ante-Nicene Fathers*, Vol. III. Trans. S. Thelwall.

Chapter 7:

Note 30: *"An hour of hard rowing brought us to the Northmen's village."* By 890, Vikings, known to Franks as Northmen (eventually, Norman), switched from more than a century of harrying the coastline, and began to establish themselves in the land. Charles the Simple enfeoffed Rollo the Viking around 910 and had him protect the coast against other Northmen. Noirmoutier, near the mouth of the *Leger* (*Loire*) river, had fallen over half a century before, as described in Father Leovigildus' discussion above.

Note 31: *"showed a white handle and sheath of a cream-white similar to the ivory of Father Leo's diptych."* A Norse sorceress is similarly described in the *Saga of Erik the Red*, Ch.4.

Online: http://sagadb.org/files/pdf/eiriks_saga_rauda.en.pdf.

Chapter 9:

Note 32: *"chicken soup, a curative found in the Vita of Saint Benedict of Aniane."* A late 8th-century source from southern France, *Saint Benedict of Anianes: His Life and Times* describes a noble who left the military life and built a monastery on his own land. The work provides details as to the interior furnishing of a church, the charter system that bequeathed the land by the order of Charlemagne to the monastery in its own right, and other tidbits such as this remedy for illness commonly used today. Dutton, Paul E., ed. "Saint Benedict of Anianes: His Life and Times." *Carolingian Civilization: A Reader.* 2nd ed. University of Toronto Press, Toronto. 2009.

Note 33: *"Impress of the woman's heel, Fearing her, who feared her lord."*

H.J. Thomson's translation is more accurate, but the more poetic translation quoted here is R. Martin Pope, trans., *Liber Cathemerinon* (London: J.M. Dent & Co., 1905), found online through Project Gutenberg, www.gutenberg.org/14959. Hymen was the Roman god of marriage.

<u>Chapter 10:</u>

Note 34: *"the solemnity of an Easter vigil, and the gaiety of a wedding feast."* The euphoria of relic translation, including spontaneous joining of local crowds, is attested to in Einhard's *The Translation and Miracles of Marcellinus and Peter* (see note 8). The equality and fraternity these processions generated is found in Prudentius' *Crowns of Martyrdom (Peristephanon Liber)*, and elsewhere as described by Peter Brown's *The Cult of the Saints: Its Rise and Function in Latin Christianity.* The 6th century Bishop Gregory of Tours wrote *Glory of the Martyrs* (see note 26), which describes the translation of the entire sarcophagus of a likely-invented saint, revealed in a dream after being long ignored by locals as the sarcophagus was thought to be a pagan's due to its size (50). A church was erected over the new crypt. Incidentally, he also records the story of a would-be relic thief whose head was trapped and wounded by a sarcophagus lid (43), reinforcing the concept that any acquisition needed creative legitimacy to avoid the label of theft.

Note 35: *"He placed his left hand on the ebony box."* The *Translation of Sts. Peter and Marcellinus* (see note 8), describes a variety of miracles accompanying the saints as they traveled to their new home, to include the ending of a feud.

<u>Chapter 11:</u>

Note 36: *"the Dormition of the Blessed Virgin."* The 15th of August.

Note 37: *"admonishing all to return his scattered parts to burial under the altar."* From *The Martyrdom of Fructuosus and his Deacons* as described in Prudentius' *Liber Peristephanon*, Ch. VI.

Chapter 12:

Note 38: *"until Wrath wore herself out and threw herself down on her own spear point."* Prudentius, *Psychomachia*, lines 109 ff.

Note 39: *"Christianus sum, but as one stillborn."* Repeatedly in early Christian martyr accounts, the martyrs would bear witness to their faith by explicitly declaring before whichever Roman official, *"Christianus sum"* (I am a Christian). See Musurillo for a list of 28 early-source martyrdoms not including those found only in Eusebius' *History of the Church*.

Note 40: *"maybe Valerie's power transferred to someone else's bones."* Early medieval hagiography is replete with stories of saints' relics transferring their holy power to objects they've touched, or places they lay, especially if the contact was lengthy. A comparison easier for the modern mind to understand, presented by John Wortley, is the transference of radioactivity from radioactive materials to any encasement. Wortley, John. *Studies on the Cult of Relics in Byzantium Up to 1204*. Burlington: Variorum, 2009.

Note 41: *"Egilolf thought little of the option of praying to God for the appearance of a second body of Saint Valerie."* Such a convenient miracle, face-saving for sparring monasteries, was recorded in the *Vita Sancti Abbani*, as described in *Furta Sacra*. See note 22.

Chapter 13:

Note 42: *"when the saint did not want to leave and took his revenge"* The listed saints' retaliations against thieves are as described in other early medieval relic theft attempts in Geary's *Furta Sacra* (note 22), p. 114 and 152.

Note 43: *"to taste and compare his raw and roasted sides."* These details are all taken from actual martyr stories of the first centuries of Christianity, as described in Musurillo's *Acts of the Christian Martyrs* and Prudentius' *Crowns of Martyrdom.*

Note 44: *"musk, dragon's blood, mummy" Out of the East* by Freedman gives a wonderful insight into all types of herbs and spices thought useful as medicine, to include the mummified remains described here, as well as culinary ideas. See note 8.

Chapter 14:

Note 45: *"A child eater…"* The *Lex Salica Karolina*, XXXVII, after declaring a punishment of 62 ½ *solidi* (a gold coin worth 12 silver *deniers*) for accusing someone of being a sorcerer and being unable to prove it, sets out a punishment of 200 *solidi* if a witch is convicted of eating a man. The word there is "striam," but a similar word for a female witch described in *Rise of Magic* is "strix," a "horrible flying creature which devoured babies, leaving a straw doll in their place." (p.124) I have here conflated the medieval fears of someone eating a child with my experience as a child abuse detective; the abandoned, dying child has bite marks and symptoms of abusive head trauma. The psychological motivations of a severe child abuser is still so alien to modern minds that it is easy to understand medieval peoples' assumption this could only come from satanic possession.

Note 46: *"to never return in this life or the next."* The *Rise of Magic* (see above) provides evidence of bishops emphasizing the helplessness of humans facing demonic temptation of magic use, and thus imposing spiritual remedies and tempering harsher secular punishments, particularly for women (p. 156, 297). As an example of Church leniency, the only punishment a bishop assigned was penance for a murder assisted by a witch; p.232, n. 113, citing *edit.* W. D. Macray, *Chronicon Abbatiae Rameseiensis*, RS (London, 1886).

Note 47: *"thus the eternal judgement for murderers."* Like Dante's *Inferno*, the *Apocalypse* imagines group punishments fit to the type of sin. *The Apocalypse of Peter*, 23-24; an apocryphal text of the first half of the 2nd century. Considered Scriptural by Church Father

Clement of Alexandria (d. 215AD).
Online:
http://www.earlychristianwritings.com/text/apocalypsepeter-roberts.html.

Chapter 15 Marginalia:

Note 48: *Marginalia "…adding this peripheral note."* Materials for scrolls and codices being rare and valuable, scribes often wrote addenda or complete works in the intervening lines or side margins of the main texts.

Note 49: *"Lost them both to Saint Anthony's fire."* St. Anthony's fire was the medieval name for ergotism, a then-fatal disease caused by a fungus on rye. Symptoms included hallucinations, vomiting, and a sensation of burning in the limbs as blood vessels restricted, gangrene of the limbs set in, and extremities began rotting away. Online. http://www.medicinenet.com/script/main/art.asp?articlekey=14891

Note 50: *"Haven't you, of all people, heard of Anskar?"* For further on the fascinating hagiography of this northern missionary expansion, where politics and miracles hold equal influence, see *The Life of Anskar*, by Rimbert, in *Carolingian Civilization: A Reader*. Ed. Paul Dutton. University of Toronto Press: Toronto, 2009.

Chapter 16:

Note 51: *"to place his hands within Ebalus' own, to become his vassal."* Homage of vassal to lord was conducted in a ceremony that started with the vassal placing his joined hands between the hands of the lord, symbolizing submission. Bloch, Marc. *Feudal Society*, Vol. 1. (London: Routledge & Kegan Paul Ltd., 1961), 145.

Note 52: *"our iron is stronger, or stronger forged."* Charlemagne forbade his subjects, particularly merchants, from selling Frankish arms and coats of mail to Saxons and other foreigners, presumably for fear of them gaining better weaponry. "Capitulary of Herstal, 779" and "Double Capitulary of Thionville for the *Missi*, 805", in P.E. Dutton's *Carolingian Civilization: A Reader*.

Chapter 18:

Note 53: *"My own Saint Perpetua, stepping into the gladiator's ring…"* In the 3rd-c. *Passion* of Sts. Perpetua and Felicity, the Roman noble Perpetua, jailed and awaiting her martyrdom, wrote of her dream of stepping into the gladiator's ring to fight an Egyptian, a foreshadowing of her forthcoming spiritual last battle. Salisbury, Joyce E. *Perpetua's Passion: The Death and Memory of a Young Roman Woman*. New York: Routledge, 1997.

Chapter 19:

Note 54: *"on the subject of swords…"* Alcuin, client-scholar to Charlemagne, and abbot to St.-Martin of Tours from 796-804, wrote a reply to a question from one of the king's nobles about perceived discrepancies in the Gospels, such as the command to the disciples to buy two swords and the later advice that all who lived by the sword would die by it. Alcuin's reply, like much medieval exegesis, finds spiritual symbolism for the diverse mention of swords. Alcuin, "To the King on the Meaning of Swords in Scriptures," Letter 5, "Letters of Alcuin," in Paul Dutton's *Charlemagne's Courtier: The Complete Einhard*. Ontario: Broadview Press, 1998.

Epilogue:

Note 55: *"This calls for some wine."* Similar thanksgiving and intentions to celebrate have been found at the conclusion of many copied medieval manuscripts, testifying to the immense labor of copying entire books.

ACKNOWLEDGMENTS

I would like to thank all those who encouraged me in the long process of formulating, writing, and revising this book, especially Shanna H. and Rob C. for braving the jungle of those first drafts.

ABOUT THE AUTHOR

Alan Van't Land grew up as a business kid in a missionary boarding school in Malaysia. His interest in history was sparked by his study of the early Church, leading to his conversion to Catholicism in his early 20s. He honed this interest with a Masters in History from the University of Colorado and loves exploring ancient and medieval saint cults and the evolution of the Christian warrior ethic. Between bouts of historical inquiry, he's earned his day's *denarius* as a US Marine, police officer, and detective.

Eternal Light of the Crypts is his first novel.

Published by
Full Quiver Publishing
PO Box 244
Pakenham ON K0A2X0
Canada
www.fullquiverpublishing.com